MW00466850

STEFAN TOOK STOCK of the horde now driving, full-on towards him. Of the fifty, a good dozen bore standards, flags or colours rippling in the breeze behind them.

Some were undoubtedly Norscan, others had the shape and size of mortal men, but disfigured by the hideous mutations of Chaos. Stefan shuddered. Was this the fate that awaited Alexei? Was it possible, even, that he was somewhere amongst them now?

He shook the thought away. All that mattered was the coming battle, the storm of blood and steel that would soon engulf them all. Desperate and cornered, the Chaos horde had nothing left to lose. Stefan released a long roar of rage, kicked in with his spurs and rode on, accelerating rapidly towards battle.

*Also by Neil McIntosh*

STAR OF ERENGRAD
The first Stefan Kumansky novel

*More Warhammer from the Black Library*

## · WARHAMMER NOVELS ·

RIDERS OF THE DEAD by Dan Abnett

THE DEAD AND THE DAMNED by Jonathan Green

HONOUR OF THE GRAVE by Robin D. Laws

ZAVANT by Gordon Rennie

THE CLAWS OF CHAOS by Gav Thorpe

THE BLADES OF CHAOS by Gav Thorpe

BLOOD MONEY by C. L. Werner

BLOOD & STEEL by C. L. Werner

MARK OF DAMNATION by James Wallis

HAMMERS OF ULRIC by Dan Abnett,
Nik Vincent & James Wallis

GILEAD'S BLOOD by Dan Abnett & Nik Vincent

## GOTREK & FELIX by William King

TROLLSLAYER • SKAVENSLAYER

DAEMONSLAYER • DRAGONSLAYER • BEASTSLAYER

VAMPIRESLAYER • GIANTSLAYER

## THE VAMPIRE GENEVIEVE NOVELS
by Jack Yeovil

DRACHENFELS • GENEVIEVE UNDEAD

BEASTS IN VELVET • SILVER NAILS

A WARHAMMER NOVEL

# TAINT OF EVIL

## NEIL McINTOSH

**A BLACK LIBRARY PUBLICATION**

BL Publishing,
Games Workshop Ltd.,
Willow Road, Nottingham,
NG7 2WS, UK.

First US edition, September 2003.

10 9 8 7 6 5 4 3 2 1

Distributed by Simon & Schuster
1230 Avenue of the Americas,
New York, NY 10020.

Cover illustration by Clint Langley

© Copyright Games Workshop Ltd, 2003. All rights reserved.

Black Library, the Black Library logo, Black Flame, BL Publishing,
Games Workshop, the Games Workshop logo and all associated
marks, names, characters, illustrations and images from the
Warhammer universe are either ®, TM and/or © Games Workshop Ltd
2000-2003, variably registered in the UK and other countries around
the world. All rights reserved.

ISBN 0-7434-4361-6

Set in ITC Giovanni

Printed and bound in Great Britain by
Cox & Wyman Ltd, Reading, Berkshire.

No part of this publication may be reproduced, stored in a retrieval
system, or transmitted in any form or by any means, electronic,
mechanical, photocopying, recording or otherwise, without the prior
permission of the publishers.

This is a work of fiction. All the characters and events portrayed in
this book are fictional, and any resemblance to real people or
incidents is purely coincidental.

See the Black Library on the Internet at
# www.blacklibrary.com

Find out more about Games Workshop
and the world of Warhammer at
# www.games-workshop.com

THIS IS A DARK age, a bloody age, an age of daemons and of sorcery. It is an age of battle and death, and of the world's ending. Amidst all of the fire, flame and fury it is a time, too, of mighty heroes, of bold deeds and great courage.

AT THE HEART of the Old World sprawls the Empire, the largest and most powerful of the human realms. Known for its engineers, sorcerers, traders and soldiers, it is a land of great mountains, mighty rivers, dark forests and vast cities. And from his throne in Altdorf reigns the Emperor Karl-Franz, sacred descendent of the founder of these lands, Sigmar, and wielder of his magical warhammer.

BUT THESE ARE far from civilised times. Across the length and breadth of the Old World, from the knightly palaces of Bretonnia to ice-bound Kislev in the far north, come rumblings of war. In the towering World's Edge Mountains, the orc tribes are gathering for another assault. Bandits and renegades harry the wild southern lands of the Border Princes. There are rumours of rat-things, the skaven, emerging from the sewers and swamps across the land. And from the northern wildernesses there is the ever-present threat of Chaos, of daemons and beastmen corrupted by the foul powers of the Dark Gods. As the time of battle draws ever near, the Empire needs heroes like never before.

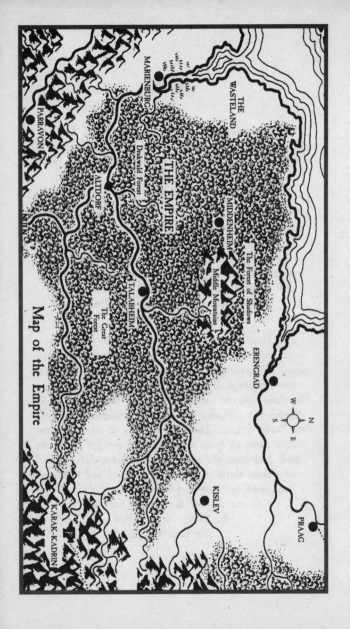

# CHAPTER ONE
## Hunter's Moon

LOTHAR KOENIG TUGGED back on the reins with a practiced ease, bringing his horse to a rapid halt upon the stony path. With the pounding of the hooves suddenly stilled, the land seemed improbably, unnaturally quiet. Lothar sat motionless in the saddle, head tilted towards the sky, scanning his surroundings. It was a cold, crisp night, poised on the cusp of autumn. Up above, the sibling moons Mannslieb and Morrslieb shone like newly minted coins in a star-flecked sky, dappling the rolling hills with a pale silver light.

In that moment everything looked so pure and untainted. The world, Lothar reflected, could be a cruel and deceitful place. And lonely. Here, on the edge of the mountains, within sight of the great river that snaked its path from the borders of Kislev to the very heart of the Empire, a man might well believe that he was the very last soul alive upon the face of the world. But he would not be alone. Not for much longer.

Lothar Koenig kicked in with his booted heels and drove his mount forward, on towards his destination. He rode quickly, threading a path through the barren forest that skirted the edge of the hills. He would leave nothing to chance. Not now, when he was so near.

Soon he reached his vantage point, a narrow ledge hidden within a cluster of trees which overlooked a second, better-trodden path that ran through the base of the valley some twenty yards below. Lothar pulled a spyglass from the pocket of his padded hide jerkin and scanned the length of the valley. At first he could see nothing beyond a tar-like blackness tinged at its extremity by the moonlight. Koenig cursed, cupped a hand around the lens so as to shade it from the prying moons, and tried again. Now he could see the outlines of the trees lying directly below. The rising profile of the mountains stretched out like a boundless ocean of blackness, in each direction as far as the eye could see. The expanse of land known as the Ostermark was vast, vast enough for a traveller to lose himself in utterly. But Lothar Koenig was not lost. He was exactly where he needed to be.

He made use of the few moments that remained to take stock of his tools in trade. Neatly stowed about the saddle of his horse were all the means by which he earned his living: a sword, light but honed to a keen sharpness, always ready: a length of rope, and a shorter length of linked metal chain wound tightly around a wire net strong enough to hold the wildest of beasts; a glass bottle, tightly stoppered, containing a potion capable of subduing a man in seconds and a short steel knife, useful only for close combat, the sort of combat that could only end in death. This was Lothar's tool of last resort. He was a bounty hunter, not a killer. If death was to be the only currency, then he could deal it as well as any man. But his clients generally paid better money if their prizes were delivered alive, not dead. What happened to them after that was another matter, and one that Lothar was careful never to pry too far into.

He shivered, aware as if for the first time of the biting chill held in the still night air. Cold or not, he would have to wait for as long as it took. Patience. He must have patience. That was a quality that his trade depended upon.

He lifted the spyglass again, tracking back along the length of the path below. Not long now, surely, if his calculations were correct. Soon his quarry would emerge from between the hills into the bottleneck of the valley below. Then the familiar ritual would begin again. Sometimes it ended in death. And eventually, he reflected, the Gates of Morr would open for him too. He lowered the glass, contemplating the prospect of his death at the hand of an as yet unknown opponent. It would probably come in a place such as this, a vast expanse of wilderness in a distant part of the Empire. His body would fall and rot amongst the trees, unnoticed by all except the devouring worms. No one would miss him, no one would mourn his loss. Such friends as he had ever known had gradually melted away, and his wife and child lay long dead in the cold earth.

For a moment something akin to self-pity washed over him, a bittersweet savouring of loss and a life that might have been. Lothar allowed himself the moment of weakness then crushed the emotion down, locking it away with the impatience, the fear and the weariness that lay heavy in his bones. This job called for a clear head and a cold, empty heart.

Patience, patience. His calculation had been exact. They would appear along the path below any minute now, emerging into the bright moonlight. He thought again about his target, the man who would put enough money in his purse to spare Lothar the need for these nocturnal adventures for many a night to come.

The man he was waiting so patiently for was a bandit, a common cut-throat set apart from his peers by his singular reputation for cruelty. A man who plundered lives and property indiscriminately, for gain or for fun, as it suited him. Normally, and – from Lothar's perspective – thankfully, their paths would not have crossed. But this particular cut-throat had gone too far. He had kidnapped a girl, noble-born, a proctor's daughter from Talabheim. The ransom demanded had been paid, but it hadn't ended there. It seemed the kidnappers hadn't known where to stop with their fun. Things had gone too far. Now the girl was dead, and her captor had a price upon his head, a generous purse laid by the grieving father.

There was no doubting that his quarry was a loathsome and despicable man, but Lothar Koenig carried no especial hatred in his heart. He thought of his target dispassionately, perhaps, even, with a strange affection. It was through men like this he earned his living, and for that Lothar gave thanks. He looked skywards and said a prayer to whatever gods might bless him this night.

CARL DURER WAS not a complex man. He rarely had room in his head for more than one idea at the same time. Tonight his mind was upon hunting, not being hunted.

They had picked up a trail a little way west of Baumdorf – a lone rider, heading south. These days few travellers were stupid or foolish enough to travel the mountain trails alone at night. People were running scared – though scared of what Carl Durer was never quite sure. There was vague talk of trouble brewing, of war beyond the border, of strange beasts and mutants stalking the land.

None of it much interested Carl Durer. All he knew was that merchants and traders rarely ventured out other than in convoy now, and pickings for men like him were growing thin. But this one, this one was surely a beauty. Durer and his men had followed him from the outskirts of the village, a single horseman oblivious or indifferent to the perils of the Ostermark. The bandits followed at a distance at first, content to let their victim run awhile. A few miles ahead the path narrowed, then dropped down into a valley. The only way out was up a steep climb at the far end. That was where they would take him and whatever treasure he carried.

Durer enjoyed the anticipation almost as much as the kill. As the four of them closed in on their prey, he started to think about the sport ahead. Usually they put up a bit of a fight, at first. If they did, so much the better, Carl enjoyed a fight. Then, when it became obvious they weren't going to escape, they would beg, beg for their lives to be spared. Sometimes – often, in fact – Carl would silence the begging with a blade through the guts, and keep twisting it until the wretch shut up. Other times, if he were in the mood, he might listen to what they had to say. They might have a bit extra to offer – money stashed away where Carl might not have thought to look. He enjoyed watching wealthy gentle-folk grovel at his feet, on their knees, pleading for their lives to be spared. Carl thought about it and laughed. It made no difference, really. He killed them all in the end.

Soon they'd reach the valley. He spurred his mount on, ready to overhaul the horseman ahead, and glanced around at the riders on either side of him. Filthy Erich Wahl: as fat and gluttonous as a pig, a man who would watch his mother starve if it meant he could feed his belly. His brother Kurt, who'd killed more men than he could remember, most for no particular reason. And the strange, whey-faced boy, a northerner known only as Lief, with a deep, unfathomable something about him that scared even Carl. They were Durer's men, but he wasn't stupid enough to think they were his friends. In truth he despised the lot of them, and they'd knife him in the back as soon as he would them – which was soon enough. But so long as they were useful to each other, then they were in it together.

Right now they probably hated his guts, blamed him for the foul-up in Talabheim. That business with the girl had got out of hand. They should have got out as soon as they had the ransom, but Carl had wanted a bit of fun, and then it had gone too far. That didn't matter in itself – nobody gave a damn about the girl. But even Carl hadn't reckoned on the little whore's father being such a vengeful bastard. Carl wasn't used to being a fugitive, and it didn't much agree with him. The hungry ache in his belly agreed with him even less. It was time he lived off the fat of the land again.

As they crested the top of the valley Carl looked down to see the other rider barely fifty yards ahead of them. He was either deaf, had no sense of instinct, or both, or he would have had some sense of the riders behind him by now. But the horseman varied neither his speed nor his course, just kept on at the same steady pace, riding bolt upright in the saddle, staring out at the night ahead.

He was a tall man, Carl noted. Tall, and heavily built with it, the sort who might give a good account of himself. So be it. All the better in fact. Carl Durer enjoyed a decent scrap, so long as the odds were good. In any case – he glanced round at his comrades again – more than one of these scum were dispensable now.

Any man out on the trail in these parts had to be heading from somewhere, to somewhere. And they had to be carrying something too: money, silver, gold, whatever. It would do. Carl met Lief's wall-eyed stare and grinned. He could almost smell the blood.

How to deal with Durer's gang was a problem that had been playing on Lothar's mind for most of the day. There had been no chance of taking him on his own. It had taken Lothar long enough to pick up the bandits' trail after Talabheim, and since then it seemed Durer was rarely if ever alone. Lothar would have to wait for his opportunity, then make the most of it.

He had slipped quietly and unobtrusively into the gang's wake just outside Baumdorf. He had weighed his chances of taking Durer – dead or alive – with three other armed men in tow, and decided that his best chance was to wait, staying just in touch, until they struck camp. An hour, two hours passed in stealthy pursuit. The sun had drawn down its light below the distant mountains, and still Durer and his men gave no sign of breaking their journey. The bounty hunter had grown anxious. If the bandit gang were to reach the forest under cover of nightfall it would be all too easy to lose them forever.

Then he had seen the fifth rider, the single horseman, bearing south-west at the same, unvarying pace, with Durer and his savage disciples slowly closing in. Then he knew that the bandits would not head into the forest. They would chase this unwitting rider down into the Ostravska Gorge, rob him and murder him. And whilst Durer's gang were busy with their butchery, Lothar would have the element of surprise on his side. If he was lucky, the traveller might manage to wound or kill some of Durer's men before he himself was killed. At worst, the gang would be distracted for a few precious moments. It might be the only chance he would get.

It had taken him only a moment to make his decision. He would ride ahead, to the far end of the gorge, then double back on them from the south. The strategy wasn't without risk. But then, he had told himself, everyone had to die sometime.

THE LONE HORSEMAN pressed on into the valley, shadowed by his four pursuers. Keep going, Carl thought, with quiet satisfaction. Soon we'll have you exactly where we want you. He looked around, taking in the physical dimensions of the valley. To his left and right, towering walls of rock. Ahead, the path snaked through the valley before exiting in a steep, winding climb that would take an agile rider at least half an hour to navigate. No way out of here in a hurry. Like a cork into a bottle. We've got you trapped now, my friend.

Carl Durer started to relax, settling into an old and comfortable routine. No harm now in making sure their quarry knew they were here. He slackened off the pace and bellowed out a command: 'Hey, you up there. Turn about!'

The words echoed off the facing cliffs, filling the valley. But the horseman made no acknowledgement of the summons, nor varied the steady pace of his horse by as much as a step. If he was aware at all of the riders closing in on him, then he remained completely indifferent to his fate. A surge of anger welled up inside Carl Durer. The horseman – trader in trinkets, courier or whatsoever he was – would pay dearly for his insolence. Any lingering thought in Carl Durer's mind that he might allow the man a mercifully quick death was now forgotten. No, he'd let the boys play a while with this one, practise their carving skills. It was remarkable how much pain you could inflict and still keep a man alive.

Durer looked left and right, and signalled to his men, initiating a familiar manoeuvre. The Wahl brothers spurred their horses on, leaving Lief at Durer's side. The two riders steered out left and right, moving to overtake the horseman on either side. Carl watched them speed past their target, the blades of their swords glinting in the moonlight. If their victim had been oblivious to his fate before, he wouldn't be now. And yet, still the solitary figure did not deviate from his path through the valley. The same, steady pace. The same, unswerving direction. Well, let him enjoy his little game, Carl thought. Soon enough, we'll be enjoying ours.

Fifty yards on, the two bandits pulled up, dragging their horses around in a cloud of dust and stones. Now they faced the oncoming rider, blocking off any escape from the valley. Carl Durer looked on with satisfaction as, finally, the horseman checked his speed and came to a gradual halt.

Durer slowed his own horse to a gentle trot until he was within hailing distance of his men.

'Mark him all you want, boys. But keep him alive for me. I want some time with this one.'

Still the rider sat, immobile on his towering steed, gaze fixed ahead as if only seeing the path that led out of the valley.

'Turn about,' Carl commanded. 'Turn around so I can take a look at you.' After what seemed a long time the horseman finally turned, slow and ponderous, until he was facing Durer.

The rider was half in shadow, but Carl Durer caught a glimpse of a weather-beaten face framed by a shock of unkempt, jet-back hair. A pair of eyes the colour of night itself stared directly through him without any acknowledgement of his existence. For the briefest of moments he looked like a statue carved out of living stone, rather than a mortal man. In the same moment a thought raced, unbidden, through Carl Durer's mind: *This is a mistake.*

Absurd. Imagining things. Carl swept the thought aside and tugged his sword out from its harness. The other man, he noted, had made no attempt to draw his own sword yet. Maybe he knows it's hopeless, Durer reckoned. Or maybe he's one of the ones who think they can talk their way out. Well, let him talk. They'd have him singing before they'd finished with him, but all the pretty tunes known to the gods weren't going to save him now.

Durer nudged his horse forward so he could get a better look at their prize. He was big all right – thickly muscled and stockily built, but that was of no concern whilst they were four to one. Carl sliced the air with his sword a matter of inches from the other man's face. The rider didn't flinch, but kept his dark eyes fastened on Durer. There was no hatred there, but no fear either. He was looking through him, not at him, Carl realised. As if he didn't exist at all.

Maybe the man had gone mad, wandering the plains of the Ostermark for days or weeks on his own? Well, he had some company now, and they'd see if they couldn't waken him up a little. He reached for the flask inside his tunic and drained its contents into his mouth, swallowing them down in one gulp. It was the last of the rotgut brandy, the last of their provisions. But it was enough to get the blood-fires boiling inside him, and not so much as to dull the killing edge. He tossed the empty flask away, the battered pewter clattering on the hard flint ground.

'Give us your money,' Durer demanded. He could sense the other men around him growing impatient, eager to get on with their handiwork. 'Give us your money, and we'll let you be on your way,' he lied. The other man looked around him, slowly, seeming to take in Durer and his three henchmen for the first time.

'No money.' The voice was cold and toneless, void of emotion. By now Durer had decided their quarry certainly was mad, and the realisation disappointed him a little. Perhaps this wasn't going to be fun after all. The night was cold and his belly was griping incessantly. Perhaps they should just kill the idiot and be done with it, then strip the body of whatever they could find. Carl Durer was already starting to tire of his evening's sport. A ride to the nearest village – even a scumhole like Mielstadt, with its sour beer and its pox-ridden bawd-house – was beginning to sound a better prospect than this.

The tall rider turned away and took up the reins, making ready to ride on, oblivious to the men blocking his path. As he moved, the sleeve of his tunic slid up to reveal his arm. At that instant Carl Durer registered something odd about the arm – the flesh extensively bruised or stained – but it was not the flesh that caught his eye. Fixed upon the man's wrist was a band of gold metal, the like of which Carl Durer had never seen before. He glimpsed it only momentarily, glittering under the moonlight, but for that moment it shone with a depth and lustre that told Carl he must possess it at all costs. Even if the madman was travelling without so much as a copper penny in his pockets, this would surely be an ample reward for their night's work. Carl Durer fixed the other man with a leering, crack-toothed grin.

'We'll start with that little trinket there,' he said. 'Give it over.'

The rider raised his arm a fraction, as though examining the golden band by the light of the two moons. 'Go on,' Durer continued, warming to his theme. 'Slip it off nice and slow and maybe we'll go easy on you.' Perhaps there was some fun to be had in this after all.

There followed a moment of absolute stillness. The rider sitting as if frozen in the saddle, eyes fixed upon an indeterminate point in the far distance. Behind him, the barrel-shaped bulk of Erich Wahl and his sadistic brother, waiting for the command that would let the slaughter begin. In front of him, Carl Durer, the bandit king with the blood of more than fifty on his hands. And Lief, the scrawny man-boy, polishing the face of his axe upon his breeches. When they'd done, Carl decided, he'd let Lief skin him alive if he fancied it.

Without warning, the rider suddenly brought his horse about and rode off, resuming his journey, apparently without a thought to the men barring his way. Carl spat a curse.

'A plague on the gods!' he yelled. 'We're finished with this fooling. Cut his arm off, then bring me that gold bangle.'

Erich Wahl drew his sword with evident relish and moved to block the path of the oncoming rider.

Carl Durer would not have believed what happened next, had he not witnessed it with his own eyes. The fat man hefted his blade and swung it in a swift arc towards the exposed right arm of the rider. As the blow fell, the other man drew out his own sword with his left arm. It was not the speed of the answering blow that dismayed Carl Durer so much as its unimaginable force. Force enough to knock the blade clean out of Erich's meaty grip and then keep moving, slicing the night air in an unstoppable trajectory.

There was no howl of pain, nor bellowing of wounded rage from the fat man. Only the dull thud of an object hitting the ground, then a second, far heavier crash, as the severed head fell to earth, followed a moment later by the rest of Erich's body.

Carl Durer stared in paralysed disbelief at the bloody carnage seemingly wrought out of thin air before his eyes. But Kurt Wahl was not so dumbstruck. Screaming murderous vengeance, he charged full tilt towards the man who had killed his brother. The stranger kept his sword hanging down by his side, resting against the horse's flank. There was no attempt to defend himself against the assault. He waited passively whilst Kurt bore down upon him, the flailing hooves of his horse raking clouds of ochre dust from the valley floor. The stranger still hadn't moved when Kurt cut across his path and lashed out, delivering a sweeping blow with a sword heavy enough to cut through armour. The stranger nudged his mount to one side with a delicacy that belied the bulk of both horse and rider, dancing away from the blow. The sword-stroke sliced uselessly through thin air as Kurt Wahl shot past.

Carl Durer glanced across at the youth sitting by his side. Lief's bloodless face was as it ever was, as bereft of emotion as his tongue was of words. But he could read the way the battle was running as well as his master, and when Carl Durer nodded he pushed his horse forward, moving in a slow circle around the combatants like a snake closing upon its prey.

Twice more Kurt surged forward towards the traveller, seized by an unquenchable rage, desperate to avenge the blood of his kin. Both times the result was the same, the tall stranger holding his ground, drawing the attack to him, before pulling out of range of his enemy's blade at the last possible moment.

Playing with him, Carl realised. Toying with the fiercest and most dangerous of his men. This was not how it had been meant to be. On the third pass, the playing came to an end. This time Kurt correctly anticipated the manoeuvre. This time his blow was on target, the sword scything down

towards the other's unprotected face. The stranger raised his
sword, and met the blow, effortlessly. Steel bit upon steel.
The stranger lifted his blade higher, twisting Wahl's arm, lifting the bandit clear out of the saddle and tossing him onto
the ground.

Things moved quickly now. Before the stranger could turn
his horse about to finish off Kurt, Lief took his chance, leaping from his own horse to fasten like a limpet upon the
man's back. Lief's bird-claw nails closed around his enemy's
neck, closing off his windpipe and scouring the flesh from
his throat. From the ground, Kurt saw what was happening
and climbed briskly to his feet, encouraged that the tide of
the battle was now turning. His optimism was rewarded
with a blade that traced a perfect line from his breastbone to
the line of his scalp, spitting him then paring him open like
a ripe fruit. His blood mixed with his brother's, draining
into the dry earth.

The pale boy now redoubled his efforts, trying to choke
his opponent with his left arm, freeing the right to lift the
axe free of his belt. Sensing the blade about to fall, the
stranger twisted to shake him off, and, in the struggle that
followed, both fell from the saddle on to the ground below.

Carl Durer dismounted and strode forward smartly, sword
in hand. Sport be damned, he was in no mood to fool with
a madman like this. He'd cut the trinket from the fellow's
wrist whilst the two of them were still fighting, and then be
off. The boy could take his chances. The figures on the
ground broke apart and Lief stood up, trying to escape. As
he stepped away the stranger reached out and caught hold of
his arm, hauling him back. The youth turned and lashed out
with the axe, but the stranger appeared to meet the blow
with nothing more than his bare hand, knocking the
weapon out of the boy's grip.

Carl watched the two figures standing in the moonlight.
Lief was now battling for his life to break free of the stranger
standing over him, one hand fastened upon his arm, the
other cupped around the boy's shoulders. There was a pop-
ping sound like splintering wood as the stranger broke the
boy's neck, and Lief tumbled lifeless upon the ground.

Carl Durer launched himself at the anonymous figure, this maniac who had laid waste all three of his men in a matter of moments. As he ran, he noticed the stranger's sword, a flash of silver in the moonlight, lying where it had fallen, well out of arm's reach. He knew this was probably his only chance. His clumsy sword-stroke fell well wide of the mark, but the impetus of his run carried him, charging into the other man and knocking him off balance. Carl struggled maniacally to stay on his feet and keep hold of the sword. He was filled with a sudden, giddy elation that, after all, his was to be the final victory.

The stranger started to get up again, moving with that same mechanical precision. Carl Durer aimed a heavy, satisfyingly accurate kick into the man's chest, sending him back into the dust.

'No you don't, you bastard. You've given me quite enough trouble for one night already.' The cheap brandy had long worn off and he felt all too vividly sober, but, for all that, he was beginning to warm to his task at last. The muscular figure shrugged off the blow and climbed off the ground a second time. Durer lashed out with his boot again. Once more the blow connected, knocking his victim back. The earth shuddered beneath the stranger's heavy frame.

Carl Durer stepped forward, casting a moon shadow across the outstretched body of the other man. He levered the point of his blade against the other's chest, pressing it lightly against flesh and bone. The other man made no response.

'Come on, then,' Carl spluttered, fighting for breath. 'Let's hear you sing.'

The other man's features were masked in shadow. Carl could make nothing of him beyond the profile of an angular, unshaven face. Yet, eerily, he sensed there would be no fear registering on the stranger's face. No fear, no recognition of his now desperate plight. Not the slightest readiness to yield.

Very well, Carl decided, let's help him find his voice. He pressed the sword in harder against the other's chest, turning the blade as he did so in a slow, corkscrewing motion.

He watched the stranger's arm lift, assumed he was ready to beg for mercy. But he assumed wrong.

The other man locked his hand around the naked steel of Carl Durer's blade. The bandit cried out, more in surprise than anything else, and tried to pull the blade back. But he could not twist it, could not move it at all. The stranger was holding the razor steel gripped in his bare hand, holding it as fast as a vice. Seized with a sudden panic, Carl pulled again on the sword, but the stranger tugged first, and much, much harder. Suddenly Durer was on the ground, spitting dry dust from his mouth, the sword gone from his hand.

He lay for what seemed like an eternity, face down in the dust, his mind grappling to find answers to this impossible reversal of fortune. The only response came in the shape of a leather boot, weather-beaten and crusted with the filth of long journeying. The booted foot flipped Carl Durer over onto his back as easily as though he were a baby.

He was now looking directly into the eyes of the man bearing down upon him: the man now carrying his sword, the man who now held his life in the balance. The dark eyes radiated a terrible strength and a harsh indifference quite unlike Carl's own cruel greed.

'Get up.' The voice, when at last the man spoke, was cold and distant, like an echo from a far country. Carl Durer struggled to his knees. He was powerless to resist the command, powerless to stop the tremors taking hold of his body. He knew how it would go now. He was an old hand at this. Except that now it was he who would do the begging.

He looked up into the man's face, meeting the other's dark, unyielding eyes. Still the other man seemed to look straight through him, as though his gaze was fixed upon another world. Blood oozed steadily from a weeping gash across the man's left hand, but he seemed immune or indifferent to the pain. *He's insane,* Durer guessed, *but maybe I can talk him round.*

'Listen,' he began, cursing himself for his faltering voice, 'let's call it quits, eh? No hard feelings. We'd be a good team, you and me. We could clean up round these parts, easy.'

He knelt, hand held out, waiting for a response. When it came there was no anger, no thirst for vengeance colouring the other man's voice. Carl heard only the flat tones of the executioner, words tinged with the faintest disgust.

'You are nothing,' the stranger said. 'You are weak.'

As the stranger drew his sword arm back, Carl Durer was granted one final sight of the amulet fastened upon his arm, the prize that he had promised to himself above all else. The polished gold sparkled in the air, as though filled with unnatural energy. For a moment Carl was filled with a sick longing, a half-glimpsed knowledge of the power the amulet could grant him, a power which would never now be his.

He saw a second, last, glimmering as the sword passed through the air. Carl followed its shimmering arc, his body held fast by a horrified wonder. He watched the movement whilst he could, then screwed his eyes shut. He knew he had been granted his final sight of this world.

THE BOUNTY HUNTER had watched the destruction of Durer's gang with growing incredulity, a disbelieving spectator at a grotesque carnival of death. He had been edging closer to the scene of the battle, keeping well hidden beneath the cover of the trees. By the time Carl Durer spat out his last, blood-flecked breath, Lothar Koenig and the killer were no more than twenty feet apart.

Looking on from the safety of the trees, Lothar had first thanked Sigmar for what was surely divine intervention. The stranger had proved to be far more than a distraction; without Lothar lifting a finger he was doing his work for him, whittling away the odds separating the bounty hunter from his prize. But it was clear that Durer was not going to survive, Lothar Koenig wouldn't be taking the bandit back to Talabheim alive. He felt a rush of something like grief stab through him as he realised Carl Durer's value would be halved by virtue of his imminent death.

A voice inside Lothar urged him to intervene, step into claim what remained of the bandit leader, alive or dead. The traveller could have no quarrel with that. He had only been protecting himself from a murderous assault. Would he not

be happy to see Durer led away, a prisoner, to face his retribution? But he held back whilst the slaughter reached its
bloody conclusion, sensing that he was witnessing something abnormal, a display of berserk beauty from a cold,
mesmerising force. He held back, yet he knew that he could
not delay indefinitely. If he could not have Durer alive, then
he must have him dead. His body, delivered intact for a
bounty of eighty crowns. That was the deal, and he knew his
grieving yet fastidious patron would brook no other
arrangement.

Wait, Lothar told himself. Wait until the other man has
climbed back into the saddle. Give him time to be on his
way. He has no business with you. But now he was moving
forward through the trees, moving from shadow into the
stark light cast by the watching moons. Moving towards
confrontation with the all-conquering warrior. Later he
would say to himself that it was determination that drove
him on. Who was to say that the madman would not
butcher Durer's dead body, every frenzied blow from his
sword devaluing what was rightly his – Lothar Koenig's –
property. He had not come so far to be denied his rightful
bounty.

But, even as the other man turned, almost casually, at the
sound of his footsteps upon the stony path, Lothar knew
that it was greed that had brought him to this moment of
recklessness. Greed, and the knowledge of what certain people – the right people – might pay to possess a creature such
as this, a killing machine the match of any mercenary Lothar
had ever seen.

A thousand possibilities were tumbling through Lothar
Koenig's mind as the two men came face to face. To the
value of Carl Durer's corpse he now added a sum at least
double that for the bounty he might earn, if he could but
take the warrior captive. Could he take the man alive? Of
course he could. He was Lothar Koenig. Not just a bounty
hunter. He was *the* bounty hunter. The best. He would find
a way. He always did.

Then Lothar looked into the eyes of the other man; and,
in that moment, all of his imaginings crumbled away. It was

he, not the other man, who was mad. Mad to ever think he would have a chance of pulling this off.

Lothar Koenig's hand moved towards the hilt of his sword, then dropped away. Almost by instinct he raised both arms in a gesture of conciliation and contrition.

'I'm sorry,' he said, aware of how stupid his words now sounded. 'I mean you no harm. That man–' he pointed towards the bloodied carcass that was all that remained of Carl Durer. 'I need the body, that's all. Just the body.'

The traveller glanced briefly in the direction of Durer's body, then turned towards Lothar Koenig. His face was unshaven, weathered by what looked like many weeks upon the road, but his eyes burned bright with a hungry fire. Lothar saw in that face neither good nor evil, only power. Unassailable power. The stranger gazed at him without favour or pity, and his features formed into something that might have been a smile. There was a moment of stillness as the stranger paused, as though listening to a distant sound, a voice that spoke to him alone. Then he raised his sword, and polished the blade slowly against the fabric of his tunic. Lothar saw the burnished gold of the amulet, but it was what lay beneath that held him transfixed. In the shadows the man's arm had appeared almost black, covered with a vivid bruise. But now he saw that it was no bruise. Almost the entire length of the man's lower arm was covered in some kind of tattoo, a tableau of runes and images etched upon the killer's skin.

As the killer raised his sword, the images began to move, suddenly animated with a life of their own. Figures came together in combat, the dark hues of the tattoo suddenly flushing blood red. With a sudden shock of recognition, Lothar realised he was watching a re-enactment of the battle with the bandits, and the death of Carl Durer.

Lothar Koenig took a step back and looked around for any aid or refuge amongst his surroundings. Finding none, he sought a last, desperate comfort from his thoughts. We all have to die, he reminded himself again. We all have to die sometime.

But, in the final moment of truth, he found that the words held no comfort at all.

# CHAPTER TWO
## Rough Justice

FOR SOME REASON, Stefan Kumansky found he was not, after all, very hungry. They had been on the road for weeks, travelling through the northern marches of Ostermark, the barren wilderness that straddled the borders of the Empire and Kislev. Much of that time, living off what little could be taken from the land, he had sustained himself with dreams of feasts to come once they returned to what passed for civilisation round these lonely parts. Now, seated at their table in the tiny inn, he and Bruno finally had hot food in front of them, and Stefan found he wanted none of it. It might have been the wretched food itself – though there had been times on the trail when he'd have eaten just about anything. More likely it was the nagging ache of disappointment in his gut that had dulled his appetite.

Stefan took another spoonful of the thin, oily gruel and spat a knot of gristly meat back onto the table. Save for a few other drinkers – a group of labourers making a poor job of pretending not to stare at the two swordsmen – the inn was deserted. From the ramshackle look of the place, it hardly ever saw any custom. With food like this, it was

24

hardly surprising. Stefan slid the bowl towards his companion.

'Here,' he said to Bruno. 'You have it if you want.'

Bruno Haussmann gave his comrade the briefest of glances and then took the offered bowl, his own being already empty. 'If you insist,' he said, and set about spooning the contents hungrily into his mouth.

Stefan looked kindly upon his friend as he ate. Their ages were practically identical – both men had known twenty-four summers – but in other ways they were quite different: Bruno being the shorter and fairer of the two, and – despite the lean weeks on the road – still noticeably the stockier. And likely to stay that way, Stefan reflected. Bruno, always true, always dependable. Solid by look and solid by nature. And himself? Listless, forever searching. A traveller on a journey with no certain end.

Stefan leaned forward, resting his head upon his cupped hands, his expression exactly mirroring his poor humour.

'Cheer up,' Bruno said at last. 'We'll find him, Stefan, sooner or later.'

Stefan took a measured sip of his beer. It was stale and slightly sour, but he drank, nonetheless, to wash away the film of grease coating his mouth. He sat, pondering his friend's words. It was a familiar routine by now, each taking turn to encourage the other whenever their spirits fell low. He didn't know whether Bruno was right, but he took some comfort from his optimism.

'The world is large,' he replied at length. 'In truth, he could be anywhere.'

'We'll pick up the trail again,' Bruno said, firmly. 'There'll be clues, somewhere. He can't hide from us, not forever.'

Stefan Kumansky leant back, eyes closed, and tugged fingers through hair that had grown long and matted over weeks of travel. There would be clues, there had already been clues. Too many clues, that was the problem. Too many trails, like this one that had carried them east from Kislev back into the Empire. Too many trails leading nowhere, going cold.

Across the border in Kislev they had fought a war – he, Bruno and the countless others who had taken arms against the dark armies of Chaos. Erengrad had been saved, the forces of light had prevailed over the darkness. That should have been the end, but fate had offered an unexpected and unwelcome twist to the tail of their adventure. Alexei Zucharov had been amongst the bravest and strongest of their comrades at Erengrad. One of the first to lead the line, and the last to quit the battle. Zucharov had left the field alive, but not unscathed. Greed had found a weakness, a way to harm him where his enemies could not. The golden band upon the body of the Chaos knight had been too much to resist. Alexei had stripped it from the body as a prize, a trophy of war. In that moment, Stefan feared, the poisons of Chaos had entered his comrade's blood.

Zucharov had fled Erengrad a changed man. Now, Stefan had pledged, he could not rest until he had been found.

'Do you know what day it is?' he asked. Bruno looked at him, quizzically.

'No,' he said. 'Do you?'

'It's Kaldezeit's Eve,' Stefan told him. He had been counting off the days. Even though their journey had taken them roughly south they had not been able to outrun the seasons. Steadily the days had been growing shorter and the nights colder, and now they had reached the very cusp of fading summer, and the dawn of the autumn season.

'Kaldezeit's Eve,' Bruno repeated. He smiled, wistfully. 'That'll be a fair excuse for much beer and company back home.'

Stefan nodded in agreement. Back home was where they, too, could already have been, many hundreds of miles to the south-west, in Altdorf. By his reckoning it was almost six months since they had left the city. On Kaldezeit's Eve he could have been back, sitting in his favourite corner bar of the Helmsman, sharing a pot of beer with his brother.

That had been one choice. And there had been other choices, other paths he could, perhaps, have chosen to take. He had been offered another. With the battle at Erengrad won, Stefan had been asked to join a war, a hidden, never-ending war against the powers of Chaos. A war waged in secret by a circle of men such as Gastez Castelguerre, the general who had led the army at Erengrad. There, perhaps, his restless crusade against the darkness would have found a home, a place where he was accepted, not mocked as a zealot who saw shadows where there was only light. But the choice Stefan had made had led him here. Right now, he wasn't sure he didn't regret it.

'I doubt we'll see much in the way of joyous celebration in this dump,' Bruno continued, sourly. He set the bowl to one side, even his hearty appetite now blunted. He looked around disdainfully at the bare, empty quarters of the tavern. 'I can't imagine they go much in the way of celebration around here.'

Stefan smiled. He knew that Bruno, at least, was not mocking him. 'What do they call this place, anyway?' he asked.

'Mielstadt,' a flat, soulless voice answered. The innkeeper snatched the two bowls off the table and glared accusingly at Stefan and Bruno.

'Another?' he said, indicating the mugs of beer still left on the table. Stefan looked up at the man. It was more of a challenge than an invitation, but, in any case, Stefan wasn't interested in staying around.

'No thanks,' he replied. 'We wouldn't want to outstay a welcome. We'll finish our beer and then–'

He was interrupted by a sudden commotion coming from somewhere outside the tavern. A scream, followed by voices raised in anger or agitation, and a clatter of wood and steel. Stefan and Bruno exchanged a single glance and got up quickly from the table.

'Here,' Stefan said, throwing down some coins. 'Thanks for your hospitality.'

They stepped from the door of the inn onto the street. Something in the clamour of voices coming from the town square away to their left communicated a sense of urgency, and soon they were running. Mielstadt wasn't big – not much more than a warren of cluttered streets clustered

around a central square. Stefan and Bruno were soon at the
heart of the disturbance.

The streets around the inn had been deserted, but the
dusty clearing that served as the town square was full to
bursting. The crowd was about the size that might gather in
a place like Mielstadt on a carnival day. On Kaldezeit's Eve,
indeed. But there was nothing festive about the mood of the
people – mostly men – jostling each other in the square.
Fear and anger hung in the air, and Stefan sensed that, yet
again, he had found trouble without looking for it.

They pushed forward, the crowd parting grudgingly for
the outsiders. Instinctively, Stefan scanned the faces
obscured by cowls or a mask of grime, searching for that one
familiar, elusive face. Nothing, as always. No sign.

The crowd was milling around a crude wooden structure
that had been set up in the middle of the square. As Stefan
and Bruno looked on, a thickset man with a face blotched
red from exertion, hatred and too much drink muscled his
way through and stood facing the newcomers, hands
planted squarely upon fleshy hips.

Here we go, Stefan said to himself. He'd met this type
plenty of times before. His hand stroked the hilt of the
sword hanging at his side. To a man, the watching mob fell
silent.

Red Face extended a finger, and jabbed it towards Stefan.
'You! You're in the way,' he said. His breath smelt of something that should have been long buried. Dabs of spittle
flecked Stefan's face as the self-styled leader addressed him.

'I've got a job to get on with,' the man said. He extended
one stubby finger, and pointed at his chest, self-importantly.
'Witch-hunter, me,' he said. 'Business to attend to.'

'If you're a witch-hunter,' Bruno muttered under his
breath, 'then I'm the Emperor Karl-Franz.'

'I'll give you a chance, since it's clear you just arrived.' The
man ran a yellowed eye over the two of them. 'Young gentlemen, I don't doubt,' he sneered. 'Fancy yourselves as
explorers, maybe, adventurers. Thing is–' he gestured
towards the wooden platform up behind him. 'You can't
come *adventuring* round here.' He smirked at Stefan, and was

rewarded by a ripple of laughter from the men standing round.

'Really?' Stefan replied, politely. He made a rapid sweep of the activity in the square. 'And why would that be?'

But he already had the answer to that question. A young woman, slight and wiry with cropped, bronze hair was being jostled through the crowd towards the platform. Her blouse was torn and dirty, her expression defiant but very, very scared. Up on the platform, a length of rope knotted into a noose hung expectantly from a crossbeam.

'This looks like a rough kind of justice,' Bruno said.

'Looks like no justice at all,' Stefan corrected him. Red Face twisted his mouth into a snarl, infuriated that the intruders were still there.

'I told you once,' he said. 'We've got a witch to deal with here, and you're in the way.'

'Well,' Stefan replied, evenly. 'We're sorry about that, aren't we Bruno?'

'Absolutely,' Bruno concurred, drawing closer to his companion as he spoke. 'We hate getting in people's way.'

There were uniformed men milling uncertainly round at the edge the square, at least a dozen of them. Stefan reckoned them to be local militia. Most were busying themselves trying not to notice what was happening under their noses. Stefan guessed they would wait to see which way the wind was going to blow before wading in. No use looking for any help there.

Red Face had drawn a few like-minded townsfolk to his cause. Now Stefan and Bruno were inside a tightening ring of six or seven heavily built men, all clutching daggers or wooden staves.

'Maybe your ears are no better than your eyes,' one of the roughnecks said. 'Maybe you've not heard about the troubles over in Kislev. Cities burnt to the ground. Armies of mutants running amok. All manner of trouble, no mistake, and creeping this way.' Voices joined in loud agreement.

'On the contrary,' Stefan told him. 'We know all about that.' Somewhere in the crowd, he heard a voice mutter, 'Easterners,' and another, 'Snow in their beards.'

'Aye,' Red Face went on, taking encouragement from his supporters. 'And we're not about to let evil take root around here! No witchcraft in Mielstadt!'

The crowd roared their approval. 'So then,' Red Face drew a long knife and waved the pitted blade before Stefan's face. 'Why don't the two of you turn around and get out of our way. We've got a hanging to finish.'

Stefan met Bruno's gaze. The look that passed between them was almost imperceptible, but it signalled agreement.

'I don't think so,' Stefan replied, firmly. Red Face took a step back. The tiniest of doubts mixed with the disbelief on his face.

'*You* don't think so?' he demanded. Stefan ignored him, and turned towards the figure tethered on the gallows. 'Hey, you!' he called, 'What's your name?'

It took the young woman a few seconds to realise that Stefan was now talking to her. Then she replied, in a clear but faltering voice: 'Beatrice. Beatrice de Lucht.'

'Very well, Beatrice. Tell me this: is there anything in your heart that is not loyal to the memory of our Emperor Sigmar or true to the teachings of the goddess Shallya?'

The young woman shook her head, vigorously.

'Have you done any wrong?' Stefan demanded of her. He looked around at Red Face and his unsavoury companions. 'Anything to harm these good people?'

'Nothing,' the girl answered. 'Nothing, I swear.'

Stefan turned to Bruno and shrugged. 'See? A simple case of mistaken identity.'

'That's how it looks to me,' Bruno agreed.

Red Face spread his arms wide in a gesture to the crowd. His face cracked into an unpleasant grin. 'Better make room for two more on the gallows, friends. Looks like we've got our work cut out today.'

The big man moved with surprising speed, grasping hold of Stefan's tunic near the neck. Stefan was tugged forwards, fighting to hold his balance. He fastened onto Red Face's wrist with his right hand, and drew his sword with his left. Red Face was fast, but Stefan was faster. Unlike his opponent, his judgement wasn't clouded by drink. He could kill the other man in an instant, but he didn't want to do that, at least not yet.

Still gripping Red Face by the wrist he swung around, striking the other man with a carefully aimed blow from the flat of his sword. Red Face toppled back into the crowd as Stefan closed in upon him. Behind him, Bruno brandished his sword for the benefit of other would-be aggressors. The crowd backed off.

Red Face had fallen to his knees. His face streamed with perspiration. He lunged at Stefan, aiming the knife at his gut. The younger man side-stepped the blow and brought his own blade down in a single stroke, skewering his attacker through the hand. Red Face squealed like a pig as blood flowed out onto the dry dust of the town square.

'Murderer!' he screamed, scanning the faces around him for support. 'Ralf! Helmut! Get the bastard!' But his friends had now gone very quiet. Like the rest of the mob, they sensed the change in the wind. Stefan pulled his sword clear. His opponent scrambled to his feet, his wounded hand stuffed inside his shirt. Red Face was about to try his luck with the dagger again, but, before he could move, Stefan had the point of his sword tucked neatly underneath the other man's chin.

'Believe me, friend, if I'd wanted to murder you we wouldn't be having this conversation now.' He looked round for Bruno and found his comrade circling the gallows, clearing a space between the platform and the crowd. 'All well?' Stefan asked.

'Quiet as the grave,' Bruno assured him. Stefan turned his attention back to Red Face and pressed home his sword until it nicked at the leathery flesh on his opponent's neck. 'Don't let's repeat this,' he suggested.

Red Face started to gather himself for a final onslaught then thought better of it. He turned away from Stefan with a muttered curse and vanished into the crowd.

'Right,' said Stefan. 'I think this woman's been up there long enough. Who's going to help her down?'

Faces in the mob looked cowed rather than bloodthirsty now. Red Face's capitulation had had a sobering effect. A few men and women stepped forward, hesitantly, at Stefan's command. As if on cue, the militia now waded in, suddenly keen to impose their authority. Stefan found a brace of crossbows aimed at his head. He sheathed his sword and raised one arm to head height.

The militia chief cleared his throat self-consciously. 'You and your friend better come with us' he said. 'And you others–' he glared at whoever in the crowd was prepared to meet his eye. 'Get back to your homes before I decide to take some of you in too.'

AUGUSTUS SIERCK, ACTING graf of Mielstadt, was a man who disliked change, especially the kind of change which, of late, had caused him to fix iron bars across the once elegant windows of his office, the only half-decent building in Mielstadt. Change which had persuaded him, against his better judgement, to allow the daubing of crude protective runes on the walls of houses in the town. Now change had brought him two outsiders, and a little matter of a domestic problem which otherwise might have sorted itself out.

'The point is,' he said, leaning against the expanse of oak desk for emphasis, 'we don't really want or need your sort troubling us here in Mielstadt.'

Stefan stood before the graf impassively, Bruno and Beatrice flanking him on either side. Since their 'rescue' by the graf's militia, they hadn't been badly treated, but welcome was still being kept to a minimum. The chamber they were standing in was shabby and austerely furnished but for a gilt-framed oil painting on one wall. The picture showed a fashionably dressed man posed on bended knee before an aristocratic, pale-skinned woman. It looked oddly out of place amongst the ugly trappings of Mielstadt.

Stefan bowed, non-committally. He assumed that the graf was applying his remarks to all three of them. Sierck pulled back his chair and drew himself up to his full height, which wasn't that much. On tiptoe he would barely reach to Stefan's shoulder, though his girth went some way to lending weight to his aura of self-importance. His face was fleshy but unlined, his hands likewise. Someone, perhaps, who had overseen hardship but not, Stefan reckoned, one who had had to endure it. Sierck made a slow circular tour around his visitors, appraising them with obvious mistrust.

'So, I'm to believe you're just humble travellers,' he said at last, 'travellers just "passing through" on your way back west? You came to Mielstadt looking for a friend?'

'Another traveller,' Stefan corrected him. 'He may be ill, perhaps a danger to himself, or to others. We need to find him, make sure no harm is done.'

Sierck snorted. 'We've had more than our share of that sort. But I doubt you'll find your man here.'

'Nonetheless,' Stefan replied, 'We thought it worth our while looking.'

Sierck circled again, fingering his chain of office. Stefan imagined the graf doubted his story, but lacked the wit to imagine what the truth might be.

'Dab hands with a sword, for everyday travellers aren't we?'

'The road's a perilous place,' Bruno replied. 'We need to be able to look after ourselves.'

The graf paused, distracted by some thought or calculation. 'I'm not a simpleton,' he said at last. 'Don't think I've spent my entire life cooped up in a Morr-forsaken hole like this. I'm a civilised man.' He gestured towards the painting on the wall: 'A distant cousin, you know. The playwright, Detlef Sierck.'

Stefan returned his look, blankly. 'Thought you might know the name,' the graf continued, 'because you seem so fond of play acting yourself.'

Stefan shook his head. 'I don't know what you're talking about.'

The graf's face reddened with irritation. 'Let's stop the pretence,' he barked, abandoning his own pretence of civility. 'We both know why you're here. Why your sort always come here, sniffing about, consorting with troublemakers like – like *her*,' he spat, indicating the girl.

'Which is?' Stefan asked, genuinely bemused now.

'Tal Dur!' Sierck snapped back at him. 'Source of all wonders, and all things to all men. Well, let me tell you something.' The graf pushed his face closer towards Stefan's, his voice rising. 'Here's a bit of free information, to save you your precious time. You won't find Tal Dur here,' he said. 'Not here, nor anywhere round here.' He pounded the desk once with his fist. 'Get that into your heads – there is no Tal Dur – no mystical pool or whatever you want to call it. It doesn't exist!' he shouted. The graf sank back into his chair, exhausted by his exertions. Stefan shrugged, and exchanged a mystified look with Bruno.

Augustus Sierck looked the two strangers up and down. 'You look regular enough to me, I'll give you that. But then–' he cast a glance in the direction of Beatrice – 'you never can tell. The fact is, we're getting more than our share of strangers in Mielstadt. Shadows and ghosts, sniffing around our town. People don't like it. *I* don't like it.'

'As I said before,' Stefan said, quietly, 'we came here looking for someone. If he's not here, then we'll be on our way.'

Augustus Sierck stood up, and puffed out his chest self-importantly. 'See to that,' he said. 'Because if you're still here at dusk, then *I'll* see to it that you're dealt with.'

Stefan bowed once more. 'You are very kind.'

'And you–' Sierck stabbed an accusing finger towards Beatrice, 'you'll be gone too, if you know what's good for you. There's no place for sorcery here, not now, not ever.'

'But I'm not–' started the young woman, but Stefan cut her protests short.

'Save your breath,' he advised. 'Let's get out of here.'

OUTSIDE, THE DAYLIGHT was fast fading, the thin warmth of the afternoon sun already giving way to a chill dusk. The three walked back towards the tavern, where their horses were still tethered.

'Well,' Stefan finally said to Beatrice. 'You certainly don't seem to have made many friends around here.'

'People are fearful,' she replied. 'Fearful, and ignorant, many of them. Word spreads of trouble in the east, and they start to turn against anyone who is – well, different.' She paused. 'I do have a power of healing, that much is true. But I'm no sorceress.'

'I don't doubt it,' Stefan replied. 'You don't look much of a witch to me.'

Beatrice's face softened. 'For that matter,' she observed 'you don't look much like regular travellers. But whoever you are, I owe you my life.'

'Perhaps you can be of help to us,' Bruno told her. 'What Stefan said back there is true. We are looking for someone. A man – perhaps a very dangerous man. Maybe you've heard some word of him.'

The girl looked up at Bruno, then, to Bruno's surprise, took his hand, turning it within her own. Finally she squeezed it firmly, and smiled. 'You have good within you,' she said. 'I can tell your cause is just. How would I recognise this one that you're seeking?'

Stefan held out his arm, and pulled back his sleeve. 'He has a mark upon him,' he said, pointing to an area just above his wrist. 'A kind of tattoo, like a rune etched into his skin. At first he hid it beneath a gold band. But the mark is growing, starting to cover his whole arm. He may be trying to find someone, or something, to rid him of the tattoo.'

Beatrice looked thoughtful. 'Come to me,' she murmured, as if to herself. *'Come to me and wash away your sin.'*

'What was that?' Bruno asked her.

'Nothing,' she said, hurriedly.

'Even without the tattoo, he'd be distinctive,' Bruno went on, with feeling. 'As tall as Stefan – taller perhaps. Tall, and heavily built. In combat he's every bit as formidable as he looks.'

'You wouldn't mistake him,' Stefan affirmed. 'Not someone you'd mess with lightly.'

'I'm sure that's true,' Beatrice agreed. 'But I think Sierck was right on one thing. Mielstadt's not so large that a stranger can go unnoticed for long. I'm sorry, but I don't think he's been here.'

They had reached the horses, and the point where a decision had to be made.

'Do you want to take a look around the town?' Bruno asked. Stefan glanced around. The crowds had gone, leaving Mielstadt deserted. He took in the crumbling houses, their windows barred and shuttered; the surrounding streets populated only by a few pigs and wild dogs.

'No,' he said. 'I'm sure Beatrice is right. If he'd been here, we'd know. The question is, what now?'

Bruno looked at Stefan and shrugged, then began to untie the rope tethering his horse to the railing that fronted the tavern. 'We travel on, I suppose,' he said. 'But as to where–' he stopped short, mid-sentence, and turned to the girl. 'What about you, Beatrice?' he asked. 'What will you do?'

'Actually it's Bea,' she said. 'I shorten it to Bea. Sometimes I shorten it to "B", sometimes to nothing at all.' She laughed, not quite convincingly. 'Sometimes I disappear altogether. That comes in useful at times, round here.'

'Have you got family?' Stefan asked of her. 'Somewhere where you'll be safe?'

Bea's response was part nod, part half-hearted shake of the head. The movement betrayed her uncertainty. 'I used to live with my aunt, a place on the edge of the town. I only came to Mielstadt to live with her. After she died I stayed on, living on my own.' She looked up, arranging her features into a semblance of a grin. 'I'll be all right,' she insisted. 'I'm used to the sort of games they play around here.'

'That didn't look like a game to me,' Stefan commented. He looked at Bruno, the two men weighing the same, unspoken options between them.

'Can you get a horse?' he asked Bea.

The girl nodded. 'Why?'

'You can't stay here at the mercy of that mob.'

'What else can I do?' Bea asked, blankly.

'You can ride with us,' Bruno said. 'At least until we find somewhere where you can stay in safety.'

Bea thought about it for a moment. 'Where are you headed?' she asked them.

'I don't know,' Stefan replied, truthfully. 'I wish I did.'

'All the same, best that you come with us, for now at least,' Bruno said. 'Maybe you can return home again, when things are safer here.'

Bea stood in silence, looking around at the town.

'No,' she said at last. 'If I decide to leave now, then it will be for good. I'll never come back to Mielstadt.' She expelled a breath, then turned back towards Stefan and Bruno. Her smile was tinged only with the faintest sadness. 'I think my heart has already made that decision,' she said. 'Give me an hour, and I'll be ready to ride with you.'

# CHAPTER THREE
## Retribution

THEY RODE FOR three days beyond Mielstadt, three long days of wearying travel. Three days crossing the same, endless barren vista, a green and brown patchwork of vast, empty plains populated with nothing but the occasional stream or clump of trees. Any direction was much the same as any other, no better, no worse. But they chose to steer south, searching for the path of the mighty river that would lead them, at length, back to the heart of the Empire, then home to Altdorf. Stefan still held to the belief that Zucharov would have come this way. That, in the end, he would turn towards the only place he knew as home.

But in those three days upon the road they had encountered no one, nor passed through anything that could be called habitation. The world had suddenly emptied. Stefan had never encountered desolation on such a scale.

That morning they had risen shortly after dawn, riding early to cover as many miles as they could in the light. But the days were shortening with winter's stealthy advance, and, after barely seven hours in the saddle, the sun was already drawing down below the cusp of the distant hills.

Bea had proved to be an easy travelling companion, happy to do her share and suffering the hardships of the road without complaint. But most of the conversation between Bea and her new companions had been small talk, guarded, incidental. In truth she was still a stranger to them, and they to her. Stefan was happy for the moment to respect the distance between them. There would be time enough yet to get to know one another.

Bea glanced around at the darkening skies, and drew her cape in tighter.

'Getting cold, and dark,' she remarked. 'When will we stop for the night?'

'An hour more, maybe two,' Stefan replied. 'We'll wring a few more miles from the day if we can, get as far south as possible.'

Bea nodded, seemingly satisfied, and rode on in thoughtful silence for a while. Stefan had the feeling there was something else on her mind, but it was a few minutes more before she said, 'So, Sierck was wrong, then. You weren't looking for Tal Dur?'

'Tal Dur?' Stefan had heard the name for the first time in Mielstadt. Now it took him a few moments to recollect it. 'No,' he said at last. 'Why do you ask?'

'It's what most who come here are looking for,' Bea told him. 'They've heard the stories. Stories of a place with magical powers.'

'A lot of nonsense, according to our friend the graf,' Stefan reminded her. 'Tal Dur doesn't exist.'

'But he's wrong,' Bea countered. 'It does exist. I know it does.'

'Stefan, look at this!' Stefan was shaken out of his thoughts by Bruno's shout. He turned to see his comrade a little way ahead of them, his outstretched arm pointed towards the horizon.

'Dead ahead,' Bruno called out. 'Smoke rising from the trees.'

Through the fading light Stefan saw three or four separate wisps of grey-white smoke rising above a canopy of trees that marked the boundary of a distant forest. He stared,

momentarily captivated by the lazy beauty of the coils
snaking skywards.

'What do you think?' Bruno asked. 'A camp fire?'

Stefan peered into the now fast gathering gloom. Buried
deep in the forest, the source of the fire wasn't going to give
up its secrets easily. But the pillars of smoke seemed to
spread across a wide area. It couldn't be a camp fire.

'It's more than one fire,' he told Bruno. 'And there's been
no attempt to conceal them.'

'That might be a good thing'

'It might.'

'Well, anyway,' Bea said. 'It's the first sign of life we've seen
in four days. That has to be good at least.'

'It's a sign of something,' Stefan replied. 'I wouldn't
assume any more than that.' He kicked in his spurs and
started forward. 'Let's take a closer look. Then we'll know
what we're dealing with.'

It took another hour in the falling light before they
reached the edge of the forest. All that time knots of thick
smoke continued to rise skywards, white against the darkening backdrop. As they entered the forest and rode beneath
the canopy of the trees, all trace of the fires disappeared.
Bruno brought his horse around in a circle, scanning the forest floor.

'There's a clear path over here, a well-trodden one,' he
announced. 'It must lead somewhere.'

The riders followed the path deep into the forest. Now, at
last, there were clear signs of habitation. Neatly stacked piles
of stones and hewn logs, the wheel from a cart, the debris of
everyday living. Nothing out of the ordinary, but Stefan had
the sense that all was far from well. Soon they could smell
it: the slightly sweet scent of wood-smoke mixed with something else: the sharper odour of charred or burning meat, a
smell that was becoming thicker and more pungent by the
moment.

Bea had sensed it too. 'This isn't right,' she said, her voice
small and anxious.

Stefan made no reply, but he was now certain his fears
were justified. There was something very wrong here. Soon

they came to the first building, its shape emerging out of a smoky mist woven around the trees. Sturdily built from thick-cut stone, the house had probably stood for a hundred years and might well stand for a hundred more. But it was a home no longer. The walls were blackened, scorched by the fire, and yellow tongues of flame still licked across what remained of its brushwood roof. The single door hung open, a gaping, broken mouth.

Further along they came upon a second burned out shell, and then a third. In front of the fourth house they found the first body, lying face down upon the forest path. A dark red bloom was spreading from a wound in the man's back. Stefan climbed down and turned the body over. The dead man was of middle years, with solid, weather-tanned features. Dead, vacant eyes stared up at Stefan. If the man had ever been armed, then his weapon had been taken from him. He had not died in battle. This was murder.

The toll of death mounted as they neared the centre of the village. The bodies were not soldiers or mercenaries. They were farmers, simple labourers. Men dressed in peasant smocks, some still clutching the tools of their trades: pitchforks, spades or hunting knives. Tools they had used to mount a last, futile defence against their executioners.

There were perhaps a dozen more houses in the village. All had been destroyed, all surrendered to the flames. At the heart of the village the trees had been cut down to make a small clearing, a patch of bare earth barely big enough to call a square. In the centre of the clearing was a neat stone chapel, and inside the chapel they found the women and children.

Bea turned away, covering her face with her hands. Bruno left Stefan alone for a moment or two, standing in the doorway of the desecrated shrine.

'How many?' he asked at last. Stefan turned to face him, pulling the door to the chapel closed behind him. 'Twenty, maybe more,' he said, his voice subdued.

Stefan imagined their terror as the attackers closed in. Imagined them praying for Sigmar to spare them, or for their tormentors to show them some small vestige of mercy.

'Are they all—' Bea began. 'I mean are there any—'

Bruno shook his head. The chapel had become a tomb. 'None survived,' he said. 'Whoever was here made quite certain of that.'

'It looks like the village has been plundered,' Stefan observed. 'Food, provisions. Anything of any use taken.'

'A raid, then. But why destroy the whole village into the bargain?' Bruno asked.

Bea shivered. 'It looks like some cruel punishment,' she said.

'Cruel indeed,' Stefan agreed. Cruel, and methodical.

Across the village the fires still crackled, otherwise a silence, almost serene in its totality, hung over the place. Stefan moved away from Bruno, and sat alone upon the bed of an abandoned cart, staring at the ruins in silence. When at last he looked round, Bea was seated next to him.

'This is a terrible thing,' she began, then hesitated. 'It touches something for you, doesn't it? Something buried deep. A deep, terrible sorrow.'

Stefan raised his head, and looked at Bea intently, taking in her features. She was young, but there was a wisdom there that outweighed her years.

'Do you know me that well already?'

'I have a power of healing' she said. 'To heal, you must be able to know pain.'

She met his gaze steadily, waiting patiently for whatever answer Stefan might give.

'I came from a place like this,' he said at last. 'A small village. A place far away, in Kislev. It was a simple life, not much to it. But people worked hard, and they looked after each other. It was enough. Then, one day, raiders came – savage riders from Norsca. They came, and when they'd left, there wasn't any village any more. I was eleven years old.'

'Your family,' Bea said. 'Were they all…'

'My brother and I survived,' Stefan said. He smiled, briefly. 'Mikhal's a merchant now, back in Altdorf. But our father died along with all the others, defending the village. They were just ordinary, hard-working people. Fishermen, not warriors. But they fought just the same, fought to save their village, their home. They fought, and they died. Just like they died here.' He scanned the smoking ruins. 'You asked me why I have to keep searching until we've found the man we're looking for. This is why,' he said. 'My life changed forever on that day. That was the day I made my vow to avenge my father, and all those who had suffered like him.'

He lifted his head, and looked around at the smoking ruins of the village.

'Whoever did this,' he said, 'we'll find them. Find them and make them pay.' He stepped forward, and ran the length of his hand across the façade of the chapel, just above the door. The brick was charred and blackened, but, carved into the pitted surface, a single word was still legible.

'Grunwald,' Stefan spoke the word softly, with reverence. 'Remember that name,' he told Bea. 'Hold it in your heart. For that is all that remains of this village now.'

Bruno appeared, running back towards the chapel from the trees at the edge of the village. 'Stefan,' he called out, breathlessly. 'Come and have a look at this.'

It was another body, all but hidden in the long grass on the edge of the village. The body was burnt, so badly charred as to be almost beyond recognition. Bruno had thought at first it was another of the villagers. But it was not a villager. In fact, as Stefan now clearly saw, it wasn't even human.

'Sigmar protect us,' Bea said, quietly. 'A mutant.'

Stefan raked through the ashes with his sword. The charred remains gave off a pungent, rancid smell, and where not totally burnt, the flesh was a grey-green in colour. Whatever the creature was, it had once been human. But twisted horns protruded from what was left of its skull, and the creature's single remaining eye was a disc of sickly yellow.

'That's our answer then,' Bruno said grimly. 'This is what happened to Grunwald. Some consolation at least that the villagers managed to destroy one of the vermin that attacked them.'

'There must be others,' Stefan said. 'The rest of the mutants can't be far.'

'There are tracks,' Bruno told Stefan. 'Horses' hooves, heading away from the village. They look pretty recent to me.'

'How many?' Stefan asked.

'Hard to be sure, but at least half a dozen.'

Stefan said a silent prayer for the dead of the village and climbed back into the saddle.

'You might want to think about staying here for now,' he said to Bea. 'We have to go after the mutants.'

But Bea was already back on her horse, following Bruno out towards the woods. 'I'd rather take my chances with you than stay here alone. Besides,' she added, 'you may have need of me before long.'

'Wait a minute,' Stefan caught up with the other horse and took hold of the reins, bringing the animal to a halt. 'Whatever we're about to get into, it's going to be dangerous,' he said. 'You'll need something to protect yourself at the very least. Here,' he slid a blade from the saddlebag slung at the side of his horse. 'Take this. It's light enough to wield, and it could save your life.'

The healer looked at the blade held out before her and seemed, Stefan thought, to back away from it. 'It's all right,' she replied at last. She patted a side pocket with the flat of her hand. 'I carry my own weapon,' she said. 'One I'm used to. I'll be fine with that.'

Stefan was unconvinced, and looked towards Bruno. His comrade turned his horse back on to the path. 'We need to get moving,' he urged. 'They already have a head start on us. Don't worry,' he said to Bea. 'We'll see you safe.'

She smiled. 'I know you will,' she said. 'Come on. Bruno's right. We need to get going.'

They followed the tracks through to the far side of the wood and back out onto the open plain. By now day had given way to night, the two moons shining like ghostly orbs through a thin curtain of mist spread low across the empty land. The hoof prints they were following cut a trail across the thin grass then disappeared abruptly as the grass gave way to stone

'We've lost them,' Bruno declared. Stefan searched the desolate landscape, looking for any clue left by the riders. Just when it seemed their pursuit was to end in frustration, a shout rang out across the plain. A shout, followed by two long notes on a hunting horn.

The three riders raced towards the sound, closing the distance between them and their quarry. The horn sounded again, two, three more times. Soon they could hear voices and the unmistakable sound of clashing steel. Stefan had no idea exactly what they were riding into, what kind of men or monsters they were about to encounter, or how many. But at the moment that didn't matter. After weeks of futile searching they had found a purpose again. The creatures who destroyed the village would not elude them now.

The mist had thickened to a choking fog, snuffing out all light from the moons. Stefan could barely see Bruno riding five yards ahead of him. Then, out of the gloom, came the outline of a horseman riding hard towards them, his progress marked by a flaming torch held low by his side.

Stefan felt his heart pounding in his chest as his body tensed itself for the coming battle. Moonlight glinted on polished steel as he drew his sword from out of its scabbard. Had the other rider not seen them? If he had, the sight of Stefan and Bruno closing in upon him had given him cause to vary neither his course nor the thunderous pace of his horse. Inevitably, the thought flashed through Stefan's mind: could it be him?

The possibility vanished almost as quickly as it appeared. Too small, too lightly built. This was not Alexei Zucharov. But if this horseman had been with those who had ridden into the village of Grunwald, then Stefan would kill him all the same.

'Hold fast,' he shouted to Bruno. 'Here he comes!'

At the last moment the other rider looked up, and seemed to see Stefan and the others as if for the first time. He called out, words that were lost in the wind. But as Stefan swung his sword, ready to aim the first strike, he heard Bruno call out to him.

'Don't strike, Stefan!'

Stefan pulled back from the blow, and the rider thundered past. There was a flash of vivid red, and a shouted cry.

Stefan now saw the ugly gash that was causing the rider to clutch his side just below his ribs. Blood was flowing freely from the wound, all but invisible against the bright scarlet tunic that he wore over his chainmail vest. A moment later the rider lost control of his horse and tumbled from the saddle onto the ground.

The rider lay, groaning in pain, then twisted his body round to look up at Stefan and Bruno. The look of anguish in his face suggested he was unsure whether they were going to attack him or not, but his strength was all but spent. He sagged forward, clutching feebly at the fallen torch with one hand, and pointing back the way he had come with the other.

Just in time, Stefan heard the heavy pounding of horses, riding in hard pursuit. The beasts and their riders materialised out of nowhere to appear on the path ahead of them. These were the living, breathing incarnations of the body left behind in the village. Stefan thrust out his sword to fend off a blow. Somewhere to his left he heard Bruno cry out, and the sound of metal slicing the air. In the next moment four – no, five – riders streaked past them, creatures clearly marked by the hand of Chaos. They rode upon hideous, altered steeds: horses with cloven hooves and eyes that glowed like burning coals.

The mutants thundered past, disappearing into the fog. The drumming of hooves receded, then grew louder again, beating a pounding tattoo upon the hard earth.

'Get ready!' Stefan shouted. 'They're coming back.'

This time he was ready for them, but the mutants rode with astonishing speed. His blade cut nothing but thin air, but the answering blow found its mark, razor sharp steel cutting a line across Stefan's cheek. As the riders sped past he had a fleeting glimpse of a gaunt, bloodless face, and an arm that looked more like the claw of a crab. Then they were gone again, melted into the murky gloom. Stefan heard the hooves recede, then turn to launch yet another assault.

Blood from the cut on his cheek dribbled into his mouth, a warm, metallic taste of mortality. Stefan spat and cursed. Again the pounding beat of onrushing hooves. Stefan held his nerve as the hideous riders bore down upon them yet again, at the last possible moment striking out with his sword. He made only glancing contact, unseating one rider from its monstrous steed.

The mutant bellowed its rage at Stefan. It had the body and features of a man, but the pale, almost translucent flesh of one arm tapered off into a curved claw-like blade where the hand should have been. The sinuous limb flexed and lashed at Stefan, the claw-end missing his face by inches. Stefan pressed home his attack. Still the mutant fought back, coiling and unleashing the tentacle-like limb in a single movement. Stefan met the blow and cut cleanly through the creature's arm, severing the lethal claw. The mutant pulled away, but Stefan blocked its retreat and aimed another blow square into the creature's neck. A gout of dark blood sprayed from the creature's mouth, and the mutant crumpled upon the ground.

Stefan cast his gaze about, ready for the next attack. But the mutant riders had vanished yet again.

'The scum are losing their appetite for killing,' Bruno commented, sourly.

'Any sign?' Stefan asked 'Have they gone?'

'Not gone,' Bea said. 'They're still out there, watching. Waiting.' She got down from her horse and picked up the still burning torch that lay beside the dead soldier. She turned her head slowly from side to side, as if following an invisible line. 'That way!' she shouted suddenly, leaping back onto her horse and gathering the reins. 'Over there!'

Without further warning, she surged forward, Stefan and Bruno close behind. Bea rode straight ahead a few yards further, then swung her horse about, drawing a wide circle around her body with the burning torch. At that moment the clouds drew back from the moons, and a wash of light pierced the smothering fog. Where before there had been only darkness, they now saw four or five riders approaching, towering mutant steeds closing fast upon Bea.

'Come on,' Stefan urged Bruno. 'They won't hide from us now.'

The mutants howled, determined to avenge their fallen comrade. The four riders converged in a pincer movement, but Bea moved with astonishing agility, steering her horse through the gap between two attackers. Two mutants collided in a tangled mass of flesh and steel. A third wheeled around, straight into Bruno's path. Bruno held firm on a collision course with the mutant, at the last moment jinking to the left, his sword cutting through the mutant's guard. The blade sliced cleanly through the creature's neck, slicing its ugly, deformed head from its shoulders.

The remaining two mutants turned back towards Stefan in a last desperate attempt to break free. Stefan felled the first, a pale creature with a glistening pig-like face, cutting him down with a single stroke as he rode past. The second held his ground, parried Stefan's first strike, and aimed a blow at the horse's flank. Stefan's horse reared up, unseating him. The last of the mutants now charged down at him, wringing the last ounce of speed from its ghastly horse.

Stefan scrambled to his feet as the apparition bore down upon him. Moments before he was trampled beneath the hooves he dodged to one side. As the mutant horse thundered past he grabbed at the rider, and pulled the mutant from the saddle.

The mutant hit the ground hard, but sprang back onto its feet almost instantaneously. It turned and growled at Stefan, a yellow, gangrenous venom dripping from its open jaw. The mutant's face bore acquaintance with humanity, but the black, beaded eyes and scale-crusted flesh had more in common with a lizard than a man.

For an instant the two stood motionless, facing each other. Stefan held his sword low, leaving his guard temptingly open. It was a temptation the mutant could not resist. It lunged forward, torso flexing in a single, snake-like movement as a clawed limb raked at Stefan's face.

For the second time Stefan tasted blood as the talons tore at his face, but he made sure the opportunity cost the mutant dearly. He drove his sword up into a fold of blistered flesh at the base of the creature's neck. There was a sound half way between a scream and a rush of air as the reptilian face split open. A foul spray misted the air as the creature toppled back, clutching at its throat. It lay upon the ground, its body twitching and juddering.

Stefan sank to one knee, resting his weight upon the hilt of his sword.

If I kill a thousand of your kind, he reflected, there will still be more. He got to his feet, wiping the putrid gore from his jerkin and legs. It would never be enough. No matter if he killed a thousand, or ten thousand abominations such as this, it would still never be enough. Each small victory was an attempt to balance the scales of natural justice, an act of retribution for the dead of villages like Odensk, like Grunwald. But, for Stefan, the sense of justice earned was always short-lived. It could never be enough, and that thought troubled him deeply.

He felt Bruno's hand on his shoulder. 'You all right?' his friend asked.

Stefan gripped his comrade's arm. 'I'm fine,' he said.

Both men looked round at the sound of a horse approaching. Bea's expression was neutral, neither elated nor fearful. Only the tremor in her voice betrayed the ordeal she had come through.

'Well,' she said. 'I'm glad that's over.'

Stefan reached up and took her hand.

'Well done,' he said. 'Truly well fought.'

'It was the two of you who did the fighting,' Bea corrected him. 'I just stayed out of the way. I told you before,' she said. 'I've a talent for making myself vanish.'

Bruno fixed the girl with a look of honest admiration. 'Well,' he replied. 'Don't plan on vanishing on us just yet.'

'Don't worry,' she assured him. 'I won't. Whatever–'

Her words were cut short by the sounds of voices and clashing steel, the unmistakable music of conflict. Somewhere close by, battle was being joined. Stefan reached again for his second sword, and offered it across to Bea. 'No excuses this time,' he told her. 'You're going to need this.'

Bruno tracked the direction of the sounds. 'Just over the brow of that hill,' he announced. 'Quite close I think.'

Bea fixed her gaze upon Stefan. 'The man – the one you're looking for,' she said, 'do you think he could have had anything to do with this?'

Stefan gave no answer. Perhaps it wasn't a question he was ready to answer. Not yet. Instead he gathered up the reins and turned his horse about to face the sounds of battle.

'Come on,' he urged his companions. 'This isn't over yet.'

# CHAPTER FOUR
## The Common Cause

IN THE END, the mutants had not got far beyond the village. Barely two miles north of Grunwald, Stefan and his comrades rode into the heart of a pitched battle. A dozen more scarlet riders bearing torches were fighting shadows, locked in a life or death struggle with the night-cloaked phantoms. The odds favouring the soldiers were at best even. Their bravery could not be doubted, but it was far from clear that they would win through.

Bea pulled ahead of Stefan, snatching the burning torch from his hand as she passed him. 'Let me be your pathfinder,' she shouted. 'I'll draw them on – you can do the rest.'

She left him little chance to protest, riding like the wind into the thick of the battle. Stefan followed hard on her heels, pushing his horse hard to sustain the furious pace. Out of nowhere, a mutant rider materialised in front of Stefan, intent upon striking out at Bea. It didn't see Stefan until much too late. Stefan saw the brief flicker of shock in the cold eyes before his blade slashed away the mutant's sword arm and sent the creature spinning from the saddle, the mutant's horse going down beneath it.

Stefan jerked on the reins, pulling his horse out of the way. For the moment he had lost sight both of Bea and Bruno. A soldier loomed out of the darkness towards him, his gashed and bloodied armour testimony to a long and desperate battle. Their eyes met in a brief, unspoken acknowledgement. Before Stefan could speak, the soldier turned away, reacting to something Stefan could not see. The soldier raised his guard, reacting quickly, but not quickly enough. Stefan heard the man scream, then saw light glinting off the blade that seemed to come out of nowhere, piercing the thin mail corselet in a single, fatal thrust.

Stefan pushed forward into the mutant's path. He aimed his sword into thin air, but it found a solid mark, cleaving a path between flesh and bone. Stefan drew the blade back and struck again. He had a momentary glimpse of a figure with the proportions of a man with scaly, black skin. The mutant reeled under the force of Stefan's blow. Before it could melt back into the night, Stefan connected with a third stroke of his sword. The scaly-fleshed warrior toppled back in the saddle and its horse wheeled away, carrying its dead cargo away into the night.

'Stefan, behind you!'

Stefan reacted instinctively at the sound of Bruno's voice, dropping his head and pulling his horse away to one side. He felt a rush of air come towards him, then something strike the flank of the horse like a battering ram. Stefan gripped tight but could not hold on. There was a moment of confusion as he was thrown clear then a sudden impact as he struck the hard ground. Creatures – horses, men and mutants – thundered around him in every direction. Stefan looked up, but his horse was gone. He was marooned, as likely to be trampled to death as cut down by a sword. There was a rush of hooves and Bruno appeared, a half-man, half-bird mutant falling beneath his sword.

Stefan shouted his comrade's name. To his relief, Bruno heard him and turned, reaching out to haul Stefan up into the saddle behind him. In the confusion Stefan had lost his sword, but a replacement was soon offered.

'You can do more with this than I can,' Bea shouted to him. 'Take it!' she insisted, holding out the blade. Stefan took the sword. 'Slow down a moment,' he told Bruno. He climbed from Bruno's horse onto Bea's, and they rejoined the battle. Another two mutants were put to the sword, but still they came on.

But their presence had given visible heart to their new allies. The men in scarlet were fighting with a renewed vigour, turning defence to attack as more and more of the shadowy creatures fell to their blades. The odds moved in their favour. Now the mutants sought escape, not conquest. But there was no longer any hiding; no shelter to be found within the shadows. The barren landscape would become their burial ground. Blood raced in Stefan's veins as he sent the last of the mutants to the Gates of Morr.

THE BATTLE WAS over, the victory won. Stefan recovered his horse, which had been wandering aimlessly at the edge of the battle field. Scattered fires flickered like beacons where the soldiers were burning the broken bodies of the mutants. Only when Stefan was satisfied that the creatures were truly all dead did he seek out the leader of the scarlet-clad soldiers. As yet, he had not the slightest idea who their allies might be, or, more importantly, where they had come from.

Half the soldiers lay dead or dying where they had fallen in battle. The survivors stood clustered around one of their injured comrades, trying to tend to his wounds. Stefan watched them, unsure now of how far he should intrude. He knew little of the surgeon's art, but it seemed clear that what remained of the soldier's life would be measured in minutes rather than years if nothing could be done.

He sheathed his sword and stepped forward. The soldier who seemed to be in command looked up.

'He's dying,' the man announced, briskly. 'Can you help him?'

'No. He can't.' Bea pushed past Stefan and approached the wounded soldier. 'He can't,' she reaffirmed. 'But maybe I can.'

The soldiers regarded Bea with a mixture of curiosity and suspicion, but they let her through, standing back as she stooped low over the wounded man. She worked quickly and silently, cutting away the remains of the blood-soaked tunic to expose the ruptured flesh. She laid her hands firmly upon the open wound, and closed her eyes. Her lips moved around the words of a prayer.

'I hope she knows what she's doing,' the man who'd first spoken to Stefan commented.

'Can you do any better?' Stefan asked him. The soldier said nothing, but shook his head slowly, then stood back to watch. The wounded man's cries subsided a little. Bea stayed at his side, pressing her hands to his chest. When at last she moved it was to look up, and seek out Bruno.

'Over in those bushes,' she said to him, indicating with her head. 'You should find a plant growing in amongst them. Thick fleshy leaves. Small yellow flowers.'

Bruno looked around. 'How much do you need?'

'As much as you can find. And quickly,' Bea urged him. 'You others,' she said to the soldiers standing by. 'Set me a fire and boil as much water as you can find or spare.'

Bruno set off in search of the herb, accompanied by one of the soldiers. Stefan stayed with the others as they gathered wood together and set a pan to boil over the fire. He turned to pick a conversation with the man on his left. From his bearing, Stefan guessed that he was their captain.

'One of your good men?' he asked, indicating the wounded man.

'They're all good men,' the soldier replied. 'Each life is precious to us.'

'What were you doing out here?'

The soldier looked him up and down, as if weighing up his new companion to satisfy himself that Stefan could be trusted with the information. 'Out here? Hunting. Hunting the mutants.'

Bruno and his companion arrived back, bearing handfuls of a dark herb speckled with tiny bright gold flowers. Bea directed them to put the gathered herbs upon the ground, then divided them into two piles, one about a quarter of the size of the other. She scooped the larger pile carefully into the bubbling water, collected the smaller pile into her fist and pressed it into the wound. The soldier moaned. His breathing deepened, then became easier and more regular.

ONE OF THE soldiers passed Bea a battered metal cup filled from the boiling pan. The steam rising from its brim gave off a pungent, bitter scent. Bea took the cup and handed it to Stefan.

'See if you can get him to drink,' she instructed him. 'The more the better.'

The man coughed and spluttered as Stefan forced the hot liquid between his lips. His eyes flickered open, but he still seemed to be barely aware of where he was or who he was with.

Stefan paused and looked around. The watching soldiers were keeping a respectful distance, as if fearful of upsetting the delicate balance of the healing worked by Bea.

'These men,' Stefan said to her. 'They appeared as from nowhere. They may be our allies, but we know nothing about them.'

Bea pressed the last of the herbs into a poultice for the wound, then took the cup from Stefan. 'I'm not sure who they are either,' she said, 'but I've seen them, or others like them before. In Mielstadt. I think they came to barter, to trade.'

'Trade?' Stefan asked. 'Trade what?'

She shook her head. 'I don't know. Ah – good.' The wounded soldier had opened his eyes again, and was gazing up at Bea and Stefan. He took a little more of the liquid from the offered cup, moistening his cracked and bloodied lips.

'I was brought unto the Gates of Morr,' he whispered. 'You have carried me back. May almighty Sigmar grant you fortune.' He started to lift his head but Bea pushed him back, gently but firmly.

'You need rest,' she told him. 'You're not going anywhere.'

The soldier's clear blue eyes flicked from side to side. 'The mutants?'

'Destroyed,' Bruno told him. 'They've met their retribution.'

The soldier expelled a deep breath. 'Then Sigmar has favoured us. Our work is done.' He sank back upon the ground, and his eyes fell closed. Bea motioned to the soldiers standing round.

'Make sure he gets all the water he needs. And keep the wound clean. The dressing will need changing every hour or so. Above all he needs rest,' she told them. 'Don't even think of moving him before daylight.'

The men conferred briefly. The one whom Stefan now identified as their leader nodded agreement. 'Then we'll make camp here for the night,' he announced. 'You'd earn our gratitude if you would stay with us.'

Bea looked to Stefan. 'Well?'

Stefan considered. Most of the hours of darkness still lay ahead of them. They could ride on for another hour or so before pitching camp, though the risks of travelling by night were considerably higher than by day. And, if they were to continue on, where would they be travelling to? Stefan thought back to the battle with the mutants. For a while he had had a purpose, powerful and all-consuming. For a moment all other thoughts, even of Zucharov, had been obliterated.

Now, perhaps for the first time since they had left Mielstadt, Stefan acknowledged the uncomfortable truth. They were on a journey without maps, trying to recover the trail of a man who had long since vanished. A man who, for all that they knew, might even be dead. Right then, any decision, any direction, seemed as good as any other.

For now, the best decision was probably to stay put for the night. And, in the morning – well, the morning could look after itself.

He looked to Bruno. His comrade shrugged his shoulders. 'It's as good a place as any. At least we'll have safety in numbers.'

'Agreed,' Stefan said. 'We'll set down here, then see where the day takes us.'

The two friends worked quickly and methodically, fixing a shelter from wood and canvas with the practiced ease of men long upon the road. By the time they'd finished, Stefan realised he was desperately tired. Riding on would have been the wrong decision.

He stretched out upon the hard ground, waves of aching weariness suddenly flooding his body. Bruno sat beside him, and both sat watching the brisk efficiency of the soldiers as they constructed their own camp. Bea still knelt by the side of the wounded man, her hands resting upon the freshly bandaged wound.

'Amazing,' Bruno commented. 'You wouldn't think she was tired at all.'

'No more than you would tire if you had a sword in your hand,' Stefan said. 'It's her calling, just as the sword is ours. We serve the same purpose, I think. But in very different ways.'

Bruno nodded agreement. 'I know we didn't plan it this way. But we couldn't have chosen a fairer companion.'

Stefan looked at his friend, reading the expression in his face. It was a look he'd grown familiar with over the years. 'Careful,' he cautioned. 'The last woman you took a fancy to betrayed us. Turned out to be a pawn of Chaos that nearly got us all killed.'

Bruno sat silent for a moment, the darkness sparing his blushes. 'That was different,' he said at last. 'Bea's no pawn of Chaos. I don't think she's going to betray us, either.'

'No,' Stefan agreed. 'Nor do I. I don't think so at all.'

The two men sat side by side as the evening waned, the twin moons melting into the night sky. Gradually the fires dotted across the camp faded as well, until finally all around was darkness. At length Bea joined them, settling herself at Bruno's side.

'Quite a day,' she observed.

'We'll have easier ones,' Stefan replied. 'And harder ones as well, no doubt.'

'Looks like your patient will pull through,' Bruno said. 'I'd have marked that man for dead. You excel at your craft.'

'And you at yours,' Bea replied.

'Stefan's the finest swordsman you'll see,' Bruno affirmed. 'The best.'

'So is every man,' Stefan countered. 'We all think that. Until we meet the one swordsman who's better still. Somewhere, death waits along the road for us all.'

Bea sat contemplating Stefan's words. 'This man you're pursuing,' she said at last. 'Alexei Zucharov. Could he be that one?'

The words struck home with Stefan, with surprising force. 'What makes you ask that?' he said, sharply.

Bea shrugged. 'I'm not sure. But sometimes I wonder if in some way we all pursue our end, our undoing.'

'A troubling thought.'

'Don't get the wrong idea. Zucharov isn't invincible,' Bruno said, firmly. 'And anyway, we're jumping to too many conclusions. We don't even know for sure that he is our enemy.'

'We don't,' Stefan agreed. 'But that's one question I can't leave unanswered. That's why we must keep searching,' he told Bea. 'Until we find him.'

'And then?'

Stefan had no ready answer. Since Erengrad, he had been consumed by the hunt for the man who had once been his comrade. But every journey must have an end. He could not yet see what that end might be, but in his heart he knew that it was impossible for both him and Zucharov to survive. Bea's words echoed in his mind, an unwelcome harbinger of death.

'Let's talk about you,' he said steering the conversation towards other things. 'You heal people, I kill them. You have the better part of virtue, I think.'

The briefest of smiles crossed Bea's features. 'You didn't kill me,' she said. 'In fact, if it wasn't for the two of you I doubt I'd still be alive. I haven't the power to disappear completely.'

She reached out towards Stefan, her fingers tracing the cuts on his face. Stefan flinched back as her touch drew a stinging pain from the wound.

'That could leave you scarred,' she said at last. 'Put your head back.'

'Why?'

'Just do it,' she said, briskly.

Too tired to argue, Stefan did as he was bidden. He smelt a strong medicinal scent in his nostrils, and a sudden, stinging pain as Bea rubbed what remained of the herb into the cut running down the side of his face. The effect was immediate, and surprising. The pain was still there, but softened by a gentle, suffusing warmth that flowed down the whole of his body, soaking into his aching limbs.

'Ulric's toil!' he murmured. 'What is that stuff?'

'Just an ordinary flower, the sort you can find growing almost anywhere.'

'Well the effects aren't ordinary, I can tell you that.'

Bea pressed her palm firmly against the side of Stefan's face. 'It's how you use it that matters. And who uses it,' she added. 'That's what makes a healer. Now sit still and let the herb do its work.'

Stefan closed his eyes, enjoying the sensation of the pain melting away from his body. 'I could get too used to this,' he observed.

'Don't worry,' she assured him. 'You'll feel nothing of it by morning.'

'What about our friend over there. Will he live?'

'He's a strong man. He'll pull through.'

'What about his companions?' he asked. 'Did you learn any more from them?'

'Not a lot. I got the feeling they were waiting to see whether I was going to heal their comrade.' She lifted her hand clear, and inspected her work. 'Or kill him,' she said. 'There. You'll do. Now you need sleep, like Bruno here.'

Stefan looked round. Bruno had curled himself under a blanket and was indeed solidly asleep. Stefan had the sudden sense of time passing unnoticed. He made a half-hearted attempt to calculate how long he must have been sitting with Bea, but he was fast succumbing to a seductive drowsiness.

Sleep. Suddenly sleep was very appealing. He began to slip into a soft, blurred world where nothing but sleep was of any consequence. When he tried to speak, his tongue felt thick and slow.

'Bruno,' he murmured. Wasn't there something he was going to mention about Bruno? But Stefan lost his grip on whatever it might have been as he slipped into a deep, dreamless sleep.

HE WOKE WITH the sun low in his eyes, and a biting wind blowing across the open plain of the Ostermark. Stefan felt refreshed, wonderfully rested. As he stripped away the covering blanket he put his hand, instinctively, to his cheek. He probed the line of the wound where the mutant's sword had cut through the flesh. The incision was still there, but very faint, and all pain was gone. He looked around, and saw Bea sitting close by, watching him carefully.

'Keeping an eye on your patient?'

Bruno appeared, walking in tandem with one of the soldiers. 'The wounded man has made a good recovery. Their captain would like to speak with us.'

Stefan got up and brushed himself down. 'Gladly,' he said. 'I'm sure there's much we'd like to know about each other.'

'I'll wait here,' Bea offered. The soldier made a short, deferential bow. 'If you please,' he said, 'the captain asked to speak with you in particular.'

'In that case, lead on,' Bea replied, graciously. The three followed the soldier through the remnants of the previous night's battle: broken carcasses, grotesque collages of twisted bones, cracked and blackened by the flames. Red-clad soldiers moved amongst the debris, carefully moving the remains of any mutants into pits to be burned. Wisps of smoke still trickled skywards where fires had been kindled.

The wounded man was sitting upright, supported by another soldier and a second man that Stefan recognised as the captain. He saluted Stefan and his comrades, and beckoned them across. He offered his hand to each of them in turn, and smiled a broad welcome.

'I must offer my gratitude to you first of all,' he said to Bea. 'But for you another of my men would not have seen this dawn.'

'His constitution is strong,' Bea told him. 'And his spirit wasn't ready to relinquish this life just yet. You have a powerful will to live,' she told the wounded man.

'Nonetheless.' The captain looked her up and down with clear grey eyes. 'We are in your debt.' He turned to Stefan and Bruno. 'And to you, too, gentlemen. Your intervention in our struggle was decisive.'

'Our paths crossed, and we met with the same purpose,' Stefan replied. 'Between us we've wiped more foul creatures of Chaos from the face of this world. For that we can all take credit.'

The other man smiled, pleased by Stefan's words. He held out his hand. 'Hans Baecker at your service.'

'Stefan Kumansky. This is Bruno Hausmann, Beatrice de Lucht.'

'Where are you headed?'

'Ultimately, to Altdorf,' Stefan replied.

'And immediately?' The steely eyes fixed Stefan with a quizzical stare. Stefan paused, thinking about his answer. 'The honest answer,' he said eventually, 'we're not sure. South, and west, I suppose.'

Baecker nodded, thoughtfully.

'And you?' Stefan asked him. 'May we know where you come from?'

'We serve the rulers of Sigmarsgeist,' Baecker replied. 'We are honoured to wear that livery.'

'It's an honourable name, and a memorable one,' Stefan agreed. 'But not one I've heard. This town – or city – lies somewhere far distant?'

Baecker shook his head. 'No more than a day and a night's ride at most,' he replied. 'I'm not surprised that our citadel is unfamiliar to you. As yet, the name of Sigmarsgeist is known to few beyond the walls. But that will change,' he assured Stefan. 'Believe me, friend, the time will come when all the Old World will know and bless that name.'

'That may well be,' Stefan replied, slightly startled by the scale of Baecker's boast. 'Certainly, your valour speaks favourably for your allegiance. We share your abomination of evil. I wish you and your people well.'

'Why not ride with us?' Baecker suggested. 'You would find much to commend in Sigmarsgeist. The citadel is only a few days distant. You would be made welcome–' he looked at each of them in turn. 'Each of you has virtues to be valued.'

'Well…' Stefan exchanged glances with Bruno. Baecker was a brave man who had shown them nothing but courtesy, and he had no wish to offend him. But a diversion to a city he had never heard of was not part of his plans. 'Your offer honours us, but–'

'I should like to see this citadel of yours,' Bea interrupted. 'I should like that very much.'

Hans Baecker bowed. 'And Sigmarsgeist would be honoured to receive you. Will you not come?' he asked Stefan. 'I promise you, the citadel is a jewel worth beholding.'

Stefan thought about it. He was still unsure exactly where Sigmarsgeist lay, but it was at least a full day's ride, and possibly in the wrong direction. But, then again, what was the right direction?

Bea read the hesitation in Stefan's eyes. 'You're wondering about him, aren't you?' she said. 'The man you've been pursuing. You're wondering where you should go next?'

Stefan nodded. If he were honest, they had lost all trace of Alexei. A part of Stefan felt relieved that Zucharov had not been with the mutants. Perhaps he was not yet ready to face that final moment of confrontation.

But it could not be delayed indefinitely. Stefan knew that, before long, he must track down Zucharov. And, in truth, he could have gone in any direction. For now, perhaps, Sigmarsgeist would offer a chance to reprovision, perhaps to rest for a while before taking stock and moving on. If the battle-hardened men they had just encountered were any measure of the place, then Sigmarsgeist might be as good a direction as any, for now.

'We'll ride with you as far as your citadel,' he told Baecker. 'We'll gladly take of your hospitality, and buy food for our further travels if we may.'

Hans Baecker gripped Stefan's hand, and shook it enthusiastically. 'Sigmar was truly smiling upon us last night, Stefan Kumansky. Sigmarsgeist awaits us. It will not disappoint.'

# CHAPTER FIVE
## The Dying of the Light

THE MAN WHO had once been Alexei Zucharov was on a journey.

It was a journey which had no defined end, and no beginning that he could remember any longer. It was a journey that had no direction of his own choosing, yet the path that he travelled was unswerving and unalterable. It was a journey that could be measured by the passing of days, and by the miles unravelled upon the road. But, more than all of this, it was a journey through his inner world, a journey taking him from the mortal man he had once been, towards a being he could not yet comprehend. Change was coming upon Alexei Zucharov, and it was relentless and unyielding.

On his journey, Alexei swam through dreams that invaded his waking thoughts and filled his hours of sleep. Dreams of what was, and what might have been. Dreams of what might yet be, and dreams of what now would never come to pass. He saw there were hundreds of futures, futures seeded from the random fates of hundreds of pasts. Any of them might have been true, or none of them. All certainty was lost and nothing was yet decided.

Somewhere in a time now past, he remembered a battle, the clash of steel that had marked the point in his history where the change had begun. That had been the beginning. The place where the great river of chance had divided, and swept him along a different path.

At night gazing sleepless at the stars, he would recall another sky, the blood red sky above the battlefield, smoke rising from the crumbling spires of the beleaguered city. Whether he had been fighting to save the city, or to destroy it, Zucharov no longer knew. But upon that field, as the fog of battle cleared to reveal the cruel fields of the dead, he had come upon his defining hour.

Time after time upon the journey across the empty plains of the Ostermark, Alexei Zucharov relived the moment in the battle that the horseman had appeared. The lone rider, emerging from the enemy lines, riding directly towards him. His callow indifference to Zucharov's presence. No attempt to flee, nor to defend himself from the blow that would surely cut him down. Alexei Zucharov remembered his disappointment; his sudden, raging fury that this, his final, crowning glory upon that day should be diminished by an opponent who would not even fight back.

He recalled his rage, that glory should be so unjustly denied him. This should have been the ultimate test, the final battle of champions. Instead, the combat was ended in moments. Alexei watched, as he had watched a hundred times before, the dark knight fall beneath his sword. The distaste, the bitter distaste for this unworthy opponent, so easily despatched. He would strip what he could from the corpse. His sword, his dagger, his other tokens of allegiance to the Dark Powers. He would take his horse, a monstrous beast that stood twice the height of a mortal man. But none of this would be enough to sweeten the bitter taste of victory so easily won.

And then, Zucharov had seen the amulet. The circle of pure, lustrous gold upon the Chaos warrior's wrist. In all his battles, amongst all the trophies claimed from his vanquished dead, Alexei had never seen anything like it. Sunlight poured from the clouds and fell upon the golden band, illuminating the runes etched upon its surface. Runes and words that spoke in an unknown tongue, the ancient tongue of the Dark Gods. Of all the treasures Zucharov had found, this, he knew, was the lodestone of his dreams. It had to be his at any cost.

Zucharov had been ready to cut the gold from the champion's flesh, but there had been no need. The shimmering band had slipped, smooth and easy, from the dead knight's hand. But, once he had put it on, Zucharov found that the amulet could not be removed. It sat fast upon his wrist, as if stitched into his flesh. Now it was part of him forever.

He began to grow stronger. He could feel the raw energy channelling from the gold band into his body. All pain, all weariness, was banished. Soon there would be nothing he could not do. At the same time, the mark of transformation had appeared on his flesh. It had started as a tiny blemish, a mark no more than a bruise, upon the skin beneath the amulet. After a while the bruise had begun to change and grow, altering in shape and line, dissolving and resolving until it became recognisable as an image, like a tattoo. It was the image of a warrior on horseback, rising triumphant above a fallen foe. As Alexei stared down upon it, the image began to move.

As the days passed, a new world began to unfold in miniature on his living flesh. These were the pictures from his dreams, the images of his past and of all his futures. Through those images Zucharov watched destiny unfold, pointing him upon the road to a future he could yet barely imagine.

And, as the living tattoo grew, so, in strange tandem, the memory of his former life faded away. Faces, names and events were disappearing, vanishing like the light fading from the dying day. Some things he still remembered, like the name of a place, Altdorf, that had been his home. A name scrawled upon a scrap of paper he had found in a pocket, a letter started and then abandoned, a message never sent from a life that had ceased to exist. Natalia. Natalia, his sister, from a time and place once long ago.

Other names, other faces. Those he had ridden with into battle. Comrades from home, from Altdorf. All of them would fade soon, fade and be forgotten. A part of Zucharov knew those names were important, a part of his identity, and he struggled to hold on to them as a drowning man clutches at flotsam. But he was locked in a new battle now, a battle for the dominion of his very soul. Alexei Zucharov fought to hold fast to those memories with the tenacity of a man who had never known defeat.

And then, at other times, he saw that it did not matter. It did not matter because his was a journey of transformation, and all the names and places of fading memory were nothing more than broken fragments, the debris of a life that had been transcended. He was on a journey to a new life, and he had a new companion, a mentor to guide him upon that journey. A voice that spoke to him inside his head. A voice that told him of his history, and of his destiny yet to unfold.

The voice whispered to Alexei through the long waking hours and across the troubled lands of his dreams. Alexei tried to banish it from his head, shut out the incessant barrage of whispered words. But he could not. It was inside him. It had become part of him. Soon, before long, it would become him, and he it: inseparable, indivisible.

The voice told him things he had never heard before. It explained to him the true nature of man, and the struggle between light and darkness. It showed him how, beneath that simplistic façade, there lay another battle, far older, far more significant. A battle not between good and evil, but between the strong and the weak. On one side, those vigorous and brave enough to transcend the shackles that tethered man to his mortal misery. Pitted against them, those who would drag mankind down: the weak, the sick and the lame. The indolent, duplicitous parasites who fed upon the bounty gathered by the strong.

Alexei Zucharov had always known he was one of the strong. Now the voice inside his head would be his guide, and his counsel, upon the long road to the final battleground.

Over time, Alexei grew accustomed to the sound of his mentor, cajoling him, driving his tired flesh onward through day after endless day. He learned his name: Kyros, all-powerful disciple of the great Lord of Transformation, Tzeentch, almighty God of Change. Kyros had plucked Alexei Zucharov from the fields of war and blessed him with the gift of Chaos. Zucharov was to be his champion, his servant upon the mortal world. Through him, the strong would conquer all.

First, Zucharov had had to get out of the city. He had ridden hard from the gates of Erengrad, across the borders of frozen Kislev and beyond, out into the barren wilderness of the Ostermark. He rode with no knowledge of his destination, only knowing that he was pursued. The men who once called themselves his comrades had become his enemies, and they would pursue Zucharov to his grave if they could. They were the champions of lesser gods: the jealous, covetous gods who laid the shackles of callow mediocrity upon the spirits of men. They were the gods of humility and feeble ambition, the humble, chastening gods of the weak. Kyros would defeat them, and Zucharov would destroy all who took arms against him.

But his champion was not yet ready. The seeds of Chaos had yet to blossom in the soul of Alexei Zucharov. Until then, Kyros would nurture his champion, nurture and protect him whilst he grew in mind and in body. Until he was ready to fight, and to destroy. For only when all else was laid to waste, when the decaying cities of man had been brought down, only then would the purging fires of Tzeentch work their miracle of transformation, and make the world anew. A world where only the strong would survive.

So he rode, always keeping ahead of the shadows that snapped at his heels. Sometimes he would still rage against the voice that whispered so sweetly inside his mind. But with each day that passed, he was succumbing to the seduction of its sweet music, its quiet, unyielding logic.

*Change is inevitable, it is the very wheel of life. From change comes strength, comes opportunity.*

I am strong, Zucharov told himself. And I am master of my own destiny. Neither god nor man can subjugate my will. I am free.

His answer would come as laughter, the laughter of Kyros, and of his master, the Dark Lord of Change.

*Freedom is nothing but illusion. The consolation of the weak.*

ONCE BEYOND THE borders of Kislev, the land opened out, and the world became a vast and empty place. Soon Zucharov was travelling both day and night, resting only when the massive horse that carried him could give no more. He rode until he came, at the dying of the day, to a path that snaked along the spine of a narrow valley. The sun set below the hills and a great shadow fell across the land.

Zucharov rode on in solitude. The gods had sucked all sound, all life, from the dark hills and left them quiet. He slowed his pace, waited for the word. But the silence of the hills had penetrated his mind. For the first time in as long as he could remember, the voice inside his head was stilled. Now the silence was absolute, his mind an empty, becalmed sea. Alexei Zucharov was alone.

But not for long. As he held the same slow, unchanging pace, two riders overhauled him, one on either flank, cold moonlight glinting on the steel of their drawn swords. The sound of horses pounding hard upon the trail told him of others, too, bringing up the rear. Alexei Zucharov remembered his time as a warrior. The besieged quarter of his mind that was still the soldier took stock, making order out of the mayhem around him. He was under attack. He pulled his horse to a halt, scanning the the valley, the dark cradling hills.

Four riders had surrounded him. One of them was shouting, trying to draw his attention. Zucharov heard them as he might hear the distant buzzing of insects, a drowsy burr of sound. He listened only for the voice of Kyros, and, when still nothing came he decided at last to ride on, on through the far side of the valley and up the steep incline that led back onto the plain. As he moved forward, two of the riders converged towards him, attempting to block his path. Now, at last, the whisper came. The murmured words of the one who would be his master; part direction, part permission.

Alexei heard the voice, and smiled. He turned to face the oncoming riders, and was at once upon familiar ground.

HE WAS GOING to die. Lothar Koenig was sure of it. The bounty hunter had made a mistake, he had let greed, or need, get the better of him. There must have been a point where escape still remained a possibility. A point where he could have leapt back upon his horse and fled back up the hillside out of the valley. However powerful, however demented the tattooed warrior, there must have been a chance that he could have outpaced him. Forget the butchered body of Carl Durer. Forget his bounty, just get out.

But he did not turn, and he did not flee. Instead Lothar Koenig stood, transfixed by the beauty of the gold band, by the images that danced upon the other man's flesh, and by the terrible power of the warrior himself. Now there would be no escaping. He watched the sword lift into the air above his head as he might watch an execution from afar, noticing how the steel of the blade was tainted red from the blood of the slaughtered men. He heard the sound like a tiny sigh as the blade fell, gaining speed as it sliced through the air. It's over, Lothar, he told himself. Your life, all of this, is over.

ZUCHAROV HAD DESTROYED the bandits, destroyed the worthless vermin who had thought it so simple to rob and murder him. He destroyed them not out of anger, nor in simple defence of his own life, but because they belonged with the weak. If not weak in body, then weak in mind and spirit. Kyros had showed Zucharov the deeper weakness that festered within mankind. The weakness of crude ambition, worthless aspirations. Durer and his men were pitiful wretches, and Zucharov detested them. He cleansed the bandits from the face of the living world, despatched them with his blade and his own bare hands.

Only when he was done did he see that there was still one other to be accounted for. A fifth player had entered the arena, a solitary figure who now stared at Zucharov like a rabbit snared by a serpent. This one did not belong with the bandit gang. The smell of fear coming off him was different to the grovelling terror of Carl Durer. This man was a clever, thoughtful marauder who would steal unnoticed into the heart of a battle to carry away his prize. This was a man who had calculated his risk, and knew that he had lost.

But he, too, was weak. He might rank higher than the bandits with their myopic greed, but only within the simple hierarchy of the damned. Zucharov would kill him as he had killed the others. He lifted his sword, measuring a blow that would cleave the other man clean in two. As the blade began to fall, he felt a jolt like a fork of lightening run from his spine to the base of his neck, paralysing him. The voice of Kyros exploded inside of him, a single, bellowed word of command: *No!*

Zucharov struggled to take control of his sword, battling to close the movement that would power the furious blade into the body of Lothar Koenig. He would have no master other than his own will. He would not submit, he would not.

But he had no choice. His body would obey only one master, and the dark lord had decreed the sword would not fall. The spasm passed, but he knew he could not strike at Koenig. He now knew that Kyros had other plans for them both.

LOTHAR KOENIG HAD watched in disbelief as the falling sword hung suspended in mid-air. The spell was broken, and Lothar fell back, out of range of the blow. It lasted barely an instant, but the fire had gone from the other man's eyes. So invincible in battle only moments before, he now looked diminished, almost mortal.

Emboldened, Lothar had drawn his own sword, unsure whether he was attacking or defending himself, but knowing that the odds had shifted suddenly, and inexplicably, in his favour. His mind had raced with the possibilities opening up. Surely he should flee. He would get no second chance of redemption. The urge to run, to leap upon his horse and ride for his life, had been strong indeed. But Lothar had been a bounty hunter for perhaps too long.

There were other, even more powerful instincts that seized him at moments like these.

The ring of metal fire glowed like the sun through the gloom of the night. Lothar had stared, greedily, at the gold amulet, devouring it with his eyes. That alone would surely keep him in comfort until winter's worst was spent. Standing between him and that comfort was the man who bore the band. The warrior with the strange, writhing tattoo disfiguring his arm. The awesome power had been dimmed, but the man still cut a formidable figure. Whatever he was – soldier, mercenary, or some freakish creation of the gods – Lothar Koenig knew there were plenty who would pay handsomely to be the master of a man such as this. If anything, this was the greater prize.

Caution had vied with greed in the racing mind of Lothar Koenig, and greed had won.

ZUCHAROV'S MEMORY HAD broken into a series of jumbled, fragmented scenes. But there was one seam that ran true through all his recollection: he was a fighter, a warrior who had never yet met his equal. In battle he had earned scars and borne pain but he had always prevailed. He had known many conquests, and the taste of victory had become commonplace, only too familiar. But one thing that Alexei Zucharov had never known was captivity. To submit now – to this man, this creature whose life he could extinguish with a single blow – would be an unthinkable humiliation. And yet he found himself stepping back from the confrontation.

His grip upon the hilt of his sword slackened. The weapon slipped from his hand. Zucharov heard it strike the hard ground, metal upon stone. And he heard himself gasp as he slumped to his knees, the strength draining from him like water through a sieve. Nothing that Zucharov had ever experienced had prepared him for this. He saw the look on the other's face: disbelieving, elated.

Alexei's head fell to his chest. He tried in vain to raise his eyes. Every muscle in his face felt leaden, and a great weight had been spread upon his shoulders, pressing him down. Only now, with Alexei bent low in unwilling supplication,

did Kyros address him once more. Zucharov listened to the
voice, and when the time came for reply, he heard the sound
of his own words inside his head, words that could be heard
only by the dark lord of Tzeentch.

*You have chained me through your magic. Shackled my body
with a spell.*

*This is not the time to fight,* Kyros answered him. *Now you
must be truly strong.*

*You mock me with witchcraft. Free me from this web and I'll
show you what strength can do.*

*No. You choose the wrong path. The path of the strong lies
along another road.*

Still Alexei railed at his master's bidding. *I will not submit,
like some beast to be tamed,* he raged. *I have free will.*

*Free will is a delusion,* responded Kyros. *A crutch for the weak.*

Alexei finally managed to raise his head far enough to look
up at the figure standing over him. The other man had his
sword drawn at the ready. He was shaking with fear, little
knowing that his adversary was powerless. Zucharov waited,
trying to fathom how this pitiful stranger could play any part
in his destiny. He was Alexei's inferior in every apparent way,
smaller, lighter and older. No match at all for Zucharov in
open combat. Even if he had been a master of the sword, it
would surely only have served to prolong his end.

He saw Koenig hesitate, saw the fear that still lived in his
eyes. Even now, Zucharov realised, he thinks I may destroy
him. Zucharov raged silently against his impotence. So this
was to be his fate. This was the man that Alexei Zucharov
was about to yield to. He had no fear of death, but to yield
like this, passively and without so much as even a word, was
worse than any death that he could have imagined.

LOTHAR KOENIG, QUITE simply, had not been able to believe
his luck. His first thought had been that the other man's collapse must have been the result of injuries he'd suffered in
the fight with Durer's men. Indeed, he had a gaping wound
that ran across the palm of his hand up the length of his
wrist on his left tattooed arm. Koenig remembered with a
shudder how that wound had been earned, and saw again

the stranger grasping hold of the razor-edged blade in his bare hand.

But otherwise he'd swear the man was untouched. Whatever it was that had stricken him, it was surely not his injury. What was more, he carried his sword in his other hand, his right. Or, rather, had carried it. Lothar watched the sword fall from the man's grasp. Time passed, moments seeming to stretch forward into an eternity. Only when it became clear that Zucharov was not going to move did Koenig finally gather his courage and snatch the sword from the ground.

Koenig stood over the kneeling figure of his would-be captive. For all the apparent supremacy of his position, the bounty hunter was filled with a terror he had barely known in all the perilous years of his profession.

'Surrender,' he commanded, his voice as firm as he could muster. 'Offer me your surrender and I promise you'll be treated fairly.' He watched as the other man raised his head, the ponderous, slow movement masking the power that lay beneath. Lothar had a sense of a great menace, temporarily subdued. He must hurry.

'Come on,' he demanded. 'On your feet.'

The other had turned his face towards the night sky. The bounty hunter felt a jolt as their gaze met. In that moment he had experienced the fleeting sense of another being, a far darker, malevolent soul, peering out at him through the eyes of the man kneeling before him.

'You are weak,' Zucharov said.

At that point, something had snapped inside of Lothar Koenig, something he would best describe as professional pride. The insult stung him into action, reminded him who he was. Lothar Koenig. Not just a bounty hunter. *The* bounty hunter. The bounty hunter, what was more, who was on the point of claiming not one, but two or even three bounties. Not bad for a couple of days' work.

'That's your opinion,' he replied, 'but right now I'd say you were the weak one, wouldn't you?'

He had swung into action, instinct and years of experience guiding him through a series of almost mechanical movements. He kept one eye firmly upon his captive as he took what he might need from his horse. The shackling chains, or perhaps the mesh of wire that could encase a man like a chicken in a net? Better both, he concluded. He patted the pocket of his jerkin, feeling for the glass bottle. If all else failed, the potion would be sure to subdue him for a while. As he set to work, he had been filled with a sudden confidence. This was going to be easy, and he wasn't going to ask why.

ZUCHAROV HAD WATCHED the shackles going about his body, the steel biting into his flesh. He neither resisted nor colluded with his fate. He was detached from it, watching it from afar. When his arms and upper body had been chained he was put upon a horse, slung across it like a commodity at market. Then he was lashed to the saddle with strong ropes, so that he would not fall. Through all of this, he was in the hands of the bounty hunter, his captor. And yet he was not; this was just his flesh, his body. His spirit had been carried far away, to the dread halls where Kyros held court.

Kyros had heard Zucharov's despair, listened to his silent rage against his subjugation.

*You still have much to learn,* the dark lord told him again. *This is not the end.*

AT LAST THEY had got under way, the bounty hunter riding ahead, leading the second horse bearing the chained body of Alexei Zucharov by a rope along the steep path that wound up out of the Ostravska valley. The going was difficult and slow, but gradually they had found a momentum, and Koenig's heart had grown lighter. He started to whistle, a tune half-remembered from his childhood.

And far away, in a place far distant from the mortal realm, Lord Kyros had looked down upon Lothar Koenig, and smiled upon his labours.

*This was only the beginning.*

# CHAPTER SIX
## Sigmarsgeist

FOR TWO FULL days and nights, Stefan and his companions had ridden south with the soldiers of the Red Guard. Finally, at the dawn of the third day, they approached their destination.

Through most of the hours of darkness, they had been climbing. A steady, gentle ascent had led along a wooded mountain trail, the way twisting and snaking like a path through a maze. As the first glimmerings of light began to streak the night sky the riders crested a hill and emerged from the cover of trees into open land. They were on top of a high hill on the edge of a mountain range, the ridge curving away to either side of them, drawing into a circle on the far side of the valley, forming a vast cradle. As if on cue, the sun rose from behind the crest of rock, suddenly and dramatically bathing the valley in a flood of warm, amber light.

The land below was swaddled in early morning fog. Through the haze, the scattered spires and towers of a town or city were just visible, rising up out of the mists like ships riding a golden ocean.

'Behold,' Baecker announced. 'Sigmarsgeist.'

From on high it was impossible to guess the exact size of the citadel, but it was undoubtedly big. Stefan's travels had taken him from Altdorf, at the heart of the Empire, to the mighty city of Middenheim, and to Erengrad, at the western edge of the lands of Kislev. Sigmarsgeist might not yet rival them, but this was no mountain village.

Stefan cast his eyes across across a complex pattern of roads and streets, a dense forest of buildings of all shapes and sizes, built from flint and stone. A cluster of tall, domed structures set high upon the northern face of Sigmarsgeist dominated the view of citadel. Beyond the domes the streets were laid out in tiers, shelving down towards the southern end of the citadel. It seemed all of Sigmarsgeist was built upon sloping ground, with the domed buildings – which Stefan took to be a temple or a palace of some kind – at its uppermost point. The sun began to burn away the early mist, cutting through the chilly shroud to glint off the slate roofs of hundreds of separate dwellings, halls and workshops.

There had to be a thousand souls living within those walls, maybe many more, Stefan estimated. And it was clear that Sigmarsgeist was still growing. At least a third of the citadel was still being built, with row upon row of new dwellings standing in various states of construction.

Stefan was puzzled that he had had no previous knowledge of such a place. The day before he had checked upon his map; there had been  no mention of Sigmarsgeist, nor of any other place of comparable size. The map that they were using was undoubtedly crude, but Stefan was still surprised to find it missing such a detail.

'You are impressed?' Hans asked of him.

'Yes,' Stefan readily agreed. He was impressed. If nothing else, Sigmarsgeist bore ample testimony to the ambition and craft of man.

He shaded the sun from his eyes, peering down into the valley. He tried to compare Sigmarsgeist with the great cities of the Empire, cities such as Middenheim, a mighty, fortress sat high upon its plateau of rock. In many ways Sigmarsgeist was the mirror opposite of the city of the White Wolf. Where

Middenheim sat high and impregnable, nestling amongst the clouds, Sigmarsgeist was buried at the very foot of the valley, hemmed in by towering walls of rock. It seemed – to Stefan's eye at least – a strange choice.

'Why was the city built here?' he asked, 'so deep within the valley?'

Baecker did not answer the question directly. 'The site was carefully chosen,' he said. 'There were many considerations.'

'Such as?'

'The Guides may wish to tell you more of that,' Baecker answered.

'The Guides?'

Baecker raised one hand. 'Come. Save your questions for later. Sigmarsgeist is waiting.'

Bea glanced at him, an inquisitive look stealing over her features.

'Was there something else?' Baecker asked her.

'Yes,' Bea replied, uncertainly. 'That is, no, not directly. I was just curious to hear more – more of how the citadel came to be built here.'

Baecker nodded, and smiled. 'Later, perhaps.' He took up the reins and started his horse down the stony path that would lead them to the citadel below.

'Let's move on,' he said. Baecker gestured again at the path that wound down the hillside ahead. 'Sigmarsgeist waits to welcome you as its honoured guests.'

'Lead on,' Stefan told him. 'For we are equally honoured to be invited amongst you.'

Sigmarsgeist took shape as they followed the path down the mountain. The descent became more shallow as, gradually, the land levelled out, opening on to a patchwork of fields, huge green and golden squares, ripe with crops. Bruno marvelled at the sight.

'There must be enough produce here to feed many hundreds,' he remarked. 'You have done well to cultivate so much from such barren land.'

Baecker surveyed the expanse of fields, each with its neat lines of labourers all working the land. 'Not nearly well enough,' he said at length. 'As fast as we cultivate, Sigmarsgeist grows still larger. Try as we might, it is never enough. Sigmarsgeist is a belly which can never be filled.'

'How do you survive?' Stefan asked.

Baecker shrugged, as though the question had no real answer. 'As best we can,' he said, and gave short laugh. 'We do whatever we must.'

Beyond the fields, teams of workers were quarrying stone from the mountain side, men working hard and apparently ceaselessly, piling wagons with chunks of rough-hewn granite. A succession of wagons was filled then towed away on the network of roads that led towards the citadel, whilst, all the while, empty vehicles moved in the opposite direction, out towards the rock face. The men worked with an indefatigable zeal, prising rock from the hard earth, piling the wagons high.

'Building the future,' Baecker commented. 'Heroes, to a man.'

Stefan didn't doubt that for a moment. Even in the relative cool of the early morning, it must have been back-breaking work. Not for the first time, he gave silent thanks that he earned his living by the sword. Dangerous work it might be, but there were harder paths in life. Any man who could spend each day labouring like this was a hero indeed.

More than three hours after they had begun their descent from the mountain, they finally stood by the walls of the citadel. From above, the walls had looked impressive enough. Now, close to, they seemed truly daunting, built from heavy stone and taller than any fortification Stefan had encountered in the Empire. Clearly, this was a place built to withstand the most sustained onslaught, and outlast the lengthiest siege.

Massive iron gates set into the walls swung open to greet them. Hans Baecker waved his men on, and led Stefan and his companions into Sigmarsgeist.

WORD OF THEIR arrival had spread fast within the city. People on the streets stopped and cheered to give thanks for the safe return of the captain and his men. The noise drew mothers and children from their houses, and craftsmen and artisans from their shops and workshops. As the procession of riders made their way into the city, more and more people poured onto the streets to add their voices to the commotion.

In amongst the townsfolk going about their business, Stefan noticed more soldiers dressed in the scarlet livery, as well as others – fewer in number – whose tunics were white rather than red. Each bore the same insignia: the image of the Imperial eagle, its wings spread wide over Sigmarsgeist. Bruno took note, approvingly.

'Feels like being back amongst our own, doesn't it?'

'In many ways, yes,' Stefan agreed. But, he kept reminding himself, he was not amongst his own. He would keep an open mind – for the moment, at least.

One thing was beyond doubt. Everyone they encountered upon the streets – soldiers, craftsmen, women bearing baskets of fruit or bread – looked healthy and well-nourished. Every town in the Empire had its share of sickness and disease, but if it was present here, then it was well-hidden. The people looked healthy. And young.

'Curious,' Stefan commented. 'I've not seen a single person above middle years since we set foot through the gates.'

'We are a young people,' Baecker replied. 'Many of us travelled here together as pilgrims. We've not had the time to grow old yet.' He pulled up, leaning from the saddle to shake the hands of the townsfolk who rushed to greet him. 'The Guides will explain how it came to pass.'

'I look forward to meeting them,' Stefan said.

'And they will be glad to welcome you.'

Bruno turned towards Bea, fighting to make himself heard above the bustle of the streets. 'Not quite like Mielstadt, is it?'

Bea gave an almost imperceptible shake of the head, but didn't respond.

'What is it?' Bruno asked, a note of concern in his voice. 'What's the matter?'

'Nothing wrong,' she assured him. 'But this place has an energy. A positive energy,' she added. 'It is a force for good.

But it's so strong...' She paused, and took a gasp of breath. 'I've not come across such a thing before.'

Stefan looked around at the neat, timber-framed houses, homes laid out in tightly-packed rows along the clean-swept streets. Everywhere the citadel had the look of a great labour that was still in progress. Many buildings were unfinished, none looked more than a few weeks or months old.

'These houses,' Bruno observed. 'The whole place looks newly-built.'

Stefan agreed. That was how it seemed. Every street they passed down looked fresh and clean, with a sense of vigour and purpose he had rarely, if ever, noted in cities such as Altdorf or Middenheim, or indeed any other place he had visited. But, in parts – particularly at the edge of the citadel near the walls – Sigmarsgeist had a disordered look to it, with too many houses crammed into too short a space. That, Stefan supposed, explained Hans Baecker's comment about feeding his people. The citadel was growing fast, almost too fast for its own good.

Nearer the centre of the citadel the streets resumed a more orderly look. The design of the streets appeared more structured and less cluttered, and the surrounding workshops and houses older, though hardly long-established. Here, as elsewhere, statues cast in marbled stone abounded. Many of them were in homage to the Emperor Sigmar, and showed him astride his horse, or standing triumphant in victory. But others – almost as many – depicted a second figure that Stefan did not recognise. The carvings showed an older man, standing proud and upright, with what looked like the citadel in miniature cupped within his outstretched hands. In the course of an hour moving through the streets of Sigmarsgeist, Stefan saw the image at least a dozen times, both in statues, and carved into the façade of buildings.

FINALLY, THE STREETS opened out into a wide courtyard facing a high-walled building, fronted by iron gates. Stefan recognised the cluster of domes that he had picked out from above. The presence of much larger numbers of militia suggested that it was indeed a palace of some kind.

'We must remain here for just a moment.' Baecker waited with Stefan and the others whilst one of his men approached the sentries standing guard either side of the gates. After a brief conversation, they were waved through. They passed through a stone archway into an open court-yard, where their horses were collected by stablemen clad in the same red livery.

Baecker dismounted, then extended a hand to Bea.

'Time to get some rest,' he said. 'Afterwards, we shall learn more of you, and you of us.'

Stefan had a hundred questions in his mind that he wanted answering, but they had been riding since dawn the previous day, and he was more than glad now to be offered some respite. The questions, on both sides, could wait a few hours yet.

THEIR QUARTERS WERE on an upper floor of the great building – single rooms, sparse but clean. A bed, a basin with an attendant pail of freshly drawn water, and a window that looked out across the rooftops. Before Stefan finally lay his aching body down, he stood for a while gazing out of the slitted window, taking in the panorama of streets, houses and workshops that lay beyond. Standing there, at the heart of a place that, a day before, had not existed for him even in his imagination, it occurred to Stefan that he had put him-self entirely at the hospitality of people he barely knew, and whose motives were at best uncertain.

Stefan Kumansky had grown up at odds with much of the world he had walked through. He had seen shadows where others had seen only light, and suspicion and doubts had walked with him as constant companions. But, as he finally lay his head down, he searched his heart for those doubts and found none. Instead he found rest, and a feeling that had been alien to him for much of that short life. The feel-ing known to the fortunate traveller at the end of a long and uncertain journey. A feeling of coming home.

HE AWOKE FEELING more refreshed than he had any right to hope for. When he finally opened his eyes Bruno was standing over him, a playful look of impatience resting on his face.

'Ulric's toil!' Stefan exclaimed, sitting bolt upright upon the cot. 'How long have I been asleep?'

'The best part of a day,' Bruno replied, keeping a straight face. 'Actually,' he admitted, 'little more than an hour, two at most.'

Stefan stretched and yawned. Certainly he felt as though he might have been asleep for the best part of the day. The air here clearly agreed with him.

'Is Bea awake yet?'

'Yes. We all are. They're ready for us now, apparently.'

'They?'

Bruno shrugged. 'Baecker and his men speak of them only as "the Guides".'

Stefan sat up and pulled on his boots. He splashed cool water from the basin onto his face, rubbing away the last of his sleep from his eyes. 'In that case,' he said, 'let's not keep them waiting.'

THEY WERE RECEIVED in a spacious, low-ceilinged chamber somewhere near the core of the palace. The attendant who had escorted them from their rooms executed a brief, low bow as he entered into the room. Stefan repeated the gesture. As he looked up, he scanned the chamber to take stock of who or what they were about to be presented to.

The chamber had few concessions made to luxury. If this was the office of the high council, or whoever ruled Sigmarsgeist, then it was austere indeed. For all that, the room was airy and well lit, possessed of the same spartan health as the citadel itself. Stationed along the walls around the edge of the chamber were soldiers decked in the same red livery as Hans Baecker's men. Each bore a brightly burnished sword, held upright and close to the chest, in the formal posture of vigilance. But where Stefan might otherwise have expected to see a table of high office, there was only open space and a stone floor bare except for a wide circle marked out in runes bearing pious homage to the gods. Seated within the circle was a group of about a dozen people, Baecker amongst them, some wearing the white livery that Stefan had noted earlier.

Hans Baecker got up, offered greeting, and bid them join the circle. Two officers wearing scarlet moved aside, making room for Stefan and his friends. Only as he sat did Stefan notice the man and woman who, although part of the wider circle, seemed by their presence to dominate. The man, Stefan saw at once, was the one he had seen depicted all through the citadel.

'All honour to our Guides,' Baecker began, addressing the couple directly. 'I beg to present Stefan Kumansky, Bruno Hausmann and Beatrice de Lucht, who joined arms with us in glorious battle. They have travelled far to this land, from beyond the borders of Kislev.'

'Not I,' Bea corrected him, hastily. 'I hail from Mielstadt, a place not so very distant from here.'

The man that Baecker had addressed as Guide nodded, signalling familiarity with the lands to the east, or with Mielstadt, or both. He studied Stefan and his companions with the steady, unhurried ease of a man grown comfortable with holding power. His lean face and fine, almost aristocratic features, gave his face a look of power tempered with wisdom. Stefan put his age at about forty years, or possibly even more, his years betrayed by the flecks of grey in his hair and beard.

'Welcome to Sigmarsgeist,' he said. 'Through the naming of our citadel, and through the works of all its people, we glorify the spirit and memory of our great emperor.' He turned to the woman next to him. 'We extend the hand of friendship to these, our most honoured guests, do we not?'

The woman was some ten years or so younger, with dark hair swept back from an unblemished, olive-skinned face. Her heavy-lidded eyes would have given her an almost languid look, but for the expression in the eyes themselves: bright and piercing. Like her companion, she exuded authority. She sat, hand-in-hand with her neighbour, yet some similarity in the delicately chiselled features of the two suggested they were not husband and wife. The woman inclined her head and favoured the newcomers with a smile.

'You are welcome indeed,' she concurred. 'We have had reports of your valour in coming to the aid of our people – both with your swords, and–' her smile broadened as it fell upon Bea – 'with your sacred powers of healing. We are thankful indeed, and indebted.'

'Your thanks are appreciated,' Stefan replied, 'but you owe us no debt. Your enemies are ours, too.'

'Indeed they are,' her companion concurred. 'I am Konstantin von Augen, the Father of Sigmarsgeist.' He indicated the woman seated beside him. 'And this is Anaise, my beloved sister.'

Stefan bowed again. 'You rule over a most remarkable city.'

Von Augen raised both hands as if to fend away the words.

'No, no,' he insisted. 'We do not rule. Here in Sigmarsgeist we have moved beyond the crude rudiments of rule and servitude.' He looked to his sister. 'The title of Guide is carefully chosen. We provide guidance to the people of this citadel: spiritual, moral, practical guidance. If the people follow that lead, then it is through choice.'

'Choice,' Anaise concurred, 'and a shared view of the troubled world we walk upon.'

'I beg your pardon,' Stefan demurred. 'I see there is much we have to learn about your city.'

'There is, and you shall,' Konstantin agreed. 'But first, we would learn a little of you, if you have no objection.'

'Of course.' Stefan's heart told him to be as open with his hosts as possible, yet his head told him there were aspects of their recent history that he should hold back yet a while. He would see; something told him that Konstantin and his sister had already guessed at much of their tale.

'You have been in Kislev,' Konstantin began. 'Perhaps you were at Erengrad?'

'We were,' Stefan confirmed. 'We fought with the army of men led by Gastez Castelguerre.' A ripple of conversation spread across the room in response to Stefan's words. Remote the citadel might have been, but it was clear that news of the battle in the east had reached Sigmarsgeist.

'The army that denied the Dark Ones in their assault upon the city?'

'Yes.'

Konstantin nodded, approvingly. 'And now Erengrad is made whole again,' he said. 'A new alliance is forged between the great families that would rule that mighty city.'

'We had a part in that, too,' Bruno added, before Stefan could consider his response. 'It was Stefan and I – amongst others – who returned the daughter of one family, safely home from exile.'

'Truly?' Konstantin's eyebrows arched in surprise, his calm countenance broken for a moment. 'Then you are due honour indeed.' He conferred briefly with his sister. Stefan heard the word 'Altdorf' repeated, together with other cities within the Empire. 'But tell me,' he went on, 'if you are now on your way back to Altdorf, how did your journey bring you here? By my calculation, your road should have taken you due south from Kislev, along the trading route that runs to the city of the White Wolf?'

Stefan hesitated. This was the part that instinct would have had him hold back, the purpose behind their quest since quitting Erengrad. But, then again, he could think of no good reason why now he should not be candid. They shared a common cause, he reminded himself. More than that, it was surely not beyond possibility that the men of Sigmarsgeist would choose to aid them in their search for Zucharov.

'If we were bound for Altdorf our road would indeed have been for Middenheim,' he conceded. 'But we cannot go home yet. We fear that one of our closest comrades may have been taken at Erengrad.'

'Taken?' Anaise queried. 'You mean killed?'

'We believe he still lives,' Bruno said. 'Lives, but only so far as a man can be said to live when tainted with the poison of Chaos.'

His words sparked further animated conversation around the circle. Konstantin called for silence, and cupped his head in his hands in contemplation. 'Like you, I would be disquieted at such news,' he said. 'But to come this far for one man? The world is large, and – as I'm sure you need no reminding – there is much evil to be found. Why this man?'

'This is – or was – no ordinary man,' Stefan told him. 'Alexei Zucharov was a formidable fighter in his mortal life. A man seized with an unquenchable fire for battle, for struggle. We greatly fear that Chaos will only have added to that power, and have turned it way from light, towards the darkness.' He paused, deep in thoughts of his own. 'Besides, Alexei was a comrade, a brother of the sword. I have a debt to discharge, a debt to the man I once knew.'

'So, your search can only end in ultimate resolution, for you or for the man who was once your friend.' Konstantin observed. His sister peered intently at Stefan.

'You are a driven man, Stefan Kumansky,' she concluded. 'You see what others often will not see. You have decided you will not rest while there is evil upon the face of this world.'

Stefan said nothing for a moment. The feeling that Anaise von Augen had so easily captured the very essence of him was far from comfortable, but he could not disagree.

'It never seemed like a choice to me.'

Anaise rose to her feet. 'A noble tale,' she exclaimed. Her face was flushed, her voice strident and enthusiastic. 'Your cause is just and valiant, and it is your valour that has brought you here to us.'

'The same valour may take us from here before long,' Stefan observed, cautiously. 'We cannot relinquish our search for more than a day or two.'

'Of course, of course,' Konstantin concurred. 'But you must remain with us a while yet, draw strength and such provisions as we can offer. Then you can ride on with full belly and good heart. Will you consent to rest with us at least until the halving of the moons?'

'Enough talk for now, brother!' Anaise chided, resuming her place. 'Time to tell our guests something of the history of our citadel. I assure you,' she added, turning to Stefan, 'it is a history worth hearing.'

Konstantin von Augen smiled, and took his sister's hand. He laughed, a soft, gentle sound. 'As ever, you guide your errant brother back upon the just course,' he said. 'Apologies, dear friends. I had not meant to cause offence, nor press you unduly concerning the length of your stay with us.'

'No offence taken,' Stefan assured him. The halving of the moons was little more than three nights distant. Whilst they had no trail to pursue, nor any lead remaining that they might follow, it hardly seemed like time wasted to stay that long in a place such as Sigmarsgeist.

He glanced at Bruno, and read the assent in his comrade's eyes. 'We would be honoured to accept your hospitality until the halving night,' he said.

Konstantin clapped his hands together, firmly. 'Then let us all here break fast together,' he declared. 'For there are few stories told that do not sit better upon a full stomach.'

# CHAPTER SEVEN
## Against the Dark Tide

THEY BREAKFASTED ON bread, fruit and cheese, and drank from
flagons of water. Whilst they ate, Konstantin and Anaise
recounted their history to Stefan and his two companions.

'We know your lands well enough,' Konstantin informed
them. 'Though it is – how long?'

'Ten full years,' his sister supplied.

'Ten years,' Konstantin continued, 'since we began our pil-
grimage from those lands.'

'Where in the Empire are you from?' Stefan asked them.

'Middenheim, Nuln, Altdorf, we have known most of the
great cities,' Anaise replied. 'And many other places in
between. But none of them could we call home.'

'You see,' Konstantin went on, 'we became refugees in our
own land. My sister and I, and others like us. There were few
enough of us at first, but, over time we grew steadily in number.'

'We grew in number until we decided the time had come
to go in search of a place where we could build ourselves a
home,' Anaise explained. 'A place where we could live in
peace, free of persecution.'

'A place where we could devote all our energies to our greater purpose,' Konstantin added, eyeing the newcomers carefully.

'And what was that purpose?' Bea asked. 'What cause could sustain you across all those hundreds of miles, then make you to build a city like this?'

'Knowledge,' Anaise replied. 'Knowledge, and our fears for the dark times to come.'

'Understand this,' Konstantin interjected. 'Sigmarsgeist is a place of purity, of devotion to the ideals enshrined by our ancestor and emperor. But it is also a fortress ready to stand against all the dark might of Chaos.'

Stefan sat, absorbing the words. It was not often that he heard the name of the dark powers spoken so openly. Nor had he known a people whose whole purpose seemed so defined by the existence of evil. The revelation thrilled and troubled him in equal measure. In the end it was Bruno who voiced the doubts in Stefan's mind.

'But, surely,' he insisted, 'the threat from Chaos has been overcome? You cannot tell me the battle for Erengrad was for nothing.'

'It was not,' Konstantin agreed. 'And yet Chaos is far from overcome.' He picked a piece of fruit from the bowl at his feet and began to eat, slowly, methodically. 'Erengrad was an important victory, and your part in that victory will surely stand amongst the great deeds of history. But the war in Kislev was a beginning, not an end, and Erengrad but a single piece in the larger design yet to unfold.'

'The larger design?' Stefan asked. He much feared he would not like the answer he would hear. The Guide looked up, scrutinising each of their faces in turn.

'The larger design is absolute, all-engulfing war,' he said solemnly. 'War that will sweep like a black tide across the face of the known world. At its centre will be the Empire, the prize coveted above all prizes by the Dark Gods. It will be a conflagration set against which the wars in Kislev will seem like nothing but a minor skirmish. A rehearsal for a tragedy the like of which mankind has only imagined in its worst nightmares.' He paused, letting the heavy silence settle upon

the chamber. 'Unless we act now, it will be the final enact-
ment of our existence.'

Bruno reached for his cup, then set it to the ground without drinking. 'Then victory in Erengrad–'

'Bought us time, no more, no less.' But the powers of
Chaos will have learned lessons from their grievous
wounds. When they return, they will be stronger, more cunning, and more cruel than ever before.'

Stefan reflected upon the Guides' words. The vision that
they conjured appalled him. But in truth, it only accorded
with what in his heart he knew to be true. That all life would
become struggle; that the battle between light and dark
would only intensify, not diminish. He had been born to
sustain that struggle, to ensure that there would be another
dawn to fight for, and another after that.

Even this did not fully explain the existence of
Sigmarsgeist. He looked from Konstantin to his sister
Anaise.

'I share your fears for the world. But would not your cause
– and the cause of all mankind – be better served by bringing the swords of your men to bear in the service of
Middenheim, or Talabheim, or any of the great cities you
have named? If what you say is true, then they will have
grave need before long.'

'We would do so gladly,' Anaise replied, 'were the rulers of
those cities not blind to all reason.'

'The Empire has seen clear warning of the dark flood to
come,' Konstantin said, gravely. 'Seen the warning, and chosen to ignore it. When I look upon my former homeland, I
see a land that has become lazy and corrupt. Too busy with
its own conceits to see the mortal danger now facing it. We
here are pledged to defend the inheritance of our mighty
Sigmar. To defend it, if necessary, by building the world
anew after the dark tide has finally ebbed.'

'But surely,' Bruno protested, 'all true men are loyal to the
memory of our great Emperor?'

'No!' Konstantin thundered. 'Not all, not by any means.
Look anywhere, and you will see decadence, indifference
and self-obsession. Mark my words, the Empire will not

waken to the threat until it is too late.' He paused, his face reddened with anger. 'I take no pleasure in this,' he declared, 'but I must speak what I know to be true. You are honest men. Can you say otherwise?'

Stefan hesitated. Dearly as he might want to contradict this bleak vision, in all honesty, he could not. He himself had grown used to being branded a madman or a fool, a zealot who saw evil lurking where others saw none. He understood exactly what the Guides meant, and he feared for the peril that the world might face.

'Do not misunderstand,' Anaise continued, her soft tone a contrast to her brother's. 'When the time comes, we will help our brothers and sisters in the Empire in any way we can. But we will not trust our survival to complacent, bloated leaders who might choose to look the other way. In building Sigmarsgeist, we have taken our destiny into our own hands.'

'Not completely, surely,' Stefan interjected, thinking of a comment Bea had made. 'Don't you still trade with the world outside?'

'True, for the moment,' Konstantin conceded. 'Sigmarsgeist is growing faster than we have capacity to feed ourselves. So, yes, we trade with the nearer villages.'

'We take whatever we cannot produce ourselves,' Anaise added. 'Water, particularly, is scarce here.'

'But take against what?' Bruno asked. 'What do you offer in return?'

'Our strength,' Anaise replied, matter-of-factly. 'We can protect them from the dark hordes that prey upon them. At least,' she added, 'as far as they will allow us to protect them.'

'Remember, not all see the struggle between dark and light as starkly as we,' Konstantin reminded them. 'I regret we are not welcome everywhere, however good our intentions.'

His voice trailed away, lost in contemplation. Anaise continued the story. 'In time Sigmarsgeist will become our fortress,' she told them. 'Our great ship, upon which we shall ride out the turbulent seas of change soon to afflict us all. We are the True Faith of Sigmar.' She spread her arms wide, towards the sentries standing guard upon the chamber.

'These are his soldiers. Their tunics are the red of Sigmar's blood.'

Anaise indicated the smaller group of men sitting with them in the circle. 'Those gathered around you are from our elite inner guard,' she explained. 'The white that they wear signifies the purity of their faith.'

The dozen or so white-clad men had so far sat silent, but one now turned towards Stefan and addressed him directly. 'Our purpose is to protect the Guides,' he said. 'Protect them from all danger.'

Stefan bowed politely in the man's direction. The answering look he received was cold, and far from friendly. Stefan had grown used to the welcome they had received in Sigmarsgeist. It came of something of a shock when he realised that the comment had been meant as a warning. Before he could reply, Hans Baecker spoke up, the emotion apparent in his voice.

'They are here as our guests,' he proclaimed. 'And, lest we forget, they have already proven themselves on the field of battle.' He looked around the room before fastening his gaze upon the man who had spoken. 'I see no mischief in any one of them, only good.'

'That is why you wear the red of Sigmar,' the other said, coldly. 'And I wear the white.'

Stefan stood up, determined that they should not be the cause of any ill-blood. 'It is right and proper to remain vigilant,' he said, in deference to the first man. 'And in truth you know no more of us, than we do of you. But I swear by almighty Sigmar, we come in friendship, and wish no harm upon any of your people.'

'You will do no harm,' the man replied, offering Stefan a brief, humourless smile. 'We will see to that.'

Konstantin brought the exchange to a halt with a single, abrupt gesture. 'Enough,' he commanded. 'All of us here speak from the heart. Doubtless, what we hold in our hearts for us is true.'

Anaise apologised to Stefan and his companions. 'Rilke means you no ill,' she said. 'He was chosen for his diligence, not for his manners.'

There was a moment of tense silence which was broken by a gentle laughter, begun by Konstantin, then spreading through the circle as others took their cue from their Guide. Finally, and with some reluctance, Rilke himself joined in.

'No offence was intended,' he said gruffly. 'I speak my mind, that's all.'

'No offence is taken,' Stefan assured him. 'Candour is a virtue to be valued like all others.'

Anaise von Augen clapped her hands. 'We have spent too long talking,' she declared. 'Sigmarsgeist must be experienced. Words alone cannot do justice to its glories.' She stood up. 'Now that you are fed and rested, you must look upon our works at first hand.'

'Gladly,' Stefan affirmed.

Konstantin looked to his sister. 'Shall I be their guide, sister?'

'Or I?' Baecker asked. 'I would be happy to show our friends the glories of our citadel.'

'No,' Anaise said, firmly. 'I'll take them myself.' She turned towards Stefan and the others and smiled, knowingly. 'That way, I get to have our friends all to myself for a while.'

FOR ALL THAT, they were not to be entirely alone with Anaise. Two escorts were assigned to them, one wearing the white of the elite guard, the other the red of the regular militia. They went to a courtyard facing the palace, where a carriage and horses waited. 'You will want to see what lies within the palace itself,' Anaise told them. 'We'll finish our tour with that. First, let me show you our citadel.' She ushered them inside the cabin. The guards joined the footman up above, and within moments they were away on their journey.

For the next hour or so the carriage took them through the maze of streets that was Sigmarsgeist. Close up, what from a distance had appeared as a unified design looked anything but. Some streets were made wide, and ran straight as an arrow, whilst others were narrow lanes that would suddenly wind back upon themselves in twisting curves. Similarly the buildings. Many were plain to the eye, clean but austere, built surely with only function in mind. But more than a

few had been built from stone that had been carved with
elaborate, often beautiful shapes or inscribed with tableaux
depicting the gods of the Empire, or Konstantin himself.
Stefan didn't quite know what to make of it. It was as
though the plans for several cities had come together in one.
The results were fascinating, but confusing as well.

But whatever the purpose that lay behind its design,
Sigmarsgeist exuded an undeniable vitality. Every corner of
every street, and every building, was occupied, busy with
activity of a particular and purposeful kind. Stefan had
grown used to viewing city life as at best a happy accident –
a muddled confluence of hundreds, sometimes thousands
of individuals, with their own business to follow, their own
battles to be won. Life was untidy, wasteful and noisy, and
conflict was inevitable. Sigmarsgeist had no lack of bustle,
but the populace seemed wedded to a single purpose, their
labours orchestrated and meshed together like a well-drilled
army. An army of builders.

All across the city, they found teams of men and women
labouring amongst the shells and wooden frames of new
buildings. A fine dust hung about the air, and hardly ever
seemed to settle. On the streets, carts and wagons loaded
with timber struts, flint and steel rolled past in an endless
procession.

'When will all this work be finished?' Bruno asked. Anaise
made a non-committal gesture, as though the question were
one without precise answer. 'Each day brings new converts
to the True Faith,' she said. 'At the moment it may only be a
few pilgrims, a mere trickle. But when the great conflagration comes, that trickle may become a flood. We must build
now for the future.'

Nowhere was the work more intense than upon the city
walls. Already substantial, the walkways and ramparts were
being reinforced and strengthened and, in places, extended,
widening the stout belt around the city. It looked, Stefan
reflected, like a place preparing for a long and difficult siege.

As they travelled through the streets, rows of houses alter-
nating with shining new foundries and workshops, other
differences also became apparent. Bruno, perhaps still

mulling over the plain water they had been given to wash down their breakfast, was the first to comment on an odd deficiency.

'Do you know,' he said after a while. 'We've been on the move all this time, past every manner of dwelling and building, but I don't think I've seen a single inn or tavern. Are they somehow disguised?'

'Not disguised,' Anaise told him. A look of almost playful reproach crossed her face. 'There are no taverns. The drinking of liquor isn't encouraged in Sigmarsgeist. It makes man weak, leaves him open to corruption, and opens doors to the soul that are better left closed.'

Bruno sat back, aghast at the idea of a world without ale. Stefan looked at his friend and raised an eyebrow. Anaise leaned forward across the seats of the carriage, her voice lowered to a whisper. 'It's Konstantin's thing, really,' she explained. 'His heart is so pure, but that purity brings strictness. He believes that all of us are vulnerable to the dark powers, and he has ruled against anything that might sow the seeds of weakness.'

'Even a mug of beer?' Bruno asked, incredulous.

'Even a mug of beer.'

'It's not such a terrible thing,' Bea commented, slightly stiffly. 'Remember what drink did for the kind burghers of Mielstadt.'

'That's true,' Stefan said. He caught his friend's eye and shrugged. 'Things are indeed different here.'

He looked out from the carriage window as they rode past yet another work party, half a dozen loaded wagons being followed by a gang of workers, marching two abreast, shepherded on each side by a row of soldiers. Stefan found himself puzzled by the sight.

'Are those men prisoners?' he asked Anaise. 'Why are there so many guards?'

'Prisoners?' she responded. 'I wouldn't have thought so. Perhaps they're going to work outside the city walls.' The carriage steered left, bringing it back onto the main highway that led through the centre of the citadel. 'We'll be back at the palace in just a little while,' Anaise continued. 'That's where things get interesting.' She leant forward and pointed out of the carriage window. 'Now, look out here,' she exclaimed. '*Those* are prisoners.'

She rapped upon the compartment wall, bringing the carriage to a sudden halt. On the opposite side of the road was a group of about half a dozen, tall, blond-haired men wearing the tattered remnants of dark armour, some bearing the insignia of a horned beast. The men shuffled forward slowly in a line, each one shackled to the next. They were being shepherded by a row of soldiers, swords drawn at the ready. The prisoners hurled curses at their guards and anyone else within earshot in a coarse, guttural tongue that was uncomfortably familiar to Stefan.

'Who are they?' Bea asked.

'Wait a moment,' Anaise replied. She opened the carriage window and leant out, exchanging a few words with the men seated above. The coachman descended and went to speak with the guard escorting the prisoners. After a brief conversation he returned to the carriage and reported to Anaise.

'Norscans,' she explained. 'A party of marauders found wandering a day or so ago on the eastern plains. Doubtless they've come from Kislev – part of the Chaos army that you helped destroy. If so,' she concluded, 'their days of mischief are now at an end.'

Bea watched the bruised and bloodied faces of the captives. A look of pity mixed with disgust passed across her face. 'What will happen to them?'

'That depends,' Anaise said. 'The strongest will be put to work upon the walls. Or the quarries or the mines beyond the walls, if we think they're capable of it. Others – well...'

As Stefan looked from the window, one of the prisoners turned towards the carriage, and their eyes briefly met. The Norscan stared at Stefan with a disdainful loathing. The man's lips moved in an inaudible curse, and he hawked a gobbet of blood-flecked phlegm upon the ground.

'There were certainly Norscans at Erengrad,' Stefan confirmed, turning away. 'Kin to the same marauders who plundered my village when I was a boy. I know only too well what they're capable of.'

'Don't worry,' Anaise assured him. 'These will make full atonement for their sins before we're done with them. Now–' She rapped again upon the pane behind her. 'Let's away. There's plenty yet that you must see.'

The carriage swung back into the square where their tour had begun, passing through the guarded outer wall that led to the palace. Without waiting for their escorts, Anaise climbed out and began walking towards a set of double doors set to one side of the main gate into the palace. Bruno helped Bea down, and with Stefan they followed their host across the courtyard, the two escorts a discreet distance behind. Anaise flung wide the door on one side to reveal a set of gates, locked and barred. The guard in white now stepped forward, bearing a set of keys, one of which he inserted in the lock. The other guard approached with a second key, and repeated the procedure. The heavy gate swung open and a gust of air wafted out, bearing with it a smell of antiquity reminiscent of an ancient place of worship.

'We're about to enter the oldest part of the city,' Anaise told them. 'The only part which remains from the time–' She broke off, a look of concern clouding her features. She strode forward and caught hold of Bea just as the girl was about to topple.

'What's the matter?' she asked Bea. 'Are you sick?' she motioned to a guard. 'Fetch her some water.'

'No, there's no need,' Bea assured her. She steadied herself for a moment, leaning into Anaise for support. 'Give me a moment. I'll be fine.'

'Are you sure?' Stefan asked. Bruno placed a protective arm upon Bea's shoulder. 'We've done too much travelling. You need more rest.'

'No, really,' Bea insisted. She took a deep breath, and wiped her brow. Anaise was studying her intently.

'What could have brought on such a thing?'

'It's nothing, really,' Bea replied at last. 'Or, rather, it's not nothing. Just–'

'Go on.'

'I felt it even as we were standing on the hillside, looking down upon the citadel,' Bea explained. 'An energy – a great, powerful energy.' She looked around at Stefan and the others. 'More than that,' she went on, sounding faintly embarrassed now. 'It felt like it was calling to me, as though I was meant to be here. I thought at first it was my imagination. But I felt it again here just now. Only this time it was much stronger – almost overwhelming.'

Anaise turned Bea gently, and led her towards the open gates. 'I'm sure this was no imagining on your part,' she said, quietly. 'I'm sure that you are, truly meant to be with us here. Come,' she said, ushering them on. 'Come, all of you. See what lies at the very heart of Sigmarsgeist.'

BRUNO HELPED BEA through the portal into the darkened interior of a small antechamber. There they waited whilst one of the guards brought a lamp, then followed in single file behind Anaise, down a spiral stairway that corkscrewed deep below ground. Something was different here: in the faint, musty odour that hung upon the air, in the very fabric of the building that they were inside. From the condition of the walls, and the stairway under their feet, it was clear that part of the building was newly made, and some of it was quite old. New brick and mortar were fused with older, mould-encrusted stone, in such a way that it was impossible to say where one became the other. Much of the walls was decorated with runes carved into the stone. Most were so worn away with age, they were impossible to read.

'It was important we kept some link with the age gone by,' Anaise commented. 'Down here our bright future meets with the shadows of our past.'

'Then these are the remains of the city that was here before,' Bea said. 'Before Sigmarsgeist?'

'A city, or perhaps cities,' Anaise replied. 'There may have been many.'

'What was its name?' Stefan asked. 'The place that stood here before.'

'No one knows – there have been settlements here since before the time of men.' She turned and smiled at Stefan. 'There were only dead ruins here when we came to lay the foundations for Sigmarsgeist.'

'And when was that?' Stefan asked her. 'When did that labour begin?'

'The first stone was laid at dawn,' Anaise replied, pausing briefly upon the step, 'two years after our quest for a home had begun. Dawn on the morn of Geheimnisnacht, eight years ago.'

Geheimnisnacht, the day of mystery. It struck Stefan as somehow appropriate.

'You have toiled mightily hard,' Bruno commented, 'to build such a place in so short a time.'

'Hard indeed,' Stefan echoed. To have constructed a city this size from nothing, and in only eight years, seemed almost beyond belief.

'We have worked hard,' Anaise agreed. 'And our work is only still beginning.'

They had reached the foot of the stairs, which opened out onto an antechamber much like the one above. Before them lay another set of locked gates. Once again, the guards turned keys in each of two huge locks. Stefan was reminded of a brief but uncomfortable visit to the grim Imperial dungeons of Altdorf.

'This is a prison,' he said.

'In part,' Anaise replied. 'And much more.'

They passed through the gates, the heavy steel clanging shut behind them. From somewhere deep within the subterranean expanse there came the faint sound of voices crying out in pain or in anguish. Stefan thought of the Norscan prisoners they had passed on the street, and of Anaise's words: *they'll make full atonement for their sins.* He knew there was no atonement that would purge the hatred for their kind from his heart. He could slake his thirst for vengeance, but he knew it would always return.

They followed Anaise along a wide passage, past other dark corridors that led off into the gloom beneath the city. The roof was just high enough for a man to pass through walking upright. It was dark, lit only by the faint glimmerings of daylight that penetrated from airshafts, and by lanterns posted at intervals along the passageway. 'This would be our place of last resort, our final refuge,' Anaise explained. 'A place of final defence in the face of the black tide. Of course,' she added, 'we hope it will never come to that.'

'Pray to Sigmar himself it will not,' Bruno concurred.

Anaise came to a door set in the left wall of the passage and waited whilst they gathered round. 'By the way,' she said, 'there's said to be water somewhere down here too. A hidden spring. What do you make of that?' The last words seemed to be addressed to Bea in particular. The healer made no reply, but her face betrayed a sudden flicker of emotion.

'I'd say, let's hope it stays hidden,' Bruno declared. 'At least until we're safely above ground.'

Anaise smiled. 'I'm sure it will,' she said, and eased the door open.

Beyond was a chamber, lit by the thin, jaundiced light of the lamps. A rush of air escaped as the door was levered open, air pungent with the sour tang of death and putrefaction.

'Merciful gods,' Bruno exclaimed, quickly covering his nose and mouth with his hand. 'What abomination is this?'

Anaise stepped inside, wrapping a portion of her gown about her face to form a mask. 'It is evil,' she said. 'In here we confront our darkest fears.'

She disappeared into the gloom of the inner chamber. Stefan took a deep breath, and followed, steeling himself for whatever might be inside.

Standing in the twilit gloom were three figures, men clad in dark robes, their faces obliterated by masks. They carried instruments of shining steel in their hands, and Stefan thought momentarily of surgeons, their blades blessed in the hope of curing, not killing.

But this was no house of healing. The room stank of the charnel house. This was surely a place of death, not life. The three men stood stock still, their eyes betraying surprise at the entrance of the strangers. One, whose mask had slipped, quickly pulled it up to cover his face once more.

'It's all right,' Anaise called to them. 'These are friends, come to see our great works at first hand.' The men eyed Stefan and his companions with continuing suspicion. They stood with their backs to some kind of raised table or galley, shielding it from view.

'These are men of science,' Anaise said, in a measured aside. 'Forgive their lack of social graces. Come, Joachim, do not hide your art from us.'

The three robed men stood back, and, in a frozen moment Stefan took in the scene laid out before him. On either side of the men there were tables, some filled with knives and instruments, others with bottles and vials. Beneath the long galley table was a tray that brimmed with a viscous liquid. And laid out flat upon the galley itself was a body, very clearly dead.

It was not the body of a man, though possibly it might once have been. The cadaver had the proportions and structure of a man, but the leathery hide of a reptile. The body had been sliced open along one side, the incision running from the base of its torso to the top of its misshapen skull. Several of the creature's organs had been cut out and placed within the clear glass jars, or laid out upon silver trays positioned on either side of the body. From the open incision, a stream of something oily and viscous oozed from the body, falling into a vessel below the galley. It wasn't blood, though the milky flow was flecked with red. The stench from the body was beyond belief. As they watched, the contents of the vessel shifted and stirred.

'Shallya save us,' Bea whispered. 'There's something alive in there.'

'Maggots,' Stefan said, fighting the urge to retch. Anaise looked at him, and nodded. 'The mark of Nurgle,' she said. 'Dark lord of infestation and decay.'

Stefan stared at the scene, quietly aghast. 'What is going on here?' he demanded. 'What in the name of Sigmar are they doing?'

'This is no casual examination,' Anaise replied, coldly. 'Our physicians are studying the ways of the Dark Powers. Only through understanding evil can we hope to destroy it.'

She turned towards Stefan, a defiant challenge burning in her eyes. 'Or would you rather we knew nothing of our enemy, until they were feasting on the corpses of our dead?'

'I feel as though I already know too much,' Bruno said, keeping his hand clamped over his mouth. Bea turned away, a trembling in her body. Her face was a confusion of disappointment and anger. 'This is horrible,' she pronounced, her voice very small.

Stefan found he did not know what to think. The sight of the mutant, dissected upon the surgeons' table, repelled and fascinated him in equal measure. Part of him could not believe that man could work in such intimate proximity to evil without becoming evil himself. But, if, truly, Chaos could be understood, measured and weighed like the pieces upon a scale – what then? Perhaps one day, finally, it could be overcome. Forever.

There was a brief, and uncomfortable space in the conversation, a tension finally broken by Anaise. 'Come,' she said. 'This is a shock to your senses, and I should apologise for inflicting it upon you without warning.' She hesitated. 'We should return to the Seat of the Guides. Konstantin will be able to explain this to you so much better than I.'

None of them had any objections. It was a relief to get beyond the door of the chamber, putting the physicians and their grim endeavour beyond both sight and mind. The four and their guards retraced their steps a distance through the passage. The sound of voices began again to grow louder.

'We are near the cells now. Do you want to come and look?' She extended a hand towards Stefan. 'I think of you as our friends. I want to keep no secrets from you. I want you to know exactly what Sigmarsgeist is, what it stands for. Only then can you truly judge.'

'After what we have seen, I doubt little else can shock us,' Stefan replied.

'It cannot fail but be easier on the stomach,' Bruno agreed. He took Bea's hand. 'Come on,' he said, encouragingly. 'We'll be back above ground in no time.'

The prison cells lay beyond a further set of gates, their iron bars thicker and sturdier than either of the two they had passed through before. Any captive would surely look upon them and despair of ever regaining his liberty. As they made their way through the chill grey of another passageway, the isolated cries gradually grew to a cacophony.

'Their agony comes from within,' Anaise commented. 'The Dark Gods began their torture long before they ever found themselves here.'

There were series of iron doors along the length of the passage, a dozen or so on each side. Many of the lightless cells were empty, but, in others, something malevolent stirred. Creatures thrashed at the chains that held them fastened to the walls, or roared belligerent hate at the sound of footsteps outside. Stefan caught glimpses of the creatures that only evil could beget: an orc, the green-skinned killer staring at its captors with brutish defiance; two beastmen, bull-headed mutants locking horns in snarling, futile combat in the narrow confines of their cell. Creatures so wedded to violence that they would tear each other apart if they could find no better foe.

But amongst the monsters there were also men. More of the Norscans, the mark of mutation not yet apparent on all of them. And others, some in armour, some not. Soldiers, perhaps, or mercenaries. Who knew what they were, or what they had been? They were all prisoners now.

'Where have they all come from?' Bruno asked.

'Some are the flotsam of the war in Kislev,' Anaise told him. 'Those who fled south, hoping to find easy pickings in the unprotected lands of the Ostermark.' She pulled back from the narrow bars of a cell as a face loomed out of the darkness, venomous fangs snapping at her hand.

'Yet some of these are men,' Bruno protested. 'Ordinary men.'

She looked at him, one eyebrow raised, then turned to Stefan. 'You do not think that evil can take human form?'

Stefan knew only too well what the answer was. Evil could take on almost any form. Chaos was never more dangerous than when it cloaked itself in familiarity.

'What will happen to them?' he asked.

'Many will be put to work, building against the day when their kind will return to threaten the world. Others...' she inclined her head back the way they had come.

'Others will serve in other ways.'

Something in the thought appalled Stefan, appalled and disgusted him. And yet he knew that reason was all on Anaise von Augen's side. If the mastery of Chaos was the end to which they were striving, who was to say that the ends did not justify the means?

'Please,' Bea steadied herself against Bruno's side, and gasped for breath. Her face had turned a deathly pale.

'She needs some air,' Bruno declared. 'And for that matter, so do I. I've seen enough here.'

Anaise turned to Stefan. 'Have you seen enough?'

Stefan took in the rows of cells, the inhuman wailing from the creatures trapped inside. It was the stuff of nightmares. But if, within that nightmare, there existed a seed of hope that that evil could not only be contained, but conquered? Was that a nightmare, or a dream?

'I've seen things we've never seen before,' he said. 'And, for that matter, never thought to see.' He looked at Anaise, and nodded. 'Yes, I have seen enough.'

Anaise signalled to one of the guards. 'Take our guests back above,' she instructed. 'See that their needs are attended to.'

ANAISE WAITED WHILST the guard led Stefan and the others away. She listened as they ascended the steps towards daylight, listened to the sound of their footsteps echo and fade. Then she turned back along the passageway, the second guard following at a distance. As she passed along the row of cells the cacophony of hate erupted again. The captives screamed out at her in their torment, their hatred for all her kind. Anaise inclined her head one way, then the other, and kept walking with the serenity of the invulnerable.

Near the end of the row she stopped by a cell, and slid back the narrow panel in the door. A powerful scent wafted from the cell. Not the stench of decay, but something quite different: a sweet, animal scent, earthy and cloying. The smell of both fear and desire, of dread, and of anticipation. Anaise flinched away, but drank it down all the same. She edged closer, and looked inside.

Crouched upon the floor of the cell were two or more bodies, their smooth skins glistening in the gloom. Their bodies were intertwined, in some kind of grotesque embrace. Sensing Anaise, they broke apart. One of the creatures stood and turned to the door. The figure was slender and quite hairless. Neither quite human nor animal, neither male nor female. Its body was covered with what at first looked like wounds, a scattering of swollen, cherry bruises all across its arms and chest. It peered out at Anaise, its pale, almond eyes holding her in its liquid gaze. The bruises swelled and parted, splitting open like ripe fruit. A dozen miniature mouths opened in a facsimile of a smile; tiny tongues forking through needle-pointed teeth. Anaise pulled her gaze away but stayed fixed by the door, breathing in the musk-drenched odour of the cell.

'My lady.' She turned at the voice of the guard, standing several steps behind her in the passageway. The white-clad soldier stood waiting for instruction, his face blank of emotion. 'My lady?'

Anaise cast a final, long, look at the apparition. She shivered, then looked away. 'No,' she said to the guard. 'Not this time. Let us away.'

# CHAPTER EIGHT
## The Well of Sadness

'YOUR COMRADES HAVE found these things shocking, Stefan. I understand that. But you must try to understand us, understand our purpose. The forces we will face in that final battle recognise no fairness, no noble ideals of honour. They will use every opportunity, every cruel turn of fortune against us. If we are to survive the coming storm, then we must be prepared to do likewise. We must fight fire with fire. There is no room in our armoury for compassion.'

Konstantin von Augen waited to see how his words would play with Stefan. His worn but still vigorous face betrayed no hint of guile or duplicity. Stefan had no doubt that he meant every word of what he said with a passion and a conviction that could only be admired.

For all that, Stefan was feeling less at his ease in the Guide's presence that morning. He had become uncomfortable with Konstantin's zeal and certainty, and uncomfortable, too, with the thought that he had found himself so readily seduced by it. There was no disputing that there was much in what he had seen and heard that found a place in his heart. In so many ways, Sigmarsgeist offered a vision of the world that he had been unable to find any-where else in his years of searching. He should feel at home here. And, the gods knew, he had waited long enough for that.

But instead, Stefan was feeling vaguely troubled. Something was worrying him, some nagging memory that lay just out of reach. Had he found what they had seen, deep below ground, shocking? Stefan would not have thought it possible. All his life, since the night of childhood when life changed forever, Stefan had lived to see the world purged of the forces of Chaos. Anything, surely, that led along that road must be right, must be honourable? And yet, and yet...

Konstantin read the doubt clouding his features. 'What is it, Stefan? You must tell me honestly what is in your heart.' The Guide cast his eyes around the small chamber. 'It's all right,' he added. 'We speak privately here. Whatever you have to say to me goes no further.'

'I don't know,' Stefan told him. 'Perhaps I'm just tired, that's all.' It was true, he was tired. He had slept badly, the night hours punctuated by dreams of running through the streets of a village, between houses wracked with flame, thick, oily smoke pouring from every window. In the dream, Stefan had been chasing someone, a person who always kept ahead of him, just out of sight. That in itself did not perturb him much. Dreams of smoke and fire had been his nocturnal companions on countless occasions since that night in Odensk, and given what had happened in the last few days it was perhaps little surprise that they had returned to haunt him now.

'You look tired,' Konstantin agreed. 'There is something lacking in your quarters, perhaps?'

'No, no,' Stefan assured him. 'It's just–' he paused, search-ing for the right words. 'I'm just wondering whether soon we must take our leave of Sigmarsgeist.'

Konstantin nodded, sympathetically. 'I know, you have a quest to fulfil,' he said. 'I would be the last to stand in the way of that. But do you truly know where that quest will take you from here?'

'No,' Stefan answered him, truthfully. 'I do not.'

'Then why not stay?' Konstantin urged. 'Sigmarsgeist is still young, Stefan. What you have seen is only the birth, the seed that has yet to grow into a mighty tree. You could be part of that.' He placed his hands firmly upon Stefan's shoulders. 'We have great need of men such as you, Stefan. Your skills would be prized here.'

'Maybe so,' Stefan conceded. 'But my life belongs upon the road, I think. I'm happier seeking out trouble than waiting for it to find me.'

It was a good answer, and not without truth. Over time he could have chosen any number of well-paid, and probably comfortable, lives as a bodyguard, armed retainer or chief of a private militia. And before he left Erengrad, Gastez Castelguerre had made him a better offer yet. To join the secret few, the men known as the Keepers of the Flame, pledged to stand in eternal defiance of the forces of darkness. Then, as now, Stefan had been honoured. But he had said no, as surely he must now. It was his destiny to be the restless soldier, always on the move. And as long as Alexei Zucharov and his kind were waiting, somewhere in the world beyond, it would have to remain that way.

Konstantin sat weighing Stefan's words, and considering his response. 'Of course,' he replied at length, a knowing smile upon his face. 'You must leave whenever you see fit. But if your thirst must have you seek out evil, then you need seek no further than here. Evil is all around us, Stefan, it is everywhere.'

'I understand,' Stefan told him. 'I appreciate what you believe you must do for the coming time. But I'm not sure I can wait that long.'

'No,' Konstantin said, gravely. 'You do not understand. We are not simply sitting here waiting, waiting like sheep in the field for the wolf to come. We are taking our struggle to the acolytes of darkness, Stefan. Seeking them out. Destroying them wherever we find them.'

Stefan had experienced most of his life as a series of clear decisions. Often life or death had hung upon the outcome, but the way had always seemed clear. To find himself torn between two paths was something new, unusual. Instinct told him that they had already spent too long in Sigmarsgeist, that they should be back upon the road before they outstayed a generous welcome. But something urged him still to stay. It was true: what he had seen in the dungeons of the citadel *had* troubled him. The rules of conflict by which he had lived most of his life had been turned upside down.

'What you stand *against* is clear,' the Guide said. 'You stand against all evil, against the foul, corrupting tide that threatens to engulf our lands. I give praise for that. Would that there were more like you.' He paused, letting the silence add weight to his words. 'But let me ask you this. Can you tell me what you stand *for*? What causes will you champion? Where will your road lead you?'

Stefan said nothing. In his heart, he knew he had no answer to give.

'Join us,' Konstantin entreated. 'Join with us and share our goal, our vision of the world to come. You belong here, Stefan. You are as one with us.'

The words struck a chord with Stefan that could not be denied. Here, in Sigmarsgeist, he had no need to try and explain himself. No need to justify his driven, single-minded quest. No need to explain why he could not rest whilst the followers of Chaos still hid within the shadows of the Old World. No need, because that was exactly the spirit that had given birth to the citadel. He could never go home from Sigmarsgeist, Stefan reflected, because he was already there.

'I'll need to confer with my comrades,' Stefan replied at length, conscious that he was only buying time by such an answer.

'Of course,' Konstantin agreed. He truly seemed to have no wish to pressure Stefan into a decision. But the look on his face signalled his belief in what the answer would be. 'I promise you,' he said, 'joining the True Followers of Sigmar will be the defining moment of your life.'

Stefan bowed, and turned to leave. He opened the door to find himself face to face with Rilke, the White Guard who had spoken against them at the meeting of the council. The look on the other man's face suggested that nothing had softened his opinion of the newcomers, and Stefan had the distinct impression that he had been standing by the door for quite some time. Rilke stood staring at him for a moment, quite unembarrassed to have been discovered. Somewhat grudgingly, he moved aside to let Stefan pass. Stefan didn't move.

'You should have come in,' Stefan said. 'That way you'd have better heard what passed between the Guide and myself.'

Rilke held Stefan's gaze, unflinchingly. There was no humour or apology in his eyes. 'I hear everything I need to hear,' he said, acidly. 'Nothing you do or say is likely to escape me.' He made to push his way past Stefan, who was now barring his way into Konstantin's chamber. 'Let me pass,' he demanded. 'I have urgent news for the Guide.'

Stefan held steady, keeping his body as a barrier between the man in white and the door. 'You and I seem to have got off on the wrong foot,' he commented. 'I hope it proves to be just a misunderstanding.' He barely caught Rilke's muttered reply.

'There is nothing to understand,' he said. 'I have a duty to do, and I'm going to do it.'

BRUNO HAD RISEN early with the idea of exploring Sigmarsgeist on his own. Although it was still barely past dawn, the heart of the citadel was already busy. Bruno stepped from the quiet of the palace on to streets full to overflowing with people going about their work. He had no particular direction or destination in mind, although a part of him was still reluctant to believe that in all Sigmarsgeist there wasn't a single beer-house or tavern. And if there was even one, then he would find it.

He emerged from the palace gates and started to walk down the broad avenue that passed directly through the heart of the citadel. Bruno's sense of direction was good and it was no idle boast that he would only need be taken somewhere once in order to commit it to memory. So he followed the same sequence of streets that they had passed along in

the carriage the previous day, this time taking in his surroundings at his own leisurely pace.

After an hour, he was lost. None of the streets he now
passed through seemed to bear any resemblance to those he
had seen the day before. Bruno couldn't fathom it; he was
sure that he had followed the same precise route, street by
street. But it didn't worry him unduly. Before long, he was
sure, he would recognise a landmark. If not, well then, there
was no shortage of people to help him find his way.

In the meantime, he took good note of what he saw
around him, and what he didn't see. No inns or beer houses,
for sure, not a single one. And no dwellings, at least none
resembling the haphazard, ramshackle collections familiar
from home. When he at last came to the residential quarter,
it resembled nothing he had ever seen before. Instead of single houses there were great misshapen stone edifices, each
large enough to house a dozen families or more.

Bruno gazed up in wonder at the carved facades, each with
its array of tiny windows. He stood for a few moments, marvelling at the strangeness of it all. People, men, women and
a few children poured from every doorway in a steady
stream whilst those returning from their labours were coming the other way, ready to take their place in the communal
homes.

Like a nest of termites, Bruno caught himself thinking.
The comparison seemed harsh, but somehow apt. To a man,
the workers were immersed in their daily routine, those now
leaving the houses hurrying to relieve the workers returning
home. But all seemed to Bruno to be in good heart, and, if
most ignored him or greeted him only with the most cursory of nods, then he guessed it was because they were
focused upon the day to come, or else the rest that would be
their reward for their labours. He stood a while longer taking in the extraordinary scene, then walked on.

The communal quarters gave way to a road lined with
storehouses, and then, in turn, to a street occupied by a
huge, smoke-belching armoury, its red-bricked chimneys
standing like sentries against the sky. Bruno took his time,
stopping to look through the open gates and between doors,

marvelling at the intensity of the heat generated by the mighty furnaces within. Outside the gates, teams of horses hauled wagons slowly up the hill past Bruno, each wagon laden with the produce of labour: heavy broadswords, axes and pikestaffs fashioned from fresh-minted steel. Truly, Bruno reflected, this was a people readying themselves for war. Could the rest of the world really have left themselves so unprepared?

Turning the corner at the head of the road, he came to a plot of open ground framed by tall, spindly trees. It was a rare enough sight in the citadel. Bruno remembered noting the scene during their journey the day before, and congratulated himself on regaining his bearings. He remembered the square as empty save for the trees, and a squat, rectangular structure at its centre, flanked by statues of the gods Taal and Ulric. Bruno had marked it for a temple or shrine of some sort.

Now, he looked on, puzzled, wondering if his memory had deceived him. The yellowish shell of the building had been almost split apart, ripped open by a tall finger of bleached white stone shaped like a pillar that had burst through the roof of the other building. Both of the statues had been felled. The holy gods lay upon the ground, their likenesses broken into several pieces.

Bruno stood and stared at the improbable structure that seemed to grow from out of the ruined temple. It looked to be made of some kind of marble, and rather than climbing straight as a chimney might, bent and twisted along its length, giving Bruno the absurd impression that it had grown up out of the ground. The column stood taller than any of the trees, and was carved from top to bottom with runes of the most intricate design. There was no way that he could not have noticed it before, and equally surely no way that such a large and elaborate structure could have been built so quickly. The white marble glinted in the sunlight, teetering above the older structure like a predator over its prey.

So distracted was he by the sight that Bruno did not notice Hans Baecker walking towards him until the two of them were almost face to face.

'What's the matter?' Baecker demanded of Bruno, cheerily. 'Are you lost?'

'No,' Bruno replied, shaking his head forcefully, hoping either memory or vision would resolve itself. 'But I'd swear that yesterday that pillar – or whatever it is – wasn't there.'

Baecker edged forward, and took a few steps around the temple, keeping a careful distance. 'What are you saying?' he asked at last. 'That all this has been built overnight?'

'Not all of it,' Bruno said. 'Just the pillar.'

Baecker looked the pillar up and down, taking in its considerable height and the carvings etched upon its surface. 'That seems unlikely,' he replied, doubtfully. 'We work hard here in Sigmarsgeist, but, all the same…'

'I'm sure I'm not imagining it,' Bruno went on. Then laughed. 'But, perhaps I am! Perhaps I'm actually seeing things. In which case,' he added, 'only one way to find out.'

Hans Baecker began to utter some kind of caution, and he reached out to catch hold of Bruno. But Bruno was too quick, he slipped through Baecker's grasp and darted towards the temple. If the strange, snaking pillar of stone was real then he would touch it with his own hands. Or, better still – his sword. He marched forward. At the same time he heard a sound from somewhere above his head, a sound like something cracking or splintering off. Bruno looked up, raising a hand to shield his eyes from the direct sunlight.

The next thing he was aware of was something dropping down out of the sky, a sliver of stone the shape and size of a blade. The fragment struck his outstretched hand and broke into a dozen smaller pieces. Bruno cursed loudly and staggered back, blood pouring from a deep cut in his hand. 'Taal's breath,' he swore. 'That's my sword hand.'

Hans Baecker ushered him back from the courtyard of the temple, muttering condolences. 'I was trying to tell you,' he said. 'Maybe that wasn't such a good idea.'

BEA, TOO, HAD chosen to use her time that morning for exploration of a sort. The young healer had set off in search of solitude, a quiet place where she could try and come to some understanding of the conflicting emotions at war inside her. She explored the grid of narrow lanes that ran beyond the palace, high above the rest of Sigmarsgeist. Finally she found a bench which allowed her a view that stretched across the lower levels of the citadel, towards the outer walls. She sat down in the warm sunshine, and stayed for a while watching the incessant movement in the distance. Lines of men, and women too, bearing their loads of stone, raising the line of the wall towards the sky, ever higher, ever more impregnable. Elsewhere, further along, the existing structure was being demolished and a new wall was being built beyond it, like a belt being loosened to accommodate an ever-swelling belly.

Bea stared at it all, the figures of the labourers and their scarlet escorts, stared at them hoping to find an answer to the question that would not leave her. Why had the gods brought her here? She was certain this was not the work of chance. But, for as long as she waited, she found no answer in the silent toiling of the tiny figures upon the walls. All they spoke of was the relentless march towards war, final and inevitable.

Bea turned abruptly at a light touch upon her shoulder. Anaise von Augen was standing over her, an expression of gentle curiosity upon her face.

'Oh!' Bea said, startled. 'How long have you been standing there?'

'A while. I didn't want to disturb you. You looked so peaceful.'

Bea stood up, feeling suddenly awkward and exposed under the other woman's gaze. 'Not so peaceful, actually. I think I was in search of peace, but I'm not sure I found it.'

'I'm sorry if it was I who disrupted that peace,' Anaise replied, contritely.

'Not at all,' Bea assured her. 'The cause is all my own.'

Anaise turned her expression to one of concern. 'What are you feeling?' she asked.

'Confused.' She saw no need to be other than truthful. Anaise took Bea's hand and sat by her. 'Now, tell me,' she began, smoothing her skirts. 'I want to know what is troubling you.'

'I'm confused. Confused about myself,' Bea began, after a pause for thought. 'Don't misunderstand me, Anaise. All this–' she made a sweep of the citadel beneath them with her hand. 'All of this makes perfect sense. I understand what you are doing here, I really do. And yet, yesterday, below ground – I'm sorry, I–' she broke off, lost for words.

'It's all right,' Anaise said, softly. She reached for Bea's hand again. 'I know. I could tell it disgusted you. It made you think you could never be a part of such savagery, whatever the motive that lay behind it.'

Bea nodded, almost imperceptibly. Anaise sighed. 'My brother and I have spent many nights of conversation, arguing into the small hours about such things. I do not expect you to understand, nor to accept. I understand your revulsion, Bea.'

'But do you understand this?' the younger woman countered. 'Do you understand why I find myself drawn to this place, drawn by a force so powerful I can feel it even here? Drawn for no purpose that my reason can explain?'

'Well,' Anaise replied. 'Much talk here has been of warriors. Of men like Stefan and Bruno, who could perform great service for Sigmarsgeist. But I think you would be of equal, if not greater value to us, Bea.' She squeezed the girl's hands between her own. 'Truly, I do.'

Bea shook her head in emphatic denial. 'That's exactly it,' she said. 'I wouldn't. Look at all this–' she indicated the citadel again. 'I'm a healer. My work is amongst the sick, the diseased, the dying even. Sigmarsgeist fairly bursts with vigour and health. You have no need of me here, no need at all.'

Anaise got up, and stood for a moment, letting the sunlight play upon her upturned face. Then she looked down at Bea. 'I think there's something you ought to see,' she said. 'Something I did not share with the others yesterday.' She looked around. 'My carriage is close by,' she said. 'It'll be quicker that way.'

She extended her hand, and smiled, encouragingly. 'Will you come?'

\* \* \*

THEY RODE BACK towards the centre of the citadel, and the palace. Neither spoke. Bea passed the time looking from the window, marvelling at how Sigmarsgeist seemed busier by the hour, like a voracious bloom, constantly growing. Inside the palace it was cool, and quiet after the bustle of the streets. Anaise led the way to a suite of chambers a single floor below ground. A soldier in the white of the elite guard escorted them through a set of heavy oak doors, and then they were alone. No guards, no distant screams. The two women stood within the eerie stillness of the inner sanctum.

'Few people ever come here,' Anaise murmured. 'Not even my brother.'

Bea looked around. They were inside a circular chamber, lit by the dim glow of candles fixed at intervals around the walls. The room was unfurnished except for four chairs set facing a rounded turret or basin that sat waist-high in the centre of the chamber. The whole place smelt of dry antiquity, and was obviously far older than the rest of the citadel. Bea immediately knew that beneath the stillness in the room, the energy was stronger here than anything she had sensed before. She steadied herself against the upright back of a chair.

'What is this place?' she whispered. 'Why have you brought me here?'

Anaise gave no direct answer to her question, 'I know your secret,' she said instead, and smiled, knowingly. Bea's face flushed a guilty red. She turned away from the other woman. 'What do you mean?' she demanded. 'What secret?'

Anaise drew the younger woman to her, taking her gently in her arms. 'It's all right,' she assured Bea. 'We're the same, you and I. The others don't understand us. But we know. We can feel it, can't we?'

Bea broke away in a sudden panic. She had the feeling that Anaise was looking directly into her soul. 'I don't understand,' she protested. 'What–'

'Magical energy,' Anaise said. She clasped hold of Bea's hands, and steadied her, forcing her to meet her gaze. 'You can feel it, can't you?'

Bea looked up at Anaise and a signal passed between them, an unspoken complicity. 'I feel it,' Bea confirmed. 'I can feel it here more than anywhere.'

Anaise led her towards the centre of the chamber. The two women stood with their backs to the raised, circular wall. Bea was at once aware of something flowing into her, powerful and irresistible.

'Turn around,' Anaise commanded, softly. Bea waited a few moments longer, then obeyed. She knew, sooner or later, she would have no choice. She found herself gazing down into a shaft which disappeared into the darkness far below. The faintest of breezes wafted up from the bottom of the shaft. Bea breathed in, and gasped, involuntarily, as her mind connected with an invisible force.

'This is why you came to Sigmarsgeist,' Anaise told her. 'All that you have been searching for is here.' She pulled Bea back from the edge of the parapet. 'Steady,' she advised. 'It will overpower you if you're not careful.'

Bea took a step back. Her head was still swimming. 'What... is that?' she asked.

'This is the most ancient part of the old city still remaining,' Anaise told her. 'The shaft passes right through the core of Sigmarsgeist. It goes deeper than we went yesterday. Far, far, deeper. I did not bring your comrades here,' she said. 'They wouldn't understand.'

'I'm not sure that I understand,' Bea said, slowly. But she felt impelled to look again. Gingerly, she edged towards the open shaft and stole another glance inside. Immediately, she felt something spark inside of her. The sensation lasted no more than a moment, but it was unmistakable, nonetheless. Anaise caught sight of her confusion, and laughed.

'Careful!' she cautioned, smiling broadly. 'You are like I was at first. You cannot resist it. Take care, or it will consume you.'

Bea's heart was pounding. She took a deep breath to free herself of the sudden intoxication. 'What is it?' she asked.

'It is a well spring of magic,' Anaise said. 'The shaft runs right to its source. Whoever built it long ago was tapping into the unimaginable power that lies buried deep beneath the world. People are frightened of such things, but you and I understand the good that they can do.'

Bea nodded, confused and awed. She knew, and yet she did not know, not really. 'I have given it a name,' Anaise continued. 'The Well of Sadness.'

'Sadness?' Bea asked. 'How can such a wondrous thing speak of sadness?'

'Because the well is dry,' Anaise explained. 'At some time in the past the shaft has been blocked, or else the waters that fed it have ebbed away.'

'The waters,' Bea echoed. Somewhere in her mind the pieces of an ancient puzzle were coming together.

'You know,' Anaise said. 'You believe. You speak its name, even to those who do not believe.'

Bea had to cling on to the other woman to keep herself from falling. She felt overwhelmed. The words were on her lips but now she could not speak.

'Tal Dur,' Anaise said at last. 'The waters of Tal Dur that once rose here.'

Bea nodded. It must be so. Nothing else could account for the power she had felt flowing into her body. 'Imagine,' Anaise went on, 'imagine what we could achieve, what ills we could heal, if only we could tap into its mighty power once again.' She turned Bea's face towards her until she was looking directly into the other's eyes.

'Like me, you have longed to find Tal Dur. Tell me it's so.'

'In my dreams I have often stepped into its waters,' Bea whispered. 'And through its divine will, I have brought healing to the world.'

Anaise smiled at her, indulgently. 'So pure,' she murmured, 'so beautiful.' She ran her fingers through the copper curls of Bea's hair. 'You should grow your hair long,' she told her. 'Grow it long like a priestess of Shallya.'

Bea twisted away. A frown crossed her face. Anaise stepped back, giving the healer space. 'No, not a priestess,' she corrected herself. 'The sisters of Shallya do not countenance the healing powers of magic.'

'No,' Bea said quietly. 'They do not.'

'But we believe,' Anaise said. 'And our belief will endure. Tal Dur is here, somewhere very close,' she said. 'And, with your help, I shall find it.'

STEFAN HAD STEPPED to one side to allow the stocky figure of Rilke past. But now he found himself more than curious to hear whatever it was that Rilke was so anxious to discuss with the Guide. As the White Guard went to close the door to the chamber behind him, Stefan held firm, keeping it open. Rilke glared at him with an undisguised loathing.

'If you want to pit your strength against mine, *mercenary*, then we'll find a place that will do justice to the argument.'

'I've no interest in fighting you,' Stefan told him. 'But if you've come to say something to the Guide about my comrades or I, then I want to hear what it is.'

'What I have to say is none of your business,' Rilke spat. 'Whether it concerns you or not.' He hauled upon the door, putting all of his strength into pulling it away from Stefan, but Stefan held his ground. The two men stood with the door between them, going nowhere.

'Enough!' the voice from within the chamber commanded. 'Both of you, step inside.'

Konstantin's face was a mask of contained rage. 'Men of good faith must not enter into conflict,' he told them. Stefan and Rilke exchanged wary glances. Neither spoke.

'That is how our enemies will divide us,' the Guide stated, curtly. 'You are both of you fools if you cannot see that.'

'I apologise,' Stefan said at last. 'If you wish, I'll withdraw.'

Konstantin waved his offer away. 'No,' he said. 'Rilke has been ill-mannered. Our guest will stay, and hear whatever it is you have to tell me.'

Rilke executed a short, graceless bow. He looked far from happy.

'It would be better that we spoke in private,' he said.

'I'll be the judge of that,' Konstantin concluded. 'Now, speak.'

Rilke looked from the Guide to Stefan, and back again. The expression on Konstantin's face made it clear he was not to be swayed.

'So be it,' Rilke said, stiffly. 'I bring news from our scouts on the western plain. They have found a gang of marauders, close on two score of them, riding south.'

'Do we know who they are?' Konstantin asked. Rilke glanced again at Stefan before continuing. 'They may be remnants of the defeated Chaos army at Erengrad.'

'Good. Very good, Rilke.' Konstantin turned his gaze towards Stefan. 'It seems the opportunity for you to exercise your blade has come sooner than either of us could have expected,' he said. 'You wanted to take the fight to our enemies. Now you have the chance.'

# CHAPTER NINE
## Seek and Destroy

THROUGH THE LONG days of captivity, Alexei Zucharov had had at least one thing in abundance. Perhaps for the first time in his life he had time to contemplate his past, and his future, to search what memories remained of the man he had once been and to explore the first stirrings of the creature that he was to become.

He had time, too, to try and adapt to his captivity, an existence he never expected to experience. Zucharov spent his waking days bound in heavy chains constricting his body like an iron serpent. His nights he spent lost in a wilderness of dreams, locked inside his own imaginings by potions fed to him by his captor. Like a wild beast he was tethered and controlled. In his lucid moments, amongst the fragments of his passing memories, he gazed in upon himself with an unquenchable fury. The tattoo growing across his flesh chronicled his downfall in every detail. Again and again he was forced to look upon his surrender to the bounty hunter, disgust mingling with fascination.

And yet, stirred in amongst his rage there was confusion. At first Zucharov had tested the limits of his captivity. He knew it was not beyond his capability to escape. The chains that bound him were strong, but he would surely prove the stronger. Each day that passed found him growing ever more powerful. Before long he would be able to snap the iron links as though they were no stronger than gossamer. And yet, somehow, he knew that he would not. There was a reason to his captivity, and a purpose to this journey, that he did not yet understand. But he would learn. Most of all, through the long days travelling across the forsaken plain, he would learn. He would be a pupil, and the voice of Kyros, the dark echo forever inside his head, would be his teacher. This was to be his journey. He must wait, and allow the alchemy of change to turn defeat into lasting victory. *You are strong*, Kyros had told him. *Great will be your reward.*

THE DECISION HAD been simple enough. Stefan was not going to refuse the chance to ride with the soldiers of Sigmar, to hunt down the mutant host, and destroy them. It was a moment to forget doubts, and put aside questions. As Stefan joined the men in scarlet riding on to the bridge across the ravine, he was reunited with them in common purpose: to root out the spawn of evil, and purge them from the face of the world.

So he rode, and rode gladly. But he rode without Bruno. The damage to Bruno's hand wasn't serious, but it was enough to make his joining the hunt out of the question. Instead of riding with the soldiers of Sigmar, Bruno had had to content himself with joining the people lining the streets to bless the parting hunters.

'Good fortune,' Bruno shouted through the din of the crowd. 'And safe return.'

'Be sure of both,' Stefan returned. It was an ill-timed misfortune, and his comrade would be sorely missed, but Stefan was determined to make good the loss. He vowed his sword would do the work of two men.

He had fully expected the squadron of riders to be led by Rilke. But although there were two of the elite White Guard at the head of the twenty or so men in red, neither was the man that Stefan was already coming to think of as his enemy. He wasn't sure if that was a good or a bad thing. If he had truly made an enemy of Rilke, then perhaps it would be better if he were there where Stefan could see him. There was no Rilke, but he had seen Hans Baecker, riding up near the head of the column. The rest of the men were strangers, but if they acquitted themselves half as well as their comrades, then they would not lack for valour.

The riders passed through the gates of the citadel, then halted. 'What now?' Stefan asked. 'What are we waiting for?' By way of answer, one of the others indicated back the way they had come. A single rider was approaching at speed, beating a thunderous rhythm upon the ground. It was Anaise, dressed for combat in a suit of mail and light armour, the insignia of a blood-red sword emblazoned upon her white corselet.

'Surprised?' she asked Stefan as she pulled her horse level with his. There was a slight note of teasing in her voice, a playfulness that Stefan had noted at least once before. 'Perhaps, amongst your people, women aren't for fighting?' she asked.

'Honoured, rather than surprised,' Stefan assured her. 'I had been given to understand that Rilke would be leading this mission,' he added.

'Rilke?' Anaise lifted her eyebrow just enough to hint at disdain. 'Konstantin's pet,' she said. 'He's better off home with his master.' She lifted her hand in a signal to the riders around her. The smile vanished, and with it any light-heartedness.

'We have a great distance to make up upon our enemies,' she called out. 'We must ride hard. Ride like the wind!'

IT HAD BEGUN so promisingly for Koenig the bounty hunter. Just at the critical moment the man had crumpled, brought to his knees as though struck down by a blow from Sigmar himself. Lothar was able to claim his sword as easily as prising a bone from the jaws of a sickly dog. The man's eyes had blazed with violent intent, but his body had nothing to offer. In that moment, Lothar had given thanks to the gods for their gift. Now he was beginning to wonder if they had not played him the cruellest of tricks.

The first task he had set himself, once his prisoner had been secured, had been to part the gold band from the wrist of its owner. Lothar was no merchant – not in any other commodity than human flesh – and he couldn't have put a price upon the amulet. But he knew it would be worth a lot, the sort of sum that he wouldn't normally see in a season, let alone a single week. The sculpted gold was thick and lustrous, and there was a rarity, and just a hint of darkness to its strange design that would surely attract no end of wealthy suitors.

First he had to get it off his prisoner's arm, pull it free of the ugly flesh, the skin defaced by the livid colours of the tattoo. Lothar Koenig could hardly bring himself to think of touching it, but he would have to if the amulet was to be his.

He was not stupid enough to try and take it from the other man whilst he was awake. Once, and only once Koenig had made to reach for the gold band in view of his prisoner. The reaction had been instantaneous, the message unmistakeable: *Touch the amulet and I'll kill you.* Lothar was sure that, even bound in his chains, Zucharov would somehow be capable of delivering on that unspoken promise. The bounty hunter had quickly learnt to keep his distance. A boundary was established, a set of rules between captor and captive. And whilst Lothar kept to those rules, it seemed his prisoner would offer him no resistance.

But getting the amulet was another matter. There was only one time when it would be safe to get close enough to take it, when Zucharov was unconscious, knocked senseless by the potions Lothar dosed him with every night, though it seemed to take ever-greater quantities of hempwort and camphor salts to affect his prisoner.

That night, to be doubly sure, Lothar had administered more than double the usual dose. From now on he would need to ration his supplies – or else dispose of his human cargo before very long. At length, once he was certain that the brutish warrior was far beyond consciousness, the bounty hunter made his move. The gold metal of the amulet looked so pure. He imagined how it would feel in his hands, the caress of the gold as he slid the band upon his own wrist. He already knew it would bring him not only wealth, but power beyond anything he had dared to dream.

He crouched beside the other man, savouring the moment. Gingerly, he reached out and made contact with the gold band with the gentlest of touches. Instantaneously he was thrown backwards, as some unseen force punched into him with the force of a battering ram. Lothar writhed upon the ground, screaming out from the nauseous pain flooding through his body. Still in agony, he examined his throbbing hand by the light of his campfire. The skin was blistered and red raw, as though he had thrust his fist into the heart of a mighty fire.

Lothar cursed the gods, and sat rocking upon his heels, trying to cool his burning flesh in the night air. It was some moments before he realised that Zucharov's eyes were open, watching his every movement with a blank, expressionless gaze. Later, he would swear that the words he heard next were spoken inside his head: *Next time we will give you no warning.*

There wouldn't be a next time. That much Lothar had already decided. The pain was excruciating beyond all experience. He would not touch the amulet again. His shrewd mind flitted through the alternatives. There weren't many. Of course, he could always cut the wretched thing from the creature's limb. This might be easier, but it would devalue his only other, human, asset. No buyer was going to be interested in a cripple. Besides, what strength of narcotic potion would he need before his prisoner succumbed to his dreams? Had he *ever* been truly asleep? The thought chilled Lothar Koenig to the marrow.

From that moment on he turned his mind to finding a way of disposing of the tattooed warrior, and earning whatever bounty he could. It ought to have been easy. Every private army, every mercenary gang along the border with the Empire would be looking for men like this, men with the grotesque musculature of a wild beast, and an unquenchable thirst for slaughter to match. Men who killed

with remorseless efficiency, only stopping when they themselves were destroyed.

So Lothar Koenig plied his wares through the scattering of
villages and towns that covered the bare plains of
Ostermark, winding a gradual, meandering course back
towards the city of Talabheim. Along the way, people
stopped to stare in wonder or disbelief at the two-horse
train: the figure of the bounty hunter leading the monstrous
painted man. But few came close, even the simplest of folk
seemed able to sense the danger in Alexei Zucharov, and
kept a wary distance.

But enough prospective buyers came to mind. Some the
bounty hunter knew as good men, some were scum, vicious
parasites who terrorised their people and robbed them
blind. Frankly, Lothar couldn't care less. Whoever was willing to pay a reasonable sum for his prisoner was welcome to
him, with or without the amulet. He would let others worry
about the consequences.

Zucharov put up no resistance as he was led, still
enmeshed in his chains, into the presence of adventurers,
warlords and chieftains. Sitting, bound and defenceless
upon his horse, he was a picture of abject defeat, a beaten
man waiting to be sold into slavery. And yet, and yet...
something of the menace inside him still managed to com-
municate itself to his would-be masters. And the message
that was communicated was clear, and unambiguous: *I will
destroy you.*

The would-be masters were men possessed of arrogance,
cunning and greed. But, to a man, they read the message in
Alexei Zucharov's eyes, and backed off. By stages, the asking
price came down, and with it Lothar's dreams of a comfortable retirement. But still the message from the buyers was
the same. Lothar Koenig and his proposition were not welcome.

Finally, the price fell low enough for one small-time warlord to take a closer look. Gunter Albrecht was the tin-pot
tyrant who held villainous rule over a stinking hovel of a
town known as Stahlhof. Albrecht had a deserved reputation
for cruelty and violence, and imagined, with good reason,

that there could be few men alive more dangerous or less trustworthy than himself.

Zucharov was hauled off the horse, and thrown upon the ground for the warlord's inspection. Albrecht manoeuvred his heavy form into position over the prostrate body. He aimed a kick into Zucharov's gut, and waited for some kind of response. When none came he grunted, dismissively.

'What's the matter with him?' he demanded of Lothar. 'Scared of what I might do to him?' He kicked Zucharov again, considerably harder this time. Zucharov still made no response, but raised his gaze to face the warlord.

'He looks the part, I'll grant you,' Albrecht commented. 'But a cur who lies there without so much as a whimper isn't going to be much use to me.'

'The gold band alone is worth more than I'm asking,' Lothar protested.

Gunter Albrecht tugged at his straggly beard, and regarded Zucharov and the bounty hunter in turn, with equal distaste. 'Maybe,' he conceded. 'Maybe.'

'Loosen the chains, then you'll see what he's made of,' Lothar blurted out. As soon as he had spoken, he was regretting the suggestion. But the idea had taken root in his patron's mind.

'Free his hands,' he commanded. 'And stand him up.'

'On second thoughts–' Lothar began. A sharp dig in the ribs from a sword wielded by one of Albrecht's men cut him short. 'Get on with it,' Albrecht said, sourly. 'I haven't got all day.'

Two of Albrecht's men pulled Zucharov up on to his feet. A third pushed Lothar Koenig forward. The bounty hunter said a silent prayer. Through closed eyes he saw exactly what would happen. He watched his own hands unfasten the shackles that bound the prisoner's hands. He saw Zucharov standing there, his hands now hanging down free at his sides. There would be a moment of stillness, of silence. Then Albrecht would break the spell, his patience exhausted, and give the fatal order for his men to draw their swords.

In his mind, he saw Zucharov move. He would move so fast that Lothar would barely have time to make sense of

what had happened. Amidst the blur of bodies he saw
Zucharov take hold of the men either side of him, and lift
them into the air as though they were dolls. The first was
impaled on the blade as it swung towards him. The second
he hurled through the air, slamming him into the body of
the third man, knocking both senseless.

He saw Albrecht turn to flee, already too late. Zucharov
stepped forward, snapping the chains around his legs in a
single move. In three strides he had seized hold of the warlord and lifted him clear of the ground. Lothar counted the
blows as Zucharov fastened a grip upon the warlord's leathery neck, then smashed his head down, two, three times,
hammering it upon the ground in a fury, until his skull had
been rendered into a bloody pulp. Then, finally, when it was
done, he saw Zucharov turn, and come for him.

Lothar opened his eyes. His body was trembling like a
leaf, but he was too scared even to feel shame. Nothing had
happened. No one had moved. Zucharov stood before him,
a terrifying statue carved from human flesh, the shackles still
fast upon his wrists.

Gunter Albrecht was still very much alive, but he looked
as though he had been to the gates of Morr and back. The
blood had drained from his face, and from the corner of his
mouth a drool of spittle ran unchecked into the matted tan-
gle of beard. Lothar looked at him and knew at once that he
had seen the same vision he had. They had all seen it,
Lothar, Albrecht, and all of his men. The warlord turned to
the bounty hunter and spoke in a voice that was thin and
cracked.

'Get out of here,' he said, quietly. 'Take that abomination
from my sight, and don't ever come back.'

The bounty hunter left without protest, without saying
another word. Once he was well away from Albrecht's men
he stopped, dismounted, and found every last piece of rope
and wire that he could to add to the chains already fastened
around Zucharov's body.

He tried to believe his prisoner was secure, at least for
now, but in his heart he knew he was only deluding himself.
He had been deluding himself all along about the true

nature of the spawn of darkness that had come into his keeping. Whatever was holding this man captive, it was not the puny bonds of rope and metal that were placed around him. A power way beyond Lothar's own feeble imaginings had brought him to this point in time, shaped his choices and steered him upon his course. The same power now spoke to Lothar, sweeping away the fear and confusion in his mind. In a moment of stark clarity, he saw what he must do, and where he must go.

Now there were no more choices. Now, a single destination beckoned.

THE COMPANY OF twenty rode out beneath the lonely skies, with the far hills and the green blur of forests the only punctuation within a barely changing landscape. This was a land that could swallow up a hundred men as easily as a handful. The band of Chaos renegades had last been seen crossing the border from Kislev a full five days past. Could they truly still hope to intercept their enemies in such a vast and empty place?

If any amongst the twenty had doubts, Anaise von Augen was not one of them. From the moment that they had ridden from the citadel, she had not wavered in her conviction that the Chaos warband would be found and destroyed. The open spaces of Ostermark were vast, but they were not without boundaries. The mighty river that marked the land between Ostermark and Talabecland was one. The Chaos warriors were riding south. When they reached the tributary of the great River Stir, they would have to head either east, into the forsaken lands of Sylvania, or cross the river into Talabecland, there to lose themselves in the forests until they could re-group. But there would be no escape, Anaise had promised. Long before they crossed the river, the soldiers of Sigmar would be amongst them.

At first there had been no signs, no trace of their enemies' path. But finally the pursuers came upon a village, a handful of houses clustered around a shrine. They were not the first to have visited. The Chaos riders had been there too, and not long before. They had stamped their mark upon the village in blood and fire, killing every living thing and levelling the simple homes in an orgy of senseless destruction. Anaise rode through the ruins without stopping, looking down upon the terrible carnage.

'Their lust for blood has betrayed them,' she commented, quietly. 'Now we know we are close.'

They rode on, faster now, fuelled by anticipation and a righteous anger. Barely two miles beyond the village, they sighted their enemy for the first time.

'There!' Hans Baecker shouted. 'Crossing the brow of the hill right ahead. By Sigmar,' he exclaimed, 'there must be at least fifty of them!'

Stefan looked to the horizon. From a distance the other riders were dark specks silhouetted against the hillsides, and looked little more than slow crawling ants. The word that had reached the citadel had said thirty. But there were at least fifty, possibly more. The men of Sigmarsgeist were seriously outnumbered. But Anaise left them in no doubt, there would be no turning back from battle.

'Whether they are five or five hundred, it makes no difference!' she exclaimed. 'They shall not escape us, not now.'

The line of riders broke forward, a wave of red pouring across the open plain. Ahead of them the soldiers of Chaos, a jagged line of riders following the green ribbon of the river that divided the land. A mile or so more and they would come to the bridge at Bahlkurk. Once across, the dark forests of Sylvania beckoned. They must not get that far.

Stefan pressed on, his heart hammering in his chest, adrenaline flushing through his body. Ahead lay uncertainty: death, or glory. And in that heady moment he embraced them both.

The Chaos force had superiority in numbers, but the pursuers had surprise and speed on their side. The distance between the two was narrowing quickly. Stefan and his comrades were travelling as light as distance would allow. The horses bearing the Chaos riders were weighed down by their riders' heavy armour and, the plunder of their bloody, merciless conquest. The moment of crisis was near.

Stefan's head cleared and he grew calm, filled with a quiet, almost serene contemplation. He was on the cusp of battle, amidst the calm at the very eye of the storm. Now, Stefan vowed, we shall show you such mercy as you deserve.

With a cool detachment, he watched the riders grow steadily larger. They were not yet close enough for Stefan to make out whether they were men, beasts or some grotesque fusion of the two. But it did not matter. If they had the mark of Chaos upon them, then he would not rest until he had destroyed them all.

Closer still. A burst of speed and a break in formation told Stefan that the Chaos warriors had realised they were being pursued. In the distance he could see the ancient stone causeway that forded the waters of the River Stir. Too far, surely, for the Chaos band to make the bridge before they were overtaken.

The dark ones would realise that too. There would be one last desperate attempt to wring enough speed from their tired steeds, to try to reach the bridge. Stefan knew what would happen next. Accepting that escape was impossible, they would abandon the attempt. He felt the muscles in his body tighten in anticipation as he watched the enemy riders slow then gradually wheel away from the river, back towards them.

'Get ready,' Stefan yelled at the top of his voice. 'They're attacking!'

'Charge them down,' Anaise commanded, her voice shaking with excitement. 'Let the river be their grave!'

Stefan held back for one last moment before the conflagration engulfed them all. He pulled back on the reins, and took stock of the horde now driving, full-on towards him. Of the fifty, a good dozen bore standards, flags or colours rippling in the breeze behind them.

Some were undoubtedly Norscan, others had the shape and size of mortal men, but disfigured by the hideous mutations of Chaos. Ragged antlers sprang from human heads, and limbs sprouted cloven hooves where feet should have been. Stefan shuddered. Was that the fate that awaited

Alexei? Was it possible, even, that he was somewhere amongst them now?

He shook the thought away. All that mattered was the coming battle, the storm of blood and steel that would soon engulf them all. The murdering Chaos horde would have been dangerous enough on the fields of Erengrad. Now, desperate and cornered, they had nothing left to lose. Stefan drew breath deep into his lungs and released a long roar of rage from his heart. He kicked in with his spurs and rode on, accelerating rapidly towards battle.

# CHAPTER TEN
## The Turning Tide

DRAWN INTO THE fury of battle, it was as though Stefan stepped from the mortal realm into a different world, a place where space and time lost all sense and meaning. Where a few seconds of desperate struggle could span an eternity, or a lifetime be cut brutally short, ending in a matter of moments. As he tore into the ranks of the Chaos riders, Stefan surrendered his fortune to the gods. They would be his counsel, steer him and guide his sword. They would bless his victories and sit in judgement upon his deeds. The day would come, Stefan knew, when their judgement would fall against him. On that day it would be he who met the falling blade. Too late to shy from the blow, or take refuge behind a shield. Too late to fall back, bloodied but still valiant, to return again victorious to the fray. Stefan would barely see the shaft of steel as it blazed its fateful arc across that final sky. Somewhere in his mind he would say a last prayer, and walk towards a vision of his father, waiting for him beyond the Gates of Morr.

One day, but not today, Stefan swore. Sweet would be the day when he stood within the halls of the dead, and

embraced his father once more. But that day was not come
yet. Today would be a day for vengeance, another small victory in the eternal war between darkness and light. Today he
would reap a bloody harvest amongst the creatures of
damnation.

The twenty of Sigmarsgeist rode headlong into the enemy,
the odds that faced them at least two to one. But Anaise's
men were faster, and they were united in will and purpose.
The fifty or so they faced were the remnants of a defeated
army, men and mutants held together only by adversity.
Stefan tore into them in a fury, his sword felling two slow-
moving riders in the first assault. There were Norscans
amongst them, possibly even kin to those who had burned
his village and murdered his father. Stefan would take care
to send as many as he could to the deaths they so richly
deserved.

Others amongst their opponents were mortal men no
longer, no more than a ghastly parody of human form.
Amongst the wheeling confusion of horses and men, Stefan
saw creatures with bodies ripped open, living cadavers
whose bones protruded like ivory spears through raw, gangrenous flesh. Many had their faces torn away, jewel-like
eyes staring out at him through bleached skulls stripped of
skin. Worst of all, Stefan now saw the flags that they carried
were not flags at all. The fluttering pennants had been fashioned from human skin; grim trophies flayed from the
bodies of the fallen. A wave of anger and disgust rose up in
Stefan. These abominations would not see out the day.

He lashed out with his sword, a scything blow that cut
through the guard of the creature bearing down upon him.
He had a glimpse of a face, a grinning skull that snarled with
the teeth of a dog. The blow cut away the monster's arm in
a single stroke, but the mutant did not veer from its collision
course.

'Stefan, to your right!' He turned quickly to see another
rider racing in on his flank. Anaise von Augen was a blur of
speed as she closed upon the mutant. Sunlight flashed upon
the steel of her blade as she tore the leering skull-head from
its shoulders. The creature buckled and fell, breaking apart

in a mass of splintered bone. Anaise was now under attack, two Norscan mercenaries closing in on her from either side. Stefan spurred his horse forward, putting himself between the Norscans and their intended target. The first rider struck out at him hastily, a wild sweep with an axe which found only thin air. Stefan made him pay for his wasted opportunity, aiming a blow squarely into the other man's guts. The second Norscan was younger and faster than the first, and for a few moments the two men traded blow for blow.

The Norscan got lucky, a thrust found its way through Stefan's guard and pierced the thin chainmail of his corselet. He felt the cold bite of the steel as it cut into his flesh, and saw the sneering satisfaction on the blond warrior's face. The Norscan aimed what he intended to be the decisive blow, but was too hasty. Your lust for death will be your undoing, Stefan promised. He parried the blow easily and struck back, adrenaline numbing away the pain. The Norscan tried to anticipate the direction of Stefan's attack, but guessed wrong, caught the full force of Stefan's blade in his face.

Stefan charged the other man's horse out of the way, spilling the blinded Norscan from the saddle. Anaise had vanished again, sucked away into another pocket of the battle. Stefan made a rapid assessment of the unfolding scene. He counted two scarlet-clad riders down, but against that at least ten of the enemy had already been accounted for. The Chaos warriors were fighting with an animal desperation, but the odds were turning against them now.

Hans Baecker emerged from the crowd ahead, weaving between three mutants, making every thrust of his sword extract a price. One by one, his opponents were cut down. Slowly, the soldiers of Sigmar were gaining parity with their foes.

Something shot past Stefan's face, grazing the surface of his cheek. He spun around to see a second missile fly past, only inches away. He found himself looking into the face of a young warrior, his ghostly skin covered in an ugly net of grey-green veins. The apparition jolted forward, accelerating toward Stefan. What had looked at first like the flaps of a coat hanging open around him were now revealed as folds of red raw flesh. The whole of the creature's upper body had been pared away, leaving the ribcage exposed. The monster was plucking the bones from between its ribs, and hurling them like jagged, bloody spears, with a casual, but deadly ease. Stefan tugged desperately at the reins, weaving from side to side to evade the deadly missiles, closing in upon his adversary.

The creature of Chaos cast three times, each razor-edged shard of bone flying just wide. Now the two riders were at arms' length. The Chaos warrior ripped another bloody blade from its carcass and stabbed out at Stefan, aiming at his throat in a short, slashing motion. Stefan flung his head back, a sudden, violent motion that all but toppled him from his horse. For a moment he fought to stay in the saddle. If he fell now, it would all be over. He grabbed frantically at the reins and regained balance.

The mutant struck out again, but this time wide of the mark. As the creature swung back, Stefan aimed a firm blow into the mutant's body, wedging the point of his sword into the open cavity. Flesh tore and bone splintered and cracked as Stefan twisted the blade. The mutant swore and writhed, desperately trying to free itself, but Stefan held firm, driving his sword ever deeper into the monster's body. When he was sure it was dead he pulled his sword clear to lash it one final time across the body, hurling the shattered corpse to the ground.

A wave of nausea washed over Stefan as the shock of the encounter kicked in. He looked around, gasping for breath, and found himself in a clear space. The plain was littered with the bodies of the fallen. Stefan counted four Chaos marauders dead for each of the six soldiers of Sigmar that had given their lives. The tide had turned, the battle was all but won.

A horseman burst through the skirmish of riders just ahead of him. It took Stefan a few moments before he recognised Anaise. Her white singlet was now a filthy red, and her face was spattered with the bloody gore of her enemies. But she was filled with an energy that was almost frightening to behold. Her face was wreathed in smiles, and her eyes shone with an almost manic excitement. She saw Stefan and saluted him, her voice trembling.

'Seven dead by my sword!' she shouted to him, elated. 'Seven sons of darkness who'll never taint the light of day again!' She pulled her horse about, coming into tandem with Stefan. 'How many have you taken?' she asked, breathlessly.

'Five, I think,' Stefan replied. 'Maybe six. It seems you have the better of me.' He tried to shape some sense of celebration into his words, but he could not. He felt cold, almost numb. There was something stark, something shocking about the raw blood lust he saw in Anaise. For a moment he found himself looking at her, but thinking about himself, in a way he had never done before. Was this how it was for him, as he emerged, victorious from battle? Was this how he *felt*? And, in that moment, he was seized with a sense of awe, and a quiet horror.

RILKE STEPPED FROM the shadows into the circle of light at the centre of his master's chamber. In the gloom behind him stood a cluster of Red Guards and two other figures, one of them weighed down with every manner of rope and chain imaginable. Rilke bowed before the seated figure of Konstantin von Augen, his grave expression mirroring that of his master.

'They are here, my lord.'

Konstantin peered into the gloom and beckoned for the guards to approach. They shuffled forward, ushering Lothar Koenig and his prisoner into the interior. Once in place, the guards stood round the prisoner with their swords held ready, drawing a ring of steel around the figure of Alexei Zucharov.

Konstantin von Augen sat, taking in the man stood before him. A look of sorrow, and deep and ancient enmity crossed the Guide's face.

'The creatures of the night come to Sigmarsgeist,' he murmured. 'Like moths to the eternal flame, they come.'

The prisoner looked down upon the Guide as though staring through him, gazing upon something in the far distance.

Konstantin returned the gaze steadily and without fear. The terrors of darkness would hold no dominion here. Finally, he turned to Koenig, who had been standing on one side, his head lowered in a posture of supplication.

'Tell me your story,' Konstantin commanded. The bounty hunter executed a low bow before the Guide. 'My lord, I captured this man with my own hands, and at great risk to my life, after a ferocious battle at the foot of the Ostravska valley. I knew at once where I must bring him.'

'Does he not speak?' Konstantin asked.

'My lord, he has uttered barely a word whilst in my keeping. I believe the Dark Gods have poisoned his tongue.'

Konstantin looked to Rilke. 'Was he alone at the gates?'

'Quite alone,' Rilke said. 'Apart from this.' He raised his arm. Lamplight fell upon a battered and blood-caked object: the severed head of the bandit lord, Carl Durer.

'The mortal remains of a thief and a murderer,' Lothar explained, hastily. 'I was taking proof of his death to Talabheim, hoping to earn some favour for my deeds there.'

Konstantin nodded to Rilke. 'Have your men dispose of it,' he said, waving aside Lothar's pleas. He looked long and hard at the prisoner. Alexei Zucharov hadn't moved so much as a muscle since being led to the chamber.

'A fearsome looking warrior,' Konstantin observed. 'And doubtless the poison of evil run deep in his veins. But what of it? The dungeons of Sigmarsgeist are full of creatures such as this. What do you think?' he asked Rilke. 'Shall we have this one put to the sword and be done?'

'Please,' Lothar protested. 'Look closer, I beg you. My lord, look closer at his arm.'

Konstantin said nothing for a few moments then, slowly and deliberately, rose from his seat and took a few steps towards the prisoner. He nodded to the guards, signalling that they should lift Zucharov's arm for him to see. The metal of the amulet shone like fire under the lights, but it was not the golden band that caused the Guide to draw in a sharp breath.

The living tattoo upon Zucharov's flesh covered all of his arm, mapping every inch of his skin. Konstantin took another step closer, unable quite to believe what he was seeing. As he looked at the tiny figures and images etched in the lines of the tattoo, he could swear that they began to move, coming to life before his eyes. He looked up, into Zucharov's eyes. For the first time Zucharov seemed to acknowledge him, and something akin to a smile crossed his dark features. Zucharov rotated his arm, the metal chains groaning as he opened the palm of his hand. Konstantin looked down, and let out a gasp of shock.

He was looking at the citadel, his creation reproduced upon the man's flesh. At the centre of the tiny image, two faces, their likeness unmistakable.

Konstantin jolted back, the shock upon his face clear for all in the room to see. The Guide took a moment, struggling to regain his composure.

'Take him to the cells,' he commanded, his voice shaking. 'Our physicks must know more of this. They must divine what manner of witchcraft this is, and what it portends.' He looked around the room. 'Rilke, do you hear me?'

The White Guard nodded, acknowledging his master. But he was not looking at Konstantin any longer. His focus was elsewhere, his gaze locked upon the figure of Alexei Zucharov, intense and unflinching.

'I FEEL TERRIBLE,' Bruno declared, getting up and pacing the floor for a second or third time. Bea regarded him without too much sympathy.

'Come on,' she cajoled. 'It's only a scratch.'

'I don't mean *this*,' Bruno said, holding up his bandaged arm. 'I mean letting Stefan down. I should have been there with him when they rode out.'

'Well, I'm sorry,' Bea replied. 'I'm a good healer, but I can't work miracles, not yet. If you will go lumbering around near falling buildings then you've only yourself to blame.'

'It's just bad luck,' Bruno continued. 'Getting myself injured at the very time I need my sword. The worst of luck.' He settled himself back by Bea's side, but continued to look out of the turret window, towards the citadel walls.

'I should be there,' he said, mostly to himself. 'I should have been with them.'

'Sorry yet again,' Bea answered, a hurt tone creeping into her voice. 'Sorry for being such poor company.'

Bruno looked round, and his face flushed. 'No,' he said, hurriedly. 'That's not what I meant at all. I meant that I didn't want to let Stefan down, that's all.' He looked away, unable to meet Bea's eye, his face growing ever redder. 'You're not poor company at all. Quite the opposite, in fact…' His voice trailed off and he sat in silence, lost for words. Bea waited a moment then took Bruno's hand.

'I'm the one who's sorry,' Bruno muttered. 'I'm not exactly making myself clear.'

'I think you are,' Bea said, her voice warmer, more gentle now. She smiled, and moved closer towards him. Something fastened at Bruno's neck flickered gold in the low light of the lamp.

'Let me see that,' Bea asked. 'Please.' Bruno hesitated. From beneath his shirt he pulled a thin gold chain bearing a pendant. 'It's an icon of the Goddess Shallya,' he explained. 'It means–'

'I know what it is,' Bea said, softly, 'and I know what it means. May I?' Without waiting for an answer, she took the chain in her hand, leant forward, and lightly kissed the icon. 'It means you are a pious man,' she said. 'And a good man. But I knew that. I knew it as soon as I first set eyes upon you.'

Bruno turned until they were face to face in the lamp-light, their bodies all but touching. The tension of unspoken words hung in the air between them. Finally, Bruno broke away. 'It's stupid,' he said, running his fingers through his hair. 'Or, rather I'm stupid. But I could swear that tower, or whatever it was, had sprung out of nowhere.' He glanced at her again. Bea was looking at him intently, no hint of mockery on her face. 'Perhaps I'm going mad,' he suggested.

'No, you're not,' Bea replied, sounding suddenly very certain. She paused, as though weighing something up. 'Actually, I've seen them too. Lots of them. All over the citadel.'

'You have?' Bruno asked. 'These columns, you mean?'

'I'm not sure what I'd call them,' Bea said. 'But whatever they are, it's like something growing out of the ground, pushing through whatever was there before, breaking it apart.'

'Yes,' Bruno agreed, excitedly. 'That's exactly it. Like – like a carcass, broken open, and something bursting out.' He broke off, reflecting on his words. 'That doesn't sound very healthy to me.'

Now it was Bea's turn to be silent. She looked at Bruno, then away again. She realised that she wanted to share everything with Bruno: her thoughts, her hopes, her secrets. Most of all, she wanted to share what she had learnt since they had arrived in Sigmarsgeist. For a moment the urge to tell Bruno battled with her loyalty to Anaise. Hadn't the Guide confided in her precisely because no one else would understand? But, finally, Bea decided that she could stay silent no longer. Anaise would understand. After all, she hadn't directly asked Bea not to mention their conversation to the others.

'You remember a while ago, soon after we left Mielstadt. I mentioned something. A place.'

Bruno thought for a moment. 'No,' he said. 'Sorry, I don't.'

Bea clasped his hand again, more tightly this time. 'Yes,' she insisted. 'You do remember. Tal Dur. The healing waters of Tal Dur. A magical place.'

Bruno shrugged, tentatively. 'Yes, all right. But I don't understand–'

'Tal Dur is *here*,' Bea blurted out. 'I mean – somewhere here. Once, long ago maybe, the waters of Tal Dur flowed right beneath the citadel, perhaps before it was even Sigmarsgeist. But they ran here. Maybe right through the city. Maybe they filled the moat that we can see all around the walls.'

Bruno shook his head. 'Are you saying that has something to do with the pillars, or whatever they may be, springing up everywhere?'

'I don't know,' Bea conceded. 'I can't be sure. But of one thing I'm certain. This is a place of great confluence. A place where flows of magic met, fusing together into a mighty power. I know it. I can feel it. And if Tal Dur is no longer here, then it isn't far away. I'm sure of it, Bruno.'

She stopped and pulled away from him, trying to read what was in Bruno's face. 'Now I'm the one who's mad,' she said, disappointed. 'You think so, don't you?'

Bruno looked at her, meeting her full gaze. After a while he took her hand again, and turned her to face him. Bea started to protest, but he put a finger to her lips, to silence her.

'I think you have something very special, a real gift,' he said, slowly. 'More than that,' he took his finger away, and moved closer. 'I think you're beautiful.'

Bea frowned, then smiled. She was about to contradict him, almost a reflex response. But then she stopped, and allowed herself to do what her body was urging her. Bruno cupped his hand behind the nape of her neck, and drew her gently towards him.

THE BATTLE HAD ended as quickly as it had begun, breaking up into a series of single combats as the mutants and their Norscan allies fled, each trying to find their own avenue of escape. For most it was a road that led only to death. The men of Sigmarsgeist hunted them down with a bitter, dogged determination, giving no quarter to the remnants of the Chaos horde. But, inevitably, a few still managed to break away, shedding most of the plunder that had been weighing down their horses to make good their escape into the fading day.

Around Stefan, the victorious soldiers of Sigmar began debating what they should do. Some favoured splitting up, others urged they hunt as a pack. There were even those who thought the day's deeds now done. They had accounted for at least thirty enemies, at a cost of eight men fallen, and could return home with a great victory. But Stefan sensed there would be no going back, not yet. There was at least one amongst them for whom it was far from over, who would not rest easily whilst any of the marauders remained unaccounted for.

Anaise von Augen gathered her men round, urging them to find the strength for one final foray. 'They will not escape us,' she declared. 'Not while I still have strength.'

Stefan drew his horse up by her side. The plain was empty now, save for the broken carcasses of the fallen. 'The rest of the mutants are scattered to the winds,' he said. 'I fear they're lost to us now.'

Anaise looked around. Aside from the bloodied bodies, the ground was littered with broken sacks and saddlebags that the Chaos riders had shed in making their escape. Scattered amongst the more obvious plunder of gold and silver icons were provisions, bread and fruit, broken skins of wine staining the earth a deeper red.

'They must have got all this from somewhere,' she said, opaquely. She paused, then looked up, having reached a decision. 'Ride west!' she commanded. 'We're not done with this yet.'

THE DOZEN RODE into the dusk for an hour or more, until a sprinkling of lights in the distance gave notice that they were approaching the edge of a settlement. The decrepit buildings of a small, nondescript town came into view soon after, and Stefan realised that he had been here before. This was Mielstadt, where he and Bruno had rescued Bea from the clutches of the lynch mob, and where, in a way, their present story had begun.

It was not a place he had particularly wanted to ever return to. Mielstadt was no more appealing in the fading dusk than it had been by day. Riding through the empty streets, past the shuttered houses with their dim-glowing lights, it seemed unlikely that any of the marauders would have taken refuge here. Stefan was convinced their search would prove to be in vain.

Anaise had other ideas. She beckoned the two White Guards over and conferred in private for a few moments. Stefan tried to nudge his horse closer but found his way blocked – accidentally or otherwise – by a phalanx of riders in red. By then the conference was ended, and Anaise had turned back towards the rest of her men.

'Make a thorough search of the town,' she instructed them. 'If any of our enemies are lurking here, then I want to know about it.'

The group split up, riders peeling off in all directions. Stefan, too, turned his horse about, and tracked back through the quiet streets, looking for any stragglers from the Chaos horde. But if they were here, they were keeping unusually quiet; the only sights or sounds that greeted him were of windows being slammed and fastened tight. There was no welcome here waiting for the soldiers of Sigmar. Stefan continued to ride, but with a growing sense of unease. There was something wrong here, something that had nothing to do with the creatures that they were supposedly pursuing.

After a few minutes more, he decided he had had enough. He would go back to the square and await the others. Mielstadt was dead, as quiet as the grave. He was certain there was nothing of interest here.

That certainty was shaken by a sudden commotion coming from somewhere near the centre of the town. Stefan swung his horse around, and galloped back, a sudden tension gripping his body. He could hear voices – several voices raised in conflict with one another – and the grey gloom was lit by the glow of torches. Stefan's first thought was of the other village, the hamlet put to the flame by the night phantoms. But this was something different. Up ahead, four or five men in red were holding back a small but gathering crowd of townsfolk. The Red Guards had formed themselves into a circle, and, in the middle of that circle there were two more figures.

Stefan sprang from his horse and ran forward. A couple of the red tunics motioned for him to stay back, but Stefan ignored them, and pushed his way past the cordon. Now he was standing just a few feet away from the two protagonists. The first was a White Guard, a man by the name of Drobny that Stefan had barely spoken to. The other man, too, he barely knew, but they had met before, all the same. It was Augustus Sierck, the pompous town leader who had taken such haughty pleasure in expelling Stefan and his comrades from the town.

Sierck didn't look haughty now. He was on his knees in front of Drobny, who was berating him with a hefty staff. From the ugly welt across Sierck's face, Stefan could see that the staff had already been put to work. Sierck was babbling, pleading for help or mercy, but his words were lost in the torrent of abuse that the White Guard was heaping upon him. Drobny raised the stick to strike again.

Stefan remembered Augustus Sierck well. He remembered his table-thumping grandiosity, and his pig-headed refusal to listen to reason. At the time Stefan would have happily have struck him down himself. But this was different. This, Stefan knew instinctively, was wrong.

Before he knew it, his sword was in his hand. Stefan strode towards Drobny. As the White Guard angled to strike a second blow, Stefan shouted out a warning, clear and unambiguous. Drobny stopped short, his staff held in mid-flight, and looked momentarily at Stefan, a mixture of surprise and disdain written on his face. Then he shrugged, and turned back to his business. Drobny swung the staff but the blow never connected. Before it could reach the cowering Sierck, Stefan had sprung forward. The first flick of his sword prised the staff from the other man's grip. The second, with the flat of the blade, sent Drobny sprawling in the dirt.

The White Guard let fly a string of curses, aimed at Stefan. Stefan was already sheathing his sword, a hand extended towards the fallen man. As he stepped forward, something struck him hard, a pounding blow into the back of his head. Stefan crashed forward, senseless, and did not move again.

# CHAPTER ELEVEN
## Alliance and Emnity

FIRST LIGHT WAS breaking through the windows of Anaise's chamber as Konstantin entered the room. He bowed low before his sister, then bent down upon one knee at her bedside.

'My heart is gladdened to have you back safe in our midst. I give thanks to Sigmar for your safe return.' He took his sister's hand and stooped to kiss it.

Anaise lay sprawled upon the bed, still clad in her battle-robes. A faint, sardonic smile crept across her face.

'Do you truly?' she asked. 'Your concern touches me, brother.' She pulled back her hand. 'Careful,' she chided. 'It would not do to soil your lips with the filthy spoils of battle.'

She rolled to one side, turning her back to her brother. 'Gods know,' she said. 'I could sleep for an eternity.'

Konstantin moved away from the back, back towards the threshold of his sister's chamber. 'If you wish to bathe, then I will have water drawn ready.'

Anaise sighed, and turned over again. The clean white linen of the sheets was already soiled a rusty red from the blood caked upon her garments.

'Does my appearance so disgust you?' she asked. 'For it is only an honest reflection of my endeavour. Or would you rather not know about that?' she demanded, peevishly. 'No, spare your precious water.'

'I'm sorry that your return finds you in such poor spirits,' Konstantin replied, his tone now similarly curt. 'I wanted only to learn what fruits your labours have borne.'

'You see the fruits before you,' Anaise said, indicating her torn and bloodied tunic. 'The servants of Chaos were intercepted and destroyed. Their story ended.'

Konstantin cleared his throat, awkwardly. 'And what,' he went on, 'what of the other matter that we spoke of?'

Anaise raised herself up on the pillows. 'Mielstadt? The problem has been dealt with, if that's what you're worried about,' she said.

'Then,' Konstantin went on, tentatively, 'they have come around to the True Path?'

'I told you,' Anaise snapped. 'The problem has been dealt with. Do you want me to give you the details?'

'No,' he concluded. 'I don't need to know.'

'No,' Anaise repeated. 'Of course you don't.' She yawned. 'And now, dear brother, I must rest. My righteous deeds have exhausted me.' She frowned, vexed that her brother seemed unable to take the hint. 'You don't mind?'

Konstantin nodded, but made no move to leave. 'Sister,' he said at last. 'There is something you must know. It cannot wait until you are rested.'

Anaise read the expression in her brother's eyes. She sat bolt upright. 'You'd better tell me, then,' she said, measuring her words with care.

Konstantin closed the door behind him. 'Whilst you were gone, a prisoner was brought to Sigmarsgeist,' he began. 'He has the look of a man, but I sense a darkness within him.'

'How so?' his sister asked. 'In what manner?'

'This is a creature the like of which I have never seen in all my lifetime.' Konstantin lifted the sleeve of his robe, exposing his arm. 'Upon his flesh, just here, his skin crawls with living images – tiny likenesses: pictures of wars, histories unfolding. It seems as though each person who looks upon the images sees something different.'

Anaise was giving him her full attention now, all trace of weariness vanished. 'And what did *you* see, brother, when you gazed in this dark mirror?'

'I saw Sigmarsgeist, our glorious citadel,' Konstantin replied. 'I saw myself. And I saw you, sister, at my side.'

Anaise stood up, and started to pace the room. 'This is a sign,' she proclaimed, excitedly. 'A sign that all we have planned for will come to pass! A sign that, truly, the time of our destiny is upon us.'

Konstantin clutched at his sister, forcing her to stop and turn towards him. 'Anaise,' he said, firmly. 'This is surely the creature that Stefan told us of. The mutant that they have been hunting since Erengrad.'

Anaise pulled herself free. 'What of it?' she asked. 'The great powers that even we cannot comprehend have brought them all here, to Sigmarsgeist. This is our story, brother. Stefan and his friends are only players within it.'

'That may be so,' Konstantin agreed. 'But we should still tell–'

'Wait a moment!' Anaise interrupted him. 'Who else knows of this?' she demanded.

Konstantin shook his head. 'No one, as yet. Aside from Rilke and a handful of his chosen men, this is a secret known only to ourselves. But,' he persisted, his voice taking on a firmer tone, 'now that you have returned, we should tell Stefan that his quest is ended. Here, in Sigmarsgeist.'

'There is no hurry for that,' his sister replied. 'Stefan Kumansky is wounded. He should be left in peace a while yet, to rest.'

Konstantin appeared shocked. 'You did not mention this before,' he said.

Anaise smiled. 'You did not ask,' she replied, sweetly. 'And you do not need to. There is no need for concern. Kumansky will survive,' she added, matter-of-factly. 'He was in the wrong place at the wrong time, that's all.' She began to peel off the blood-stained tunic. 'I must see this man, this creature for myself,' she began, then paused. 'Who did you say brought him to Sigmarsgeist?'

'A bounty hunter,' Konstantin said. 'A man full of stories, all lies, I fancy. Of course, he wanted money for his goods.'

'And you paid him,' Anaise asked, 'and sent him merrily on his way?'

Konstantin's composure was briefly broken. For an instant he glowered at his sister. 'Don't treat me as a fool, Anaise. The man had spent days, or possibly even weeks in the company of this hideous creature. I could not vouch he had not himself been tainted with the poisons of Chaos.'

'So he has been detained,' Anaise said, approvingly. 'For his own good.'

'For his own good,' Konstantin confirmed. 'And ours.'

Anaise stepped towards her brother and lifted her face to kiss him lightly upon the cheek. 'Forgive your sister and her acid tongue,' she murmured. 'As ever, you are the wise one, Konstantin. You guide and lead us all.' She smiled, and pulled away from her brother's embrace. 'And now,' she said, 'if you wouldn't mind leaving me. I think I shall bathe after all.'

STEFAN SURFACED FROM his unconsciousness like a swimmer rising slowly from the depths of a dark lake. He had no clear memory of how he had fallen into the deep pit of sleep, nor how long he had remained there. But, as the light of day reached into his waking eyes, he knew that he had been somewhere, far away, and for a very long time, so long that the intensity of the light was at first unbearable. He screwed his eyes shut again to protect himself from the glare. When finally he was able to open his eyes and focus upon his surroundings, he found Bruno standing over him, his arm around Bea. Both of them looked worried. Stefan assumed he was the cause of their concern.

'Where am I?' he managed to say at last. 'Mielstadt?'

'Mielstadt?' Bruno exchanged puzzled glances with Bea. 'Taal's breath, Stefan, you must remember. You're back inside the palace. In Sigmarsgeist. They brought you back here, after you were injured in the battle.'

'How long?' Stefan asked, his tongue thick, his voiced slurred and heavy. 'How long have I been lying here?'

'Probably a day or more,' Bruno told him. 'And this time, I'm not joking.'

'I didn't think you were,' Stefan replied. He tried lifting his head, and quickly realised he was not quite yet ready for that. He lay back down, giving himself a few more moments. He felt as though he had been drugged, or had had his head slammed against something solid and hard, or both.

Bea placed a cool hand upon Stefan's forehead, and held it there a few seconds. 'You were running a fever,' she said. 'Your body was burning up when they brought you back. I had to find something to give you.'

Stefan let his eyes drift closed again. The light was still barely tolerable. 'Is that what's making me feel like this?'

'How do you feel?' Bea asked.

'Terrible. Like I've drunk the Helmsman dry then been sleeping it off for a week.'

'Nothing so convivial, I fear,' Bruno said. 'You've taken quite a pounding, by all accounts.'

Stefan groaned, and forced himself to sit up. He peered at his companions through half closed eyes. 'You said something about "brought me back",' he said to Bea. 'What do you mean – back from where?'

'Gods preserve us,' Bea exclaimed. 'He's lost all memory of the last days.'

'You rode out with the hunting party,' Bruno said, insistently. 'To find the Chaos marauders. You must remember that.'

Stefan cursed the confusion swilling inside his mind. He sifted through the jumbled memories, trying to make some order from them.

'I do recall the battle,' he said at last. 'We were heavily outnumbered, but we destroyed the forces of Chaos all the same. At least–' he said, uncertainly, 'I think that's what happened. Is that where I was injured? Struck down in the battle?'

Before Bruno could answer, the door opened and a third person entered the room. Stefan caught a glimpse of a stark red uniform, and a face that, though familiar, he struggled to name.

'Your injury came later, Stefan,' the newcomer explained. 'Whilst we were pursuing the last of the marauders. You were unlucky.'

'But we got them all,' Baecker continued. 'Every last one. Our mission was successful, Stefan. Once again, you come to Sigmarsgeist a hero.'

'I can't say I remember much of the getting here,' Stefan said. He turned his head, experimentally. The slightest movement corresponded with a bolt of pain, but it was becoming steadily more bearable.

'You were struck down from behind, Stefan,' Bruno told him. 'One of the Norscans, I think?'

Baecker nodded in confirmation.

'A last desperate act. Luckily he managed only to catch you a glancing blow, or the damage could have been worse. Don't worry,' he assured Stefan, 'our Norscan friend was paid in full for his trouble. I cut the vile brute down myself.'

Stefan looked around the room, his eyes now growing more comfortable with the light.

'In that case,' he said to Baecker. 'It seems I owe you a debt. I'm only sorry I have no memory of your bravery.'

Baecker grinned broadly. 'The main thing is, you are safely returned, and your wounds will mend.' He glanced at Bea. 'He is mending, your patient, isn't he?'

'The blow he suffered did more harm than I would have expected,' Bea said. 'But, gods be thanked, he is through the worst of it now.'

'That's all I need to know,' Baecker replied. 'I'll leave the three of you in peace. But you must rest. Stay here.' He saluted Stefan smartly. 'Someone will come for you when it is time.'

Stefan waited a few moments after Baecker had left the room. 'Is he gone?' he asked at last.

Bruno checked the passage. 'I think so,' he said, and frowned at Stefan, slightly perplexed. Bea came and seated herself next to Stefan, and touched her fingers against his forehead again. 'Have you truly no memory of what happened once the battle begun?'

'Not a lot,' Stefan confirmed. 'The things I can remember seem broken up – as though they don't fit together properly. Everything seems mixed up with the dream.'

'The dream?' Bea asked.

'The dream about your village, when you were child?' Bruno interjected. 'Have you been dreaming of Odensk again?'

'Yes, there was something like that,' Stefan began, then hesitated. There had been a dream, a dream of darkness and smoke, of houses burning. It was the same dream he had been having since before even they had arrived in Sigmarsgeist. And Bruno was right, it was like the old dream that haunted him, the dream of Odensk. Except that something was different. Except that it *wasn't* Odensk. And that was what was troubling him.

THE PIECES OF memory were gradually coming together. It was starting to make sense now. He had been in Mielstadt again, he remembered that now. And there was something else, something lurking just in the shadow of memory that he was clutching for, as well.

'What was his name,' he demanded, suddenly sitting up. 'Bea, the graf of Mielstadt. What was his name?'

'Sierck,' Bea replied, puzzled. 'Augustus Sierck.'

Now Stefan saw him. The pompous dignitary strutting around his office. And the frightened man upon his knees in the town square. Two different occasions, but the same man: Augustus Sierck. As Stefan made the connection, he knew then that Baecker had lied. There had been no Norscan, no savage attack fended off by Baecker's avenging blade. But important though it was, this wasn't the detail that was occupying Stefan now. He was back with the dream, with the fires and the screams of the dying. He thought the gods had been taking him back to Odensk, but they hadn't. It was somewhere else.

'Bruno,' he said. 'What was the name of the village? The name I said we must hold in our hearts?'

'The village?' Bruno asked, confused. 'You mean Grunwald, the one that had been destroyed by the mutants?'

'Grunwald, yes,' Stefan replied. With the name came the answer to a puzzle. Something that had been gnawing at him incessantly, whispering a warning that he only now began to understand. Now, he knew what the dream had been telling him.

'It wasn't the mutants who destroyed Grunwald,' he said.

'But,' Bruno protested, 'we found a body there.'

'We did,' Stefan agreed. 'But the mutant didn't die fighting the villagers. And, unless I'm badly mistaken, the villagers didn't die fighting the mutants, either.' He got up, ignoring the pain still throbbing inside his head.

'Throw me over my boots,' he said to Bruno. 'We need to get moving.'

'Just a moment,' Bea interrupted. 'You won't be in a fit state to go anywhere for a while yet.' She looked to Bruno for support. 'Bruno, tell him.'

But Stefan was already on his feet, fastening his tunic. He looked around for his belt and sword. Neither of them were anywhere in the room.

'My sword,' he said to Bruno. 'Was it with me when they brought me here?'

Bruno shrugged. 'I'm sorry, Stefan. I didn't notice.'

'What about you, are you armed?'

Bruno lifted his coat. His sword harness hung empty about his waist. 'Stefan, Bea's probably right,' he urged. 'Maybe you should rest a while yet.'

Stefan seized hold of Bruno, and brought him round to face him. 'If I'm right, then we may not have much time,' he said. 'Bruno, you're going to have to trust me on this. Please, go to the door, and see if the way is clear outside.'

Bruno hesitated for a moment, then did as Stefan had bid.

'There are guards at the end of the corridor,' he said, puzzled. 'Two of them, and definitely armed.'

Stefan nodded. 'I don't suppose they're there for our own safety,' he commented. He turned to find Bea. 'We're going to need some help,' he said.

* * *

DEEP BELOW GROUND, Alexei Zucharov prowled the airless gloom of his narrow cell, and cursed the trick of fate that had brought him to such a bitter end. In a fury, he beat against the granite walls until his fists were raw and bloodied, and strained with all his might against the irons that anchored his body to the bare stone floor. Kyros had promised him treasure beyond his wildest imaginings, a path to glory in return for his humiliation by the bounty hunter. Instead, he found himself trapped within a grey tomb, with only the tortured screams of the foul servants of Chaos for company. Was this how his life was to end, not with the thunder of battle, but with his body slowly rotting away, lost and forgotten in some Morr-forsaken hole?

Zucharov railed against the injustice, against the false god that had led him here. And he cursed the insidious power of the gold band that had lured and trapped him more surely than chains or prison walls ever could. But all his anger, all his rage was for nothing. As hour followed hour he remained as he was, alone in the darkness.

Finally, his rage was spent, leaving him with despair as his sole companion. Only then, finally, did Kyros come to him. Only then did the Dark Lord whisper to him of what would come to pass.

*Your faith is barely tested, and yet you founder,* Kyros chided. *This is not strength.*

'Set me free of this poisonous trinket,' Zucharov said out loud. 'And I'll show you what my strength can achieve.'

*That will never come to pass. Only death will part you from the amulet now.*

'Then let it be so,' Zucharov screamed out loud. Let death come, for he would rather die than live another day as a prisoner.

But death would not come, he knew that. Death would not take him, not yet, for there were tasks for him to fulfil before he left this mortal world. His life in service to the Lord of Change was only now beginning.

And as Zucharov sat within his cell he thought he saw the enveloping gloom start to lift, as though an unseen candle had been brought to light the darkness. He looked down at the gold band, glowing like cold fire upon his wrist, and at the black shadow of the tattoo. The disfiguring mark now covered all of his arm, and was already beginning to spread in a dark web across his chest. As he looked, the picture written in the tattoo started to move again. Zucharov sat, spellbound, and watched the story come alive. After a few moments the glow from the amulet faded, and Zucharov was alone with the darkness again. But he knew he would not be alone for long. He had read the future in the figures that crawled upon his skin. He waited. For a while there was nothing but the anguished wailing of the creatures chained in the blackness of their cells, a sound like a sea of torment rising and falling against the rocks of despair.

But then came another, distinct sound. Of footsteps, moving down the passageway towards his cell. Quick, purposeful footsteps. Zucharov knew where they would stop, and, when he heard the first of the keys grinding in the lock of the door, he was expecting it. He waited another moment, as the iron panel in the door was pushed back, and then looked up.

Someone was staring in at him, their face illuminated by the flicker of an oil lamp. As Zucharov met the gaze of those searching eyes, he smiled. They had never met before in this life, but it was a smile of recognition nonetheless. The time of waiting was almost over.

ANAISE VON AUGEN stood back, and waited whilst the door was hauled open. There was a few seconds' delay whilst the first, and then the second locks were turned, and the bolts placed at intervals across the door drawn back. Then it was done, and she was standing upon the threshold of the cell, almost within touching distance of whoever – or whatever – the gods had seen fit to gift her.

The figure crouched in the darkness was fastened by chains attached to both his arms and his legs, chains embedded securely in the stone floor of the cell. There was surely no risk to her safety, and yet Anaise was trembling as she took a step further into the cell.

'Bring more light,' she commanded. 'Let me see properly what we have here.'

Two guards followed her into the cell, each carrying a lantern.

'The prisoner is quite secure?' she asked them. And then, without waiting for the answer told them, 'Put the lamps down upon the floor. Leave me with him for a while.'

A shiver of fear ran through Anaise as the door closed at her back. She took a deep breath, and pulled herself up to her full height. She would not let any creature of the night intimidate her, no matter how cruel or terrifying the disfigurement that Chaos had worked upon it. She folded her arms across her chest and took a step forward, remaining just beyond the prisoner's reach.

'Do you know where you are?' she asked. The creature made no answer, but continued to return her stare with a steady, unblinking gaze. Anaise had the sudden, uncomfortable feeling that she had somehow been expected. And the feeling that it was not she who was truly in control.

'You have been brought to Sigmarsgeist,' she continued, hurriedly, 'and here you will be judged and your sins will be accounted for.' She lifted one of the lamps, so that a wash of light fell across the figure shackled before her. 'What do you have to offer us, that might possibly postpone your miserable end?'

But she already had the answer to that question. There was no doubt that this was the fugitive that Kumansky and his friends had been pursuing. Her eyes took in the thickly muscled body of the warrior, the animal power barely contained by the chains. She saw the amulet, the polished gold shimmering in the light of the lamp, more wondrous than Konstantin had described it, impossibly beautiful. And below the beauty, the ugly stain: the tableau printed upon the flesh. The tattoo was surely the visible embodiment of evil, yet somehow impossibly intoxicating.

Anaise had been edging steadily forward towards Zucharov. She suddenly stopped short, pulling herself back. 'You are an abomination of Chaos,' she declared. 'A creature of darkness. You will die here in Sigmarsgeist, and your death will purge a blight from the world.'

Zucharov turned his head to one side, the same smile still playing across his face. 'We have waited long for you,' he said at last. 'Here our destinies intertwine.'

Anaise gasped. Part of her was outraged by the profanity she had just heard. But another part, hidden within her, had jolted in shock in recognition of the deeper truth.

'How dare you presume to speak to me as an equal!' she retorted. 'I should order you to be hacked apart here in your cell, and your poisoned corpse fed to the rats.' She edged back towards the wall, a sudden wave of giddiness flooding through her.

'Whatever could link my destiny with a spawn of damnation such as you?'

By way of answer, Alexei Zucharov raised his arm towards the light. The tiny figures etched upon his arm began to twist and turn, moving in a slow dance amongst the shadows cast by the lamp. Anaise wanted to close her eyes, but she knew that she had no choice but to look. Zucharov flexed his arm, and opened his hand to Anaise like a flower coming into bloom. Anaise looked down, and saw the waters cascading down to the rocks below.

Alexei Zucharov saw the expression upon her face change. He nodded, in confirmation, and spoke the words that Kyros had placed upon his lips.

'Tal Dur,' he whispered to her. 'Tal Dur.'

THE GUARDS DREW their swords as soon as Bea emerged from the room and stood with blades pointed toward her, barring the way. 'You're supposed to stay in there,' one told her. 'Get back inside.'

'But his fever is getting worse,' Bea protested. 'I need your help, or else he may die.'

A sound of moaning came from the room behind Bea, followed by a louder cry of pain. The two guards exchanged nervous glances and took a few tentative steps forward.

'Come quickly, please,' she implored. 'There may not be much time.'

The first guard hesitated then followed Bea into the chamber, with the second some distance behind.

'What's going on?' the first man demanded. He looked around the chamber, taking in the scene. Bea stood in front of them, a look of fearful dread on her face. Bruno was seated anxiously by the side of the single cot, and Stefan lay upon the bed, the sheet drawn up to his chin, his body twisted and hunched.

'His fever has returned,' Bea told them. 'He's burning up. We must get help.'

The first guard took a step toward the bed. Gingerly, he peeled back the sheet a few inches then touched his hand against Stefan's forehead.

'Doesn't seem to be anything wrong to me,' he commented. 'Anyway,' he looked round at Bea. 'You're the healer,' he said, a note of suspicion creeping into his voice. 'Can't you help him?'

Before Bea had time to answer, Stefan had his arm around the guard's throat, wrestling him down towards the ground. Before the second man could react Bruno was onto him, the two of them battling for control of the weapon. Stefan was struggling to keep his arm locked around the first guard's head. The soldier was strong, and heavily built. On a good day Stefan might be a comfortable match for him, but this, he was quickly discovering, was not a good day.

Stefan pulled himself back, and managed to aim a series of punches to the man's midriff, hoping to wind his adversary rather than do him any serious harm. But the Red Guard had recovered his poise, and was fighting back powerfully. There was a splintering of wood as a table broke beneath them and the two men fell to the floor. The guard shrugged off Stefan's hold and swung a blow at him, and then another. Stefan was first to his feet, but now it was he who was having to defend himself. He glimpsed a flash of steel, and realised that the guard had drawn a knife. The soldier lunged, and narrowly missed, the blade slicing instead through Stefan's tunic. All Stefan's concentration was now on getting hold of the knife. He was convinced the guard was going to kill him if he could.

As his opponent drove at him with the blade for a second time, Stefan caught hold of his hand, and held on for dear life, ploughing all the energy he could muster in turning the sharp steel away from his body. For a moment the two men tottered across the room in tandem, their faces only inches apart. The other man's face was an angry, purple mask as he matched his strength against Stefan's. The pair staggered forward, then fell back, and Stefan felt something warm streaming down his hand. The look in the other man's eyes changed from rage to disbelief. Stefan lost his grip upon the other's wrist, and the two broke apart. The guard staggered back. The red of his tunic was stained with the darker hue of fresh blood. He dropped the knife, and clamped his hand to his stomach, trying to stem the flow from the wound.

On the far side of the room, Bruno finally wrested the sword from the second guard. The guard looked to his fallen comrade, and the bloodied figure of Stefan standing over him. He made a final, futile attempt to clutch at the sword, then turned towards the door. Bruno aimed the sword carefully, and struck the guard behind his head with the flat of the blade. The second man staggered forward a few steps further, then collapsed.

The eerie silence hanging in the room was broken by Bea. 'Stefan,' she said. 'I think he's dead.' Her voice sounded numb, disbelieving of what she had just witnessed.

Stefan dropped down upon one knee, next to the fallen man. 'I didn't mean to kill him,' he said, fighting to regain his breath. 'As the gods may judge me, I was trying to take the knife from him.'

'The other's still breathing,' Bruno announced. 'But he'll be out for a while.' He went to Bea, and drew her into his arms to comfort her. Stefan read the look written on his friend's face, the message clear: *You'd better be right about this.*

'We need to get moving,' he said to Bruno. 'We don't have much time now.'

Bruno lifted Bea's face towards his own. Her cheeks were lined with tears.

'It's not going to be safe here,' Bruno told her. 'Come with us.'

Bea shook her head in confusion. 'I can't,' she said, her voice choked with sobs. 'I have to stay,' she said at last, more firmly now. She looked at the second guard, lying crumpled in a heap by the doorway.

'I'm a healer. I have to stay, and do what I can for him.' She put her arms about Bruno. 'It's all right,' she said. 'They won't hurt me. I know that.'

Stefan looked to Bruno. 'There's no guarantee that she'll be any safer with us,' he said. 'It might truly be best if she stayed.'

Bruno stood facing the two of them, battling his emotions. 'Shallya watch over you,' he said at last to Bea. 'We'll come back for you. As the gods are my witness, I promise we will.'

Stefan took Bea's hand. 'I'm sorry this is happening,' he said. 'There isn't time to explain now. But you must believe me. There's something very wrong about Sigmarsgeist.'

Bea regarded him without judgement, and forced a smile. 'Go now, hurry,' she urged. 'And the gods grant you luck.'

They gathered up the weapons from the fallen guards. 'Where to?' Bruno demanded, breathlessly.

'The cells, I think,' Stefan replied. 'I want to see what else they're keeping down there. We must make all speed.'

But whatever luck the two comrades had been granted had already expired. Stefan and Bruno had barely descended a single flight of steps from their quarters when they were met by Hans Baecker, a quartet of armed men at his heel.

Baecker drew out his sword smartly and greeted Stefan with a thin smile.

'Stefan,' he said. 'I'm sorry you weren't able to take my advice about resting. I'm afraid I must insist that we return to your chambers.'

Stefan looked down at the men below, one hand upon the sword now buckled at his waist, weighing the odds. Baecker plucked the question from his mind, and answered it unequivocally.

'You're excellent swordsmen, both of you,' he said. 'You might stand a chance of overpowering us.' He cast a glance over his shoulder. 'But you should know that Rilke is waiting in the courtyard below with a dozen or more men. I'm sure he'd like the chance to put your resilience to the test.'

Baecker took another step up towards Stefan and Bruno. He smiled again, but there was no warmth in his eyes now. He extended his hand.

'Now, gentlemen,' he said. 'The swords, please.'

# CHAPTER TWELVE
## Betrayals

THEY WERE TAKEN to the chamber of the High Council, back to the place where they had first met with the Guides. It was where their encounter with Sigmarsgeist had begun, and where, Stefan now feared, it might now end. This time there were to be no speeches of welcome. This time the soldiers lined around the walls had a very different role.

Most of the places around the great table were empty. Whatever judgement would be reached here today would be reached without the wisdom of the council. Stefan wasn't expecting much in the way of justice.

Konstantin von Augen sat at the head of the table, staring impassively at Stefan and Bruno. To his left, Hans Baecker, the same thin smile still playing about his lips. On his right, Rilke, his stone face revealing no hint of emotion. Of Anaise, there was as yet no sign.

When Konstantin finally spoke, his voice was filled with an angry sadness.

'You have betrayed us, Stefan,' he said. 'You have betrayed our trust, and murdered one of our brothers. Every soul of Sigmarsgeist is treasured, you must know that. We opened our gates and our hearts to you, and you have repaid us with treachery.'

Stefan stood in silence for a few moments. Konstantin sounded truly wounded, a righteous man who had been wronged. For a moment Stefan had found his own anger punctured, tempered by something very like guilt. Could it be that he had made a mistake? Perhaps the blow that he had suffered had impaired his thinking. Perhaps, truly, he had got things badly wrong. If Konstantin von Augen was only acting a role, then he was playing his part exceptionally well.

'The girl, Bea, had no part in this,' Bruno said firmly. 'However you choose to judge us, she is free of any guilt.'

Konstantin's eyes narrowed. 'That is a view shared by my sister,' he replied, coldly. 'But we shall find the truth of that in due course.'

'Where were you going, Stefan,' Baecker interjected, 'when we found you upon the stair?'

Stefan looked to Bruno. There seemed little point in subterfuge now. They would know the truth of this one way or another, and then learn the consequences.

'To the cells,' he said, simply.

Rilke raised an eyebrow, and flashed a brief, ironic smile. 'I dare venture that your wish will be accommodated,' he said, dryly.

Konstantin leaned forward, perplexed by Stefan's answer. 'We held nothing back from you,' he said. 'Why were you intent on going back? Why did you kill a man for so little gain?'

'I wanted to see who else had found their ways to the dungeons of Sigmarsgeist,' Stefan said. He took a deep breath. 'I'd got things wrong,' he said, looking directly at Baecker. 'The night we met you we had come from a village. Its name was Grunwald, though no one will ever have cause to speak it now. There must have been forty or more souls living there. By the time we arrived they were all dead – butchered and burned.'

'We took it to be the mutants,' Bruno interjected.

'We assumed they had destroyed Grunwald,' Stefan continued. 'Our assumption was wrong.'

'Why are we wasting our time with this nonsense?' Baecker blurted out, angrily.

'Indeed,' Konstantin concurred. 'It is you, Stefan Kumansky, who stands before me accused. Do you think that you can deflect that accusation by in turn accusing us?'

'I only ask to be heard,' Stefan replied, determinedly. 'I ask that you hear me out.'

'You will be heard,' Konstantin granted him, coldly. 'And then you will be judged.'

To his right, Rilke sat strangely silent, his eyes fixed all the time upon Stefan. Stefan turned his gaze from Konstantin back towards Hans Baecker.

'What had those people done to anger you?' Stefan asked him. 'Was the toll they had paid for your so-called "protection" not enough? Or had you just stripped out all you could? Was that why you attacked Mielstadt? Was that why the people of Grunwald had to die?'

Baecker stood up and flung his cup to the floor, the clay smashing on the hard ground. 'We have heard enough of this insolence!' he roared. 'Will you let this man – this *murderer* – speak his slander against us?' he demanded of Konstantin.

Konstantin reflected, his face an inscrutable mask.

'I will not countenance lies,' he said, quietly. 'But I will hear you answer his question.'

'The mutants had been to Grunwald,' Baecker said. 'Someone there had chosen to give them succour – food, shelter – who cares? It's all the same.' He fixed Stefan with a disdainful stare. 'They gave succour to evil, and suffered the consequences.'

'There were no mutants in Mielstadt,' Stefan retorted, furiously. 'But that didn't save the people there.' He turned his gaze back upon the Guide. 'You know what your people have done,' he shouted at Konstantin. 'Or is it simply that you choose to be blind to their deeds?'

Just for a moment, Stefan thought he saw a glimmer of doubt in the Guide's eyes. Then Konstantin seemed to banish the thought, waving it away with a gesture of impatience.

'Baecker is a loyal servant of Sigmarsgeist,' he proclaimed. 'I am satisfied that he speaks the truth.' He spread his hands, drawing the matter to the close, and sighed, deeply.

'I thought Sigmar had delivered us a great gift in you, Stefan Kumansky,' he said. 'And in you, too, Bruno. Perhaps I allowed myself to see what I wished to see, rather than the truth that is now laid before me.' He closed his eyes, and sat for a few moments in contemplation.

'Is there anything more?' he asked Baecker. 'Anything at all you have not told me?'

'My lord, every deed I have ever done has been for the glory of Sigmarsgeist,' Baecker replied. 'You know the power that evil has. You know that it can take the most innocent of forms.'

Konstantin lowered his head, and deliberated. When he raised his gaze once more, any doubt or pity had been swept aside.

'You have betrayed our trust, and betrayed the cause of Sigmarsgeist,' he said to Stefan and Bruno. 'The clear penalty for such deeds is death.' He looked to his two lieutenants. 'Unless you find argument to the contrary?'

Baecker shook his head. The faint, almost cruel smile had returned, and he was looking directly at Stefan. Stefan could scarcely believe this was the same man he had been glad to call comrade. To the right of the Guide, Rilke at last broke his silence.

'Death would be more than they deserve,' he said. 'It is of little consequence to me, but I would put them to work in the mines, or upon the walls. Let them give their blood to atone for their crimes. After all,' he said to Konstantin, 'once they have given their all, they can still be put to death.'

Konstantin nodded. 'As ever, Rilke, you are wise.' He stood to address Stefan and Bruno. 'You *will* serve Sigmarsgeist,' he pronounced, 'by one means or another. Your deaths are postponed for as long as you may labour in our service.' He sat, and the shadow of sadness passed across his features once again. 'Do not think I pass this judgement lightly,' he said. 'Nor should you think that my judgement is a mercy.' He signalled to the guards for the prisoners to be led away.

'Before your penance is served, you may be wishing for death as your deliverance.'

ANAISE SAT PATIENTLY by Bea's side, waiting for the girl's sobs to subside. Bea cried unashamedly. Days of conflict and confusion had come to a head inside of her, and now the dam had burst. She felt miserable and powerless. Since they had found her, tending the wounded guard, she had spent all but a few hours confined within Anaise's quarters. She was not a prisoner, Anaise had explained, yet neither was Bea any longer free to go as and where she chose. If not guilty of the crime, then she had at the very least been tainted by it. Anaise had made it very clear how she had intervened in person to spare Bea from Konstantin's rage. Now Anaise was her protector, and, to all intents, her custodian, too.

After what seemed to her like an age, Bea lifted her face and looked around. They were sitting facing the ring of stones that lined the ancient well – the Well of Sadness, Anaise had called it. The name seemed particularly appropriate to Bea now.

Even through the numbing grief, she could feel the energy radiating from the well, like the heat from a great fire. She shuddered. She was not ready for this yet.

'Why have we come here?' she asked.

Anaise ran her hand through Bea's hair, brushing the strands back from her tear-streaked face. 'There is nowhere safer than here,' she whispered, soothingly. 'This is the one place Konstantin will dare not come. This is my place alone.'

'Konstantin is searching for me?'

'He does not understand you,' Anaise said. 'He doesn't understand us.'

Bea uttered a cry, a nervous, fearful half-laugh. 'I don't think I understand, either,' she said. 'I don't understand what's happening. And I don't understand why you are choosing to protect me.'

Anaise plaited Bea's hair between her fingers. 'Because I do understand you,' she said at length. 'You were confused. Your loyalties were torn. You felt you owed a debt to Stefan and Bruno, that's why you helped them. But you also wanted to do the right thing. That's why you stayed to tend to the wounded guard.' She smiled, and drew back. 'It's all right. I understand.'

Bea shook her head, uncertainly. Everything made sense, and yet no sense. She thought hard about what she needed to say. 'Stefan and Bruno are good men,' she declared. 'I know that their souls are pure.'

'But why did they kill a man, and grievously wound another?' Anaise asked, gently. 'Can you explain that?'

Bea shrugged. The tears started to well up inside her again. She did not know, yet she sensed that something was wrong, something that she could not yet explain. It was there in the fabric of Sigmarsgeist itself, the unceasing, barely controlled growth of the citadel each day. And it was there in the energy that swelled, like restless waves upon a sea all around her. But the explanation was still beyond her reach.

'They are good men,' was all she could say.

'You say that, but–' Anaise paused, and inclined her head, looking deeper into Bea's eyes. 'Wait – there is something else, isn't there? You hold a place in your heart for one of them.' She hesitated, put a finger to her lips. 'Is it – Bruno?'

Bea averted her eyes, and gave the slightest of nods. She felt her eyes prickling with tears again. Anaise drew an arm around her shoulder to comfort her.

'It's all right,' she said. 'It's nothing to be ashamed of.' She reached for a glass, and placed it into Bea's hand. 'Here,' she said. 'Drink some of this.'

Bea lifted the glass to her lips, and sipped. The clear liquid burned in her throat. 'Merciful Shallya,' she exclaimed, coughing. Her head felt light, faintly giddy. 'What is it?'

Anaise laughed, and took the glass from her. 'At least it brought some colour to your poor face,' she said. 'Just a simple herbal elixir,' she explained. 'All the way from Talabheim. Come, drink a little more. It'll put the fire back in your heart.'

Bea looked at the glass with a mixture of suspicion and curiosity, her troubles momentarily forgotten. 'But I thought–' she began. 'I thought you said–'

'That such things were not allowed in Sigmarsgeist?' There was a note of mockery in Anaise's suddenly stern tone.

'Quite right. We must set an example for our people, to guide them along the true path.' She raised the glass to her lips, and drained it in one draught. 'This is different, though,' she continued. 'Besides, there is no wrong in acknowledging our desires.' She refilled the glass from the stone flask at her side. 'So long as it is only to understand them.'

She offered the glass back to Bea. 'We must set examples, Bea,' she said. 'That does not mean we must be enslaved by them.' She smiled. 'Konstantin might not agree with me,' she said. 'But you can share my secrets.' She stood, and lifted Bea to her feet. 'You shall be a part of all of them.'

'I should leave,' Bea said, hurriedly. 'It is not right for me to stay here.' She tried to shrug Anaise aside, but the Guide was in no mood to let her go.

'Where will you run to, Bea?' Anaise asked. 'To Bruno, to join him in his miserable cell? You won't be of help to him that way, be assured of that.' She turned the girl's face towards her own. 'Or to Konstantin, perhaps? I hope you wouldn't be so foolish. I can only do so much to ensure your safety.' She reached to Bea's cheek, tracing the line of her tears with one finger. 'Once things are quieter, it will be safer for you,' she said. 'Until then you should rest here. With me.'

'What do you want of me?' Bea asked. 'What can I have that is so valuable to you?'

By way of answer, Anaise steered Bea towards the centre of the room. As her eyes fell upon the shadowed hollow of the Well of Sadness, Bea felt herself begin to fall, as though the ground beneath her feet had suddenly dropped away. She walked – or glided, so it seemed – towards the well as if drawn by irresistible gravity. She stopped herself, just short of the edge, and stood clutching at the low stone wall for support.

'I'm not ready for this,' she stammered. 'I'm not strong enough. The drink has made me confused–'

'The magic is summoning you,' Anaise insisted, brushing her protests aside. 'It is *your* strength that it has recognised. The waters of Tal Dur, Bea. They are waiting to be found once more. They wait for you to release their power.' She drew her on, insistent. 'It is your calling, Bea. Your gift. It is your duty to heed that call.'

For all her fear, Bea found herself staring down into the depths of the ancient well. The shaft dropped away into darkness, an empty, arid void. And yet, as she looked down, Bea felt the brush of air light against her face. A slight fluttering breeze, as if, far below, something stirred. And she thought that, just for a moment, she heard a sound, the sound of water; single drops falling upon the parched earth. A needle-thin trickle of cool water snaking across the base of the dead well.

She pulled her face away. At once the sound was gone, and the air resolved once more to stillness. She felt light-headed, giddy from much more than the sip of liquor.

'I must have imagined it,' she said to Anaise. 'I thought for a moment I heard something.'

'There is nothing false in your imagining,' Anaise replied. 'All that you saw and heard will come to pass.' She smiled. 'Tal Dur is waiting for us, Bea. Waiting for you to find the key.'

THEY WERE NOT to be taken down to the cells, not yet at least. Konstantin had decreed that their punishment was to be hard labour in the service of Sigmarsgeist. And the punishment was to begin at once.

Stefan and Bruno were led from the High Council to an outer yard of the palace, where they joined a gang of perhaps twenty or thirty other men. Some were in pairs or small groups, but most stood or sat upon the ground on their own, lost in some dream, or some private misery, of their own. Few if any were speaking, and none seemed to notice the newcomers' arrival amongst them.

Stefan cast his eyes around, trying to fathom whether these might be allies or enemies that they now found themselves amongst. There was no clear answer to that question that he could see. All of the gathered prisoners looked human, with no obvious marks of mutation upon them. But whether they were men who had marched beneath the dark flag, or simply villagers who had found themselves on the wrong side of the Red Guard, there was no way of telling.

But they were all quite unlike the healthy, vigorous volunteers Stefan had seen on their arrival in the city. To a man, the crowd in the courtyard were ragged and filthy, bowed down from days of toil. Their clothes hung in tatters, coated in dust or a dark brown grime. And they reeked, their unwashed bodies ripe with the stench of long labour, deep below ground. They looked and smelt like nothing Stefan had seen in Sigmarsgeist before, until now.

The guards moved Stefan and Bruno forward, prodding them with their swords, herding them further into the confined space of the courtyard. Soon they were jostling for space amongst the ragged mob. A figure bumped against Stefan; a lank-haired man approaching middle years, but sturdily built. He still had the hawk-like look of the hunter about him, despite having clearly taken a beating from someone only recently. He eyed Stefan and Bruno warily. He might not have been a man to trust, but Stefan sensed no particular evil in him, either. He doubted such a man had ever been part of any Chaos army.

'How did you come here?' Stefan asked the man. 'Were you taken in Mielstadt?'

'Mielstadt?' the man turned the word about in his mind, then looked at Stefan as though he were deranged. 'What would I be doing in a scum-hole like Mielstadt?' he demanded of Stefan, irritably. 'No,' he went on. 'I'm only here because of a misunderstanding. They owe me money. I captured one of the beasts, brought it all the way here.' He tugged urgently at Stefan's sleeve. 'They've made a mistake,' he insisted. 'You tell them for me. I brought them—'

Stefan heard the crack of a whip, and felt the sharp sting of the lash against his face.

'Enough talk,' the guard shouted out. 'From now on you can hold your tongues, the lot of you. Save your energy for the walls. Now, get moving.'

Stefan reached out to catch hold of the other man, suddenly anxious to know who or what he claimed to have brought to Sigmarsgeist. But he was gone, lost in the river of souls beginning their weary progress through the court-yard.

Stefan scanned the rest of the group. The prisoners were certainly not all followers of Chaos, but that didn't mean that none of them were. His eye fell upon three Norscans, walking apart from the main group, heaping guttural curses upon anyone who came within earshot. For a moment he wondered if it could be true – perhaps a number of the mutants and their Norscan allies really had found their way to Mielstadt. There was a part of Stefan that perhaps wanted to believe that. But his heart and his head were in one accord. Wherever these Norscans had come from, it was not Mielstadt, nor any other wretched village that the Red Guard had chosen to wreak their revenge upon. Baecker was lying, and therefore Konstantin, too. He began to wonder if all of Sigmarsgeist was not a lie.

One of the Norscans – a flaxen-haired man with a bull-like stature – he recognised from the gang of prisoners being marched through the streets as Stefan and the others had taken their first tour of the citadel. The Norscan looked at Stefan and seemed to recognise him too. He gestured, unmistakably, drawing a line across his throat with one finger. A shouted command from a guard brought him back from his thoughts. A gate at the end of the courtyard had been opened, and the prisoners were lining up ready to file out. At their head, a single White Guard stood ready to deliver their instructions.

'Today you will have the honour of working upon the citadel walls,' he announced. 'Building the fortifications that will one day protect us from the dark flood of Chaos.' He stared out at the crowd of prisoners, seeking out any who would make eye contact. Bruno tightened his fists into balls, his face taut with rage.

'By all the gods, Stefan,' he declared. 'Now, truly, we see the other face of Sigmarsgeist.'

– Stefan shook his head, slowly. How different things had come to look, and in so short a space of time. The line of men began to trudge slowly towards the gate. A line that would have looked not much different from any other of the bands of workers they had watched during their first days in Sigmarsgeist. Nothing, and yet everything, was changed.

'There's no middle road with these people,' he declared. 'You side with them, or against them. Truly, my friend, we've moved to the other side of that line.'

'We've got to escape,' Bruno muttered. 'We must find Bea. Pray to the goddess that she's all right.'

Stefan looked round at the guards, sizing up their number and the weapons they carried. 'Little enough chance of that at the moment,' he replied. 'They'd cut us down like dogs before we got ten paces. The opportunity will come,' he assured Bruno. 'But we're going to have to bide our time.'

The procession moved through the open portal and out into the streets. It was the first time in days that he had seen the outer reaches of citadel. Time enough, apparently, for Sigmarsgeist to change beyond all belief. Stefan's first thought was that the citadel had somehow shrunk, become smaller. Everywhere there seemed to be so much less space, so many more people. He quickly realised that, on the contrary, Sigmarsgeist had continued to grow, and grow at such a rate that the very buildings at its heart seemed to be competing with each other, jostling for precious space. Every inch of land was now given over to brick and stone, and not so much as a blade of grass had been left to grow between the tall buildings that now sprouted up on all sides.

He could not fathom how so many new buildings could have sprung up in such a short space of time. But he understood clearly now why their lives – and those of the worn-down wretches around them – had been reprieved. The equation was simple. Sigmarsgeist was growing at an unimaginable rate, far outstripping the capacity of its workforce. Labour was their most precious commodity, and for as long as he and Bruno kept their strength, he guessed that they would be spared.

He slowed his pace to take in the strangeness of it all. In several places, houses had been damaged, walls broken down or roofs ripped apart by pale alabaster columns that seemed to have nothing in common with the surrounding structures. The columns rose, straight and tall, out of the wreckage of brickwork, before looping and bending like branches of a tree, lacing together like a bizarre stone latticework.

'What do you make of that?' he asked Bruno.

'I don't know,' Bruno replied. 'But I've seen something like it before.' He held his hand out towards Stefan. 'That's how I got my injury, remember? Bea has seen them, too, in other parts of the city. It looks almost like something alive, growing, not built.'

'All part of Konstantin's grand design?' Stefan mused. 'Or something moving out of control?'

He was answered by a jab to his ribs from a sword. 'I told you once,' the guard barked. 'Shut up. Keep moving.'

Stefan eyed Bruno, and walked on in silence. For the next thirty minutes or so, they marched through the streets towards the edge of the city. The townsfolk who crossed their path weren't greeting them as heroes now, and many hurled abuse or spat upon the prisoners as they passed. Finally they had left the crowded streets behind, and had come within sight of the high walls that encircled the citadel. Walls to keep intruders out, and Stefan realised now, to keep prisoners in.

The prisoners were driven left, herded like cattle along the line of the fortification by the guards. After a while they came to a gap, a breach the width of a pair of wagons. The stonework had been deliberately demolished, knocked through so that a new wall could be erected further out, extending the outer boundary of the citadel. The new wall already stood at twenty feet, and teams of workers were labouring upon the ramparts, building up the walls layer by layer. Along the wall was placed a row of ladders, up and down which figures streamed like ants, each weighed down with sack-loads of fresh stone for the artisans working up above. It would be back-breaking work for even the fittest of men.

'That's the end of your stroll,' the guard announced. 'Get in line over there. Each of you'll be given a sack. Make sure it's filled – there's a beating waiting for any man who doesn't.'

For a moment the troop of prisoners stood where they were. The open wall stood before them. For many, this was probably as close to freedom as they would ever get again. More than one must have thought of escape, a last desperate bid for freedom. But the soldiers guarding the work party now almost outnumbered the prisoners, and all of them were armed. In any case, Stefan realised, they were in no position yet to leave Sigmarsgeist, not with Bea still somewhere inside the citadel.

'Come on,' he muttered to Bruno. 'We'll see this out.' He marched to the head of the line, and took a coarse fabric sack from the pile. The quarried stone was stacked in a series of wagons, waiting to be carried up to where other teams of prisoners were at work, raising the level of the walls. Stefan walked to the first of the wagons and began loading stones into the sack, all the time watched by a brace of guards. When the sack was filled he hefted it over his back and carried his load over to a ladder. The ladders were at least securely fixed against the walls; the builders of Sigmarsgeist had no intention of killing their slave workers, at least not by accident.

Stefan put a foot on the bottom rung of the ladder, and, after shifting his load to get a better balance, began to climb up. In a few seconds he was at the top, and swinging the laden sack down off his back.

Bruno was right behind him, both men now standing atop of the growing wall.

'This isn't too bad,' Bruno said, gulping down breath. 'We can take it.'

'At the moment,' Stefan agreed.

The second sack that he loaded upon his back seemed heavier by far than the first. By the time he and Bruno had carried three more sack-loads to the top of the ladders, the burden felt as though it was doubling each and every time. Others amongst the prisoners fell by the wayside, dropping where they stood, unable to lift another stone, or toppling from the ladders under the weight of the sacks.

The guards spared no mercy for those unable to go on. Stefan had to look on as they rained blows down upon one prisoner who had collapsed under the weight of his load. The Red Guard beat the prisoner until his whimpers turned to screams, and then they beat him some more. Casualties were of no interest to them. There would be plenty more where they had come from.

The prisoners worked on through most of the day, without food or a break. Long before the end, Stefan's whole body ached, and his back felt like it would break under the punishment, but he kept going. They had to get through this. The prisoners fell into their routine, hauling the laden sacks from the foot of the walls to empty them for the work party laying the stone up above. It was a routine that got harder with every load. All the while, the sun beat down upon them, unyielding and relentless. Finally, late in the day, they were allowed to rest, and food – bread, and a little water – was handed out. Even the guards acknowledged they would get no more work out of their prisoners until they had been given some rest.

Their vantage point gave them a commanding view over the citadel. Sigmarsgeist lay spread before them through the gap in the old fortifications. The bizarre expansion of the city was now all too plain to see. From above it looked like some inexplicable multiplication was underway, a growth that was barely controlled or contained. Structures – recognisable and unrecognisable – sprouted everywhere, crammed into every available plot or space, haphazardly blocking roads and streets.

'It looks like a city gone insane,' Bruno said quietly. Stefan agreed, but it looked like more than that. Many of the new buildings reached skywards then stopped, unfinished and without purpose, and at least half seemed to bear no relation in design or function to those that they stood next to.

'Like a city feeding upon itself,' Stefan reflected. 'Forever destroying and remaking itself anew.'

Bruno lay back, exhausted. His hands were bloodied and chafed, and his face and hands were covered in a fine white dust from the stone, giving him the look of a man already dead.

'Where will it all end?' he asked.

Stefan shook his head. He had no answers now. No way of telling where the path they found themselves upon would lead.

A party of guards moved along the line of prisoners resting on top of the walls, prodding bodies with staffs and swords, pushing those that still had strength left in their bodies back to work. Most struggled back to their feet; those that could not were thrown without ceremony from the walls. Stefan watched the bodies being collected like refuse in one of the empty wagons below.

'Is this the great bright future that Sigmarsgeist was created for?' Bruno asked. 'By the gods, they have become the very evil that they would oppose.'

'And now we must set our face against them,' Stefan replied. 'Our allies are become our enemies.'

The prisoners were being moved on again. 'Make the most of your day in the sun,' a guard sneered. 'It'll be the mines for you tomorrow. A few hours down there and you'll wish you'd never been born.'

# CHAPTER THIRTEEN
## The World Below

HOWEVER RELUCTANTLY, BEA had taken heed of Anaise's words. Her impulse at their last meeting had been to run from her chambers, run and keep running, until Anaise and every tangled, confused thought of Sigmarsgeist had been swept from her mind.

But years of surviving had taught Bea a measure of prudence. There was nowhere for her to go. Whatever Anaise's motives, for the moment Bea was safer with the Guide's protection than without it. After that last, troubling meeting, she had fled, but she had not fled far. And for the next day, Bea had confined herself to the areas of the palace where Anaise, alone, held jurisdiction. There, at least, she would be safe – if she felt anything but secure.

She had been waiting for what seemed like hours for Anaise to return. Early that morning, Anaise had gone, apparently in search of news of Stefan and Bruno. Bea had been left alone, waiting whilst the long hours of morning dragged on. Finally, when she thought that she must indeed have been abandoned, the Guide swept back into the room. Anaise glanced at Bea, but did not speak. Bea got to her feet and rushed after her, eager to hear any news.

'Have you seen them?' she asked, anxiously. 'Are they all right? When can I go to them?'

Anaise placed her hands upon Bea's shoulders, steering her gently back to her seat. 'Peace,' she implored. 'Patience, Bea. You have so many questions, I understand that. But remember that I am like you. I have gifts. But I can not work miracles.' She waited for Bea to compose herself, then sat down beside her.

'I have not seen them,' she began. Bea's face fell, and Anaise quickly put a finger to the girl's lips to cut short her protest. 'No, Bea, I did not promise you that. But I *did* promise that I would speak to Konstantin, and that I have done.'

Bea leaned forward, anxiously. 'And?' she asked. 'What did he say?'

'He promised that Stefan and Bruno have not been harmed. He was minded to have them killed, but has been persuaded against that course for now.'

'Then when can I see them?' Bea demanded.

Anaise furrowed her brow in a frown. 'You ask so much of me,' she sighed, as if in exasperation. 'Very well – I'll have to trust you. I've interceded on their behalf, I'm doing what I can. But you must understand that they killed a soldier of the Red Guard, which is a grievous offence.'

Bea nodded unhappily.

'I have convinced Konstantin that you played no part in any treachery. I have also convinced him that your gift of healing should not be wasted, and that you could be set to work, tending to those who are building the citadel. Just like our soldiers, each one of them is valuable if the glory of Sigmarsgeist is to be realised.'

'I will do that work gladly,' Bea affirmed. 'It is my calling. But–'

'Bruno and Stefan are to be put to work in the quarries and mines outside Sigmarsgeist,' Anaise interjected.

'In the mines? Will they be safe there?'

'Safer than being put to death by Konstantin's executioner? I would say so, yes.' She looked at Bea and saw the anxiety on her face. Her voice took on a more conciliatory tone. 'Look,' she said, 'you'll see them, soon enough. In the meantime, I am keeping them safe, as far as is possible. Bea, I am doing everything I can for you.'

Bea bit upon her lip. 'I know you are,' she said. 'I'm sorry. I didn't mean to sound ungrateful.' She took a breath, then sighed. 'And it's some relief to hear that they are safe.' She smiled at the Guide, recovering some composure. 'Thank you, Anaise,' she said. 'I know that you have taken risks on my behalf.'

'I made you a promise, and I always honour my promises,' Anaise told her. She took Bea's hand, and squeezed it gently. 'But trust must run both ways,' she said.

'Now, you must do something for me.'

IT WAS TOO cold in the cell for sleep, too cold for anything except to lie in the dark, nursing bruised and aching bodies. Finally, Stefan had dozed only to be woken minutes later by the sound of someone moaning in pain. He was lying on a hard stone floor somewhere within a cramped, lightless space. A thin blanket covered his body, but made little difference to the numb ache that had set deep into his limbs. His hands were shackled together with a short length of chain, anchored at the other end to the floor. Stefan tugged briefly at the metal links, expending only enough strength to be sure there was no prospect of escape.

He stretched out one hand as far as the chains would allow. Almost immediately it met resistance – a wall, coarse flint under his fingers, slightly damp to the touch. Stefan raised himself onto his knees and stretched out in the opposite direction until he found the opposite side of what he now understood to be a cell. The two walls were little more than the width of a man's body apart. Stefan began to map the dimensions of the cell in his mind, since he could still see nothing through the blackness.

He remembered coming down from the ramparts with what by then remained of the work party. Around half the prisoners had not returned, and Stefan did not imagine for a moment that he would see any of them again.

He checked himself over as best he could in the gloom. Every muscle in his body ached, and his hands felt as if they had been scoured of skin. But he was intact; as far as he could tell no bones had been broken, and any blood from his scrapes and cuts had dried. So far, so good. Stefan didn't expect it was going to get any better for quite a while.

Down by his feet, something rustled and stirred. Stefan stepped back quickly, aware that he would have to do any fighting equipped only with his bare hands. Through the gloom he made out something that looked like a bundle of rags moving upon the floor at his feet. The bundle coughed and groaned, announcing itself as Bruno. Stefan helped his comrade to sit up, and waited for his coughing to subside.

'Are you all right?' Stefan asked.

'No,' Bruno replied, shivering. 'I feel like death.'

'Make the most of it,' Stefan said. 'I imagine this is the only rest we'll get.'

Bruno coughed again, a dry, rasping sound. 'My throat feels like I've been drinking dust,' he complained. 'Is there no water in here?'

Stefan explored the narrow cell in the darkness. Aside from the two thin blankets on the floor, there was nothing but themselves and four bare walls.

'Not so much as a drop,' he said. 'But if they're going to get any work out of us, they'll have to bring us something.'

Sounds of life – or what remained of it – were beginning to drift from other cells nearby. Men crying out in pain, begging for food or, more often, simply water. Men pleading against their captivity, and cursing the name of Sigmarsgeist. There was no way of telling who or what they were. Half the cries sounded barely human, but that was hardly surprising. They might equally be friend or foe, but they had a new common adversary now. There was a bitter irony to the path that the fates had chosen for Stefan and his comrades.

After a while the cries ebbed away. There was a clattering of iron from somewhere outside the cells, as the gates by the entrance were opened. Footsteps followed – it sounded as if guards were moving down the length of the passageway, stopping for a few moments by each door before moving on.

'Food?' Bruno suggested, hopefully.

'Perhaps,' Stefan agreed. He tugged again at the length of chain shackling his wrists. 'Whatever they're up to, there'll be little chance of escape until we can get rid of these.'

The footsteps reached the door of their cell. Light from a lantern flooded through the iron grille, washing the walls a sickly yellow. Stefan waited for something to appear through the narrow slit, some bread perhaps and – if the gods were merciful – something to drink. But instead he heard a key being turned in the lock, and then the cell door was pushed open.

Two figures stood in the open doorway. With the light of the lantern shining directly into his eyes, Stefan could not properly make out either of them. One – a man wearing the scarlet tunic of the Red Guard – was carrying what looked like a tray of food. The second man took the tray then turned to the guard.

'Leave us for a few minutes,' he said. 'We'll see whether a little honest work has loosened their tongues.' Once he had dismissed the guard, the second man stepped inside the cell, and drew the door closed behind him.

As the lantern was lowered to the floor Stefan looked up and saw that the man bearing the tray was Rilke. Among all the people he might have imagined, this was surely the worst.

'What's this?' Stefan demanded. 'Come to gloat?'

Rilke squatted down until he was face to face with Stefan and Bruno. There was a look on his face that Stefan had not seen before. Tentative, almost apologetic.

'Actually,' Rilke began, 'I'm here to help you if I can.'

'Yours is the kind of help we can do without,' Bruno told him, coldly. 'What did you have in mind? Poison in our food? Thanks, friend. We'll take our chances in the mines.'

Rilke's response was to lower his voice until it was barely a whisper. Without understanding why, Stefan realised that he was trying to make sure the guard outside the door could not hear him.

'I'm sorry,' Rilke went on. 'Sorry that I didn't come to you sooner. But I wasn't sure I could trust you.'

'Trust us?' Stefan asked, incredulous.

Rilke got up and checked the door. Apparently satisfied, he turned back and sat down. Perhaps even close enough, Stefan noted, for him and Bruno to overpower Rilke, shackled or not. But something in Rilke's tone convinced Stefan he should hear the man out. 'I had to be sure that your story – Erengrad, and the aftermath – was true. I couldn't risk revealing myself to you if it wasn't.'

'Revealing yourself as what?' Bruno asked, curiosity creeping into his voice.

Rilke looked directly at Stefan for a few moments. 'You said you had the confidence of the commander at Erengrad, Gastez Castelguerre. Did he mention a name to you, the name of an order pledged to wage a secret war against the hidden forces of Chaos?'

Now it was Stefan's turn to hesitate. He knew the name. Castelguerre had spoken it to him in the last days at Erengrad. He had asked Stefan to join that order in their eternal struggle against the dark powers. Stefan had refused, not because that battle was not close to his heart, but because he had his own battle, his own quest that he must first complete. Since that day Stefan had uttered the secret name to no man other than Bruno. The last few days had seen plenty of unanticipated reversals. But to speak those words now, and to the one man that he had counted above all as his enemy, seemed an act beyond reason.

And yet there was something in Rilke's voice, in the expression in his focused gaze, that Stefan could not bring himself to disbelieve. More to the point, if Rilke already knew of the existence of the order, then little harm could come from uttering its name now. Rilke waited, patiently. He seemed to understand the magnitude of the decision Stefan was trying to make.

'He mentioned a name,' Stefan said at last. 'But I will not betray that confidence by speaking those words.'

Rilke nodded, and smiled. 'I am glad to see your sense of loyalty undimmed.' He looked over his shoulder, scanning the corridor beyond the cell. 'Then let our transaction be that I speak that name unto *you*, Stefan Kumansky. The name of the order is the Keepers of the Flame.'

Stefan expelled a breath, heartened and astonished in equal measure by Rilke's disclosure. 'If you're telling us that you are in some way connected to the order, then what in the name of the gods are you doing here?' Stefan demanded.

Rilke raised a finger to his lips. 'Quietly,' he urged. 'All you need to know is that Konstantin and his sister came to the notice of the Keepers long ago. I was sent here to learn more of their plans, their intent. To do that, I had to be able get close to the Guides, and earn their absolute confidence.'

'You've done that, all right,' Bruno muttered darkly. 'Why should we believe him, Stefan?'

'Whether you believe me or not, there's no time to answer all of your questions now,' Rilke insisted. He glanced round at the door. 'There's no chance of your escaping from the cells,' he said. 'Konstantin was adamant. Nothing I can do will get you out of here now.'

'So,' Stefan asked him. 'What are you here for? Just to offer apologies?'

'Today you will be taken to the mines,' Rilke said, speaking quickly now. 'They are a terrible place, and few who go there ever return alive.'

'More good news,' Bruno said, sourly. 'Our path to damnation awaits.'

'But they can also be your salvation,' Rilke insisted. 'The ore needed for the foundries is being exhausted faster than it can be dug out. The Guides are forced to mine ever deeper to find new seams. Far below ground, many of the shafts meet with ancient tunnels and passageways, part of the old city that existed long before. That is your chance of escape.'

Footsteps sounded again outside the cell. The guard was coming back.

'I will find you in the mines,' Rilke whispered. 'Somehow I will fashion the opportunity to get you out. It may not come this day, nor the next. But you must be ready, for there may be one chance only.' He got up, taking the lantern from the floor.

'Wait,' Stefan whispered urgently. 'You said you didn't believe our story. What changed your mind?'

By the light of the lantern, he saw a terse smile pass across Rilke's face. 'The proof I needed is here,' he began, 'It–' Before he could finish the door of the cell swung open. The guard eyed Rilke warily. 'You've been a while,' he said, natural deference weighing against the irritation in his voice. 'Thought I'd best check.'

'Very wise,' Rilke said, patting the guard upon the shoulder. 'But no need for concern. I'm finished with these wretches.'

He looked round, and kicked the tray of food further into the cell towards Stefan. 'Enjoy the comfort of your cell whilst you can,' he advised. 'I assure you, after an hour in the mines it will seem like paradise.'

THE CHART SPREAD out in front of Bea mapped Sigmarsgeist in its known entirety. The healer looked at it one final time, then drew a deep breath and turned towards the dark mouth of the Well of Sadness. Within moments she was locked away in her private contemplation of a world invisible to the mortal eye. Inside her mind, she had flown the palace, flown from Sigmarsgeist, had been transported to a place where no living soul dwelled. A place where there was only light and dark, and the ebb and flow of pure energy. There was no judgement here, no right or wrong. Here the boundaries between good and evil were all but indistinguishable. The future presented itself to Bea as a churning, vacant sea. Everything was possible; no outcome was yet pre-ordained.

Bea focused her inner gaze, then imagined herself falling into the fathomless sea of light, searching for one single stream amidst the swirling flow of energies. She spread her arms wide and let the energy channel through; a bright, pure force surging into her, filling her with a divine, all-knowing power. Bea held on until she thought she could bear no more, then sprang back, her eyes wide open and her body locked tight.

Anaise stood over her, eyeing her like a predator watching its prey. There was a look of almost manic desperation on her face.

'Well?' she demanded. 'What did you see? Did you find the source?' She caught hold of Bea, gripping her wrists so tightly that the girl cried out in sudden pain and alarm. Anaise backed off immediately, and allowed her features to soften.

'I'm sorry, Bea,' she said, contritely. 'I'm letting my feelings take control of me. But I can sense that we're so close now. So close to the source of Tal Dur. I must know what it was that you saw.'

Bea nodded, but took a few moments longer to compose herself. The power she had just experienced had shocked her. Whether for good or for ill, it was a raw, brutal force that would not be easily tamed. For a moment, she found herself wondering if, after all, the elemental powers of Tal Dur were a secret best left undiscovered. But that, surely, could not be so. Through all her life she had grown up believing in the redeeming waters. To deny that now would be like denying her very existence. She hesitated, looked up at Anaise, and smiled, apologetically.

'It was different this time,' she began. 'Much more powerful.'

Anaise smiled. 'And do you know why?' she asked. 'It is because of you, Bea. You are the channel for the energy flowing back into the city.'

Bea pulled back, nervously. 'No,' she said. 'This is not my doing. I can sense the growing powers of magic. But I have not created it. This isn't my doing.'

Anaise clasped Bea's hand. 'Do not deny your powers, nor your destiny,' she implored her. 'The time is all but upon us. I must know what you were able to see.'

'I saw – something,' Bea said, tentatively. 'Something very strong.'

'Go on,' Anaise urged her. 'Was it here, beneath the citadel? Show me upon the chart.'

Bea looked down at the chart spread out below her. The lines drawn upon the parchment depicted lanes and streets, passageways and sunken shafts drilling down below the surface of the city. It was nothing but a visualisation of the known, material shell of Sigmarsgeist, and as such meant nothing to the healer. But whatever mystic force had touched her had gifted her with a temporary glimpse of second sight. Beneath the literal charts she saw another map, one that charted the flows of the unseen energies below. She passed her hand across the surface of the parchment, tracing the paths of invisible lines. Bea repeated and retraced the motions several times, before turning back to Anaise.

'There are lines that intersect deep below the citadel,' she said. 'The waters that once flowed through their channels carry great magic energies.'

'The confluence,' Anaise whispered. 'Tal Dur.'

'No,' Bea said, surprised by her own certainty. 'The healing waters are close, very close. But I cannot sense them below Sigmarsgeist itself.'

Anaise bit upon her lip, and scrutinised Bea carefully. 'Are you sure?' she asked. Then, without waiting for an answer, 'but if Tal Dur lies close, you could find it, couldn't you?'

Now Bea hesitated. Part of her felt emboldened, blessed with a new certainty. Tal Dur had touched her; the waters had called to her, beckoning her to them.

'Perhaps,' she agreed. 'Perhaps I can find it. Yes, give me time, and I can find it.'

'You'll be given everything you need,' Anaise assured her. 'We shall be sisters, you and I. Sisters bonded by the healing powers of Tal Dur. Together, there will be nothing we cannot achieve.'

Bea smiled, weakly. She had a sudden sense of something draining from her body. She clutched hold of Anaise's hand to steady herself.

'Bruno,' she muttered, 'and Stefan. I must see them.'

'And you will,' Anaise promised. 'But first–' she held Bea out at arm's length and stood back to appraise her. 'Look at you. Your face is so drawn and pale. I've put you through an ordeal, it was selfish of me to push you so hard.' She drew her arm around Bea's shoulder and started to lead her away. 'I'll find a way of getting you to your friends,' she said. 'But first you must rest a while.'

She snapped her fingers. A maidservant appeared in the doorway.

'Perhaps you're right,' Bea replied, wearily. 'Perhaps I should rest?'

'Of course you must.' Anaise beckoned the servant into the chamber, towards Bea. 'And don't think of anything else until you have done so.'

As soon as Bea had been escorted from the room, Anaise closed the door behind her. She waited, alone, in the room for a few moments more, then summoned the waiting guard into the chamber.

'Get some men,' she said, simply. 'We're going to the cells.'

THE FOOD WAS as bad as could be imagined – rank, rotten meat and a hunk of grey bread – with only a bowl of fly-specked water to wash it down. But Stefan and Bruno ate, and they drank, for neither knew when they might get the chance to do so again. They had barely finished when the guards returned to rouse the prisoners from their cells, to face whatever torments the day held in store.

A row of covered wagons was waiting in the courtyard above, pulled by braces of oxen. Stefan guessed that the wagons were intended to save time rather than spare the prisoners' strength. The mines must lie some distance beyond the citadel walls. The prisoners climbed up into the wagons in pairs. Once they were all boarded, the guards moved amongst them, shackling each man securely to the next. There would be little or no chance of escape during this journey.

Stefan sat towards the back, trying to glimpse what he could of the world outside as their wagon rolled through the citadel towards the outer walls. It was still dark, the first rays of the sun's light had yet to break above the hills that crested Sigmarsgeist. Even so, the streets were already brimming with people heading towards their day's labour. None paid any heed to the passing wagons or their cargo. It was as though they had ceased to exist.

As night gave way to grey dawn, Stefan peeled back the edge of the canvas hanging over the back of the wagon to get a glimpse of what was happening outside. He saw little to give him comfort. Aside from the dozen guards sitting with the prisoners inside the wagon, there were at least a dozen more on horseback surrounding the wagons as they made their slow progress through the streets. He soon gave up watching the guards and looked instead at the citadel itself.

They were following the same route as they had taken the previous day on the way to the walls, and yet the place looked already altered. Buildings, houses and shops that had looked barely half-built only the day before now stood virtually intact, their construction completed with incredible speed. Then there were other buildings – those that had been already standing – that now appeared partly demolished, broken down for no obvious purpose other than to accommodate the new, partly-built structures growing up out of their midst. Some of the new structures were recognisable in shape. Others – bizarre lattice-works of alabaster marble twisting about one another like sleeping serpents – were not. Everything, every edifice, was competing with others for the increasingly precious space around the citadel.

'It's getting out of control,' Stefan said quietly to Bruno. 'The place is feeding upon itself. The growth can't be contained.'

'Why do they keep building?' Bruno asked, awed and perplexed in equal measure. 'They must see that they're starting to tear the place apart?'

Stefan turned to his friend in the shadows of the wagon. 'Who knows?' he said. 'But my senses tell me that Konstantin and Anaise have unleashed something here that they cannot now undo.' He watched as the streets behind them receded into the distance. 'Something which sprang from honour and virtue, and has become something other.'

The wagons passed beyond the city walls onto the open plains that lay beyond the citadel. A wan light began to penetrate the interior of the wagon, and Stefan was able to see the rest of his companions for the first time. Aside from Bruno and the guards, they shared the cramped space with twenty or so more prisoners. Their pale, emaciated faces looked battered and defeated. Flesh hung off their frames like empty sacks. Many were not long for this world, Stefan could see that. He wondered how much of this he could take before he, too, came to look like the same.

There was another hour's journey beyond the walls before the wagons rolled to a stop, and the prisoners were ordered down into the pale morning light. The land around them was desolate and barren, hemmed in by bare grey hills stretching up towards a leaden sky. Some way in the distance, deep within the cradle of those hills, lay Sigmarsgeist. Stefan looked upon it, and saw it no longer as a jewel, but as a canker. A canker, steadily, remorselessly spreading.

Nearly fifty men in all were gathered by the wagons, shivering in the early dawn. Many of them flung back their heads to the open sky, drinking in the light as though it were for the last time. The guards allowed a moment's respite, then marched the men towards a yawning fissure, a cleft carved in the rock like an entrance to a gigantic cave. In single file, and still shackled one to another, the men walked down a steep slope towards the entrance to the mine. With each step the air around them grew ever more stale and foetid. The dark mouth of the mine disgorged a steady flow of men, caked in filth, some hauling laden barrows and wagons, others with sacks loaded upon their backs.

Stefan gazed into their bruised and broken faces, and saw nothing but a vacant numbness written there. They were the lucky ones, Stefan supposed, men who were still able to walk from the mines on their own two feet. Piles of bodies lay stacked like so much ballast either side of the gravel path, awaiting disposal. The stench of death mixed with the odours of sweat and grime pouring off the exhausted souls trudging out of the mine.

All we are, Stefan realised, is more fuel for the furnace. Sticks of human tinder to feed the flames of Sigmarsgeist. His life was worth precisely the sum of the labour that could be wrung from it. No more and no less.

He was pulled back from his thoughts by someone – or something – barging into him from behind. He turned about and found himself staring into the face of a tall Norscan, a scar running the length of one cheek. The Norscan stared at Stefan, a murderous expression on his face.

'Erengrad,' the man said. 'You were there. We don't forget.'

'Neither do I,' Stefan replied. 'I won't forget Erengrad, or you and your kind, for as long as I live.'

'Which won't be for long,' the other countered. Stefan braced himself, ready to fight there and then if necessary. But he wasn't to have the chance. Two guards standing close by had seen the altercation between Stefan and the Norscan. Now they weighed in energetically, lashing out with their staffs, and pulled the two men apart.

'Save it for later,' the guard snarled. 'First we want some work out of you.'

The Norscan backed off, but shot a look towards Stefan that clearly signalled his intent. A look that said, *this is not over.*

The guard at the head of the column of prisoners shouted for silence.

'Behold the Mines of Sigmar,' he announced to the waiting men. 'Behold them, and despair. For those of you who work hard–' he looked around at the prisoners, and laughed. 'Who knows? Maybe you'll find some food and rest as your reward at the end of the day.' The guard looked down the line, scanning the faces. 'For those who don't, take a good look about as you climb down the shaft.' He looked down, and spat upon the ground. 'Because they'll be your tomb.'

The guards standing to either side of the column of men cracked down upon their whips, and slowly, with something approaching dread, the line moved forward into the darkness.

'Gods spare us,' Bruno muttered. 'The Gates of Morr themselves couldn't be a crueller place.'

'Courage, my friend,' Stefan replied tersely. 'The worst of this still lies ahead.'

# CHAPTER FOURTEEN
## The Mines of Sigmarsgeist

KYROS, THE DARK lord of Chaos, looked out upon the world through the eyes of Alexei Zucharov. Through those eyes he examined the citadel men had named after Sigmar, that old and obdurate enemy of the dark powers. In times past Kyros would have taken no comfort from that cursed name, but what he saw now gratified him beyond all measure. The forces of change, servants of his master, the dread god Tzeentch, had been loosed upon the citadel, irreversible and, ultimately, irresistible.

He gazed through eyes the colour of storm-beaten seas as Zucharov was led, his limbs still weighed down with chains, through the courtyards and corridors of the palace. He looked out upon the streets, across the face of the citadel. The Chaos Lord could sense what was – as yet – still invisible to the mortal eye.

The tide of anarchy, barely contained within the physical bounds of the citadel. Sigmarsgeist was growing too fast; it was close to tearing itself apart. The men who had built this folly had released a force which they barely comprehended. Soon, surely, the walls would crumble and blood would wash through this dry place. Sigmarsgeist would fall, and another piece of the puzzle would have been completed, another step taken upon the road towards the inevitable victory.

But the citadel of Sigmarsgeist was only a token, a gilding gift for his master to add to the greater prize. Kyros was concerned with what lay somewhere, far below the folly of timber and stone, a place possessed of powers that the rulers of the citadel could only dream of. Powers that would render his glorious master all but omnipotent. Kyros had vowed to claim the waters of Tal Dur for the glory of almighty Tzeentch, and Alexei Zucharov was going to lead him there.

Zucharov was strong, his will had proved stubborn and obdurate. Even now, weeks after the amulet had infected his veins with the elixir of Chaos, Zucharov still struggled to hold on to his former self – a man possessed of his own, indomitable will. Kyros would subdue that will, remould and recast Zucharov's spirit until his single remaining purpose on this earth was to serve Kyros, his eternal lord and master.

Through Zucharov's eyes, Kyros followed Anaise von Augen as she strode several paces ahead of the man she considered her prisoner. Surrounded by her retinue, she exuded a calm authority that Kyros admired and mocked in equal measure. She did not yet understand that the strongest shackles were those the eye cannot see.

The Chaos Lord studied her movements. She was so proud, so confident, possessed of absolute certainty and an iron resolve. Kyros would probe that certainty until he had found each and every weakness, uncovered the keys that unlocked the gateways to her soul, then he would put her resolve to the test, bear down upon it and not desist until it had been utterly, irrevocably broken.

But first came Tal Dur. Between them, Zucharov and the Guide would lead Kyros to the source, each of them drawn to its light by yearnings too powerful to ignore. Like moths to the fatal flame, they would lead Kyros there. And when Tal Dur had been delivered, the followers of Tzeentch would have need of no one, nor would anyone be able to stand in their way.

First, THE LIGHT had faded until all that remained was the residual glow of the tallow lamps set at intervals along the length of the mineshafts. Then the air had begun to grow so stale and scarce that Stefan had begun to wonder if there could possibly be enough to sustain so many men. And this was not to be a brief stay below ground. The ordeal had begun with the descent into the underworld. The prisoners had descended a series of shafts linked by narrow, inter-connecting corridors carved out of the rock. Each successive shaft took them deeper, plunging them further into the belly of the earth. Some had the luxury of a few crude steps, like a ladder cut into the sides of the shaft. Others offered nothing but a rope dropping down into the darkness. Either way, they were a single slip from their deaths. Stefan cast a wary eye about for the two Norscans from the wagons, but there was no sign of either man. In any case, Stefan reck-oned, there were more pressing matters of life and death to occupy all of them for the time being.

He and Bruno joined the line of men descending down angled ladders into the gloom. For a while, on the surface, conversation amongst the prisoners had been animated, despite the attentions of the guards. Now, an almost eerie silence fell upon the men. One by one they disappeared into the dark void of the mine, interspersed between the guards. No one spoke. Each man was left alone with his own imag-inings of what might lie ahead.

For what seemed an eternity, the descent continued, men clambering down into the suffocating darkness, whilst the newly-mined ore was hauled relentlessly up through the shafts towards the surface. Stefan counted at least a dozen heavy rope nets filled to the brim with rough hewn stone, passing above his head on the way back up the mine. He tried to keep some measure of how far below the surface they had travelled, but after the fifth shaft had given way to a sixth, he gave up. It was far enough, further below the face of the world than he had ever ventured before.

He had expected it to be cold below ground, but it was not. A thick, sticky heat had been apparent from the moment he reached the bottom of the first shaft, and with each successive descent it grew worse. Long before he had reached the bottom of the climb, Stefan was drenched in sweat.

For a while the darkness was near total, the men finding their way by touch alone. But as Stefan neared the bottom of what he counted as the seventh shaft he saw a faint glow of light beneath him, and heard the sounds of iron beating upon stone. At long last they reached the face of the mine itself, and joined a queue of prisoners shuffling slowly forward along a cramped, narrow gallery. Up ahead the space opened out, temporarily at least, and there was enough room to walk two abreast, and more or less upright. At one end of the gallery, guards were handing out a supply of tools, spades and pick-axes.

Bruno came alongside Stefan. 'One of those could be turned to a useful weapon,' he commented, quietly. 'Maybe we have a chance of getting out of here.'

They came level with the guards, and Stefan reached out to take one of the picks. The guard issuing the tools gave him a knowing look and pulled the tool from out of his grasp.

'Not you, friend,' the guard smirked, unpleasantly, then raised his eyes. 'Orders from up above. You don't get one of these, not today, at any rate.' He moved the line along and then gave the pick to a prisoner further down the queue.

'How do you expect us to work then?' Bruno demanded. 'With our bare hands?'

'You learn fast,' the guard replied, sarcastically. 'With your bare hands. The ones with the picks hew the ore, the rest of you gather it up. With your bare hands.'

Stefan counted the guards he could see. There were four of them positioned around the space where the prisoners were collecting their tools. There was a chance that they could overpower them. But only a slim chance. And once they were free, they still had to find their way out of the mines. The only way that Stefan knew to do that was

through the long climb back to the surface, back the way
they had come.

'Even if we could get our hands on a pick we'd be lucky to
make it,' he told Bruno, shaking his head. 'Once we started
to climb out of here they'd have us caught like rats.'

'Then our best hope rests with Rilke,' Bruno said. 'Which
hardly brings me comfort.'

'Nor me,' Stefan agreed. 'But at the moment that may be
all we have.'

'What are we digging for anyway?' he demanded of the
guard. 'If I'm going to break my back in the service of
Sigmarsgeist I'd like to know why.'

'Metal ore,' the guard replied. 'To be forged into steel in
the furnaces above.'

'How much are you expecting us to dig out?' Bruno asked.

'You'll dig till you drop,' the guard told him. 'And then
some. Here,' he thrust a sack into Bruno's hands. 'Get a move
on.'

The line pushed forward, marched briskly on into a linking galley on the other side. The heat, and the reek of the
bodies pressed in all around him, was overpowering. The
guards were herding the prisoners through as quickly as possible, but progress along the galley was still slow. The floor
of the mine was slick and wet, treacherous underfoot, and
the threat of a roof-fall looked ever present. Despite the
order to stay silent, sporadic conversations broke out once
more, as prisoners planned hopeless escapes, or offered
prayers for their gods to intervene on their behalf. A voice
spoke, somewhere right behind Stefan.

'You can believe them about the ore if you want,' the voice
muttered. 'I reckon there's more to it than that.'

Stefan turned in the confined space of the passage, and
glanced over his shoulder. In the flickering half-light cast by
the tallow lamps he could just make out the features of the
man standing a few paces to the rear of him. He remembered that sallow, knowing face. It was the man he had
spoken briefly with whilst they were waiting to be sent to
work on the walls. He looked pale and ill, but for all that
still exuded a stubborn air of survival, a refusal to give in.

'I shouldn't be here,' he reminded Stefan. 'They owe me. It's a misunderstanding.'

'You said as much yesterday,' Stefan responded. 'And something about how you came to be here.'

The sallow man grinned, but there was bitterness in his smile.

'The tattooed one,' he said. 'Damn him to Morr. A blessing that turned out to be a curse, he was.'

'He's lost his mind,' Bruno observed, not without some sympathy for the man.

'I'm not so sure,' Stefan replied. He wanted to hear more of the man's story, but he was too late. The prisoners were being separated out into two work parties. Stefan, Bruno and about a dozen other prisoners were taken down a passage to their right, their new companion taken off in the opposite direction. Stefan caught a brief glance of the flaxen-haired Norscans, towards the tail end of the second work-gang. The bigger of the two men turned, as if sensing Stefan's eyes upon him. He smiled at Stefan, his face registering neither warmth nor humour. Stefan met his gaze for an instant, then, as the guard's whip cracked down, he turned away, following Bruno and the others toward the seam. One less problem to contend with, for the moment at least.

The guards forced the pace as far as they could, but, bent almost double in the half light of the subterranean tunnel, progress was still barely more than a crawl. After about ten minutes the passage opened wide enough for the men to stand upright. Here more guards waited for them and extra lanterns had been set, but there was still barely enough light to work by. The far wall of the chamber had been hollowed out from digging, and hewn stone lay stacked in great piles to either side. One of the guards indicated Stefan and Bruno and several others, the fittest and strongest amongst the gang.

'Don't stand there staring,' he barked. 'This is what you're here for. Those that have picks, use them. Those that don't, use the tools Sigmar gave you. I want at least six sack-loads of ore out of every man today. You others can start carting the loads back to the head of the mine.'

Stefan waited whilst the man ahead of him struck at the rock-face with his pick. The first strike jarred against the solid rock, and made hardly any impact at all. The second dislodged a fist-sized fragment of stone, and the third another piece of about the same size. Stefan and the others moved in, and started to pull out the fragments loosened by the work of the pick. The interior of the mine was already roasting; a hot, stinking pit starved of both light and air. It was going to be slow, exhausting work.

But Stefan's sallow-faced friend might have been wrong about the purpose of the mine. There was certainly ore here, about half the stone quarried out was flecked with a silver metal that shone with a dull lustre in the light of the lanterns. But, for all that, it looked like a poor return. Mining enough ore to fill even half a dozen sacks would take an eternity.

They worked for perhaps an hour under the unwavering gaze of the guards. A good part of the stone quarried out was useless, and at the end of that time Stefan had managed to fill barely half a sack. At some point the guards must have decided that the seam had nothing left to offer. New instructions were issued, the gangs were reassigned a second time, and Stefan and Bruno found themselves separated.

Stefan and five others were led away, deeper into the mine, to where – he assumed – the ore-seam might be thicker. The men squeezed through another tunnel barely big enough to accommodate their bodies, and emerged into a lower chamber that was smaller and darker than the first. By now Stefan's body was drenched in sweat, and his throat parched dry. A flask of water was produced and thrust into his hand, and Stefan drank, gratefully.

It was now so dark that Stefan could barely make out who else was in the chamber with him, or how many. He stumbled, momentarily losing his footing on the slippery granite floor. When he grabbed out to steady himself, a shower of loose rock and stone fell down around him, peppering his face and shoulders. It wouldn't take much for the whole mine to collapse in on itself, and a man could easily end up buried alive.

Stefan looked around, his eyes still battling the gloom, trying to orientate himself. The voices that had been around him a moment ago had dropped away. He had the sudden, disorientating sense of being alone inside the dark cavern of the mine chamber. Then, out of the silence, a voice quiet but clear called out, 'Over here.'

Stefan's first thought was that it was Rilke. He didn't recognise the voice, but it had been in his mind ever since they had entered the mine that Rilke had promised to find them and help them escape. Perhaps this was part of that plan. He couldn't be sure either way, but took a step forward all the same. Somewhere in the space in front of him, someone moved, emerging out of the shadows. He still couldn't make out the figure ahead of him, and he certainly hadn't seen the second, closing in behind.

And he didn't see the knife coming at him until it was all but too late.

ANAISE LOOKED UPON Zucharov, fixing him with an unblinking stare.

'Don't delude yourself,' she told him. 'Your surroundings may have changed, but you are still a prisoner.' She paused, reflecting on her words. 'You are still *my* prisoner.'

Alexei Zucharov returned her stare with his own cold, unblinking gaze. Through him Kyros looked upon the Guide, appraising her with a disdain that he would never confuse with pity. How haughty she was, how proud. How greatly he would enjoy the mighty fall of Anaise von Augen, once her work was done and her purpose spent. But to do that he must win her trust. Kyros would see her drink from the bottomless cup of Chaos, drink with a thirst that could never be extinguished, then they would see who was the prisoner, and who the guardian of the keys.

Anaise had had Zucharov brought to the chamber of the high council. The guards had stood him in the centre of the circle of the council, the dozen places now all empty. Anaise circled slowly around the man who, she had decided, would become her personal slave. In truth, he excited and appalled her in equal measure. Although his body was clearly still that of a mortal man, the sinewy flesh and terrifying musculature reminded Anaise more of an ogre than any human creature.

Then there was the tattoo. The dark, fluid bruise covering Zucharov's left arm, crawling its way slowly up towards his face as if possessed of some malign existence of its own. It was hideous, disfiguring, yet at the same time a work of wonder. Zucharov knew that Anaise was both repelled and yet excited by it. He sensed her longing, her desire to touch the tattoo, to feel the blood flowing in the images beneath her fingertips.

Anaise reached out her hand, then drew back. 'The pictures on your skin,' she said, curtly. 'The pictures of Sigmarsgeist, of my brother Konstantin and me. It's all a trick. How is it achieved?'

Zucharov moved his lips, and the words flowed from him. Slow, awkward at first, but sonorous and clear. They were his words, but they were orchestrated by Kyros.

'It is no trick,' he intoned. 'My flesh is become a mirror to the truth. It reflects all that has come to pass, and all that will.'

'If that is true,' Anaise replied, fighting to hold her excitement in check, 'then you can show me what the future holds for me, and how I am to achieve it.'

'That future is not yet foretold,' Zucharov told her. 'Your destiny is there to be shaped, and for you to choose how to shape it.'

'What choices do I have to make?' Anaise demanded.

Zucharov's face folded into a semblance of a smile that faded almost as quickly as it had appeared. 'You may choose to ally yourself with me,' he said, slowly. 'But I serve no mortal being. I shall not be your slave.'

'And you shall not be my equal, either,' Anaise retorted, indignantly. 'What makes you think you can bargain with me for your salvation?'

'Tal Dur,' Zucharov reminded her, Kyros turning the words carefully upon his servant's tongue. 'Tal Dur, and the knowledge that will allow you to claim the prize that is your right. To allow you to rise above the failings of those around you.'

'Such as?'

'Your brother,' Zucharov replied. 'Konstantin. There is weakness within him.'

'My brother is a righteous man,' Anaise replied, her anger in that moment genuine and impassioned. 'Sigmarsgeist owes him everything. He is its creator, its inspiration.'

'And the architect of its ruin,' Zucharov continued. 'You owe him nothing.'

Anaise rose up, her face a mask of practiced fury. Around the room, guards drew their weapons, anticipating the command. A tense silence hung upon the council chamber. 'You are deluded, and a liar,' Anaise announced. 'The corruptions of Chaos have rotted your mind.' She looked around at the guards, then, dismissed them with a curt sweep of her arm.

'Go,' she told them. 'Leave us. This creature is no threat. His body is weighed down with iron, and his mind is enfeebled. Go about your business, you are dismissed.'

The guards exchanged glances, wondering perhaps if they had misunderstood the Guide's orders. When Anaise said nothing more, but simply folded her arms across her breast, they began, one by one to file out of the chamber. Only when they were gone did Anaise seat herself again.

'How dare you defile my brother's name in their hearing,' she began. 'You claim yourself worthy of my trust, yet at the first opportunity you seek to undermine me. I should have set my men upon you like dogs.'

She glared at Zucharov, her expression a studied mask of angry grandeur. Yet the mask was fragile. Beneath its surface was a curiosity, and an aching need that she already found hard to deny. 'You spoke the name of Tal Dur in their presence,' she added, with less certainty now. 'You are not worthy of my trust.'

Kyros was in no hurry to have Zucharov answer.

'It is those others around you that you cannot trust,' he said at last. 'This is the time of change. The time for old ways to be swept aside, for a new order to be forged. I shall guide you to Tal Dur, and I shall show you how to use its power.'

'I have no need to be taught the ways of power,' Anaise retorted. 'I know how to use it well enough.'

The smile rose again on Zucharov's face, slow and faintly mocking. 'You do not,' he said. He held his hands up in front of his face, the heavy irons glinting in the light. 'You think this is power,' he said. 'You think this is captivity.' Zucharov flexed his wrists, tensing his muscles against the shackles. The iron fastening groaned then suddenly snapped apart. The shattered links sprayed across the floor of the chamber. Zucharov lifted his unfettered arms into the air in a moment of silent triumph.

'It is not.'

Anaise flinched, involuntarily, at the sight of the chain ripped open so effortlessly, but she held her ground, and her voice betrayed none of her anxiety. 'Are you trying to intimidate me?' she asked. 'Perhaps you think you can escape from this place at will?'

Zucharov laughed, the laughter of his dark god, a dry, rattling sound like bones stirring in a grave. 'I will leave this place only when I am ready,' he said. 'And I am not ready yet. As for you, I wish only to show you the true meaning of power. How you may attain it, and what riches it may buy.'

Anaise drank down Zucharov's words. She wasn't sure yet whether the creature of Chaos could possibly be believed. But she knew that she wanted to believe, wanted with a passion that burned inside her. She had been born to power. If Zucharov was right, and Sigmarsgeist and all that Konstantin stood for came to nothing but dust, then her whole life would have been in vain. All of this – Zucharov, Bea, Kumansky and his comrade – had come to pass for a reason. And the reason was surely her. The time of reckoning was close at hand.

But Anaise was not driven by impulse alone. Not for the first time, reason and suspicion intervened. 'You haven't come here to offer me something for nothing,' she said, carefully. 'If you are offering me such riches, then you must want something in return.'

Zucharov nodded once, signalling that he had understood. 'What would you give, my lady Anaise?' His eyes flashed dark thunder. 'What would you give in return for the keys to eternity?'

Anaise hesitated over her answer for just an instant. So far, she might just have been toying with this painted monster. But if she went further, this would be real. A bargain would have to be struck. Did that matter? In her mind she was already envisaging the time when Zucharov would have outlived his purpose. That would be the moment when he would be destroyed. If she turned back now, called back the guards and had him thrown into the cells, it would be over. Zucharov would rot in the dungeons of Sigmarsgeist, and Anaise von Augen would once again be captive to her brother's dreams of – what? Mere survival?

That was not the better world for which she had sacrificed more than ten precious years of her life. That was not the promise that they had made, when the first foundation stone had been laid. Zucharov was right, though she had not conceded it. Her brother had grown weak; his courage and his vision had waned. He could no longer be trusted to carry the hopes of all his people. She must take her destiny into her own hands.

Anaise could still hear the other voices, those warning her to turn back from this course whilst there was still time. But she was no longer listening to their counsel. She had made her decision. In that instant of lightening thought, she had convinced herself. There was nothing to lose, and all eternity to be gained.

'There is a girl,' she said, calmly. 'A healer. She has gifts far greater than she knows. Tal Dur has drawn her here. It is calling to her, and she will heed the call. Her gift can lead me to the well-spring, the source of its magical power.'

She took a deep breath, and parted with the next words as though relinquishing a treasured gift. 'I will share that gift with you,' she said.

Zucharov's expression did not alter. Anaise was disappointed, and angered. It was as if her revelation held no surprise for the tattooed man. Zucharov stood, his head slightly to one side. He was not listening to Anaise now. Her voice faded away as the words of Kyros entered his mind.

*There is more…*

'There is more,' Anaise continued, insistently. 'I have something else to offer you. A chance to purge your past.'

An image flashed into Zucharov's mind, a face drawn from the pool of fading memory that was all that remained of his former life.

'Show me,' he said.

IN AN INSTANT, the other man was on top of Stefan, bearing down upon him in the darkness. Through the gloom Stefan saw the steel blade of the knife and recognised the zigzag scar running down the side of the Norscan's face. It seemed the time had come for the bloody resolution of their differences. Stefan blocked the first blow then stepped out of range of the blade. He was about to strike back at the Norscan when someone took hold of both his arms from behind, holding him as though in a vice. Rancid breath wafted in his nostrils, and a voice, heavily accented, spat out: 'Kislevite scum!'

Stefan struggled to pull himself free, but with his arms pinioned by his side there was little he could do. The guards – either by accident or design – had melted away, as had the other prisoners. He was trapped in the darkness deep below the ground, alone save for two natural enemies who were determined to kill him.

He found some movement in one arm, enough to jab an elbow back into the body of the man holding him. The blow had some force, but it was not enough. The Norscan grunted then redoubled his efforts, gripping hold of Stefan even more tightly. The first man took a step closer. Stefan could see him clearly now, even through the murk of the mine. He was a thick-set man Stefan's own age, or slightly older. His straw blond hair was matted with grease, and his once pale-white complexion was tinged with a faint luminescence, the first glimmering of the evil blooming inside of him. He fixed Stefan with a lopsided grin, and licked his lips. He passed the knife through the air in front of Stefan's face, like a butcher ready to cut away at a carcass.

Satisfied that Stefan was no longer a threat, the Norscan dropped his guard. As he positioned himself to cut Stefan with the knife, Stefan lashed out with his booted foot, putting as much of his weight as he could into a kick placed squarely between the Norscan's legs. The Norscan howled in agony and the knife clattered upon the stones at their feet. With the first Norscan doubled up on the ground in agony, the second was now torn between keeping hold of Stefan, and retrieving the knife. His hesitation was just enough to grant Stefan the space he needed. He clamped his hands around the beefy arms holding him captive, and shifting his weight, heaved the man's body over his shoulders. The Norscan hit the ground hard, causing a storm of grit and stone to hail down from the roof of the cavern. Stefan wiped the filth from out of his eyes and plunged forward towards where he hoped the knife would be.

For a moment there was nothing but confusion, Stefan and the two Norscans all scrambling upon the ground, trying to locate the blade. Stefan found it first, fastening a grip upon the short shank of the weapon and stabbing it up into the face of the Norscan who had been holding him. The man screamed, the sound echoing through the mine, and Stefan's own face was suddenly wet with hot blood. The Norscan fell forward like a toppled oak, on top of Stefan. As Stefan pushed the body aside, he felt something tug at his hand, and in a moment the knife was gone.

The remaining Norscan was on him in a second, stabbing out wildly with the short knife. A thrust missed Stefan's body by less than an inch, deflecting away off the hard rock. As he struck out again, Stefan caught hold of his attacker's wrist with both hands. Now it was a trial of pure strength: the Norscan trying to turn the blade towards Stefan's face, Stefan pushing it back toward the cavern wall. He twisted his body and found room to bring his knee up hard into the other man's gut. The Norscan gasped and flinched back.

Stefan compressed all that remained of his energy into a final push, and slammed the other man's arm against the wall of rock. The Norscan released his grip, and Stefan punched him hard in the face. The blow would have felled an ordinary man but the Norscan hardly flinched. It did buy Stefan enough time to seize the knife. As the Norscan lunged back at him, Stefan thrust the blade squarely into the throat of the other man. There was a moment of almost total silence as the Norscan stood staring at Stefan, blood dribbling from each corner of his mouth. He aimed a last desperate blow at Stefan, a blow that was never struck. The Norscan sank slowly to his knees, and his head dropped.

Stefan watched him for a few moments, then tucked the knife away beneath his tunic. He could hear footsteps now, and voices in the tunnel behind him. He didn't know who it was, and, right now, he didn't care. He had no strength left.

The Red Guards quickly surrounded him, four of them materialising out of the darkness as fast as they had disappeared. One made a cursory check of the Norscans, just to be sure that both were dead. A second kicked out at Stefan, a half-hearted blow aimed at his ribs.

'You were trying to escape,' one of them said, matter-of-factly. 'The punishment is death.'

'I was trying to stay alive,' Stefan shot back. 'I only hope you managed to collect whatever bribe my Norscan friends were offering you.'

'It doesn't matter,' said another, ignoring Stefan's comment. 'All dissent is punishable by death, for the greater glory of Sigmarsgeist. Get him up.'

Two of the guards took hold of Stefan and hauled him to his feet. The knife was plucked away from him in a single, deft movement.

'This time you're lucky,' the same guard told him again. He seized Stefan by the hair, and turned his face towards his own. 'Seems someone wants you back up above,' he said, a vexed curiosity mixed with the anger in his voice. He had the bloodied knife in his hand, but Stefan knew he wasn't going to use it. Not this time.

'Looks like you have friends in high places,' the guard told him. 'Very high places indeed.'

'Better pull yourself together,' the second man advised. 'You're on your way back to the palace.'

# CHAPTER FIFTEEN
## Battleground

STEFAN MADE THE long journey back from the mines alone save for the half dozen silent soldiers charged with guarding him. There had received no word, nor seen any sign of Bruno. They reached the heart of the citadel as dusk fell, and Stefan was led to a cavernous room in the upper reaches of the palace, a place with bare, featureless walls that rose to a high, curved ceiling. Thick ropes hung down from ceiling to floor on pulleys, giving the chamber the appearance of a huge bell tower.

A familiar figure walked towards him. Anaise looked Stefan up and down, taking in his tattered, filthy garments and his bruised and bloodied arms. Her face settled into an expression of compassion and concern.

'Stefan,' she said, softly, as though mildly surprised to see him standing there. 'I'm so heartened to see you still alive and well. I've been worrying about you, and Bea has been too.'

Stefan returned her gaze but not her greeting. He was unmoved by the Guide's show of pity, and in no mood to trade pleasantries. 'Is this how you show your concern? Having Bruno and myself locked up, and trying to have me killed?' he replied, curtly. 'Unless you have something particular to say, I'd rather we waste no more time on this charade.'

Anaise gazed at him, earnestly. 'You know your imprisonment was Konstantin's doing,' she said. 'I had no part in it. As for having you killed – you must believe I know nothing of that. But the mines are a treacherous place. I'm glad I got to you in time.'

'What's all this about?' Stefan asked. 'And where's Bea? What have you done with her?'

'Bea is fine, she is safe and resting,' Anaise assured him, trying to soothe Stefan's anger. 'She has been hard at work, tending to the sick and wounded amongst our workers. Bea is my jewel. She, at least, has embraced the true spirit of Sigmarsgeist,' she added.

Stefan cared only to see this audience over. 'I want to see her,' he said, flatly. 'Bea. I want to see her now.'

'You are in no position to make demands,' Anaise asserted. 'You will see her,' she went on, 'but not just yet.'

'So, what is all this about?'

Anaise expelled a long breath, and took a step closer. She motioned to the guards either side of Stefan, signalling for them to loosen his bonds, and step to one side.

'I want to try and mend our differences, Stefan Kumansky. Settle our misunderstanding.' She sighed again. 'Stefan, Stefan, I had such high hopes of you.' She reached a hand out towards his cheek, but Stefan pulled his face away.

'Our "misunderstanding" began when you and your men started murdering innocent people in Mielstadt,' he snapped back at her. 'Or was it in Grunwald, or some other village that wouldn't pay its dues to Sigmarsgeist?'

Anaise shook her head, sorrowfully. 'I thought you understood,' she replied. 'Clearly, you have not. Those people – the villagers and townsfolk you are so ready to defend – they are like children, Stefan. They need to be shown the true path, they must be guided, and directed.' She bowed her head. 'And, sometimes, when they stray from the true path, they must be punished. Punished for their own good.'

'You do a lot of things for other people's own good,' Stefan commented. 'But I don't hear many extolling the virtue of your good works outside the city. Take me back to the mines, or to your cells. If yours is the true path, then I will take the opposite way.'

Anaise narrowed her gaze, and her expression hardened. The demure, almost diffident manner of a few moments before evaporated. In that instant she was again the ruthless warrior he had witnessed on the plains of Ostermark.

'You will follow *my* way,' she snarled, then hastily added, 'the way of Sigmarsgeist, the true path.' She nodded to the guards standing by. 'You shall follow that path, willingly or not.' She hesitated, apparently lost in thought. Her voice softened once again and she lowered her heavy lids just enough to break the intensity in her eyes.

'But I would that we could earn your will, and your heart.' She moved a step closer. 'When you first came to us, I had you marked for our champion,' she confided. 'With our great vision, and your strength of passion there is little that we could not have achieved.'

She smiled, wistfully. 'It could still be so, Stefan,' she said. 'Just a word from you and all this could be changed.'

'I thought that "all this" was Konstantin's doing,' Stefan reminded her. 'And none of yours.'

'Konstantin is wise, but he has his weaknesses,' Anaise murmured. She took another step towards him, her gaze unwavering, unblinking, upon Stefan. 'With my counsel, he could be persuaded to see things another way.'

Stefan raised his arm, barring her way. The urge to strike out at Anaise was strong, but he held it in check. 'Spare me your favours,' he told her. 'Save your counsel for someone else.'

'Very well,' Anaise replied. 'So be it.' She lifted her gaze from Stefan to look at the domed ceiling overhead. 'In any case,' she said, 'your time has come and passed. I have no need of you now.'

She snapped her fingers and teams of guards at either end of the chamber began to haul back upon the ropes suspended from convex roof of the chamber. The room was filled with a low groaning, the sound of great slabs of stone moving one upon the other.

Stefan looked up and saw the two sides of the domed roof moving apart like a set of mighty jaws unlocking, opening the chamber to the night sky. The huge sliding panels spread apart and fastened into place. A third set of ropes drew down a cantilevered series of steps from the facing wall of the chamber, near the rim of what was now an open parapet.

Under the watchful eye of the Guide, Stefan was led towards the stairway to the stars.

'Please, make your way up' she suggested. 'Don't you have any curiosity?'

'Does it matter whether I do or not?'

She smiled again, more enigmatically this time. 'I promise,' she said, 'there are wonders awaiting you there.'

With sharpened steel a hastening reminder at his back, Stefan began to climb. The ladders bowed and flexed beneath him, but they were sturdy enough to take him safely to the top. As he reached the top of the final section, guards waiting above lifted him clear of the ladders and onto the narrow walkway that ran around the parapet's edge. Stefan looked back down into the chamber. Figures were following him up the ladders: two Red Guards then Anaise herself. Whatever fate now lay in store for him, it seemed he was to have company.

Now he understood where he was. He had emerged on top of one of the cluster of four enormous domes that capped the palace of Sigmarsgeist, the highest point in all the citadel. Three identical structures stood facing him, the four domes forming the points of a square which framed a courtyard far below. Everything had a precise, somehow ominous symmetry. But it was not the domes themselves, nor the courtyard that lay below, that commanded Stefan's attention. It was what lay between the domes, and above the courtyard.

The exterior of the palace was barely recognisable as the building he had seen on his arrival in the citadel. It had been transformed, overlaid almost entirely with a labyrinthine maze of bridges and walkways superimposed upon the existing shell of the building, an alabaster exoskeleton that seemed to glow in the night air. There were walls that jutted out at angles from other walls; bridges that began or ended nowhere, arcing upwards only to stop abruptly in mid-air. There were steps and footpaths that led down into solid ground, and those that climbed up to end in thin air. And between the four domes, where before there would have been clear space, there was now a contorted lattice-work of paths and bridges, linking the domes together like binding weeds. To Stefan it looked like insanity given solid form.

He heard Anaise's voice, close behind him. 'This is the power of Sigmarsgeist, Stefan,' she said. 'A change is coming upon the world. All who will not be part of it will be swept away.'

Stefan gazed upon the scene with stunned wonder, tempered by a growing unease at what the nightmare might yet portend. 'So,' he said at last. 'These are the wonders you were so intent on showing me?'

Anaise's laugh was high, almost girlish. 'More than this.' Her eyes sparkled, expectantly. 'There is something yet more wondrous yet.'

There was a sound – like a footfall or a series of steps – heavy and deliberate upon the walkway, out in the darkness somewhere just out of sight. Stefan turned around quickly, trying to locate it.

The face of the dome that lay directly opposite was splitting open like a shell, the two halves of the golden orb peeling back to reveal the open space below. A figure was climbing up out of the darkness, just as Stefan had done a few minutes before. As Stefan looked on, the hairs on the back of his neck rose up, and a chill dagger of anticipation stroked the length of his spine. The figure stood half in shadow, but Stefan already had no doubt of who it was.

AMIDST THE STORM of confusion that had swept through his inner world, the man that had been Alexei Zucharov was sure of one thing. His journey had reached a decisive point. He was at a crossroads, upon a threshold that, once crossed, could never be regained: a point at which he would leave his old life behind forever, and walk towards the strange land that had become his future.

But he had not finally crossed that threshold, not yet. Some residue of that old life remained, tumbled fragments of memory that held on, worried and tugged upon a place deep inside him like a memory that would not be cast off. Faces of the men who had been his comrades flickered fitfully in his mind like the light fading from dying lamps. The voice inside of him told him these were no longer his comrades, rather his bitter enemies now. Still the faces persisted.

Time and again he had removed from his pocket the scrap of folded paper, a letter, unfinished and never sent, once destined for a loved one now lost forever inside that other life. The name and place had long vanished, but the feeling had not. The feeling was love, a warmth and compassion that disturbed the new Zucharov. It was a last vestige of what he once had been, a reminder, perhaps, of what he could still be. A reminder that there was a war raging at the core of his being that was not yet finally over.

There had been no need for Kyros to explain to him that Sigmarsgeist would be that fateful place, the gateway between his old world and the one that lay beyond. He had seen it from afar, as the bounty hunter Koenig had hauled him in chains towards the city. Sigmarsgeist, the city upon the plain, its spreading mass lit by a phosphor glow that came not from any natural source, but from the tide of elemental energy that raged like a boiling sea below. The sulphurous light would have been invisible to the mortal eye, but Zucharov knew he was not quite mortal any longer. If he was to surrender his soul, then there were things he would gain in return. Zucharov saw the world as no mortal man could, he saw the things that lay below. The engines of the gods, in all their terrible majesty, were laid bare before his gaze.

He had seen his own body change, watched it sometimes with the dispassionate stare of the spectator at a game, sometimes with the dull horror of a man who knew he was losing his very soul. The malignancy of the tattoo would not be suppressed. It now covered his arm and was spreading across his shoulder to his throat and chest. Soon, he knew, it would map his entire body. He knew it was the visible stain of Chaos, the taint of evil by which he was marked for damnation. Whilst he bore the tattoo there was nowhere he could go, nowhere he could hide. His very body now proclaimed him for what he was.

For weeks, since that moment upon the battlefield in Erengrad, Zucharov had raged against Kyros and the dark master that had branded him so. The power over men that Chaos promised him was seductive; the livid mark of mutation was not. Kyros had gifted him the living tattoo. Now it was Kyros that whispered to Zucharov how he could, if he chose, be rid of it. The key, he had told Zucharov, was a place known in legend as Tal Dur. The fathomless waters of the lake held magical powers that would surpass any imagining, power enough to take the strength of a man such as Zucharov and multiply it tenfold. The power to erase all visible sign of the mark upon his body, and the power to wash away all sight of sin.

That was the bargain that Kyros had offered his servant. If Zucharov could find Tal Dur, then, in return, he would be the first to taste its fruits. Thereafter, there would be surely nothing that was not within his reach.

In the meantime, Zucharov had studied the images that danced upon his flesh. The tattoo had foretold his capture by the bounty hunter, and it had foretold that he would come here, to Sigmarsgeist.

Now, as he stepped from out of the shadows, another history was unfolding in the lines melting and reforming upon his skin. A face from memory came into resolution. Zucharov recognised it, knew it was the face of a man he had once called friend. It was the face of the man who now stood no more than twenty yards away from him. He had waited long for this, their final meeting. A meeting that, for one of them, would end only at the gates of Morr, grim God of Death. Zucharov was certain it would not be he who was about to make that final journey.

\* \* \*

STEFAN HAD NOT seen Alexei Zucharov since the battle for Erengrad. Stefan barely knew it then, but, as that battle ended, another was about to begin. The beginnings were there in the first gleaming of madness that shone, faint but insistent, in Zucharov's eyes. It was there in his sudden, violent flight from the city. And it was in the small mark, no more than a bruise, half-hidden beneath the gold band that he wore upon his wrist. Stefan knew that, if ever they met again, he would see a changed man in Zucharov. But nothing had prepared him for the extent of the change that had come upon his former comrade.

Zucharov had grown: physically he had become bigger and stronger. The man that Stefan remembered had been tall and powerfully built, more than a match for all but a few of the bravest men on the field of war. But in the days and weeks since Erengrad, every muscle in his body had expanded, and his frame had stretched and opened as though struggling to contain the awesome physical might within. The creature that was now Zucharov looked less a man than a machine of war designed with one purpose only – to deal death and destruction to any that stood in its way, and deal it without pity or discrimination. Zucharov's deep eyes stared out at Stefan, but there was no warmth, no recognition in the connection they made.

'Is this wonder enough for you, Stefan?' Anaise asked him.

Stefan did not take his eyes from Zucharov for a moment.

'This is beyond your reckoning,' he warned Anaise. 'This man is more dangerous than anything you have ever known. He will destroy you, and all of your works, and leave nothing but dust.'

Anaise laughed, a hollow, mocking sound. 'It's not me he wants to destroy, Stefan.'

Zucharov moved out of the shadows, onto the brittle web of marbled fibres that now meshed the four domes together. With his left hand he drew out his sword, and then Stefan saw the extent of the disfigurement, the dark blemish that reflected the torment that raged within. Tiny figures moved in a macabre dance across Zucharov's flesh. Stefan looked on, mesmerised, horrified. Everything he saw told him that

Alexei Zucharov was no longer human, that every fragment of the man that he had once known as a friend was gone. And yet, as he watched Zucharov step forward, sword in outstretched hand, all Stefan saw was a mirror of his own self: a being driven by an all-consuming, single-purpose. A fierce, unyielding purity of vision, and a will to prevail that would only be subdued by death itself.

He could not believe – was not yet ready to believe – that this was a mirror that reflected only darkness. He called out to Zucharov, the sound of his voice echoing in the night sky high above Sigmarsgeist.

'Alexei.' The word so familiar on his tongue. The prelude to countless shared combats, and many more mugs of beer in celebration of a battle won. The familiar was now the alien, and the battle that lay ahead would be between them, and it would be unto death.

'Alexei! In the name of the gods, don't you know who this is?'

Zucharov paused, his weight balanced precariously on the delicate walkway created by the arch of stone across the space between the two domes. For a moment it seemed as though he *did* remember. His expression shifted momentarily, and a look akin to recognition flickered in his eyes. In that moment Stefan understood that Zucharov's soul was in the balance. The realm of Chaos had not claimed him, not yet. He prayed to the merciful gods that it might yet not be too late, and called Zucharov's name again, this time with greater urgency.

Zucharov turned his head, scanning the open space until his eyes locked with those of his former friend. Stefan would never know what battles raged below those dark pools, what agonies his soul endured as it slowly fell into that chasm of eternal night. The gaze flickered, but when it finally settled upon him once again Stefan knew all would be lost. Alexei Zucharov was gone, and a monster looked out at him through his eyes.

'Stefan.' The word was spoken without warmth. It was statement of fact, an identification rather than a greeting. 'Stefan Kumansky.'

Alexei Zucharov – or the shell of the being that had once borne his name – lifted up his sword and started to cross the newly formed bridge towards Stefan.

Stefan was unarmed. He turned to Anaise, a murderous anger towards her and all the world burning in his heart.

'Is this how you would have it end?' he demanded furiously. 'Am I to be butchered by a man who no longer knows his own mind?'

Anaise simply smiled once again, and tilted her head on one side. Stefan saw something sparkle in the night sky as it spun towards him. He reached out, grabbing the hilt of the sword before it tumbled into the well of the courtyard.

'Now you are evenly matched,' Anaise said to him. 'Now we shall find out where the gods have invested their true power.' She looked from Stefan to Alexei Zucharov, and spread her arms wide. 'Now, my glorious champions. Let the contest begin.'

The lattice of tangled paths and bridges looked too frail to bear Zucharov's weight. Stefan heard it groan and crack as the man who was now his adversary advanced across it towards him. He sized up his options. If it came to a trial of brute strength, then he did not doubt for a moment that Zucharov, with his greater height and bulk, would prevail. Stefan would have to make the most of the advantages that he possessed – agility and speed. The brittle structure spanning the gap between the domes looked precarious by any standards, but, in the circumstances, it might offer Stefan his best hope of equalising the terms of battle. He took a deep breath, and, balancing his sword in his hand, stepped off from the edge of the parapet, and out into the unknown.

Immediately, he could feel it. It was nothing he could see or touch, but Stefan was immediately aware of its force. Something was leaking out of the depths of the ground, oozing from the very fabric of the buildings themselves. An invisible tide of energy, funnelling up into the space between the walls of the palace. He felt it in the shuddering pulse that ran, like a second heartbeat, through his entire body. And he felt it inside his head, an omniscient presence sitting in judgement on the struggle about to commence.

As Stefan stepped forward the walkway shivered and flexed below his feet, rolling like a boat upon the water. He now guessed that the structure was not made from stone at all, but from a substance more like bone, a living, growing substance like the frame of a great skeleton spreading itself across the city. Just for a moment, Stefan held the thought of turning back, but he knew that this remained his best, perhaps his only chance. He was committed now.

The two warriors made their way towards each other, across the skewed and twisting maze that was their battleground. Twice, three times, Stefan lost his footing as the walkway dropped away or twisted suddenly to one side. But step by fateful step, across cracks that widened without warning to yawning chasms, Stefan and his nemesis edged ever closer to their confrontation. At last, all that separated them was a single span of bridge, a brittle ivory spine no more than twelve feet across. Alexei Zucharov took two steps out upon it, and from the other side, Stefan matched him pace for pace. The two were now little more than a sword's length apart.

Stefan weighed the sword in his hand, calculating the angle and speed of his attack. Yet in his heart he was still not ready to believe his comrade had totally surrendered his soul to Chaos. He could not believe there was not still some flickering of humanity remaining somewhere inside Zucharov. He called Alexei's name a second time, and a third, hoping against hope that somehow he could yet connect with the man he had once called his friend.

Zucharov stopped, midway across, his sword frozen in mid-air. The fragile bridge rolled drunkenly under his weight, the whole structure poised between suspension and collapse. Zucharov shifted his balance, settling the bridge. His eyes fell upon Stefan, and recognition flickered, a last guttering flame of kinship between the two swordsmen, then he struck. The big man sprang forward, lithe and supple, quicker than Stefan could possibly have anticipated. Not only was he bigger and stronger than before, but he was also much faster. The one advantage Stefan had held over his former comrade had evaporated before he had cast a single blow.

Stefan retreated under a torrent of strokes from Zucharov's sword. Before he could attack, he had to defend. All his skill was being channelled into simply staying alive. Zucharov's blade slashed through the night air, carving splinters from the shuddering bridge. In no time at all, Stefan had fallen back to the edge of the parapet.

His mind raced through possibilities that grew more limited by the second. He thought about fighting Zucharov on the parapet, with solid ground beneath his feet. But there, with nowhere else to turn, he would surely be quickly defeated. So, with Zucharov still pressing down upon him, Stefan took the only option left, he mounted the side of the bridge, and leapt.

He fell ten feet or more, crystalline filaments shattering beneath his weight before something solid broke his fall. Stefan rolled, and pulled himself quickly upright. Zucharov stood on the bridge above, looking down at him, his face impassive. Then, slowly, methodically, he began climbing down through the labyrinth, scything a path through fibre and bone. Stefan found a place where his footing seemed secure, on a looping segment of path that rose and fell like a serpent's back. This was where he would make a stand. This time the initiative would be with him.

Zucharov dropped down onto the path and charged at Stefan, equally determined that the battle should be ended on his terms. He attacked with the ferocity of a madman, heaving a massive, two-handed stroke that would surely have cut Stefan in two had it connected. But it did not connect, the blade missed its mark by a hair's breadth, and suddenly Stefan had the opportunity to strike back. He dropped his shoulder and aimed a blow through his opponent's open guard.

The sword struck Zucharov at an angle, just below his ribs, but just bounced off. Zucharov barely reacted other than to redouble his own efforts, drawing upon an apparently bottomless well of strength. Stefan found the space for another strike, and again his sword grazed his opponent's tough, leathery flesh and flicked away without appearing to inflict any lasting harm.

Now Stefan was forced back onto the defensive. Under pressure, he managed to hold his ground, trading blow for blow with his adversary as Zucharov tried to power his way through. Stefan was holding him, but knew he could not continue to do so indefinitely. The fifth hammer-blow from Zucharov sent a shockwave of pain flooding through his body. The sixth prised the sword from out of his hand, and sent it sliding away out of reach.

Zucharov took the briefest of pauses then advanced on Stefan to finish things. Stefan glanced over his shoulder only to see that the path behind him had disappeared. There was no escape route. He was trapped between the void and the murderous blade of his opponent.

For the first time, Zucharov smiled. It was a smile devoid of all warmth or human feeling. He lifted his sword to despatch the final blow.

Stefan understood little of the following moment, other than that the world had turned upside down. He was aware of falling through space, and reaching out blindly to clutch hold of something – a strut, or a length of rope – that arrested his fall. By the time he realised that the walkway had spun right over, he was hanging, suspended in mid-air from what was now the underside of the path. He was clawing with his hands, trying to get a grip on anything that could support his weight. But everything that he touched felt white hot, burning with a fierce, unbearable heat. Stefan managed to hold on for a few seconds more, then, with a single scream of agony, he fell.

He fell through clear space for what seemed like an eternity before his fall was broken. The pain of the impact made Stefan want to curl his body into a ball, but he knew he must get on his feet as quickly as he could. He scrambled to his feet, desperately trying to orientate himself, and locate Zucharov. He had no idea how far he had fallen – twenty feet, or a hundred – but he had landed on a wide, circular platform, slightly concave in shape, which had nothing linking it to any other part of the structure. Nothing above or beneath looked familiar, except for the dark outline of the courtyard some distance below. He swung around at the sound of a footstep, and found himself staring directly at Alexei Zucharov. It was impossible. The big man could not have fallen that distance and landed so close by, without Stefan being aware of him. But there was no mistake. There Zucharov was, sword still firmly clamped in his hand, moving forward slowly, purposefully, to complete his task. The turmoil of the last few moments had changed nothing, Stefan was back where he started.

As Zucharov closed in on him, Stefan grasped hold of the only object within sight, a length of railing hanging down just in front of him. As Zucharov struck, Stefan hauled himself up into the air and kicked out with both feet. The blow connected cleanly, striking Zucharov high and square in the chest. Zucharov was caught off-guard, the blow knocked him back, off-balance. The floor of the platform bowed and flexed beneath his crashing weight, before springing back into shape with a supple elasticity. Almost instantaneously, Zucharov was propelled back onto his feet, and Stefan's gain was short-lived. But, whilst he held the advantage, he made it pay. He flung himself at Zucharov in a desperate attempt to wrest the sword from out of his grip.

He threw all his weight behind a punch into Zucharov's face. The big man gave a short grunt of pain, and Stefan knew that he had finally managed to hurt him. He punched again, and a third time, getting his blows in faster than Zucharov could respond. Blood began to flow, a dark red stream trickling from the corner of Zucharov's mouth. But it still wasn't enough.

The wounds that Stefan had inflicted served only to fuel the cold, relentless rage driving Zucharov. He pulled free of Stefan's grip and lashed out, swiping Stefan aside like an insect. Stefan fell heavily, reacting only just in time to roll to safety as the sword scythed down yet again, cracking the bone floor of the platform.

Stefan looked around in desperation for some means of turning the unequal struggle. All the while he was being forced back towards the edge of the platform.

Just when it seemed that Zucharov had him finally trapped, Stefan saw his salvation. A set of steps, like a ladder, zig-zagged out haphazardly from the rim of the platform. He was sure they hadn't been there before. He wasn't sure he could believe what he saw now, but, suddenly, there was perhaps a chance to gain some respite. The ladder looked filament-thin, yet when Stefan stepped back onto it the structure bore his weight without so much as bending. He retreated as fast as he dared, as Zucharov rushed towards him. As the big man set a foot upon the ladder, the brittle surface seemed to shimmer and melt away, and Zucharov was plunged into darkness. Stefan saw him clutch at the edge of the platform like a drowning man. He was holding on, but couldn't pull his body back up.

Stefan was still able to stand firm on the solid section of the ladder. He looked down where the structure had broken apart. Long, ivory shards like spears splayed out at every angle. Stefan leant forward, and broke one off. It was as sharp as any blade. Now he had the weapon, and it was he who had the advantage.

Zucharov stared up at him, his eyes a blaze of anger and confusion. He clawed frantically at the edge of the platform, but could not get enough grip to haul his bulk back up.

*I can end this now*, Stefan realised. *I have been gifted the power.* Somewhere in the darkness above, he was aware of Anaise, her expectant gaze fixed upon the confrontation. He raised the jagged blade, and aimed the point at the base of Zucharov's throat. He stared into his eyes, deep into those dark pools, searching for any last vestige of the man he had once known.

Then a man's voice filled the night air with an angry shout of command. 'Stop this heresy!'

In the same instant, the ledge that Zucharov still clung to gave way beneath him. On instinct, Stefan thrust out his hand, the makeshift sword falling from his grip. He clutched hold of Zucharov as he fell, and held on.

For a few moments the two men were locked together, neither moving. Stefan was only dimly aware of the guards climbing down towards them, and of the man's face that had appeared over the parapet above, next to Anaise.

Konstantin directed the full force of his anger at his sister.

'This abominable charade is now ended,' he proclaimed, furiously. 'Seize these murderous wretches,' he told the gaurds. 'Secure them, and take them from my sight.'

# CHAPTER SIXTEEN
## Forgotten City

KONSTANTIN WAITED UNTIL the last of the guards had withdrawn from his chamber then he turned to face the only person left in the room, his sister. As he began to speak, Konstantin realised that an anger that had been building within him for days, or even weeks, was now finally finding its voice. He had meant to stay calm; he took pride in his reason. But when he finally spoke, it was the rage that won out.

'There must be an end to this madness,' the Guide thundered. 'It must be ended, all of it, now.'

He battled with the fury that burned in his heart, determined to have mastery over his own emotions. Konstantin was a man who prided himself upon order and structure. Everything he believed in, all that he strove for in the building of Sigmarsgeist, was founded on that sense of order, and the need to preserve it in the face of overwhelming odds. Now he saw that order beginning to unravel, being torn apart by a force he could neither control nor comprehend. And his greatest fear was that the locus of this great unravelling was none other than his own sister.

'Madness,' he muttered again, to himself as much as to Anaise. 'And I will see that it goes no further.'

'Brother,' Anaise responded, gently. 'There is no madness other than the anger I see burning in your eyes.' She raised her hand to his face, and placed her cool palm upon her brother's cheek. 'I fear you are being driven to a fever, though none that I can feel,' she said. She tilted her head to one side, her expression quizzical, probing. 'There must not be strife between us,' she continued. 'If the Dark Ones can divide us, then they can destroy us, too.'

'That much is true,' Konstantin conceded. 'But I will not countenance folly such as I have just witnessed. What in the name of Sigmar was in your mind?'

Anaise raised her eyebrow in surprise. 'Nothing but the search for the truth,' she protested. 'Either of these warriors might serve our cause, and serve it mightily. But they are opposed, one against the other. Each has defamed the other. We must decide who is just, and who has deceived us. All I did was place that decision in the provenance of the gods, that they might let justice prevail in combat.'

Konstantin grunted with derision, unconvinced by his sister's oratory. 'Kumansky is a prisoner, guilty of murder. He has had his justice. As for the other – it is there for all to see what he is. The mark of mutation could not be plainer upon him.'

'Nonetheless,' Anaise continued, 'there may be ways in which he can serve. For the glory of Sigmarsgeist.'

'The glory of Sigmarsgeist is already tarnished!' Konstantin shouted at her. He pointed across the city, towards the tangled mass of structures choking the life from the citadel. 'I have kept my counsel for long enough. Too long,' he reflected, with bitterness as well as anger. 'Too long I have played the loving brother, indulging his sister's magical designs. Designs, you tell me, that will hasten the rise of Sigmarsgeist as a great power.'

In a sudden fit of anger he seized hold of his sister, and forced her to the window.

'Is *this* our great design?' he demanded of her. 'Is this what our glory has come to?'

'It is none of my doing,' Anaise responded coldly, shrugging him off.

'Are you saying it is mine?'

'You are the architect of Sigmarsgeist,' she told him. 'Are you now disowning the fruits of your designs?' When Konstantin did not respond, she continued, her tone more conciliatory. 'Listen,' she urged. 'There is a magical energy at work here, a power beyond our understanding. It is the same elemental power which drew us to Sigmarsgeist, and led us to set our first stones here. Without it, Sigmarsgeist would be nothing, just another pitiful village huddled upon the windswept plain.' She drew her brother to one side and led him back to his seat, her hands resting gently on Konstantin's shoulders. 'It is true this energy works in ways we cannot always control. But I shall master it in time, dear brother, you may be assured of that. The elemental forces shall serve Sigmarsgeist, just as we have harnessed mortal will. You must be patient, brother,' she insisted, 'and you must place your trust in me.'

Konstantin took Anaise's hand from his shoulder, and stroked it absent-mindedly. His sister could use words with the guile of a conjuror, and he knew he was being cleverly placated. But it was not a disagreeable experience, and he felt himself growing calmer. When he looked up at her again, he was unable to suppress a momentary smile.

'Your champions would have torn each other apart like dogs had I not intervened.'

'Maybe so,' Anaise agreed, non-committally. 'As it is, they both survived.'

Konstantin pondered for a while. 'No reason why Kumansky cannot be put back to work,' he said at length. 'There is use in him yet awhile, I imagine.'

Anaise said nothing, but nodded her head in agreement.

'But the one marked by Chaos is too dangerous,' Konstantin went on. 'He must stay in captivity. Unless you would have our physicks make examination of him?'

'Neither,' Anaise replied curtly. Konstantin's eyes widened in surprise. Anaise's expression hardened. 'There are things best left to my domain,' she told him. 'Things that you do not understand. You must hold your trust in me,' she said again. 'Only then will all that is promised come to pass.'

THE DESCENT BACK into the mine was little more than a blur to Stefan. His body was suffused with pain, and it took all of what little strength remained for him to safely negotiate the ropes and the steep iron ladders as he worked his slow progress down below ground. The guards gave him no quarter, nor did he expect any. But once, when he faltered upon the step and seemed about to fall, one of the men in red thrust out an arm to steady him. They don't want me dead just yet, Stefan realised. There was a purpose to this that had not yet been revealed.

Rather than being put straight to work, he was taken first to a chamber, not much more than a large, hollowed-out cave, deep in the interior of the mine. This was where the prisoners waited to be assigned to their duties and, whilst they could, take some rest. From the stink of unwashed bodies carried by what little air wafted through the gloomy galley, Stefan could tell the place was already well-stocked. He stumbled over a line of prostrate prisoners then collapsed upon the first clear space he came upon. His body had nothing left to give. The fight with Zucharov had taken him to his limit. He could think of nothing except that he had had a chance to end it, and he had not taken it. Only time would tell how costly his indecision would prove.

He stretched out as best he could, and groaned despite himself. At that moment he felt a cloth pressed lightly to his brow, and some of the pain was eased.

'Merciful Shallya,' he muttered. 'Is that you, Bea?'

'Hardly,' a voice replied. 'But the comparison flatters me.'

'Blood of the just,' Stefan exclaimed. 'Bruno.' He opened his eyes, and saw his companion standing over him. Bruno was bruised and filthy, but he had a great grin upon his face.

'Thank the gods, Stefan! Thank the gods, you're safe.' Bruno embraced his comrade joyfully. 'When you didn't return from the mine, I was filled with all manners of hopes and fears. Hope, perhaps that you had met with Rilke, and found a way out.'

'No sign of Rilke,' Stefan said. 'But there's something more–'

'Wait a moment!' Bruno interjected, abruptly. 'In Taal's name,' he said, 'What am I thinking of?'

'What is it?'

'News,' Bruno told him. 'Important news. I've been talking to our friend over there–' He broke off abruptly. Stefan looked up as a guard passed by, probing and prodding at the exhausted prisoners with his staff. The guard met Stefan's eye for an instant and then moved on.

Bruno lowered his voice to a whisper. 'I've been talking to our friend over there…' He pointed towards a figure sitting hunched by the thin light of a tallow lamp. Stefan recognised Lothar Koenig.

'The fellow we were talking to before. The one who thinks his captivity is just a big misunderstanding,' he said.

Bruno nodded. 'He wants out all right,' he said. 'And he's not stupid. He's guessed we're planning to get out. I think he wants us to take him with us.'

'Is that all?'

'No,' Bruno replied, breathlessly. 'It's not. This man's a bounty hunter. He brought a prisoner here to Sigmarsgeist, hoping to sell him. And not just any prisoner, Stefan. It sounds like it might be–'

'Zucharov? You're right, my friend. Alexei is here, in Sigmarsgeist.'

Bruno pulled back, astonished. 'You've seen him?'

'More than seen him,' Stefan replied. 'I've come within an inch of losing my life to him.'

'Taal's breath, where did this happen?'

Stefan paused, waiting for the guard to pass out of earshot. 'In the palace,' he whispered.

'The palace?' Bruno replied. 'Do the Guides know of this?'

'More than know of it,' Stefan told him. 'My meeting with Alexei was contrived. A little sport for Anaise von Augen.'

Bruno shook his head. 'Then there is a darkness falling over Sigmarsgeist.' He looked up, a flicker of hope passing across his face. 'In the palace – did you get any news of–'

'Of Bea? I'm sorry, no,' Stefan said. 'Though there is no reason to suppose her harmed. Not so long as she's useful to them.'

'I must go back for her, Stefan,' Bruno said. 'I must find a way. I vowed to do as much.'

Stefan's reply was cut short by a command shouted out by one of the soldiers standing close by. All around, the prisoners that had been sitting gnawing bread, or trying to get some sleep now began to stand up, and form into a weary line near the entrance to the chamber.

'Come on, you filthy rabble,' the guard shouted out. 'Work's barely begun.'

Stefan and Bruno were shoved forward, into the waiting line. Stefan sought out the shuffling figure of Lothar Koenig, a few paces ahead of them. He pushed his way through the slow-moving line until he was shoulder to shoulder with the bounty hunter. Koenig looked as if he'd aged several years since Stefan had last seen him. His back was bowed, and he walked with a heavy limp. The steely determination in his eyes had dimmed, but it was still alive.

'Quickly,' Stefan said to him. 'Before they split us up. Tell me about the man you brought here. The mutant.'

Lothar weighed Stefan up carefully. For a moment he was no longer a prisoner, but Koenig the bounty hunter, Koenig the opportunist. 'Everything has a price,' he said. 'Even down here.'

'What's yours?' Stefan demanded.

'Company,' Lothar told him, simply. 'If you're planning to escape – and don't tell me you're not – I want you to take me with you.'

'Maybe,' Stefan replied. He exchanged glances with Bruno.

'You wouldn't regret it,' Lothar boasted. 'I'm a useful man to have on your side. The best tracker this side of the Grey Mountains.'

'Tell us about the mutant, Zucharov,' Stefan said. 'How did he come to be your prisoner?'

Lothar drew himself up, painfully, to his full height. A look of bravado flickered momentarily on his face, then vanished as he let out a long sigh. 'I suppose if I told you

I bettered him in combat, you wouldn't believe me,' he said.

'I wouldn't. And I don't,' Stefan confirmed. 'You'll have to do better than that.'

Koenig sighed again. 'I'm a survivor, friend,' he said, looking around him. 'As Sigmar is my judge, I'll survive this, somehow I will. But I swear, the tattooed mutant could have torn me apart at any time of his choosing.'

'You're telling us he *let* you capture him?' Bruno asked. 'Let you bring him here?'

Koenig nodded. 'That's how it seemed to me.'

'Then it's no accident that he's here,' Stefan said. 'There is a purpose to it.'

'There's a purpose to everything, friend,' Koenig agreed. 'If only we can find it.' He smiled, enigmatically. 'And I can find anything, given time. I'll find a way out of here. Wait and see.'

The line of prisoners ahead of them came to a halt. They had reached the bottom of a shallow slope, leading to a quarry face. Men were being set to work, pounding at the ore with their picks, gathering it into barrows and sacks with their bare hands.

'Here we go again,' Bruno muttered.

Stefan saw a figure wearing the white of the elite guard step from the shadows and speak to two of the Red Guard standing on watch at the head of the line. As the man turned towards the light, Stefan recognised Rilke. The White Guard ran his eye along the line of prisoners until he found Stefan standing with Bruno towards the back.

'Those are the ones,' he said out loud. 'Those two. Bring them out here.'

The Red Guards moved forward and hauled Stefan and Bruno out of the line, marching them across to where Rilke stood, arms folded across his chest. Rilke dismissed the guards with a curt nod.

'Plotting another insurrection?' Rilke accused them loudly. 'How did you think you were going to get away with it?'

'If you plan to have us killed just get on with it,' Bruno countered, angrily. 'Don't waste our time with imaginary plots.'

Rilke seized hold of Bruno and pulled him closer. He lowered his voice to a whisper. 'I said I would get you out of here and I will,' he said. He looked to Stefan. 'I hadn't bargained for Anaise's little diversion with you. This may be our only chance.'

'Why should we trust you?' Stefan asked him. 'How do I know this isn't another attempt to put a knife in my back?'

'You don't know anything,' Rilke said. 'But you don't have much choice, do you?'

Stefan looked around. One of the guards at the head of the line was keeping a wary eye on the conversation, one hand hovering over his sword.

Stefan had no reason to trust Rilke but right now, there was no other choice but to trust the man. 'Very well,' he said. He saw Koenig on the fringe of the group of prisoners, still looking in his direction. 'That man over there,' he said to Rilke. 'He comes too.'

A look of disbelief passed over Rilke's face. 'Are you mad? I'm risking my life just trying to get the two of you out.'

'One more won't make any difference,' Stefan insisted. From the corner of his eye, he saw the watching guard unsheath his sword.

'Very well,' Rilke snapped. He gestured, impatiently, for Koenig to be pulled from the line. Two guards stepped forward to seize the bounty hunter. Koenig made a convincing show of resistance as he was pulled, kicking and protesting his innocence, towards the waiting Rilke.

'A third conspirator,' Rilke announced. He struck Koenig hard upon on the side of his face, stifling his protests. 'Get the rest of them to work,' he told the guards. 'I'm taking these ones back above.'

'You'll need an escort,' a guard said, half as a question and half as a statement of fact. Rilke held his sword out for the Red Guard's inspection. He glowered at the other man.

'Are you suggesting I can't take care of these wretches on my own?'

The guard shook his head, vigorously. 'Just orders, that's all.'

'Forget orders,' Rilke barked back at him. 'I can take care of them.'

The guard wavered for a moment, but finally shook his head. 'Best I come with you, all the same' he said, emphatically. Rilke stared back and him, and shrugged.

'As you will,' he said, and prodded Koenig with his sword. 'Get moving,' he snapped. 'Get moving, all of you.'

ALEXEI ZUCHAROV WATCHED Anaise like a hawk. He recorded every gesture of her hand, every movement, every line that animated her face. And, as he watched her, so the Chaos Lord Kyros watched too. Watched, and bided his time. The net was tightening.

The chamber they had gone to was within Anaise's own private quarters. This was a place where Konstantin and his guards would not, dared not go. But Zucharov was unsure of his status now. Had the words that Kyros crafted for him done their work? Did Anaise now accept him as her consort, her advisor or was he still a prisoner? The armed men she had posted around the room and beyond the closed doors did not suggest she considered him free to come and go as he pleased.

'Why did you allow the combat to be ended?' Zucharov demanded.

'To appease Konstantin,' Anaise responded. 'We must tread carefully around my brother. He does not understand, not yet.'

Zucharov felt the anger chafing at him like a wound which would not heal. 'I should have killed him,' he said, slowly. 'Kumansky. It was my right. My destiny.'

'It did not look that way to me,' she retorted. 'Kumansky had outwitted you. You were at his mercy. Perhaps you should be grateful to Konstantin for intervening when he did.'

Zucharov wanted to punish her insolence, but knew that Kyros would not allow him, not yet. He felt the hand of his master, reining in his desires. His face lifted up, and his eyes rolled back in his head. Kyros had nearly total mastery of him now, able to orchestrate his every word and movement.

Zucharov looked around the room, his gaze taking in the guards standing with their swords held upright, each man waiting on his mistress's command.

'There are some amongst you that you can no longer trust,' he said at last.

Anaise looked at him, quizzically, then realised that Zucharov was referring to her own men. She stepped closer, almost within touching distance.

'The soldiers of Sigmar have served me faithfully,' she said. She laughed, but the laugh caught in her throat, giving lie to her confident manner. 'What are you saying?' she demanded. 'That someone here is going to betray us?'

Zucharov closed his eyes. From deep within him, Kyros reached out, his sightless gaze spanning both past and future, tracking the futile endeavour of mortal souls as they struggled against inevitable fate. In that brief, flaring moment of clarity, everything was clear, and everything was known to him.

Zucharov opened his eyes, and looked down on Anaise. A faint, sardonic smile appeared upon his face.

'You have already been betrayed,' he said.

THEY WALKED, AND sometimes crawled, through the cramped, airless passageways for the better part of an hour, until they reached a shaft leading up to the next level of the mine. Rilke lifted his lantern to indicate the ladder.

'You first,' he said to the guard.

The guard looked up at the ladder then back to Rilke, keeping one eye fixed upon Stefan and the others. 'You go first, then the prisoners,' he said. 'Once you reach the top, I'll follow.'

'Of course.' Rilke forced a smile, and laid a friendly hand on the man's shoulder. 'What am I thinking of?' He steered the guard away from the ladder, and, in the same movement, turned in slightly. Stefan saw the brief flicker of steel in Rilke's right hand, then the guard's eyes widen in sudden alarm. He started to call out, but it was a gushing purple tide of blood, not words, that spilled from his mouth.

Rilke cleaned the knife carefully on the dead man's tunic, and went to tuck it beneath his belt. He hesitated, then offered the blade to Stefan,

'You're probably going to need this,' he said, 'and this.' He held out the lantern.

'By the time this wick has burnt down a finger's width,' he said, 'I'll have raised the alarm. You overpowered both of us,' he looked down dispassionately at the crumpled body at his feet. 'This poor wretch got the worse of it.' He bent down, and gently extracted the sword from the dead man's grip. 'You'd better take this as well,' he said. 'There's no telling what lies ahead for you now.'

'Armed or not, how are we going to get out of the mine?' Bruno asked, still suspicious. 'The place is thick with guards, all the way to the top.'

'You don't go up,' Rilke told him. 'You go down.' He indicated with his lantern. 'Take the passage off to your left. It works its way along for about a quarter of a mile, then comes to a dead end.'

'A good place to die, trapped like a rat,' Bruno commented, sourly.

'There you'll find rubble that's been hewn from the rock face,' Rilke continued, ignoring Bruno. 'Hidden underneath there's a plate, a trapdoor. It hasn't been opened in a while, but you should still be able to prise it free.'

'And underneath?' Stefan asked.

'A shaft, just about big enough for a man to pass through. Climb down it, and you will be in the tunnels which once formed part of the old city.'

'The old city? You mean the original foundations of Sigmarsgeist?'

'No,' Rilke shook his head. 'The rulers of Sigmarsgeist were not the first to build here. As the foundations were dug, they came upon the ruins of another city, long since abandoned or destroyed.'

'Who built this other city?'

'No one now knows for sure,' Rilke replied. 'Perhaps they were people not unlike the Guides. Perhaps they too had dreams of a great citadel, a bastion to protect them against evil. But the underground tunnels are all that remain now, and they will not survive long. Soon the seam that lies directly above is going to be mined. The shaft will be buried and access to the old tunnels will be lost forever. This is your only chance.'

'Doesn't sound like much of a chance,' Bruno commented. 'How can we find our way through?'

'Head due north,' Rilke said. 'That is, directly away from Sigmarsgeist. Find the routes that take you upwards, towards the surface. Some will be impassable, but a few, I know, are still open.'

'If there's a path, I can find it,' Koenig said, confidently.

'You must leave now,' Rilke said. 'Time is running out.' He held out the lamp. 'Take this. There should be a good hour's worth of light in it. Then you're on your own.'

Stefan took the lantern. 'It seems we misjudged each other.'

'One last thing,' Rilke said. He took a step towards Stefan, his hands down by his sides. 'Hit me,' he instructed him, 'and make it look convincing.'

Stefan hesitated, momentarily disarmed by the request. 'Not long ago I'd have gladly done so,' he reflected.

'Then act on that memory.' Rilke offered his head to one side. 'My very survival may depend upon it.'

# CHAPTER SEVENTEEN
## The Wakening Beast

KONSTANTIN VON AUGEN stood, as he had on countless mornings before, on his balcony high on the east face of the palace, looking out across the ever-growing expanse of Sigmarsgeist. Through the last decade of his life, the sight of the citadel growing from a scattering of flimsy homes into a vast, impenetrable fortress had filled him with joy, and with hope for a future world to come. It had seemed to him as though he were standing upon the threshold of a new age. But today there was no joy, and his hope was strangely muted. Today his heart was heavy, and he could not envisage when, or even if, that burden would ever lift.

This cold early morning he seemed to see Sigmarsgeist as he had never seen it before. The citadel was his: Sigmarsgeist was his creation, his child. But now, with the wind blowing off the hills setting a cruel chill into his limbs, he began to see that creation for what it truly was. Instead of order, he saw anarchy. He counted dozens of new houses and workshops which had not existed the day before, new buildings that had sprung up across the city almost literally overnight. But equally there were dozens more that appeared to have been destroyed for no reason, burst open like cracked, discarded shells and new, half-finished structures emerging from the ruins like jagged teeth.

The streets of the city were full, as they always now seemed to be. But where before Konstantin had seen only labour and purposeful endeavour, he now saw discord and strife. Men and women clashed upon the roads and walkways of the citadel, elbowing one another out of the way, jostling for what limited space remained. So many people, too many. He could hear their voices raised, a tumult of sound rising to the high towers of Sigmarsgeist. And what for so long had sounded in his ears as exaltation now rang with bitter anger. He saw the White Guard amongst them, staffs and clubs raised as well as voices. Many he no longer recognised. Even the guard were passing beyond his control.

Most of all, wrapped around nearly two thirds of the city like a choking weed, were the structures of fibre and bone that no mortal hand had built. Walls that blocked off streets; walkways and bridges that ended in empty space. Flights of steps that vanished into the ground without entrances or exits. A madness had seized hold of Sigmarsgeist, a touch of Chaos, and this was its physical form.

Had it come so suddenly, or had the change been so gradual, so stealthy, that it had crept upon him without his noticing? Or was it simply that he had tried so hard, and for so long, not to see what was unravelling before his very eyes?

The wind gusted, raw and hard against his face, and Konstantin felt a tear cold upon his cheek. There was more, something in its way, almost worse. Konstantin had lived his life battling adversity and disappointment, but betrayal had always wounded him most deeply of all. And this wound went to his very core. He had trusted this man above all others, a man who had been his lieutenant and his confidant. After Konstantin's own death this man might have carried the torch of Sigmarsgeist in the darkness. But if what Anaise had told him was true, Konstantin had been truly deceived. His trust had been extinguished like a flame, and now hope itself was starting to die.

He turned at the sound of knocking, then the door to the chamber opened. Rilke appeared in the doorway, with two of the Red Guard in close attendance. His normally austere countenance had given way to look of confusion and alarm, and he wore a crude bandage above one eye.

'My lord,' Rilke began, 'I bring news–'

Konstantin held up his hand, stopping Rilke's words. He looked at the scarlet-clad soldiers standing on either side. 'Where are your own men, Rilke?' he asked, his voice cold and dispassionate. 'Where are the White Guard?'

'My lord, my men cannot be found,' Rilke told him. 'But be assured, I shall account for them before long.' He paused, and took a breath. 'But first you must know–'

'I already know,' Konstantin interjected. 'I already know that the prisoners, Kumansky and his comrade, have escaped from the mine and that they overpowered you and your men. I have already heard your hollow apology. Spare me your disgusting fabrication.' He gripped the arms of his chair and, slowly, lowered himself into a seated position.

'I do hope that earning your wound did not cost you too dearly.'

Rilke made no reply. He heard footsteps from the corridor outside, marching towards the Guide's chamber. This time there was no announcement before the doors were flung wide.

Anaise entered, flanked by six or seven men wearing the white of the elite guard. Rilke stared at them, taking in the pale, Norscan faces; their skin the colour of winter. They stared back at him with a look of open disdain.

'These are not my men,' Rilke protested.

'You have no men,' Anaise told him. 'You have no one to protect you any longer.'

Another figure now entered the chamber, a huge, imposing man. Rilke and Konstantin looked in astonishment at Alexei Zucharov. The tattooed mutant had no shackles upon his arms or legs to temper his frightening power. Instead of chains he bore steel armour – a breast-plate fastened upon his chest, and a broadsword at the belt about his waist. He stood amidst the white-clad guards, his posture proclaiming his authority over them.

All colour had drained from Rilke's face.

'What is he doing here?'

'He?' Anaise responded. She smiled, first at her brother, and then at Rilke. 'He is your executioner,' she said.

LOTHAR KOENIG STARED at his two companions in mute disbelief. 'You want to go *where?*' he asked.

Up to that point – from his perspective at the very least – it had gone perfectly. He hadn't trusted the man the others called Rilke one jot, but he had been as good as his word, Lothar had to give him that. The journey through the mine had been difficult – rock spills and fallen roof beams threatening their progress every inch of the way. But when they finally reached the far, dead end of the gallery, everything had been as Rilke had described it. Buried beneath a carefully placed slew of rocks they had found a hatchway which led, quite literally, to another world. Once down the angled set of steps – a stone stairway that had not seen use in several years – they had found themselves in a network of old, abandoned tunnels that had once served another, far older settlement.

'Sewers, probably,' Bruno had offered, speculating about their use. 'But bone dry now.'

Lothar Koenig didn't care what they had once been, so long as they could now lead him back towards sunlight, clean air and freedom. Again, it had been exactly as Rilke had described it. The tunnels splayed off at different angles and in various directions, some boring deeper into the ground, but others following a gentle incline towards the surface. Lothar could swear he could see daylight, or at the very least, smell it. His sense of direction was unerring; he was confident he could find a way back to the surface in a matter of hours. It came as a shock to him when Stefan told him he had no intention of going that way.

'We're heading back into the citadel,' Stefan repeated. 'We're going to try to find a path through the ruins of the old city that will lead us back into the heart of Sigmarsgeist.'

'Right under its belly,' Bruno added.

Lothar spread his arms as wide as the narrow passageway would allow. 'Why?' he asked.

'Because we have friends there,' Stefan told him, 'and enemies. And unfinished business that concerns both. We're going back.'

'You're an excellent scout, you told us as much yourself,' Bruno continued. 'You could lead us there.'

'Or I could not!' Lothar laughed. 'I could leave you here to wander around lost in the darkness until you died of starvation. And more fool you for not getting out of this Morr-forsaken hole whilst you still had the chance. Look,' he said, 'your friend Rilke was telling the truth. I reckon I can use these old tunnels to find our way out. Three or four hours, five at most and you can be breathing fresh air and soaking up the sunlight. Think about it.'

Stefan thought about it. He had no particular wish to stay with Lothar Koenig, and if the bounty hunter wanted to get out now, he wasn't going to stop him. But finding their way back towards the city through the maze of derelict tunnels underground wasn't going to be easy by any means. Stefan knew they were going to need all the help they could get.

'Listen,' he said at last. 'If you want to go on alone, then go. But what will be waiting for you, up there?'

'The rest of my life, hopefully.'

'I thought you said you were still owed something,' Stefan continued. 'Walk away now and you'll have nothing. Come with us, and – who knows? We don't intend to come out of this empty handed, do we Bruno?'

'Forget it,' Bruno advised. 'He's a man who doesn't want to take a risk. Who can blame him?'

'I've known more risks than you've had pots of ale,' Lothar countered, bridling at Bruno's suggestion. 'And don't you forget it.'

Stefan turned away to survey the path ahead. 'Well,' he said. 'Do whatever you want. We go this way, back to the citadel.'

'You'll never find your way without me.'

Stefan shrugged. 'It seems we don't have a choice. Ready?' he asked Bruno.

'As I'll ever be.'

'Just a moment.' Lothar called them back. 'Just let me think about this. If you're going to throw away the chance of getting out of here to crawl through some monster-infested sewer, just to get back inside Sigmarsgeist–' he stopped short. 'Well, you're either mad, or there's something worth going back for.'

'Fair assessment,' Stefan agreed. 'I suppose you'll never know which.'

'Wait,' Lothar insisted, catching hold of Bruno. 'What are you going to do if you do get back in there? What about your tattooed friend, for example?'

Stefan stood facing the bounty hunter in the darkness. He knew the answer, but bringing the words to his tongue acknowledged a hard truth.

'I'm going to have to kill him,' he said at last.

'Oh yes?' Lothar snorted, incredulously. 'And I suppose you're going to bring down the city whilst you're about it?'

'That's the general idea,' Bruno concurred calmly. 'There should be plenty of spoils for the likes of you in the process,' he added.

'So,' Stefan said. 'Are you with us, or not?'

Lothar stared down the length of the tunnel that, not so far ahead, would surely lead to freedom... and hunger... and poverty. He drew down a lungful of air, savouring its smell, savouring the prospect of what might now never be. Then he turned about and walked on ahead of Stefan, taking the tunnel that tracked not north, but due south, back towards the heart of Sigmarsgeist. He was already regretting the decision he was about to make. But he was going to make it, all the same.

'Best get going,' he muttered, mostly to himself. 'After all, we all have to die sometime.'

ANAISE CLASPED HOLD of Bea's face, forcing the girl to look at her. 'However much you may wish it not to be true, it is nonetheless,' she insisted. 'Your friends have abandoned you.'

Bea tossed her head angrily, eager to prise herself away from Anaise's grip. The other woman was as strong as a warrior, but at last she let the healer go.

'How do you know this?' Bea demanded, haughtily. 'Did Stefan and Bruno come and tell you as much themselves?'

'They had no need to,' Anaise countered, her voice rising. 'We have snared their accomplice, Rilke,' she went on, bitterly. 'That wretched worm who sat for so long at Konstantin's side, whispering his lies in my dear brother's ear, poisoning his heart against all wisdom.' Anaise brought her hand down hard upon the table, scattering crystal glasses upon the floor. 'Well,' she said. 'He'll whisper his lies no more. Now he'll pay a reckoning for all of them.'

Bea shook her head, incredulous. 'Rilke was no friend to Stefan and Bruno,' she said. 'They had him marked as their enemy before any other man here in Sigmarsgeist. Why would I believe such a story?'

'Believe what you want,' Anaise snapped back. 'The proof is rotting even now in the cells. As for your friends, they are gone. Already far from here, eager to save their own skins.'

'Then I am glad,' Bea said. 'Glad that they are free. Stefan and Bruno were unjustly accused, and wrongly punished for their deeds. I pray that they find freedom far from this place.'

Anaise spun round on Bea, and for a moment seemed about to strike her. Then she pulled back. The Guide's face softened, and her voice took on a gentler tone.

'Bea,' she remonstrated, gently. 'We must not let these things divide us. We are sisters, you and I. Sisters joined by our pledge to bring the healing might of Tal Dur to Sigmarsgeist.'

Bea would not be placated. 'You do not understand me, and you do not understand the forces of Tal Dur. It is not a gift to be tapped, like the water in a barrel. And you cannot use me as your vessel, to channel it here.'

'Then take me to the place where Tal Dur lies,' Anaise said, eagerly. 'Let us travel together, you and I, for as far as it takes.

And let us worship together at the source of its divine power.'

'I cannot do that,' Bea replied, defensively. 'Truly, I cannot.'

'You can!' Anaise insisted. 'All you lack is true belief. Surrender yourself to Tal Dur, and it will surely draw you to its heart.'

'For what purpose?' Bea asked her. 'So that the waters may wash away the evil that has taken hold of Sigmarsgeist?'

This time Anaise did strike out, lashing Bea across the face with the back of her hand. Bea cried out in pain and surprise, but her eyes still held their look of defiance.

'I mean what I say,' she blurted out. 'You only have to look with your own eyes to see what is happening around you. You are becoming that which you claim to oppose.'

Anaise stepped forward and touched her hand, gently this time, to Bea's face. 'I wish that I had one tenth of your powers, Bea,' she murmured. 'For I would heal the hurt I inflicted on you. And I would heal this terrible rift that threatens to come between us. Will you not put it aside? The only evil here is for us to be set against each other.' She stroked Bea's cheek. 'I implore you, Bea, let us be friends once again.'

Bea shook herself free. 'You do not want my friendship,' she retorted. 'You only want what you think that friendship can bring you.' She wiped a tear from her face. 'If I am to be prisoner here, then I will be a prisoner on my own terms.' She pulled away from Anaise. 'Whilst the sick and the weary are put to work in your mines, and upon the walls, then I will tend to them.'

Anaise made no attempt to stop her leaving. 'You are truly a daughter of the goddess,' she avowed. Bea stopped in the doorway, her body shaking with anger and despair. 'The Goddess Shallya would surely weep to find me here,' she said.

Anaise watched her go, a smile still playing upon her lips. 'The goddess may weep all she likes,' she murmured, 'but, wherever you go, it is Tal Dur that will find you before long.' She lifted a looking-glass to her face, and studied her reflection in its silvered pane. 'And, rest assured, I will be there when it does.'

\* \* \*

THE LANTERN HAD finally given out. Now they would have to rely on whatever they could find to burn to give them light to find their way. Fortunately, or so it seemed, there was plenty of fuel to hand.

'It doesn't make sense,' Bruno said, surveying the mess of broken, desiccated timbers that lay around the floor of the tunnel. 'You'd think a great storm had raged through here, destroying everything in its path.' He prised another length of wood free of the debris, and lit it from the remnant of the last. The flame welled up, light filling the interior of the tunnel.

'Unlikely,' Stefan commented. He breathed in another lungful of the stale, foetid air. 'I wouldn't have thought anything had stirred down here for a generation.'

A few yards further on they found the first of the bodies, or what was left of them.

Stefan knelt amongst the soft earth, and turned the remains of the corpse between his hands. Apart from some bleached and pitted bones, and a few strands of rotted cloth, there wasn't all that much left.

Bruno whistled softly. 'I wonder what got the better of him?' he asked.

'Time, amongst other things,' Stefan replied. 'I'd say he or she has been dead a good few years.'

'But what were they doing down in a sewer?'

'The same as us?' Stefan answered. 'Trying to get in – or out?'

'Maybe,' Bruno conceded. But he didn't sound convinced.

Further down the tunnel they found more debris of the human kind. A second skeleton, this one more complete than the first. Bruno crouched down and studied the remains in silence for a few moments.

'It's odd,' he said, eventually. 'Look at the way this one seems to be gripping hold of the sides of the tunnel. Almost as though they were desperately trying to hang on to something when they died.'

Stefan looked. These were old bones, much like the first skeleton they had found. It seemed unlikely they would give up their secrets now. But Bruno was right. The fleshless hands did indeed seem to be clinging on to the wall of the tunnel, clinging with a desperation which seemed at odds with the lonely stillness of the place now.

'This doesn't feel good,' Lothar grumbled, still regretting his earlier decision. 'I should have followed my head way back there instead of letting you talk me into this.'

Stefan clapped his hand upon the bounty hunter's shoulder. 'Don't give up now,' he urged him. 'You've done well. You'll have us back inside the citadel in no time now.'

'Exactly,' the bounty hunter agreed. 'That was what I was worrying about.'

'I don't know how you can be so sure,' Bruno observed, warily. 'Any direction looks much the same as any other in this Morr-forsaken warren.'

'It's the right direction, all right,' Lothar replied, quietly. 'I've found a safe path halfway across the Ostermark Marches, without so much as a star in the sky to guide me. Don't worry. We'll find your citadel all right. I only hope it's going to be worth my while.'

'Wait!' Stefan interrupted him. 'What was that?'

'What was what?' Bruno demanded. 'I didn't hear anything.'

The three men stood, stooped and stock still in the musty interior of the tunnel. At first the only sound was the intermittent crackle of the flames licking at the wooden stave Bruno held in his hand. Then, from somewhere far behind them, came another sound. A sound from deep underground, a groaning and churning as though the very belly of the earth itself were being torn open.

'I don't like the sound of that all,' Lothar declared. 'What in the name of Taal is it?'

'I don't know,' Stefan said. He strained to listen, but all was now quiet once more. 'Whatever it was, it's a long way away,' he concluded. 'If it's headed this way then all the more reason for us to press on.' He turned to look back into the darkness, the way they had come. He saw and heard nothing, but where the air before had been utterly still, he now felt a stirring, a gust so faint as to be almost imperceptible, against his face.

'Come on,' he said to the others. 'Let's see if we can't move a little quicker.'

IT HAD BEEN no harder than taking a toy from a child. Anaise had given Zucharov the key that would unlock the whole city. Now all he had to do was turn it, and Sigmarsgeist would be delivered to his master. Already, the balance of power had shifted decisively. The humbling of Rilke had been of no interest to him, but it had served a clear purpose. In discrediting the commander of the White Guard he had also weakened Konstantin; the Guide was no longer in a position to stand against that will. And his sister's will, though Anaise did not yet know it, would be the will of Kyros.

His first task had been to recruit men who would obey his every command, and who were hungry enough to take pleasure in the bloodiest of tasks. Zucharov did not have far to look. The dungeons of Sigmarsgeist were crammed with men and beasts that had passed through the shadow of Chaos on their road to Sigmarsgeist. Many were beyond redemption, and of no use to him. There were savage orcs who would happily tear any living creature apart for sport, but whose mental strength failed to match their physical might. The dull-witted beastmen, neither man nor beast but a clumsy fusion of both, were barely better. And then there were others, creations of darkness that had once been mortal, but were now too far gone down the path of damnation to be of any use.

But the Norscans, they were different. Many of them had the mark of Chaos upon them, but the darkness surely mixed well with their cold northern blood. The mutants among their number were still recognisable as mortal men, but stronger, fiercer, far more cruel. This was the stock that Zucharov would draw upon to serve as his guard. They would now wear the white of Sigmar, but they would bear his likeness upon their breast only in hollow mockery. They would bow to only one true master, and they would acknowledge only one god – Tzeentch, the Dark Lord of Change.

Rilke was discredited, and, with his fall Konstantin, his patron, was fatally weakened. In one simple move, a vacuum had been created that Zucharov had been swift to fill. Even then Anaise could have stopped him, even as he freed the blond butchers from the cells and had them don the white uniforms of the disgraced elite guard. Even then she could have intervened, and drawn a line beneath the madness. But she did not, and she did not because she too was part of the madness now.

Zucharov had given her the thirst for power, and to slake that thirst she was prepared to see all Sigmarsgeist destroyed. With Anaise in the ascendancy and Konstantin rendered impotent, Rilke's men – the elite guard – were swiftly disarmed, and imprisoned. Rilke himself would be made an example of. Zucharov would see to it that his would be a very public death: a symbol of the new regime that would seize hold of the citadel, and then, stone by stone, break it apart.

There were other matters that now concerned Zucharov. He tormented himself with the knowledge that his battle with Stefan Kumansky had been cut short, and cut short with him apparently at the mercy of his opponent. Zucharov had already had more than enough of the taste of submission. To taste it again in combat, and against a man who was in all senses his inferior, was unthinkable. He must finish what he had begun, and the only acceptable conclusion now would be Stefan's death.

Kyros too, had cause to want the swordsman dead. Stefan had already caused trouble enough for Zucharov's malign master, and it was he who had done most to deny Kyros the prize of Erengrad. But the Dark Lord knew that Stefan Kumansky's death would be incidental, a small victory within the bigger game. It would count for nothing if his plans for Tal Dur were allowed to unravel. Through Zucharov he watched from afar as Bea fled Anaise's chambers. Only through the girl would he uncover the source of the waters. So far, he had been content to wait whilst Anaise snared the healer and turned her to their purpose. But it was taking too long; so far the girl had delivered nothing. If persuasion would not prevail, then some other, cruder means would have to be found to exploit Bea's naïve but precious potential.

Zucharov waited until the girl was well clear before entering the Guide's chambers. He found Anaise perched upon the edge of a chair, petulant and angry. She barely reacted when Zucharov appeared in the room, but continued drumming her fingers upon the arms of the chair.

*She grows comfortable with looking upon our disciple,* Kyros noted. *So much the better.*

'Your men have control of the White Guard?' she said, more as a statement than a question.

Zucharov nodded. 'What of your brother?'

'What of him?'

'Konstantin is weak. He is the stone that would weigh down our ambition.'

'My brother would never directly oppose me. Without the White Guard to support him, he has no choice but to follow my lead.'

Zucharov continued to stare, impassively.

'Is this not enough for you?' Anaise asked. 'What else do you want?'

'Progress,' Zucharov responded. 'You have had days to work upon the girl, but we are no closer to finding Tal Dur.'

'Does your dull mutant mind appreciate nothing?' Anaise snapped back. 'I have delivered you the White Guard on a plate. Rilke is yours to do with as you wish. We are masters of Sigmarsgeist in all but name. And yet all you can do is chide me on account of the girl. She is not so simple, nor so compliant, that I can bend her like the branch of the tree.'

'There are always other ways,' Zucharov responded. 'Sooner or later, she will yield.'

'No,' Anaise insisted. 'We will do this my way, or not at all. You say we have achieved nothing. That is not true. Have you not looked around you? Have you not seen what is happening in Sigmarsgeist?'

Zucharov inclined his head towards the window and gazed across the citadel, taking in the choking mass of buildings and stony growths that had become Sigmarsgeist, and the turmoil upon the streets.

'The forces of strange magic are loose upon this place,' he concluded. He looked towards the mouth of the well. 'You have set them loose.'

'I have had Bea draw the energy here,' Anaise asserted. 'She is the catalyst for all this.'

Zucharov made no response, but, behind his eyes, Kyros made note of the arrogance that would be the Guide's downfall.

'The forces at work here are not Tal Dur,' Zucharov said at last. 'They are tainted and impure, nothing but distant echoes of its mighty energy.'

'Then we shall track those echoes to their source,' Anaise responded, defiantly. 'The healer will lead us there, else she will draw the power of Tal Dur to us.'

'Yes,' Zucharov agreed. 'That she will.'

INCH BY CAREFUL inch, yard by yard, Stefan and his companions continued their subterranean journey back towards Sigmarsgeist. Progress was slow, sometimes almost impossible. Tunnels would end abruptly; the way blocked by barriers of stone or roof-falls. In other places the passageway had silted up, and they found their way blocked by a solid wall of earth, an impenetrable crust of hardened mud. But somewhere, somehow, by doubling back or searching out other routes, Lothar Koenig always found a way through. He had given up his complaints now, and was applying himself to the single task with a silent tenacity that Stefan could not help but admire. He was truly a survivor, and through him, Stefan hoped, they might yet all survive. Bea too.

For a while the three of them had had to crawl on their hands and knees through a section of the dry sewer where the tunnel was almost totally blocked by rocks and broken debris. Now at last they emerged into clear space and were able to stand upright once again. Lothar brushed himself down and looked around with a quiet smile of satisfaction.

'I reckon we're below the city walls now,' he declared. 'We'll start thinking soon about finding a way up. Don't forget,' he looked at Stefan and Bruno in turn. 'They owe me. So do you. When we get up top we'll see what's what.'

'Where should we look for?' Bruno asked. 'I mean, where do we need to be?'

'Inside the palace would be a good start,' Stefan suggested. Lothar raised an eyebrow and grunted in derision.

'Perhaps you'd like to choose a particular room!' he sneered. 'Look, friend. I said I was good. I didn't say I had second sight. We'll take what we can find. Wherever that puts us up top, that's down to luck.'

'There's that sound again,' Stefan cut in.

All three stopped and listened. The sound of tearing and rending was still faint, but insistent, like a deep vibration shaking at the very core of the earth. There could be no doubt. It was getting steadily louder.

'We must be getting nearer to it,' Bruno said at last.

'It's getting nearing to us, more like,' Stefan said. 'Whatever it is, it's coming from somewhere behind us, and getting closer all the time.'

'By the gods,' Lothar declared. 'It sounds like something dying.'

'Or something being reborn,' Stefan said, quietly. 'A wakening beast.'

He turned to the bounty hunter. 'You're right, Lothar. Let's not worry too much about where we reach the surface. Let's just concentrate on getting up. Fast.'

They moved on, in silence now, through the stale gloom. Then Bruno stopped dead again. 'That's strange,' he said. 'I can hear water.' His voice was suddenly tinged with anxiety. Lothar raised his arm to call for quiet, then strained to listen to the sound. He turned and grinned broadly at the others.

'It's the sewers,' he said. 'Not these dead worm-holes. The real, working waterways running beneath the citadel. This must be where the two systems meet up, where the tunnels below the old city meet with those of the new. Come on,' he said. 'We're close now. There must be a way through.' He started running his hands across the crusted surface of the tunnel wall. 'Somewhere near here,' he said again. 'Further on, maybe. Here,' he said to Bruno, 'give me your knife.'

Bruno handed the knife over. Lothar moved steadily down the length of the tunnel, keeping his head pressed close to the wall, listening all the time. Half way down he stopped, and began to prise the stones loose with the point of the blade. Soon he had worked a hole large enough in the tunnel wall to put his fist through. Dank air gusted through the breach in the wall, ripe with a familiar stench.

'Help me,' he called out, 'we're almost there.'

Stefan and Bruno joined in, working with their bare hands to pull out the stones. On the other side of the tunnel they found a second, almost parallel passage. As Bruno hefted the torch, light glittered upon the surface of a dark stream, flowing sluggishly at its base.

'We're home, boys,' Lothar muttered. 'Let's hope it was worth it.'

Stefan stepped through the breach into the second tunnel, taking the torch from Bruno. 'I can see a ladder,' he called back. 'Barely twenty yards further down. With any luck it will take us all the way to the surface.'

Lothar clambered through behind Stefan, dragging Bruno after him. 'Come on,' he said to Bruno. 'Didn't you hear him? We're getting out of here.'

But Bruno didn't move. He had stopped, straddling the gap between the two tunnels, his attention fixed on something back the way they had just come.

'Water,' he said. 'It's water.'

'Of course it's water,' Lothar replied. 'The sewers on this side are teeming with it. Lovely, stinking, filth-laden water.'

'No,' Bruno shook his head. 'That's not what I mean. That's not what I mean at all,' he called, more urgently now. 'Listen – can't you hear it? The sound of rushing water, like a flood... Can't you hear it?'

But they did not need to hear it, for by now they could feel it, a shock wave as a great shudder passed through the belly of the earth, and somewhere from out of the depths, an unstoppable tide broke free. Everything around them began to shake, violently. Great slabs of stone and earth tumbled into the sewers as the walls of the tunnels blurred then began to break apart.

Stefan turned to shout back to Bruno, but his words were lost in the pandemonium. Almost at the end of their journey, they had stumbled upon the end of the world.

# CHAPTER EIGHTEEN
## The Flood

ANAISE VON AUGEN had lost track of how long she had been sitting in the shadows of the chamber, staring deep into the void which was the Well of Sadness. She was not a woman given to stillness, but, for at least the last hour, as the shadows lengthened and daylight fell to grey, she had not moved from that place.

Surely, she reasoned, she had done enough for it to come to pass. She had taken each of the cards that the gods had offered her, and she had played them well. They had given her the girl, Bea, and the monster Zucharov. Two opposite and opposing forces that, combined, could nonetheless deliver her unfettered power. And they had given her the opportunity now to use that power.

Konstantin had stumbled; his judgement had been shown to be weak, fatally flawed. The gods had loosened her brother's grip upon Sigmarsgeist, prised the chalice that was power from his grasp. Now it could be hers. Everything was in place, her destiny stood ready to be fulfilled. And yet she found herself waiting, for what she did not know. Perhaps for the next, decisive chapter in the story to unfold, and for a sign, some signal that it had begun. Anaise stared down into the depths of the Well of Sadness, but found only dark silence in answer to her questions.

The sign, when it finally came, was from a quite different, and at first unwelcome, source. It came in the shape of a knock, tentative and brief, upon the door. Anaise looked up, pulled away from her contemplation by the sound.

'What is it?' she demanded, irritably. 'I gave clear instructions that I was not be disturbed.'

The door opened just wide enough to reveal an officer of the Red Guard standing upon the threshold, his head bowed.

'I beg your forgiveness, mistress. But these are exceptional circumstances.'

Anaise beckoned the man inside with a curt wave of her hand. 'Come in, then,' she snapped. 'And make it quick.'

The guard stepped into the chamber and made a further bow before the Guide.

'Well?' Anaise asked him. 'What do you want?'

'My lady,' the guard began. 'There is water in the streets of Sigmarsgeist.'

Anaise was still vexed by the interruption. For a moment the significance of the guard's words was lost upon her. 'That's good news indeed,' she replied, caustically. 'Perhaps now the miserable wretches will get on with their work and stop complaining they don't have enough water.'

She shot the man a look to indicate he was dismissed, and turned back towards the well. The guard hesitated, but did not move.

'I ask pardon, mistress. I did not express myself clearly.' He paused, marshalling his words. 'There is water pouring into the streets. A great deal of water, mistress. I have received word that the lower quarter of the citadel is flooding.'

Anaise turned around. Now the guard had her full and undivided attention. She crossed the room and seized the man by the arm.

'Have you seen it?' she demanded. 'Have you seen for yourself?'

'Madam, no,' the guard replied. 'Word has only just been received from the Watch. But if they tell true then the levels are rising quickly.'

Anaise pushed the guard to one side and went to the window that looked south, towards the lower levels of the citadel. Little could be seen beyond the flickering of the lamps. Sigmarsgeist looked calm, almost tranquil in the moonlight. Anaise uttered a curse, then reached for her cloak, and drew it around her. 'Hurry,' she commanded. 'I need to be taken there. I must see for myself. Now.'

The guard held the door open for the Guide and stood at attention.

'A carriage is waiting below,' he reported. For a moment the man forgot his deference, and stared earnestly at his mistress.

'Some of the men say it is the wrath of the gods, my lady. That gods have come to punish our ambition. Could it be so?' he asked of her. 'Has vengeance come to Sigmarsgeist?'

Anaise hurried on, no longer interested in what the Red Guard had to say.

'No,' she said to herself. 'Tal Dur has come to Sigmarsgeist.'

As soon as she heard word of the floods, Bea knew that she had no option but to go. She no longer had any fear of Konstantin, or Anaise, or of what either of them might do. She knew that she must answer her calling, and that the time for concealment was over.

The streets of Sigmarsgeist beyond the palace were as full as ever, but now the crowds flowed in only one direction, towards the higher ground on the northern side of the citadel, away from the rising waters. Nearer to the palace people were jostling each other out of the way. Some were not even sure what the commotion was about. But as Bea got closer to the lower reaches of the citadel the angry flow became a stampede of frightened, panicking humanity. Against it all, Bea pressed on, a solitary figure moving against the tide. She watched them fleeing all around her: men and women from the foundries, labourers cut loose from their gangs, children with even smaller infants in their arms, fleeing servants and dishevelled officers of the Red Guard. All kindness and patience had been swept aside. Order was breaking down. All that would soon be left was the law of survival, the strong enduring over the weak. The final act in the history of Sigmarsgeist was beginning.

Bea had no clear notion of where she should be going, only that she must go. She let the massing crowds be her guide, and, before long, the water had begun swirling about her feet. After an hour the flood reached above her ankles. Soon after that it had reached her knees. Now she knew for sure that what the people were saying was true: Sigmarsgeist was drowning.

She fought her way past the fleeing crowds towards the bottom of a wide avenue that was fast becoming a canal. At the bottom of the avenue the road forked sharply to the right then turned downhill again. As Bea reached the turn in the road, a wall of water rolled out towards her and, when it had subsided, the icy waters had risen up above her waist. Soon she would need to swim if she were to make any further progress. She could feel the current plucking at her feet, trying to pull her over. She reached out and caught hold of the first thing that came to hand, the chassis of a cart that had been thrown over and upended in the stream, one set of wheels poking up towards the sky. All around, bales of clothes and possessions bobbed up and down on the water, the remnants of a life swept away.

Bea clutched tightly to the shattered iron frame and took a moment to look around her. The streets – if they could still be called that – were emptier now, as most of the people had fled. The bodies of those who had failed to escape lay around her on every side, face-down or face-up in the water, some still clutching the sticks or bundles of rags that they hoped might save them. Further ahead, Bea could now see where the flood was entering the citadel. Great plumes of water were shooting into the air, bursting from the grates and holes in the ground above the sewers. The force of the water still forcing its way from below ground was enormous; there was no possibility that the waters were about to subside.

A terrible noise from somewhere ahead made Bea look up. She turned her face to the sky just in time to see a huge marbled shard break off from the structure above her head and tumble into the rushing waters. The maze of mad bridges and pathways that had taken a parasitic hold upon the citadel was being broken apart by the power of the surging waters. As Bea looked on, sections of the bone-like mass sheared off and crashed down into the waters, bringing great slabs of masonry tumbling down with them. Those people still looking on screamed out, in wonder or in horror at the sight. Some proclaimed it the vengeance of Sigmar, others the might of the Dark Powers. Bea kept her counsel and looked on. She already knew that it was neither of these things.

Still the waters rose, relentless, pushing up out of the ground, overwhelming Sigmarsgeist. Another surge caught Bea, and plucked her feet away from under her. She managed to clutch hold of the abandoned wagon, still just visible above the water. But when she tried to place her feet again she could find no solid ground. She would have to swim from now on.

Gradually, a kind of eerie calm settled upon the scene as most of those around her in the water were swept away. She scanned the empty windows that lined the buildings on either side. Two or three of the tallest still had floors that rose clear of the water line. After a while, from those windows, the cries started to come. The last desperate cries of those who had all but abandoned hope.

Bea drew down a lung full of air and prepared to cast herself adrift from her fragile place of sanctuary. She was at one with her calling now. She knew what she had to do.

NEWS OF THE great flood had reached Konstantin much as the waters themselves had breached Sigmarsgeist. Slowly, at first, no more than a trickle of rumour and speculation. But the rumours had quickly become an unstoppable tide of reports, all of them bad, all of them pointing towards the destruction of the citadel that had been his life's achievement.

Konstantin knew he should act. His action should be bold, and decisive; an intervention that would turn back the waters and reverse the ill fortune that had stricken Sigmarsgeist. But he did not act. He could not act. He had become paralysed by a sickness that had taken hold of both mind and body. It was a sickness seeded in the belief, deep within his heart, that all of this was his doing.

Konstantin had sat and listened in silence to the reports of death and destruction brought to him with ever-increasingly regularity by his men, those of them that he could still trust. At length, even that became too much, and he barred all messengers from his chamber. He could hear them still, beyond the door, pleading to be admitted to the presence of the Guide, begging for him to save the citadel.

Konstantin sank his head into his hands and wept. They did not understand what he now knew. It was the judgement of Konstantin that had brought things to this. All that was left for him was to oversee its final undoing.

There was a pounding upon the door, louder and more insistent than before. Konstantin did not know who it was. Perhaps it would be his sister. They had not spoken since Rilke's act of betrayal, and the overthrow of the White Guard. Anaise had taken her opportunity to seize all power, and he had let her take it, for in that same moment he had known for certain that he was broken. Konstantin raised his head as the knocking came again.

'I will speak with nobody,' he cried. But he knew instinctively that his authority would no longer hold. A few moments later, the door was opened and Hans Baecker strode in, accompanied by three or four of his men. Konstantin favoured him a weak smile. Baecker, he knew, was still loyal. He would be loyal until the death, but that counted for too little now.

'What have you come to tell me?' he asked, quietly. 'What grim news can you be bringing me that I do not know already?'

'The waters still pour into the citadel,' Baecker reported. 'There is no hope of their abating. At this rate of progress, Sigmarsgeist and all its souls will be lost by daybreak.'

Konstantin gazed up at his lieutenant. After Rilke, Baecker was the most trusted of all his men. But then, after Rilke,

Konstantin no longer had confidence in any man, himself
included.

'What of the gates?' he asked, distractedly, looking about
the room. 'Why have the gates not been opened to abate the
flood?'

The guard to Baecker's left exchanged an anxious glance
with his commander. Baecker nodded, signalling that he
should continue.

'The gate on the south wall is already submerged,' he
began. 'As for the west gate–' he hesitated. 'Sire, it seems the
west gate is no longer accessible – it has been – blocked.'

'Blocked?' Konstantin spoke the word as if unable quite to
grasp its meaning.

'Built over,' Baecker said, firmly. 'Blocked by timber and
stone. We are cut off by our own endeavour.'

'But what of the main gateway, on the north side of the
citadel?' Konstantin asked.

'That will not solve our problem,' Baecker told him. 'By
the time the waters reach that far, most of the citadel would
already have been laid waste by the floods. And all those left
in the lower reaches will have drowned.'

'Then there is no hope,' Konstantin said. 'No chance for
Sigmarsgeist?'

'That is not the news I bring, majesty,' Baecker replied. His
voice was terse, his impatience with his master barely
masked. 'But if there is to be hope, then we must act, and act
now.'

Konstantin looked about him, trying to draw some
inspiration from the spartan surroundings of his chamber. He found none, only the image of the waters as they
rose, higher and higher, until he, too, had been consumed.

Konstantin looked away. Gradually his head sunk into his
hands, and he moaned. 'I never imagined such a thing could
come to pass.' He looked up again at Baecker, a look of
pleading on his face. 'How could I have anticipated it?' he
demanded. 'It is not as we planned. These were not the
forces we built Sigmarsgeist to withstand. It is not as we
planned at all.'

'Majesty,' Baecker cut in. 'There is another way. Another chance that may yet save the citadel.'

Hope flickered like a weak flame upon Konstantin's face. 'Then what?' he asked. 'Tell me, tell me now.'

'The walls of the citadel must be breached,' Baecker said. 'As much as we can manage, they must be laid to waste. Only then is there hope that the waters can be dispersed, and the citadel saved.'

Just for an instant, Konstantin was re-energised. He got up from his seat, almost majestic again in his wrath, and would have clutched hold of his lieutenant by the throat, had Baecker not abruptly backed away.

'Destroy the walls?' Are you mad?' Konstantin demanded. His face, so drawn and pale only moments before, flushed a hot red. 'The great walls that girdle the citadel are the very symbol of all that we stand for, all that we have built and striven for. Destroy the walls and you destroy the very heart of Sigmarsgeist itself!'

Baecker glanced around at his men, and stood his ground. 'Leave the walls standing and Sigmarsgeist will be destroyed anyway,' he replied. 'In body as well as in spirit, as sure as darkness follows light.' He paused for a moment to let his word settle with the Guide, then added, 'Sire, we have no other choice.'

Konstantin turned from Baecker and walked towards the high window. Night was starting to fall across Sigmarsgeist, but the carnage on the far side of the citadel was still clearly visible. More than a quarter of the city lay beneath a raging flood that had come from nowhere. And, where the waters boiled, the crazed, alabaster structures that had taken hold across the citadel were crashing down, taking towers, walls, whole sides of buildings with them. Years of pious toil were being rolled back in the space of hours as one madness collided head on with another.

Finally he turned back, as he knew he must do, and faced Baecker again. He did not look at him when he spoke.

'Very well,' he said, his voice cracked and low. 'Do whatever is necessary. Bring down the walls of Sigmarsgeist.'

* * *

ZUCHAROV HAD HAD no need of mortal word to bring him news of the flood. His master, Kyros, had already whispered to him of the waters coming. The time of reckoning was at hand. The time for waiting was at an end. Now was the time for action. After so many long months of inaction and sub-servience, Zucharov could feel the desire rising strong inside him to get out upon the streets of the citadel, to engage with the maelstrom and taste again the spoils of bloody war.

But first Kyros had one further duty for him to perform in the cells deep below the palace where the wretched prisoners rotted, unaware of their newly altered fate.

He had left it to the Norscans to look after Rilke. As soon as he stepped into the cell, Zucharov could see that the brutal northerners had paid close attention to their task. Rilke was still standing, but only because he had been chained upright to the wall of the cell. The Norscans had stripped him of his uniform, and beaten much of his life from him as well. Rilke's once haughty features were barely recognisable, his face covered by bruises and blood. As Zucharov entered the cell, Rilke opened one eye and looked at him. With what strength he had left, he spat upon the ground to make his feelings clear.

Zucharov did not care about Rilke's feelings, or about Rilke himself. He was one of the weak, and Zucharov had not cared whether he lived or died. The task he had to perform was to deliver his master's bidding, and that was all.

He clamped one hand to the side of Rilke's head, and turned the prisoner's face towards his own. Rilke grimaced and tried to suppress a cry. There was still some capacity for pain within him, Zucharov noted. That was good. The Norscans had not, after all, over-stepped the boundaries of their command.

'Do you know who I am?' Zucharov intoned. Rilke struggled to force his swollen tongue around the words, but eventually managed to speak.

'You're the servant of evil. I don't need to know any more than that.'

Unmoved and untouched by Rilke's words, Zucharov left a lengthy pause before he replied.

'I am death,' he said. 'I am annihilation. I am the counterpoint to everything that your masters have prayed and striven for. I am the darkness that waits upon the end of your world.'

'My masters are the Guides of Sigmarsgeist,' Rilke retorted 'And they will never–'

Zucharov drew back his hand, and delivered a punch to Rilke's ribs. Not so hard that he lost all consciousness, but hard enough to draw a scream of agony from his already battered body. 'Do not waste my time with fiction,' he said. 'I know who your real masters are.' He twisted Rilke's head again, and looked hard into his eyes, deep into his tortured soul.

'I know who you are,' he said. 'And I know *what* you are.' He shoved Rilke back against the wall of the cell, and turned to the two Norscan gaolers standing in waiting behind him.

'Leave us,' Zucharov told them. 'I will finish this now.'


'I WAS WONDERING how long it would take you to find me here.'

Bea was drained of all emotion. She had found her way to the lower city, already sinking below the rising waters. She had lost herself in the warren of half-flooded streets and houses, lost herself in her work. There were plenty there who needed her help, and there would be many more. But she knew that, wherever she went, Anaise would find her. Their destinies were inextricably linked. She understood that now.

She no longer felt any kinship or warmth towards Anaise, but there was no room in her heart for hatred, either. She knew she must pour all of her soul into her devotions, into her calling. Which, at that moment, meant doing whatever she could for the wounded woman that lay at her feet. So she did not so much as look up when she heard Anaise's voice at her shoulder. Bea knew that, before long, the Guide would track her down. But she would not let Anaise distract her from her work. Not now. Not any longer.

'Where else would you be found?' Anaise asked, earnestly. 'Where else would a daughter of the goddess be, but amongst the sick and the wounded, tending to them as best she could? Here–' The Guide got down by Bea's side. 'In the name of the gods, let me at least help you.' She tore a strip of cloth from the sodden bundle lying upon the floor and began to tie a tourniquet around the injured woman's arm. Bea made no attempt to stop her – Anaise was competent, and Bea knew she could use all the help that she could get, welcome or otherwise. But there was a coldness in her heart towards the Guide that would never now be displaced.

'Why should you want to help?' she asked, icily. 'What is it to you?'

Anaise stopped what she was doing, and tugged the hair back from her face so that she could look directly at Bea. 'Don't you think I care?' she asked her. 'Don't you think it matters to me what happens to my people?'

Bea finished the work of securing the tourniquet, and lay a soothing hand upon the sick woman's brow. 'I know why you're here,' she said. 'You want me to help you channel the power of the waters.' She held Anaise's gaze, unblinking. 'As for all this suffering, no, I don't think you care at all.'

Anaise stared back at her. Her expression hardened. 'You did this, Bea,' she said. 'It is you who brought the waters to the citadel.'

Bea turned away, towards another patient, an older man who had been crushed beneath a falling building. The flesh of his arm was dark with a livid green bruise; he would certainly lose the limb if Bea did not act quickly.

'You're wrong,' she said, without turning from her work. 'It is you who have brought this doom upon Sigmarsgeist. With your desire, your naked greed for power. Now these people are suffering the consequences of that greed.'

Anaise reached out to her, but Bea pulled away. 'Believe what you want,' Anaise replied, sharply. 'I have no gain in bringing ill to my people. But if I have truly succeeded in restoring the great powers to this place–' She stood up, and started to pace the floor, taking no account now of the suffering around her, 'then it must be I who will reap its bounty.' She smiled, defiantly, at the young healer. 'I always knew that Tal Dur was close,' she said. 'There was a purpose which drove us to set the first stones of

Sigmarsgeist here, just as there was a purpose in your being delivered to me. The great powers are restored to this place!' She laughed. 'Your work is done, Bea, whether you willed it so or not.'

Bea glared back at Anaise. 'You do not understand those powers,' she asserted. 'You understand nothing. You think Tal Dur is a place. It is not. It is a state of being. To those who seek it, it gives back only what it finds within them. Take the warning that is before your eyes, Anaise,' she implored. 'Seek for Tal Dur with evil in your heart, and only evil will attend you. Turn away from this course before it is too late!'

Anaise brushed her aside and stood up. 'Minister to your sickly charges whilst you may,' she advised. 'And know this. We stand on the threshold of a new world, a world where weakness and sickness will have no place. A new Sigmarsgeist, *my* Sigmarsgeist.'

There was a sound like a roll of thunder from outside, and another great edifice collapsed into the swirling waters, great blocks of stone torn apart by the sheer force of the tide. For a few seconds the building trembled like a tree in a storm, and then subsided.

'Is this how your new world will look, Anaise?' Bea asked quietly. 'With destruction and death its heralds?'

'There must be an ending before we can begin anew,' Anaise countered, stridently. 'It is all within my gift. I can stop this whenever I choose, and begin to build anew. The strong shall survive the deluge, and I shall be there to lead them!'

ALEXEI ZUCHAROV REGARDED the plight of Sigmarsgeist and its people with a cold indifference. The bricks and stones that had been the citadel were nothing to him, nor were the souls that had taken shelter within it. He strode through the heart of the citadel, towards the ever-rising flood waters, gazing dispassionately at the carnage unfolding all around him. To the mortal eye this would seem like the end of all things, mayhem and brutal destruction, a senseless tide of anarchy that could no longer be reined in. Only a follower of Tzeentch could see the destruction of Sigmarsgeist for what it truly was: an act of mighty transfiguration. Transformation on a huge scale; transformation of the sort upon which the great wheels of eternity turn. Zucharov knew this now. Without change there was stasis, and with stasis came degeneration and decay. Change was the very essence of being. The destruction of Sigmarsgeist was an act of celebration, pious homage to the great, Dark Lord of Transformation himself.

The end game for Sigmarsgeist, and for Tal Dur, was at hand. Now he must ensure that nothing interfered with the mighty forces at work. Zucharov had assembled an army, of sorts, to do his master's bidding. The Norscans accounted for the greater number, prisoners from the defeated army at Erengrad, now freed to return to the service of the dark cause. Most of them wore the white of the elite guard. It had pleased Kyros to have them don the uniform whilst Rilke's men were rounded up and left to rot, discredited and shamed by their leader, in the cells.

The Norscan force had been augmented by such others of the prisoners who could be trusted, any who bore the mark of Tzeentch upon them, or those who had not yet mutated beyond the point of madness. Amongst the white of the Norscan guard jostled a dozen or more inhumans, mutants and other creatures of Chaos.

Some of them were still recognisably human, some altered beyond all semblance of mortal form. As they waded amid the swirling waters, the power of their dark master flowed ever more powerfully through their altered forms. Bodies shimmered and convulsed; voices rose to a keening scream, adding to the insane cacophony of the streets, driven to joyous delirium by the scenes of grief and destruction all around them.

Zucharov did not share their joy. His purpose was to see the will of Kyros done, and the job was not accomplished yet. But he knew he must let his warriors – particularly the cruelly violent Norscans – have their head. Zucharov decided to give them blood, much as he might throw meat to a pack of dogs. All around them now townsfolk were trying to flee the rising waters. Zucharov ordered the Norscans to turn them back, it would be sport enough for them, for the moment. The white-clad northerners went about their task with a brutal, ruthless efficiency, lashing out with staves at anyone – man, woman or child – who tried to get past to safety, and herding those who held off back into the arms of the flood. Any who fell by the wayside they skewered with their swords, murdering the fleeing populace without discrimination.

Zucharov let the butchers get on with their work, all the time marshalling his men deeper into the citadel. There was no reason why the townsfolk should die, but there was no reason for them to live, either. In the end, he knew, they were all dead. He marched on, the icy water swirling about his ankles running red with blood. Soon enough, he found real work for his murderous horde to concern themselves with.

They had skirted the heart of the city, and followed one of the main thoroughfares that ran from north to south, close to the high walls. Ahead of them was a large group of Red Guards – perhaps twenty or thirty in all – attacking the walls with picks and staves and – in one place – a great battering ram. The sight made no immediate sense to Zucharov, but Kyros quickly communicated to him their intent, and, equally quickly, made clear his orders. The guards must not be allowed to breach the walls. The great flood must be allowed to run its course; the transformation must be completed. Only then could the prophecy of Tal Dur be fulfilled. Only then could Kyros – and Zucharov – claim its gifts.

Zucharov raised his arm and drew his men to him. With a single shouted command, he began the attack. So absorbed were the Red Guard in their assault upon the walls, they did not see Zucharov and his grotesque troop until they were all but upon them. Zucharov drew out his sword and bellowed a cry of war that came from the very core of his being. At long last, he was delivered to his true destiny. The blood of battle coursed in his veins; he could taste it in his mouth. Soon his sword would run red with it. Too late the soldiers of Sigmar saw the Chaos horde bearing down upon them. Too late, they turned from the walls and raised their shields against the crazed attackers.

Zucharov plunged his blade deep into the body of the first guard who tried to block his path, the force of his thrust was so great that it carried the man – already dead – clean off his feet. He calculated the odds of battle – level or better than level, his followers matching the Red Guard man for man. Even with the odds against them, they would surely have prevailed. The Red Guard were weary, in their minds already defeated, desperately trying to salvage something from the wreckage of their citadel. The soldiers of Sigmar would be swept away, cut to ribbons in a flurry of frenzied steel.

Zucharov tore into the midst of the Red Guard, annihilating adversaries to his left and his right with thunderous blows of his sword. Most of those who had a chance to counter-attack could barely get near him, and even those who found their mark were unable to inflict a wound upon the leathery hide that had grown, like armour, covering Zucharov's body.

The soldiers of Sigmar were not totally without heart, and they were not without skill. Although overwhelmed, they were still taking a toll of the Norscans, and soon as many as a dozen of the northerners lay dead or dying. Zucharov regretted their loss only as much as he would regret the loss of a resource. The Norscans deserved to die, he had no kinship with their foul breed. And there would be enough of them to ensure the deed was done. And if the Norscans, and his other followers all perished, then he would still stand, undiminished and unvanquished. He was strong, he was all-powerful, he was immortal.

Zucharov swung his blade, double-handed, decapitating two soldiers as they tried to close in upon him. In the aftermath he looked about, trying to establish what had happened to the Guards' assault upon the walls. All but a handful of them had abandoned their attempt, and turned their attentions to saving their miserable skins. But, as he looked on, one of the red-clad guards – their leader – was now running back to where the great siege engine – the battering ram – sat poised ready to deliver its hammer punch to the outer wall.

Zucharov paid it scant attention at first. Huge though the siege engine was, it was surely incapable of breaching the thick stone wall. Then he saw that the wall was already weakened. Several great slabs of stone were missing or removed where the wall was being rebuilt. One well-directed thrust might be enough to break through. This could not be allowed to happen.

Zucharov broke away from the main combat, swatting aside another three opponents, and sprinted for the walls. The Red Guard was on the point of releasing the machine, and sending the column of oak smashing against the stone wall. Zucharov let out a roar and hurled a short-bladed knife, aimed square in the middle of the guard's back. In that instant the guard turned to one side, and the blade flew wide.

Zucharov recognised the man. It was one of the confidants who sat in attendance upon the Guides, the highest ranking of those who wore the red of Sigmarsgeist. Baecker. Yes, that was his name. Zucharov leapt towards him, a final desperate lunge before his enemy could loosen the catches that held the mighty beam in place. Even in that moment, he was able to look through the eyes of Kyros, into the other man's soul. Yes, it was clear. Baecker had the seed of darkness within him, the potential, at least, to cross the great divide and join with the march of the armies of the night. But for now, he was just another adversary. Zucharov already had enough men that he could call upon as his ally. The only fate that could await Hans Baecker was death.

Baecker's hand was inches away from the mechanism, another second or two would be all he needed to set the beam in motion and smash a great fissure in the wall. In the last instant he saw Zucharov coming for him, and swerved aside. The manoeuvre saved Baecker's life, but it cost him the chance to launch the battering ram. Before he could recover, Zucharov was on him, wielding his blade with awesome speed. Baecker was dwarfed by his opponent, but stood his ground, fending off Zucharov's first strikes and even finding space to strike back at the tattooed mutant towering over him. Just for an instant, Zucharov experienced a feeling akin to shock, or surprise. For just that fleeting moment, as Baecker lashed out at him with a vigour born of desperation, Zucharov remembered what it was like to be mortal, and his sense of invulnerability fell under threat. He reacted to that threat with another belli-cose howl of rage, redoubling the speed and ferocity of his sword.

Baecker parried three, then four, shattering blows in suc-cession, but his strength was waning. Zucharov's fifth stroke spun Baecker off-balance, and the sixth prised the sword from out of his hand.

Zucharov pulled back, on the threshold of the seventh, decisive strike. He looked down at his own chest, where a rivulet of ruby blood was running into the contours of the dark images etched upon his flesh. He sheathed his sword, and raised a hand to his chest, wiping the blood away con-temptuously.

Hans Baecker launched a last desperate attack, charging full on at Zucharov, his fists held high. Zucharov grabbed the man's arm and twisted, the sharp crack of splintering bone met by Baecker's scream of agony. Zucharov drew his other arm around his opponent's neck and held him firm. Baecker was twisting and writhing like a wild animal, but Zucharov was able to hold him with ease. He let Baecker struggle for a few moments more, then, with his free hand, clamped hold of Baecker by the hair, and snapped his head back, breaking his neck.

He kicked the body to one side, and stood back. The wall had not been breached. The final chance to save Sigmarsgeist had gone. The rushing waters hastened to cover the siege engine and the bodies of its crew. Soon they would all be submerged. It was time for Zucharov to move on. There was still more to be done.

He opened his hands and gazed down at his palms. The jet-black lines of the tattoo melted and reformed, swirling like the waters assailing the citadel. As Zucharov looked on, the image resting in each hand took on a similar, but differ-ent, shape and form. Finally the likeness of two faces came into view. The faces of two women, opposite and opposed, but united now in one purpose: to deliver Tal Dur to Kyros and his servant.

# CHAPTER NINETEEN
## Endgames

BRUNO FORCED OUT his words between painful gasps of breath as he lay on the upper floor of the ruined house.

'That's as close as I ever want to come to drowning,' he gasped. 'If I never cast eyes on another drop of water, then I won't be sorry.'

'Not something you'll be worrying about for a while,' Lothar panted in reply. 'I have a feeling there'll be plenty of water about for a while yet.'

'I have a feeling you're right,' Stefan added. He got to his feet and peered out through the narrow, slitted window, looking down onto the fast-flowing river that, only minutes before, had been a street.

They had escaped with their lives from the warren of sewer tunnels by the narrowest of margins, clambering clear into the daylight with the sound of the pursuing waters like the roaring of a wild beasts in their ears. They were on dry land for no more than a few seconds before the waters had burst from the tunnels with an unstoppable force, and Stefan and his companions were thrust into a battle for simple survival.

The abandoned house would provide at best temporary refuge. Stefan had calculated that, at the pace the waters were rising, the upper floor and finally the whole building would be below water in less than an hour. But, for the moment at least, it was a place that offered concealment and a chance for them to take stock. The families of workers who had occupied the building were gone, escaped to dry ground, or else drowned in the attempt. The threadbare, makeshift furnishings decorating the rooms and the remnants of a meagre meal still left on a table were all that was left of them, all that was left of the better world that should have been Sigmarsgeist.

'I wonder if they still thought it was worth it,' Bruno mused, looking over the scraps of the abandoned lives. 'The dream of Sigmarsgeist. Whether they still believed, right to the end.'

Lothar Koenig reached across Stefan and picked the rotting remains of an apple core from off the table. He put it into his mouth in one piece, and chewed on it noisily. 'It's all about winning and losing,' he said. 'If you win, your dreams are real. If you lose, then all is dust. That's the way it's always been.'

'I'm glad it's so simple for you,' Bruno observed.

'Wait a minute.' Stefan was back at the window. He beckoned the two of them to be quiet.

'What is it?' Bruno whispered.

Stefan crouched down by the window, careful not to make himself conspicuous. The light outside was fading fast, and most of the lamps in this area of the citadel had already been extinguished by the flood. But he could see something moving along the skyline marked out by the rooftops on the far side of the street.

'What is it?' Bruno hissed again. 'What can you see?'

'Company,' Stefan told him. 'At least a dozen men clambering about at roof level, just across from here.'

'The Red Guard,' Bruno surmised. 'I was wondering when they were going to show up.'

'No,' Stefan said quietly. 'These wear the white.'

'The elite guard? Rilke's men?'

Stefan peered again at the clambering figures. The pale skin and blond complexions of the men seemed to confirm his fears.

'They're dressed as White Guard, but it's not Rilke, nor any of his men,' Stefan concluded. He turned back into the room. 'Bruno,' he said. 'I think they're Norscans.'

'Taal's blood,' Bruno swore. 'That's the last thing we need. How did they get loose?'

'Things are much changed around here,' Stefan muttered. 'And changed for the worse, however unlikely that might seem.'

'Do you think they've any idea we might be here?' Lothar asked.

Stefan was saved the trouble of answering by the sound of splintering wood, and the shattering of glass somewhere nearby.

'They soon will,' Stefan said, evenly.

Bruno turned to Lothar. 'Looks like you can let your sword do your talking for once,' he declared. 'Think you're up to it?'

'I'm as ready as you are,' Lothar retorted, defiantly. 'I intend to make sure I come out of this alive.'

'Gods willing, so shall we all,' Stefan concurred. The crippled building shook to the sound of heavy-booted feet upon the narrow stairs. 'Stand ready,' he said. 'Here they come.'

Who the Norscans were looking for wasn't clear. The original inhabitants of the house, perhaps, or any other innocent citizen of Sigmarsgeist who hadn't yet perished. What they obviously hadn't been expecting to encounter was three armed men, ready to return their favours in kind. The first marauder broke down the fastened door and burst into the room, casting his gaze about for plunder or bloody sport. His eagerness earned him the length of Stefan's blade, rammed to the hilt into his belly.

The Norscan was dead before he could even cry out, but the sound of his body crashing to the floor was enough to bring his comrades stamping up the narrow stairway in pursuit.

The first of them, a red-eyed youth rash enough to take the vanguard, was cut down by a stroke from Bruno's blade. But hard on his heels were four more muscular warriors, and by now the advantage of surprise was lost. The Norscans cried out, giving their blood-lust full voice, and flung themselves into the combat. The air rang with the sound of clashing steel as the adversaries locked swords. Stefan focused upon his target, an ugly, thick-set Norscan with a pock-marked face that he took to be the leader. The man towered over Stefan, bettering him both in height and bulk. The Norscan spat contemptuously, anticipating an easy victory over this lesser opponent, and then struck out. His first blows were delivered with a savage force, and some accuracy, but Stefan kept one step ahead, slipping just out of range of each murderous strike, all the time drawing the Norscan towards him. The big man struck a third, and then a fourth blow, each time missing his mark by bare inches. Stefan grinned, and dropped his hands by his side.

'This make it easier for you?' he taunted.

The Norscan screamed out at Stefan in rage and frustration, and swung his sword in a blind fury, aiming at Stefan's unprotected flank. Stefan dodged the blow, and the sword bit deep into the stout wooden beam that stood behind him. As the Norscan tugged desperately at the blade to pull it free, Stefan struck back, finding the exposed flesh of the Norscan's throat with one, telling thrust of his sword. Now the odds were at least even.

Or better than even. Stefan had feared that Lothar Koenig would prove little match for the brutal Norsemen, or, worse, would flee in the confusion of the battle. Wrong on both counts. The bounty hunter was very much with them, and more than holding his own against his opponent, making up in cunning and skill what he lacked in bulk and speed. But that still left Bruno facing the remaining two Norscans on his own. Bruno was a match for most swordsmen, but he was being forced back by the sheer force of the onslaught from his two attackers. The Norscans had him cornered, and, amidst a hail of sword strokes, some of their blows were beginning to find their mark.

Stefan shouted out – something, anything to draw the Norscans' attention – and flung himself across the room towards them. One of the Norscans paid no heed, and continued to tear at Bruno with a manic energy. But the other pulled up, and turned, caught between attack and self-defence. Stefan made him pay dearly for his indecision, knocking the man's sword from his grasp with a mighty kick, then following through with his sword, a two-handed blow that cleaved the Norscan's arm from his shoulder. The Norscan staggered but did not fall, so Stefan struck him again, and then a third time, pouring all he had into the blows until his enemy was beaten to the ground.

Bruno was wounded, but now took new heart, digging deep to find last reserves of strength. His opponent struck at him again, but before long he was using his sword to fend off the blows, not to deliver them. Stefan saw the man glance round and take stock of the situation. The cruel grin on his face was replaced by desperation as he began to look about for a means of escape. There would be none.

Bruno landed the decisive blow, his sword biting deep into the flesh below the Norscan's ribs. Stefan met him as he fell back, two scything strokes of his blade ending the argument for good.

Stefan's first concern was for Bruno. His comrade was covered in blood, and the cuts on his face and arms were many, but they were not deep. Stefan looked for Lothar, already marshalling what energy he had left for one last, desperate, assault. But Lothar had no need of their help. In the space of a few minutes he had turned the tables on his opponent. Stefan saw him standing on the far side of the room, one foot pressing down upon the prostrate form of the Norscan, sword poised to deliver the final blow.

'Wait!' Stefan shouted to him. 'Hold off.' He crossed the room and reached out to stay the bounty hunter's hand. 'Just a minute. We might be able to learn something useful from this creature.' He knelt down and grabbed the man by his straw-blond hair, pulling his face up towards his own.

'Tell us who your leaders are, and where we can find them,' he demanded. 'Tell us, and we may spare your miserable life.'

The other man looked up at Stefan. He was young – probably little more than twenty summers, younger than Stefan himself. But a cruel savagery had run deep through that short life.

Stefan could find no kinship in the other's eyes, nor even the faintest glimmer of compassion. The Norscan sneered up at Stefan.

'If I'd cared about preserving my life, I'd have made other choices long ago,' he muttered.

'Answer me,' Stefan insisted. 'Who leads you? Who freed you from the cells?'

The dying Norscan parted his lips, and spat in Stefan's face. 'I will tell you nothing,' he said.

Stefan stood up, disgusted, and glanced at Lothar, still poised with the sword.

'Go ahead.'

As soon as the way was clear, they got out of the building. They could have delayed little longer. The waters were still rising fast, and the bottom half of the stairway was already submerged.

Stefan led the way out through one of the upper windows, and onto the flat roof. For a while the three men just sat, watching the scene unfolding around them. The citadel had a quite different look now. To the south, it had become a drowned world with only crests of stonework left poking through the churning waters like islands in the sea. They had to keep ahead of the flood, keep moving toward the higher ground, around the palace, at the northern edge of Sigmarsgeist.

'What's our plan?' Bruno asked.

Stefan thought for a moment. 'First we have to get to a place of safety,' he said. 'And try and keep out of the way of the Norscans.'

'How many more do you think there might be?'

'A lot, I fear,' Stefan replied. 'Too many for us to account for on our own.'

'Where are Rilke's men?' Bruno wondered. 'And the Red Guard?'

'Where indeed,' Stefan agreed. 'We need to find the answer to that question if we're going to stand any real chance of defeating the Norscans.'

'Excuse me,' Lothar cut in. 'But when you're talking about "we", I hope you're not including me in your plans?'

'It's your choice,' Stefan replied. 'But it stands to reason you'd be safer if you stayed with us.'

Lothar Koenig smiled, and shook his head. 'No offence, friend,' he said, 'but you seem to attract trouble like a lamp gathers moths. Besides,' he said, getting up and looking around, 'you and I have quite different quests to fulfil. You want to save the world, and all good people in it. Me–' he sheathed his sword, and fastened the buckle of his belt tight around his waist. 'I just want to get out of this a rich man.'

'I'm afraid there's no certainty any of us will get out of this at all,' Stefan said, quietly.

'Be that as it may, I'll take my chances. You go your way, I'll go mine.' He held out his hand. 'No offence.'

Stefan took the bounty hunter's hand, and shook it. 'You owe us nothing,' he said. 'And we owe you a good deal. Take whatever path you must, and take our good wishes with you.'

Bruno nodded, but said nothing. Lothar Koenig looked them up and down once more, then raised his hand in a brief salute, and was gone.

'That man,' Bruno said at last. 'Is nothing better than a looter, out to line his filthy pockets.'

'Maybe,' Stefan concurred. 'But if so, then he's a brave one.' He watched the bounty hunter for a while longer as he picked his way along the skyline with an agility that belied his years. 'Actually,' Stefan said, 'I think he's just a survivor. Not good, nor bad. Just a man doing whatever he has to do to see him through this life.'

Bruno looked round at Stefan, faintly surprised. 'A while ago you wouldn't have talked like that,' he observed. 'You'd have had no truck with the likes of him.'

'That might be so,' Stefan agreed. 'Perhaps I've started to see things differently. Perhaps the line between black and white, good and bad, isn't as clear as I once thought it was.'

He got to his feet, and helped Bruno up in turn. He clapped a hand on his friend's shoulder.

'This isn't the place or time for such discussions,' he said. 'We need to get moving too.'

'Agreed,' Bruno said. 'But to where?'

'I want to know what's happened to the Red Guard,' Stefan said. 'I can't believe they've all been swept aside in such a short space of time. I need to find Konstantin.'

'Konstantin?'

'He should have command over every man in this city. And we can't hope to turn this situation about without them.'

'Do you really think Konstantin will help us? We were hardly honoured guests last time we came before him.'

'Things have changed,' Stefan said. 'And they'll change a good deal more before long unless we can act.'

'And Anaise?'

'Anaise has contributed to this evil, knowingly or not. But we stand a better chance of dealing with her if we can sway Konstantin.'

Bruno fell silent, pondering Stefan's words. 'You're right,' he said. 'We must reach the palace then, if we can.' His head was nodding agreement, but his face told a different story. It took Stefan a moment to realise what must be going through his mind.

'Of course,' he said then. 'Bea.'

'I'm sorry, Stefan,' Bruno blurted out. 'I know there are more important matters to be resolved. But I can't just forget about her.'

'No, no,' Stefan assured him. 'It's I who should apologise.' He took hold of Bruno. 'Of course you must go,' he told him. 'You must do whatever you can. But–' he hesitated. 'Is it not possible that Bea is still inside the palace too?'

'Possible, yes, but...' Bruno shook his head, firmly. 'There's only one place she would want to be,' he said. 'Amongst the fallen, tending to the wounded as best she coan. She's out here, somewhere. I'm sure of that.'

Stefan mulled over his words. 'You may be right,' he concluded. 'Then we must go our separate ways.' He thought for a moment.

'We'll stay together until we reach dry ground,' he concluded. 'Then I'll head in towards the heart of the citadel,
and the palace.'

'And I will look for Bea,' Bruno said. 'Wherever she is, I'll
find her.'

'I pray you will,' Stefan said. 'And may the gods smile
kindly upon us both.'

ANAISE HELD OUT the battered metal bowl, and all but forced
it into Bea's hands.

'Take it!' she demanded. 'What are you waiting for? This is
water drawn from the holy flood. It can heal your patient,
can't it? Or will you now deny everything that you have ever
believed?'

'This same water has claimed the lives of countless of your
people,' Bea countered, quietly. Anaise stared at her,
unblinking.

'Water touched with the gift of Tal Dur,' she insisted. 'In
the right hands – the hands of a healer – it can restore the
powers of life. Isn't that so?' she demanded.

Bea shrugged, and tried in vain to evade Anaise's grasp,
her burning stare. In truth she no longer knew what to
believe. 'I don't know,' she said. 'I don't know anything any
more.'

Anaise cast her eyes down at the injured woman, barely
more than a bundle of rags, lying on the damp floor
between them. She had been trapped between two buildings
when one had collapsed into the other. Anaise knew little
enough of the arts of medicine, but she knew that the
woman would die soon, and she knew that Bea knew it too.

'Why do you hesitate?' she pressed. 'You know that the
waters are her only hope. "That which lays waste may also
yet make whole". Isn't that what the prophesies tell us?'

Bea shook her head, unhappily. There was no point in
denying the truth of what the Guide had said. Without
another word, she took the proffered bowl and began to dab
water from it lightly upon the injured woman's brow. She
waited a moment then dipped her fingers carefully in the
bowl again, this time letting drops of water fall where the

woman's wounds were gravest. The woman stirred, fitfully, then began to breathe more easily.

Anaise jumped to her feet, her eyes ablaze with excitement. 'There!' she exclaimed, delightedly. 'You see! The gifts of Tal Dur begin to work their magic!'

'They channel their powers through me,' Bea said, hesitantly.

'Then they shall channel that power through me, too,' Anaise declared. 'You shall show me, Bea.' She crouched down once more and put her hands either side of Bea's face, running her fingers through her curled brown hair as though she were a treasure. Bea shrugged her off and turned back to her patient.

'This is not Tal Dur,' she said, 'only a weak reflection of its magic. The true power of Tal Dur will only be found at the water's source.'

'But that cannot be far from here,' Anaise insisted. 'It cannot.'

'No,' Bea conceded, wearily. 'It cannot be far.' She was tired. Too tired for any more subterfuge, any more trying to divine what was the right thing to do. She just wanted to be left alone, left to answer the call of healing.

The woman coughed, and her body went into a sudden spasm, then, for the first time since Bea had come to her, opened her eyes. Bea turned to the woman's husband, a pitiful figure who had been sitting mute on the sidelines whilst she tried to work her healing.

'Keep her warm,' she told the man. 'Pray, and she will live, I'm sure of it.'

'The waters cured her,' the man replied, his voice cracked and thin. 'She should take more of them.'

'No,' Bea said, firmly. 'It's not safe for you to do what I did. You would cause more harm than good.'

Anaise's patience had worn thin. She tugged Bea to her feet, roughly and without ceremony. 'You know where the source can be found,' she insisted. 'Where is it, Bea? Where?'

Bea struggled half-heartedly, but knew she could never evade Anaise. Only one thing would satisfy her now, she was blind to all else.

'All right,' she said at last. 'Very well. My sense is that the waters will converge near the bottom of the Well of Sadness. That, if anywhere, is where the locus of Tal Dur may be found.'

Anaise glowered. 'Nonsense,' she retorted. 'I spent long hours sitting at its edge only this day. It was dry as tinder.'

'The ways of Tal Dur are not so transparent,' Bea said, obdurately. 'The first waters were channelled elsewhere, to surface at the lower part of the citadel. But I will wager my all,' she went on, 'when the springs at the very heart of Tal Dur burst forth, it will be through the Well of Sadness.'

'Then that is where we go,' Anaise declared. She seized Bea and started to drag her along behind her. 'We go there now. I've waited long enough.'

FORTUNE HAD FAVOURED Stefan, at least as far as the gates of the palace. His journey across the rooftops of the city towards the higher ground had taken a zig-zag course, following the paths connecting the taller buildings that still held out against the flood. There had been times, when two buildings were separated only by a short span of water, that he had been tempted to leap into the flow and swim. But he did not. Some instinct of nature told him to avoid the dark sea that was slowly swallowing up the citadel, even if it meant finding a much longer way around. Progress was steady, but slow.

For the most part, he managed to stay clear of the Norscans. Once or twice he had seen gangs of them, patrolling the distant skyline, or traversing the flood waters in makeshift boats. It seemed that they were unopposed. With no sign anywhere of the Red Guard, the Norscans had taken complete control of the citadel. Just once, Stefan encountered a single northerner, climbing from the shattered window of a building. He was laden with plunder he had stripped from the house, and hadn't been expecting to find an armed adversary waiting for him. The combat was brief and bloody, and left another Norscan body floating on the tide. But otherwise Stefan avoided contact where he could. This was not the time to fight, not yet.

In time he reached the heart of the citadel, where the waters had only just begun to penetrate. Now, as he came within sight of the palace, Stefan realised what had happened to the Red Guard. They were here, scores of them, lining every wall and standing guard upon every door and gateway, even though there was no obvious sign of Norscan attack.

Stefan sheathed his weapon as he climbed the hill that led to the great courtyard. The streets beyond the palace were teeming with people, workers no longer, now simply refugees from the unforgiving flood. But there was to be no refuge for them within the palace, the guards surrounding the walls refused to let them inside.

Stefan fought his way through the crowd and approached the gates with his hands high above his head. There was no way he could hope to fight his way in. It would have to be his word, not his sword, that served him now.

An exchange of shouts greeted Stefan as he approached the gates. Several of the guards had recognised him and had drawn their swords. They looked on, some incredulously, as Stefan drew out his own weapon then held it out towards the men in scarlet. 'I am a prisoner,' he said. 'I offer you my surrender.'

KONSTANTIN VON AUGEN had taken his customary place in the chamber of the High Council. Although at least a dozen of his men were with him, he looked very much alone. When he at last looked up, Stefan saw he was much altered. The madness that had seized hold of Sigmarsgeist had taken a different path in Konstantin. The elegant, lined face with its mane of iron-grey hair was unchanged, but his eyes were empty, devoid of hope or inspiration. Konstantin looked like a man already contemplating the aftermath of defeat.

He looked up at Stefan for a few moments before seeming to recognise him.

'Ah,' he said at last. 'It is you, then. I thought it might be Baecker. I am waiting news of his return.'

One of the attendant guards stepped forward and knelt by the Guide. He coughed, awkwardly. 'Sire,' he began, a tone of careful deference to his voice. 'You will recall the news that was brought earlier. Hans Baecker is dead. My men have recovered his body.'

Konstantin nodded, absentmindedly, oblivious to what had been said. 'Baecker has a plan,' he told Stefan. 'A plan to save Sigmarsgeist.'

'Konstantin,' Stefan said. 'I must speak with you. I need you to hear what I have to say.' The guards standing around the chamber looked from Stefan to the Guide, uncertain whether Stefan was to be treated as a prisoner or an emissary. When Stefan took a step closer to the Guide, he was not opposed. Stefan moved within arms' length of Konstantin, then settled upon the floor of the chamber, facing the Guide.

'Why do you keep your men here?' he began. 'Don't you realise that the Norscans will soon have the run of Sigmarsgeist? Your people are being tortured and killed. Sigmarsgeist is being torn apart.'

Konstantin drew himself upright and stared back at Stefan. For a moment he assumed the grandeur and authority of old.

'My men will defend the sanctity of Sigmarsgeist,' he said. 'No enemy – neither man nor flood – shall pass through these gates. Sigmarsgeist shall prevail, ready to face the dark tide to come.'

Stefan wanted to grab hold of Konstantin and shake him. But instead he mustered all of his patience. Reason, he told himself, reason must prevail.

'Look around you,' he told the Guide. 'You devoted your life to building a fortress, a great wall to keep the forces of evil at bay.' He paused, and took another breath. Konstantin still gazed at him, his blank expression unchanged. 'But all you have kept at bay are your own, frightened people,' Stefan continued. 'Somewhere, Konstantin, your purpose was lost. You became what you wanted to destroy, and opened the gates to the very thing you wished to oppose.

'The great battle against the darkness that you spoke of so eloquently. It is not ahead, in some distant time yet to be imagined,' he told the Guide. 'It is here. And it is now.'

'Baecker will reverse our fortunes,' Konstantin said again, with a hollow defiance. 'Sigmarsgeist will stand firm.'

On impulse, Stefan reached forward and took hold of the Guide. No one moved to stop him. 'Baecker is dead,' he reminded the old man. 'Your men have his body.'

'His plan was to breach the walls to release the flood waters,' one of the guards added. 'I fear it is too late for that now.'

'And where is your sister?' Stefan demanded. 'Is she here, by your side? Is she fighting for the soul of Sigmarsgeist?'

'My sister?' Konstantin looked around, taking in the figures standing about the room, as if searching for some sight of Anaise. 'My sister is lost,' he said, at last, sadly. 'And so now are we all.'

'We are not lost yet,' Stefan told him, defiantly. 'Until we stand at the very gates of Morr, there is always hope.' He paused, trying to marshal the thoughts racing about his mind. 'Do you remember,' he said, 'when we first spoke. You asked me if I knew what it was that I stood for? Not just what I stood against, Konstantin, but what I stood *for*?'

Konstantin made no response.

'I couldn't answer your question then,' Stefan went on. 'But I know the answer now.' He got to his feet. 'This – this struggle, until the very last hope is extinguished, that is what I stand for. I stand for all the people who live their lives, not by some shining ideal, but as well as they can, in order to survive. I stand for *life*, Konstantin, impure and imperfect.' He turned and scanned the faces looking on. 'And, by all that is mighty, for as long as life survives, we owe a debt to the gods to fight for every precious last breath of it.'

Konstantin looked up at Stefan, a broken man at the end of his life. But somewhere inside him, Stefan's words found their mark, or at least tugged at a memory of the dream that the Guide once held for Sigmarsgeist.

'What is it you want of me?' he asked, mildly. 'What do you want me to do?'

Stefan looked round in search of the soldier who had spoken up before. 'How did the Norscans get out?' he asked. 'Who set them free?'

'The mutant,' the guard replied. 'The one whose body bears the living tattoo. He accounted for Baecker, and Rilke too.' The man looked round, nervously, at his comrades. 'He has – he has the confidence of our lady Anaise,' he said.

'Then he will account for all Sigmarsgeist unless we act now,' Stefan replied, tersely. 'You must turn control of your men over to me,' he told Konstantin. 'All is not lost yet, but we must act now.'

A look of pain crossed Konstantin's troubled features. 'You last came before me as an enemy of Sigmarsgeist,' he recalled.

'Then ask yourself this,' Stefan urged him. 'Ask yourself how things have come to this. Ask yourself who are the true enemies of Sigmarsgeist now.'

Konstantin made no reply, but there were tears welling up in his eyes. After some hesitation, he slipped a bronze ring from his right hand, and offered it to Stefan.

'This is my authority,' he told him. 'My sovereignty and my power. Take it and you have my all.' He cast his eyes about the chamber, meeting the gaze of his men. 'Witness this act,' he commanded. 'And witness with it the end to the vain folly that has brought us here. He is your captain now,' he told them. 'Follow his command as though it were my own.'

The Guide slumped back, his eyes closed, his breath slow and deep.

'And may Sigmar grant some stay against the dimming of our light,' he whispered.

As THE LONG day of carnage gave way to grim night, so Alexei Zucharov made his way through the drowning citadel. He had no need to look for the healer girl, no need to guess where she might be found. He had Kyros to light his path, to guide him, sure and certain, to his destination. The spirit of the dark lord flowed in every fibre of his being. It was the voice that whispered incessantly inside his head, and it was the rhythm that beat, without pause or falter, inside of him, a second heartbeat next to his own. Zucharov could feel it rising from the golden amulet clamped tight about his wrist, a burning flow of pure energy pouring through his body.

His progress was slow, but inexorable. Where he met with resistance – from what few of the Red Guard were on the streets, or the even fewer townsfolk stupid enough to stand in his way – he repressed it, ruthlessly. He dealt out death, but not as the Norscans had done. Zucharov took no delight in this simple, meaningless killing. His was the greater purpose ordained by Kyros. He killed swiftly, efficiently and economically, expending no more effort than was necessary to remove the obstacle. He would leave the Norscans to enjoy their mindless plunder whilst they may. The greatest spoils of blood still lay ahead.

Beneath the sound of the surging waters, he could hear the last desperate calls of those left behind in the ruins, praying against all odds that salvation would still come. They would pray in vain; if the waters did not claim them, then the Norscans surely would. Their plight did not interest Zucharov.

He stood, head turned slightly to one side. Gradually, Kyros tuned out the plaintive wails of hunter and hunted, and the tumult of the waters, leaving only silence. Gradually, into the silence came the sound of footsteps, two pairs of feet, hurrying away from the rising tide towards the dry ground above.

Zucharov stepped back into the shadow of an adjacent street, and waited. The footsteps grew louder, and with them the sound of two women's voices, one raised against the other. Zucharov stood within the shadows, very still, and let them come. Only when they had passed, one tugging the other behind her, did Zucharov step from his place of concealment and call out, 'Where are you going?'

The two women stopped, and turned around. Zucharov moved closer, stepping fully under what light the moons allowed, recognising one of them as Anaise. He watched, with satisfaction, as the expression upon their faces turned from surprise to a disbelieving horror. The transformation that had raged like a fire inside him and out was all but complete now. Every inch of his flesh was now mapped by the lines of the tattoo. Even Anaise could not have imagined it coming to this. Besides, who knew what dark future each woman saw – or imagined she saw written in the terrible tableau of his face?

'Where are you going?' he said again, slowly, deliberately. 'Where are you going, Anaise?'

He watched the Guide carefully. In her suprise she had let go of the healer. Now she grabbed the girl back, like some precious treasure she meant to horde. Zucharov knew already what reply she would make, but it amused his dark lord to hear the worm-tongue words.

'I was searching,' she stammered. 'Searching for you.'

Zucharov nodded, an almost serene smile playing upon his hideous face. 'I am glad of that,' he said.

'Yes,' Anaise affirmed, more boldly now. She held the healer out towards him, as if in proof of her words. Bea screamed out and struggled to escape, but the Guide was deaf to her pleas.

'See. I have the girl safe. I was bringing her to you. Now the time is come. Now Tal Dur is come.'

Zucharov listened to her words, and, behind her words, heard also what was unspoken: the lies, the duplicity and the manipulation. Anaise thought she could use him, trick him. She was not so stupid as to try and directly oppose his will, not yet at least. But she still believed that Tal Dur could be hers alone. That delusion was her weakness. And there would be no room for weakness in the world that was to come.

Immersed in his contemplation of the Guide, Zucharov only now noticed the third player in the scene as he advanced upon them. A voice, raised in warning or alarm, rang out, calling the healer's name out loud. A figure came running towards the two women, sword held aloft. Zucharov edged back into the shadow and looked on. Memory stirred at the sound of the voice. An old, abandoned memory buried deep in the recesses of the mind of the man he had once been.

It was him. Kumansky. The face from the past. And from the present. The more recent memory of the battle, bitter and rancorous, rose in Zucharov's mind. Now he would finish it. Now he would be avenged.

But he was mistaken. It was not Stefan Kumansky who was now sprinting towards the two women. Another face, almost equally distant, yet still familiar, swum into view. Zucharov trawled through the debris of that fading life, and seized upon the name: Bruno, Bruno Hausmann. Not Kumansky, but almost as good. Bruno, Kumansky's oldest, most trusted friend. Killing him would be satisfaction enough, until the final reckoning came.

At the very moment that the girl Bea tried to shout out a warning, Zucharov stepped forward where he could be seen, and drew out his sword. It seemed to take an age for the rushing swordsman to see him standing beside the women, and another for recognition to strike. But when it did, the effect was profound.

'Alexei.' Bruno's voice was quiet, almost stunned. He looked upon Zucharov, at the grotesque facsimile of what his former comrade had become. Fear, confusion and disbelief all met in his face. Zucharov read each separate, jarring emotion. Smelt them, and tasted them, as clear as he could taste the blood that was soon to flow.

'Alexei,' Bruno said again, and then his expression hardened. He looked at Anaise and to Bea, still held firmly in the other woman's unyielding embrace. Bruno hesitated, wavering for just an instant, then took his sword in both his hands.

*Now it begins,* the voice whispered to Zucharov.

'Alexei, I'm sorry,' Bruno shouted, then charged towards him. Zucharov saw at once in the speed and movement of his body, and in the way that he carried his weapon, that this opponent would be different. This was no red-shirted conscript, no wretched townsman fighting in a last, crazed defence of his home. He would be stronger, more skilful and more resilient than all but one of those that Zucharov had fought. But he would make the same mistake that others had made: Rilke, Baecker and the feeble bounty hunter who had served to bring him to Sigmarsgeist. Bruno would believe that he had enough skill, enough guile, and enough bravery to defeat him, and he would be wrong.

Bruno fell upon Zucharov in a fury, his sword probing Zucharov's defences. He was not a small man, but he was faster than most, certainly fast enough to catch Zucharov off-guard if he allowed his concentration to falter. For a while the two swordsmen circled each other, trading blow for blow. But each thunderous stroke from Zucharov drained away a little more of Bruno's strength.

He is already wounded, Zucharov noted, he cannot endure long.

He swung his sword two-handed, aiming to smash his way through the other man's guard. Bruno saw the blow coming and swerved aside. For a moment, Zucharov was left vulnerable. He saw the glint of steel and felt the cold stab of Bruno's blade as it penetrated his flesh. The pain was vivid, brief; forgotten in an instant. He turned, with improbable speed, and met the second strike with his own sword. He caught Bruno just below the wrist, not where he intended. But it was enough to loosen Bruno's hold upon his weapon. His opponent cried out in agony, dropping his guard momentarily. Zucharov struck out again, this time knocking the sword clear from Bruno's hand.

Zucharov experienced a sensation of disdain, almost disappointment. It had been easy, too easy. Just for a moment, he made the error of assuming the battle already won. In that same moment, Bruno threw himself at him, raining down blows with his fists in a last, desperate assault. In the tumult that followed, Zucharov's own sword was dislodged, and parity restored.

At least half of Bruno's blows were finding their target, but it made no difference. To Zucharov they were little more than the fluttering of an insect upon his face. He hit back, battering his opponent from side to side, until blood was flowing from Bruno's face. Bruno struck out again, with all that remained of his strength, but wide of the mark. Zucharov's reply knocked the other man off his feet, and tumbling across the ground. By the time Bruno had regained his feet, Zucharov had recovered his sword.

Bruno closed on Zucharov one final time, but the look in his eyes betrayed the hopelessness of his situation. Zucharov shrugged off the challenge, and pushed his opponent away. Then, as Bea screamed out in despair, he thrust out his sword, and drove the blade through Bruno Hausmann's heart.

# CHAPTER TWENTY
## The Wrath of the Gods

WHAT COULD STEFAN hope to achieve with the small force now at his command? What little he knew of the Red Guard – so recently his adversaries – told him that they would give their all, but he had no idea whether that would be enough. He did not know if Sigmarsgeist could be saved, but the briefest tour of what remained of the citadel quickly confirmed that Baecker's death had been in vain. All attempts to force a breach in the city walls had failed. More than two- thirds of the citadel was now below water, buildings and dwellings wrecked and submerged. Only the tallest of buildings still survived, those and a steadily diminishing island at the centre of the citadel, with the palace at its heart.

But Stefan was sure of two things at least: he had to destroy the roaming gangs of Norscans that were feeding off the carcass of Sigmarsgeist, and stop Alexei Zucharov. That the two were inextricably linked, he had no doubt. Their fates, and his, were now intertwined. There would be no reasoning with the Norscans, no course of action open but to hunt them down, and then fight them to the death. He led his men on, out into the citadel, knowing full well that most would never return.

The appearance of the guards upon the streets was greeted with commotion from the surviving townspeople. Word quickly spread of their arrival, and faint hope began to supplant the despair that had settled like a shroud across the citadel. But with the hope came impossible demands. Men and women cried to them from the roofs of flooded houses. Buildings were still collapsing into the swirling waters, creating mayhem. And those that had so far survived the worst were cold, hungry, and in urgent need of care. But Stefan could not help them. First he had to deal with the Norscans. Until then, anything else would be at best a postponement of the greater horror to come.

The most important task now was to eliminate the Norscans, and find the man who led them. The man he had once known as his friend. For the moment the hopes of the people had to be ignored. In the end, it was their only true hope of survival.

There had been no time for Stefan to win the trust of the men he now commanded. But the scarlet-clad soldiers had so far fought more bravely, more defiantly than he had dared hope. Their belief in the future that was to have been Sigmarsgeist might have been built upon a falsehood, but it was deeply held, and they would cling to that belief until every last drop of their blood was spilled.

At the very edge of the flooded area, a group of women had taken shelter in a chapel, a place of humble worship to the goddess Shallya. The women – twenty or thirty of them – had huddled together inside as the waters rose around them, united in their fear, and in their hope that the watchful goddess, and the very safety of their number, would protect them. The Norscans had fallen upon them like wolves, taking what pleasures they liked before slaughtering the women indiscriminately.

Stefan and his men heard the screams from afar, the sounds guiding them like a beacon to that forsaken place. But by the time the Red Guard arrived, the grim deed was done, and the Norscans, clad to a man in mocking white, were spilling back out onto the street, already seeking the next diversion to feed their bestial greed.

Stefan and his men saw to it that that they had all the diversion they could handle, and plenty more besides. They swarmed over the Norscans, the Red far outnumbering the White, totally overwhelming them. It was a small revenge, only a beginning, but victory tasted no less sweet for it. Stefan waded in amongst the clashing steel, and settled upon his target. A large, grinning Norscan was emerging from the chapel, tightening his breeches as he went. The man was oblivious to what was going on until it was too late. Stefan didn't wait for the man to find his sword. Before the Norscan had even moved, Stefan took aim and plunged home his blade. A flower of dark blood blossomed out over the white uniform as the Norscan screamed out in agony. Stefan pulled the sword clear and, with the next stroke, sliced off the man's head.

He looked around for likely opponents, but with the Red Guard in the ascendant the battle was already all but won. A flash of movement caught Stefan's eye. He turned, and saw a figure slip out from the chapel, running for cover. Another moment and the Norscan would be out of reach. Stefan pulled the knife from his belt and took careful aim before hurling the blade. The knife arrowed through the air before catching the Norscan below one shoulder. The Norscan slowed, stumbled, and fell.

Stefan hurried across to the prostrate enemy. This one he would keep alive, for a while at least. He pulled the knife free then turned the Norscan onto his back. The pale face stared up at Stefan, defiance in his eyes.

The man started to swear at Stefan, harsh curses from his barbaric land.

Stefan slapped him hard across the face. 'Be quiet,' he commanded. 'Tell me about the mutant, the tattooed mutant.'

The Norscan struggled, trying to break free, but Stefan held him down. The marauder glared up at Stefan. 'The tattooed one? He'll swallow you whole and spit your bones out into the water,' he sneered. 'Head south if you're in a hurry to meet your death.'

'Get up,' Stefan said curtly, tugging the man to his feet.

Weak from blood loss, the Norscan was unable to put up much resistance.

Stefan wordlessly dragged his prisoner along behind him, back towards the chapel. The battle was over, all the other Norscans were either dead or dying. Of the Red Guard, all but three had come through the encounter unharmed. It was as good a start as Stefan could have hoped for, but now there were hard decisions to be made.

'You've had a taste of what it feels like to get your own back,' he said to them. 'I hope it tastes good.' His words were met by a chorus of cheers from the Red Guard.

'You'll have plenty more chances to enjoy that taste,' Stefan assured them. 'But it's not going to be so easy from here.' He looked round at the men, meeting the gaze of as many as he could. 'There are Norscans everywhere,' he told them. 'And doubtless things far worse than them, too, creatures touched by Chaos. We have to spread out, form ourselves into smaller units.' He took a breath, measuring up what needed to be done.

'I need a few men to come with me,' he said, 'five or six, no more than that. I warn you, mine will be the party at most risk. You others, form into three groups. My group will head south. The rest of you cover the other quarters of the city, as far as you can go towards the water line. Do what you can for your people, but your priority must be the Norscans. They must be destroyed at all costs.'

'What about this one?' a voice from the back demanded. Stefan glanced around at his prisoner, seized the man by the scruff of the neck and threw him back towards the gathering of Red Guards. 'Deal with him as you will,' he said.

NO LONGER WOULD there be safety, nor security, in numbers. Stefan had left the gates of the palace at the head of a formidable force, a troop approaching a hundred men. For a short while, he had felt invulnerable. Now, he headed back across the dark, watery wasteland of the citadel in search of Zucharov with a bare half dozen guards at his side. Now he was both hunter and hunted once again.

Still the exodus came, long lines of bedraggled people heading in the opposite direction, fleeing the merciless waters with whatever they could carry. Whenever he could, Stefan spoke to them, always with the same question. But none of the frightened refugees would admit to any knowledge of the tattooed mutant. Most would struggle past without making any response, and those few who did meet his eye only answered with a short shake of the head. Before long, even the last of the refugees had disappeared. Stefan and his men had reached the flood line and were wading in water that was knee deep and still rising. The citadel seemed to have emptied.

Stefan looked around, increasingly convinced that the trail had led only to a dead end. Zucharov was not here. He would have no purpose in being here.

As he searched around, desperately looking for any clue, his eye fell upon the remains of a house, its upper floor a jagged spur of stone and earth still standing above the waters. A face appeared briefly at a window, then pulled back hurriedly at the sight of Stefan and his comrades.

'You in there,' Stefan called out. 'Show yourself. We mean you no harm.'

He stood waiting for a response. The face did not reappear. 'We mean you no harm,' Stefan repeated. 'You must leave your home,' he said, determinedly. 'You will drown unless you leave now. Let us help you.'

A few moments later the face reappeared, peering over the ledge of the window. 'We cannot leave,' a voice, worn down with age and exhaustion, replied.

'My men will help you to safety,' Stefan assured them. 'We just want to talk to you first.'

The old man extended his head from the window to take a better look at Stefan. He stared at him for a few moments, then said, 'Who are you?'

'I am Stefan Kumansky,' Stefan said. 'And an enemy to your enemies.'

The old man peered at him through the gloom. 'You're one of the ones who came to the citadel with the healer,' he said. 'With the healer.'

'I am,' Stefan affirmed.

The old man disappeared back inside the room for a moment, then called down to Stefan, an urgency in his voice now.

'Come up here,' he said. 'Come quickly.'

Inside, the house was dark and crumbling, the stairs disintegrating under Stefan's feet as he climbed up. Whoever was still in the house only had a little time left to get to safety. Stefan climbed the stair quickly, but with caution. He had no idea what awaited him above. Reason told him that it could not be Zucharov, but he held his sword drawn ready nonetheless.

As he reached the top of the steps he saw the old man who had been at the window sitting by the dim light of a spluttering oil lamp. Next to him a woman, her body wrapped in a heavy shawl to keep out the cold, was bending down over something or someone lying stretched out upon the floor of the tiny room. The light was too poor for Stefan to see clearly, but he felt his pulse suddenly begin to race.

'What is it?' he demanded of the old couple. 'Why are you still here?'

'The healer loved him,' the old man said, sadly. 'He went to her aid.'

'But the dark one fell upon him,' the woman muttered. 'The dark one was sent from Morr to claim him.'

As Stefan stepped into the room, the bundle laid out upon the floor stirred slowly, and a voice, so weak as to be all but unrecognisable, called his name.

'Bruno!' Stefan cried out. He fell down upon his knees at his friend's side, and took Bruno's head in his hands. His comrade opened his eyes, and forced a semblance of a smile.

'Zucharov,' Bruno whispered. 'Sorry, Stefan. I couldn't stop him.'

'Here,' Stefan beseeched the old couple. 'Give me some light.'

The woman passed Stefan the lamp, and he bent towards Bruno's chest, to see that his tunic was sodden and sticky with blood. Carefully, he prised the fabric apart, trying to get to the wound. His hand fastened upon the locket hanging from a chain around Bruno's neck, the likeness of the goddess Shallya.

'It's all – right,' Bruno said, struggling to force out the words. 'Our lady intervened to – spare me. See?' he gasped. 'The icon – deflected the blade.'

Stefan took the lamp in his left hand and looked closely at the wound. The talisman around Bruno's neck was battered, almost folded in two by the impact. Clearly, it had taken some of the force of Zucharov's sword. But the wound was still deep, and a thick, darkish blood was oozing from the jagged incision in Bruno's chest. Stefan was no surgeon, but he had seen enough battle to recognise those who the gods would spare, and those that were bound for Morr. The locket had not so much saved Bruno's life, as prolonged his death. Stefan pressed his hand against the bloody gash, hoping against hope for his comrade's survival, despairing in his own helplessness.

'He loved the healer, with his life,' the old man said, solemnly. 'And she was our redemption, our hope. We could not leave him to die alone.'

'He's not going to die,' Stefan retorted, defiantly. But his heart and his head were telling different stories. 'I'm going to get you to safety,' he told Bruno. 'Somewhere where we can take proper care of that wound.'

Bruno's eyes flickered open again. 'No,' he said, a harder tone in his voice. 'You must save Bea,' he said. 'Zucharov – took her, with Anaise. Back to – the palace. To find – Tal Dur.' A violent cough shook through Bruno's body, and spittle flecked with blood appeared at the corners of his mouth. 'Stefan,' he urged. 'Please. You must save her.'

Every instinct inside of Stefan told him he could not abandon his comrade. He could not leave him – not now, not here in this dank, forsaken place. It could not end like this. Yet he knew also that Bruno was right. If he did not find Bea, and with her Zucharov, then all would be lost. Everything that they had endured – and Bruno's sacrifice – would have been for nothing. As he looked down upon his friend, he tried to hold his emotions back, but the tears still fell from his eyes. He looked at the woman who had been tending Bruno's wounds.

'Can he be moved?'

She shook her head, emphatically. Stefan stood up, and shouted to the soldiers standing round.

'Fetch some help,' he commanded them. 'In the meantime, in the name of the gods, do whatever is within your power to help him.' He turned to the old man and his wife.

'Will you stay with him also?' he asked.

'We would not do otherwise,' the woman said. 'We will give back such healing as we can.'

'You're going back to the palace?' a guard asked. 'Alone?'

'There's only one man I'm looking for now,' Stefan replied. 'And he will be waiting for me.'

ANARCHY HAD BEEN loosed upon the world. The whole of Sigmarsgeist had become consumed within a carnival of death and destruction. Soldiers ran amidst the remains of houses and streets, fighting running battles, their blood mixing with the boiling, foaming waters. The people of Sigmarsgeist, once so organised, so industrious, were running, too, but without purpose now. They were running anywhere that afforded shelter, running from the tides of water and steel that had engulfed the citadel.

Anaise von Augen looked around at the destruction of her life's work with astonishment, and with a crazed sense of delight. Had she not known it? Sigmarsgeist would be torn down before it could be made anew. The old would be swept aside. Only when it had been purged, utterly and completely, would Sigmarsgeist be ready to greet the new age: the age of Tal Dur.

The girl had ceased to resist. At the moment when Zucharov had killed Bruno, Bea had gone wild, suddenly consumed with pain and despair, and had fought like a wildcat to free herself from Anaise's grip. But Anaise was far too strong for her. There was never any possibility of her letting the healer go, not even for a moment, and gradually Bea's protests and struggles had subsided until, finally, she

hung limply upon Anaise's arm, an animal being led meekly
to the slaughter.

Anaise strode through the carnage, untouched and invulnerable. Zucharov, walking a few paces behind, was her
shield, her merciless sword to fend off any who dared to
come too close. There were few enough of them, and none
lived to regret their folly. The time would soon come when
her protector, too, would have outlived his usefulness. But
for now, he still served, as all had come to serve her. As the
mighty powers of Tal Dur in turn would come, so soon now,
to serve her.

Within sight of the gates of the palace, Anaise stopped,
and turned her face to the sky. She looked about, listening
intently to the sounds echoing around her. Keeping Bea
secure within one arm, she lifted the other above her
head.

'Listen,' she said, to Bea, to Zucharov, to any who would
hear her.

'What is it?' Zucharov demanded. 'Why have you
stopped?'

'Listen.' Anaise said again.

'I hear nothing,'

'That is it,' Anaise said, a new excitement rising in her
voice. 'That is exactly it.'


KONSTANTIN HAD HEARD it too. Hidden away within his
chamber in the highest reaches of the palace he had heard,
or, rather, sensed the sudden cessation of the roaring of the
waters that battered against the fabric of his dreams.

His lieutenants had entered his room without even the
formality of knocking. The elder Guide could see at once
from their faces that they believed themselves to be the bear-
ers of good news.

'Majesty,' one began. 'The assault upon the citadel is
ended!'

'The waters are no longer rising,' his comrade went on,
eagerly. 'All is growing calm.'

Konstantin smiled at them, indulging their humour. 'I
hear,' he said, quietly.

'Do you think that Kumansky was successful?' the first man asked of him. 'Perhaps the outer walls have indeed been breached?'

'No,' Konstantin replied. 'I do not think Kumansky was successful.' He watched his lieutenant's face fall.

'Then what?' the man asked, uncertainly. 'What can it mean?'

Konstantin did not answer the question, but instead turned his attention inwards, drawing deep upon the insight and wisdom that, in his madness and his folly, he had all but lost. After a long pause, he opened his eyes and looked up at the expectant faces of his men.

'It means,' he said at last, 'that it is time for you to stand down from your posts. Time for you to leave me. Time to leave the palace, if that is your will.'

The two men were amongst the oldest and most trusted of his officers. They had followed him without question or complaint, all through the long rise and swift descent of Sigmarsgeist. Now he dismissed them for the last time, with no more than a word and a gesture of his hand. The officers stared back at the Guide in disbelief.

'Sire,' one said. 'We will not go. We will stay at your side, and serve you through whatever is to come.'

'I release you from my service,' Konstantin said again, with steel in his voice. 'Only solitude may serve me now. Go.' He turned away, and when he spoke again, his words were no longer for them.

'What there is left to face, I must face alone,' he said.

He did not turn back, nor speak another word, until at last the two men had retreated reluctantly from his sight. Then he sat, and waited, alone with the stillness that had now settled like a cloud over Sigmarsgeist. He did not have to wait for long.

The rumbling started deep within the palace itself. Konstantin could not place it exactly, but he did not have to. He knew where it came from, and he knew – now – what it meant. It came from the very heart of the palace, and rose from the depths to touch the very top of its highest towers. It was a rumbling like the anger of the gods, deep and unforgiving. Konstantin watched as first the table, then the walls around him started to shake. He bowed his head.

'Anaise, my sister,' the Guide murmured. 'Do you hear it? It is the voice of judgement, calling us to account.'

Konstantin von Augen closed his eyes, and prayed. For the last time, he prayed to the holy memory of Sigmar, a prayer of atonement, heavy with regret. And he prayed that, if the gods should ever choose to grant him another life, he should never again grow to be so blind.


YARD BY YARD, and sometimes inch by bloody inch, Stefan had fought his way back to within sight of the gates of the palace. By now, all order had broken down, the hierarchy of control was defined by the outcome of single acts of combat, Red Guard pitted against Norscan, and Norscans turning their cruel rage upon anyone who came within sight. Not all the combatants were human. As Stefan edged closer he began to encounter those whose mutations had placed them far beyond the bounds of the mortal realm. These were the creatures of the dark, nameless abominations, once chained within their cells in the dungeons of the palace, now freed to exact their revenge upon humankind as they chose.

The attack came without warning, a flash of movement and colour, something tumbling from out of the sky, plunging from the ledge of a building high above. The daemon spun onto its feet in front of Stefan and stood before him, a shimmering grotesque of muscle and bone, razor-sharp talons adorning the claws on each of its sinuous arms. It shifted and settled back on its haunches, lithe as a dancer, savouring the encounter to come. Stefan sensed it had been waiting for him, its sole purpose to stop or delay him reaching the palace.

Stefan drew breath then rushed forward, hoping for a quick and decisive resolution. The Chaos creature moved with astonishing speed and agility, springing from its haunches to leap into the air above its opponent's head. Stefan spun around, disorientated, holding his sword high to fend off the anticipated attack. He felt a blow upon his back, then wiry, powerful limbs wrapped themselves about his neck, and razor talons were clawing at the exposed flesh of his throat. Stefan twisted from left to right, and managed to dislodge the creature from his back. The thing fell heavily, but regained its feet in an instant and stood eyeing Stefan, a knowing smile upon its thin, androgynous face. It winked, mockingly, then spat at Stefan, a bolt of sulphurous bile that bubbled and smoked as it struck the ground by his feet.

Stefan struck out with his sword, but the creature simply stepped away from the blow, moving faster than any mortal man. By now Stefan knew what to expect, even if there was little he could do about it. The counter-attack came with lethal speed, a sudden blur of colour as the claws raked the air before Stefan's face. Stefan felt a sudden stinging as though a thousand needles had pierced his skin. His face was damp as though sweating from every pore, but this was blood, not sweat. And if the servant of Tzeentch got any closer, he would be cut to ribbons.

Stefan thrust out his sword again, aiming for the murderous, raking claws. Bone bit upon steel, the creature had one arm wrapped like a serpent around the outstretched blade. Stefan swung the sword, two-handed, smashing the creature against the wall. Before it could recover he lashed out again, finally managing to land a blow upon the multihued body. He moved in for the kill, but the creature wasn't finished yet. Claws tore at his face and body. A cut appeared along Stefan's left arm, then another upon his thigh. The creature opened its mouth and let loose a low, keening wail.

Then the thunder came, a noise fit to wake the sleeping gods. It started as a low rumble, somewhere deep below the ground, but rose quickly to a crescendo. It was like the roaring of the waters as they first burst up into the citadel, but much, much louder. The creature of Chaos turned its hairless face to the sky and uttered a blood-curdling response. It seemed to have anticipated the sound, and turned towards Stefan as if to say, *you are too late*.

But, for a brief moment, its guard was down. Stefan had one chance, and he made sure he took it. The ground

trembled as the pounding rhythm took hold, the gates
and walls of the palace, the buildings lining the surrounding streets, everything was moving. But Stefan had only
one focus. He blocked out the thunderous roar, and all
thought of what it might portend. The monster flung its
head full back and wailed, and Stefan lashed out with his
sword, the blade slicing clean through its neck. The creature's head flew from its body, the leering grin still fixed
upon its face.

Stefan steadied himself upon his sword, fighting to stay
upon his feet. All around him, buildings were cracking and
crumbling, great towers of stone falling to the ground. The
gates of the palace stood open, unguarded. Stefan ran
towards them, not knowing if he was running towards his
salvation or his doom, only knowing that this was the locus
of the storm. Whatever outcome awaited, it would be
decided here.

A mighty crack split the air. Stefan looked up and saw one
of the great domes above the palace crack open. Plates of
iron peeled apart, spraying wreckage and dust into the shivering air. A second dome fractured, and then a third under
the relentless pounding. The palace, the very heart of
Sigmarsgeist, was dying before Stefan's eyes. And all within
it were surely going to die, too.

Then, as suddenly as it had begun, the infernal hammer
beat was stilled. An eerie, tranquil silence settled upon the
citadel. Stefan ran on through the gates, suddenly able to
hear his own footfalls amongst the steady rain of debris
falling upon the ground.

He counted five seconds of silence... six... seven.
Somewhere between the eighth and ninth, the explosion
struck. The thunderous pounding that had reduced much of
the palace to rubble had been only the beginning, a prelude
to what was to come. As Stefan looked on, a massive column
of water burst forth from the ground and punched, like a
great fist, towards the sky. The water crashed against the
walls of the palace with the force of a mighty explosion, like
a thousand storms brought together into one single, cata-
strophic event.

Sigmarsgeist had been meant to stand until eternity. But the buildings beneath the four domes had already been undermined by the sprawling mass of bone-like growths that had eaten their way through the fabric of the palace. Once-solid structures began to crumble. Great slabs of masonry were thrown into the air and smashed to fragments upon the ground below. Through the blurring haze, Stefan caught sight of the domes as they fell, dragging the walls of the palace down behind them. Ten years of mighty labour was torn apart in minutes.

Blinded by the icy spray, and showered with shards of broken stone, all Stefan could do was protect himself as best he could. For what felt like an age he crouched down with his arms about his head, the only shelter he could find from the relentless storm.

Then, as suddenly as it had come, the noise and water were gone. Dazed, Stefan clambered to his feet, gazing spellbound at the ruination all around him. The proud heart of the citadel had been swept away. The high walls, the domes and gilded towers were all gone, replaced by a drowned wasteland of rubble.

Minutes before, the streets in and around the palace had been teeming with people. Only the gods knew how many souls had been swept to the Gates of Morr in the maelstrom that had followed. Stefan looked about and said a silent prayer for them all, and for all the hopes and futile dreams of Sigmarsgeist, gone in the passing of a moment.

# CHAPTER TWENTY-ONE
## Tal Dur

IF ANAISE STILL held any lingering doubts that this was to be her destiny, then those doubts were utterly dispelled now. She had watched in wonder as the palace of Sigmarsgeist was destroyed. On all sides, walls, towers and statues fell, great edifices of stone thrown high in the air and smashed upon the earth below. The carnage was absolute, the destruction all but total. But it did not destroy her. With Bea and Zucharov she had walked into the maelstrom, to the very edge of the storm that was tearing the palace apart, and she was not harmed. Now, Anaise knew, this was the will of the gods – not the safe gods of the Empire, but deeper, darker forces. It had been ordained. At last, her time had come.

She watched in wonder as the work of years was undone in a few violent minutes, the unnatural fury of the water leaving nothing intact. Soon there was no palace, nothing left of the monument to her brother's dreams. The entire edifice, the tallest structure, the highest point in all Sigmarsgeist, had collapsed in upon itself. The palace and all its surrounding buildings had disappeared, pounded to rubble then collapsed within the great pit of its own dismembered foundations. Everything, above and below, had been washed away.

Anaise began to laugh, softly at first, then with a growing intensity until her voice became a hysterical counterpoint to the dark laughter of the gods. Her brother's dreams had been buried, and with them Konstantin himself. But she had endured. The new citadel that would follow would be in her image, an everlasting testament to her great and enduring will.

As suddenly as the deluge had begun, it was over. For a moment the great tower of water hung suspended, spinning in mid air. Then, abruptly, the pounding ceased, and the tower fell in upon itself, wave upon wave crashing down upon the wreckage of the palace.

The waters flooded across the open space and then withdrew, draining back into the crater left behind. Almost as quickly as the subterranean ruins beneath the palace had been exposed, they were drowned, subsumed as the waters poured into the gaping chasm. Where the palace had once stood there was now only a pool, the size of a small lake. The fury at its destruction was spent, not even the smallest ripple disturbed the surface of the water. Anaise was left with her captive and her consort, standing by a shore of tumbled stone beside the edge of the lake.

Nothing was left standing above the water, except for a solitary tangled mass of bleached-white bone which had tumbled from on high to lie spanning the width of the water like a ghostly bridge.

Anaise looked around. Gradually her delight gave way to a puzzled disbelief. She seized hold of Bea, and pulled the girl around to face her.

'Is that it?' she demanded, tersely. 'What happens now? Where is the Well of Sadness?'

'Gone,' Bea said quietly. 'It has served its purpose.'

Anaise shook her violently. 'Where is Tal Dur?' she screamed. 'I will not be denied, not now!'

'Tal Dur is here,' said Zucharov from behind her. 'Still you do not understand, and you will never will.' He turned his gaze upon the dark, unblemished face of the waters and stretched out a hand. The placid calm of the lake broke apart in response, rising up in a swirling wave.

'The sins of Sigmarsgeist have been washed away,' Bea told Anaise. 'The power of the waters is distilled to its very essence. This is the source,' she said, looking toward the lake. 'This is Tal Dur.'

'The girl,' Zucharov said. 'Give her to me.'

Anaise took a step back, her eyes fixed upon Zucharov. With one hand she still held firmly to Bea. The other trailed down by her side, lightly brushing against her gown.

'Of course,' she replied at last. 'I will share the gifts of Tal Dur with you. That was always our agreement.'

'Give her to me. Now.'

Anaise dipped her head in a shallow bow. 'Of course,' she replied, forcing a smile. 'One moment.' She appeared to fumble with the clasp of her gown.

Zucharov made a grab for the girl, his patience at an end. He didn't see the knife until it was flying towards him. In a single, elegant movement Anaise had lifted her hand clear of her gown and sent the blade twisting through the air. It struck Zucharov, hard and firm, in the very centre of his chest.

The tattooed warrior stumbled backwards, a look of puzzled disbelief forming beneath the hideous mask. He coughed, gasping for breath. His huge frame shook, then steadied itself. Zucharov grasped the hilt of the knife, but did not pull it free. His expression changed. Slowly, a bitter smile crept across his dark features. When he spoke it was with the voice of Kyros.

'You are wrong,' the Chaos Lord murmured. 'We were never to share Tal Dur. That was never to be your destiny.' He ripped the blade from his chest, a plume of crimson blood spouting from the wound. Oblivious to any pain, Zucharov pulled open his tunic around the wound, revealing the canopy of horrors daubed upon his body.

'See,' he continued. '*This* is your destiny.'

A scream welled up in Anaise's throat as the image shaped itself before her eyes. Right where the knife had penetrated the mutant's body she saw her own likeness, drenched in

blood. The wound that she had inflicted was a jagged scar
that ran the length of her body. She let go of Bea and tried
to run, but Zucharov caught her, and restrained her with
ease.

Alexei Zucharov brought his hands about Anaise's neck
and held them there. He traced the contours of her face,
running his fingers down the length of her cheek. Anaise
battled to free herself with every last ounce of her being,
beating at Zucharov with her fists. When all else had failed
her, she screamed.

'Enough,' the voice of Kyros murmured. 'Enough. Now
you see where your destiny has brought you. Now you see
where you belong.' Zucharov raised one hand, brushing
away the single tear running down her face.

'You are fallen,' he whispered to her. 'You are weak.'

Anaise's eyes grew wide with fear, or with anger. She began
to speak, defiant to the last in the face of the monster who
would deny her her rightful prize. Zucharov pressed one finger to her lips, stopping her words. Then, slowly, almost
gently, he cupped his hands once more around Anaise's
neck, and stilled her voice for ever.

AT FIRST, IT had seemed impossible to Stefan that anything,
or anyone, could have survived, either inside the palace, or
in the dark maze of dungeons that had once lain below.
Every living thing must surely have perished. Yet he had
been spared, and he now realised that he was not the only
one to have survived.

He now stood on the lip of a vast crater where the walls
had fallen, and the palace had collapsed in upon itself. The
waters had drawn back, retreating into the cavernous space,
filling it until all that remained of either the palace or the
great flood which had destroyed it was a lake. The only structure that still stood was a single span of the bone-like
growth that curved like the spine of some great beast across
the surface of the water.

Fragile and brittle, the bridge swayed precariously in the
faint breeze that drifted off the water. At any moment this
last remnant of the struggle would surely crack and break

apart. But for the moment, the bone-bridge held, a solitary arch above the still, silent waters. Upon the bridge, Stefan made out two figures. One was monstrously tall and powerfully built. The second, diminutive by contrast, walking two steps behind, hands fastened behind their back, linked to the first by a length of rope or chain. He recognised them instantly – Zucharov and Bea, captor and captive. Locked together in a slow dance across the waters of Tal Dur.

Stefan had asked himself what he would feel when this moment came. Would he be consumed by vengeance, raw hatred for the creature who had stolen the life of his comrade? Would he feel excitement, or fear at the prospect that his own life, too, might soon be at an end? Now the time had come, Stefan felt neither of these things. He had become quite calm, as though he had reached a sudden and unexpected point of stillness. As he slowly drew his sword he was aware only of a sense of fulfilment, and the knowledge that he had been waiting for this moment for much of his life. This would be the fulcrum, the defining struggle. Whatever the outcome now, nothing would ever be the same again.

Zucharov had not seen him yet. He was only interested in Bea, dragging the healer behind him as he moved on to the bridge. Bea looked rigid, immobile. For a moment Stefan feared that Zucharov might want her dead, but no, that was not Zucharov's purpose. Her presence made Stefan's task all the more difficult, now he must destroy Zucharov without endangering Bea. There would be a way. There had to be a way.

Finally, almost casually, Alexei Zucharov looked up and saw his former comrade. A look passed across the mutant's face that signalled that he, too, had been waiting for this moment. A flash of common understanding passed between them, the last bond they would ever share.

Stefan barely knew Zucharov now. He looked as if he were wearing a mask, a mask that clung taut against his skin, covering every inch of his face. Then Stefan saw it for what it truly was, the living tattoo that had begun a lifetime ago in Erengrad, as a tiny bruise upon his comrade's arm. There could be no question now that Chaos had now claimed Zucharov. There was no way back from the abyss for Alexei.

Stefan wasn't expecting Zucharov to smile, but smile he did, even though the tattoo rendered the smile inhuman. Stefan realised that this, after all, was what Zucharov truly wanted. To face Stefan here, at the place they would know as Tal Dur, and to kill him. Zucharov's whole body had been transformed. Sinews strained and pumped-up muscles pushed hard against tough, leathery flesh. The realisation sat like ice in Stefan's stomach. The dark power flooding into Zucharov was making him ever stronger, ever more unassailable. Every moment that passed tilted the odds of battle further in Zucharov's favour.

Beyond the fight that lay ahead, there was Bea to think of. So far she seemed to be unharmed, but Stefan knew he could not risk attacking Zucharov whilst he still held the girl.

'Let the girl go free!' Stefan called. 'This quarrel is for you and I alone.'

Zucharov's mocking laughter echoed across the water in response.

'Quarrel? With you? I've no more quarrel with you than I might have with a fly.' Zucharov raised the blade of his knife to Bea's throat. The healer's face was pale with terror.

'Is this what agitates your weak, insect mind, Stefan?' He touched the edge of the steel to Bea's skin. 'Perhaps if I dispense with the girl then the fly will stop bothering me?'

Stefan moved forward, cautiously. 'I don't think you'll do that,' he said. He paused, struggling with the gamble he was about to take. 'But if you want,' he said, 'then go ahead. Kill her. You'll have no excuse to hide behind then. You'll have to fight me.'

Veins pulsed upon the mutant's forehead. The patchwork that was Zucharov's face buckled and stretched, and blood began to leak from his dark, lidless eyes. He pulled himself up to his full height, towering over both his captive and his opponent.

'You should have killed me when you had the chance,' he told Stefan. 'As it is, you will live just long enough to regret your words.' He turned to the girl.

'Where does the source lie?' he demanded. He took hold of her arm, twisting it slowly, relentlessly, until Bea screamed out in pain.

'Tal Dur,' Zucharov demanded again. 'Where is the source of its power?'

'In Shallya's name,' Bea responded, fearfully. 'At the centre of the lake. Where the water is at its deepest. The power of Tal Dur flows from there.'

Zucharov looked toward Stefan who was still advancing. 'I have not done with you yet,' he told Bea. 'But for the moment, our business must be set aside.' The mutant unfurled the iron chain coiled around Bea's wrists, and secured one end against a thick spar of bone, pulling the iron links so tight that they cut into the flesh of Bea's hands. Zucharov ignored her cries, concerned only that she should have no chance of escape.

'Now,' he called out to Stefan. His face split into a hungry grin. 'Come and taste the power of Tzeentch.'

Stefan needed no bidding. He vaulted up upon the tottering bridge, and attacked. The many victories he had known as a swordsman counted for nothing now. This was the only fight that mattered.

The speed of his opening thrust seemed to take his opponent by surprise. Stefan's sword cut through Zucharov's tunic, exposing the patterned flesh beneath. But it made as much impact as a fingernail grazing leather. Zucharov spat a dark oath and brushed the blade aside, counter-attacking with a flurry of sword-strokes that swiftly forced Stefan back.

Zucharov drove in again, the heavy steel went just wide of Stefan's shoulder and sliced deep into the side of the bridge. The bridge shuddered violently, shards of fibrous bone breaking away to scatter into the water below. In the instant it took him to free his sword Stefan had struck back, this time finding his range and aiming a blow cleanly between Zucharov's shoulder and chest. The mutant's answering howl gave Stefan fresh hope. No longer human, perhaps, but not immortal either. Not yet.

The wound sparked Zucharov into a frenzied rage of retaliation, and Stefan had to defend himself beneath a murderous storm of steel. He was drawing on his deepest reserves of strength and skill, but still some of his opponent's blows were finding their mark. Stefan bit back upon the pain as first one arm and then his leg was sliced open, and still the onslaught continued. Each new wound, however small, was taking its toll. With every passing moment his strength was being depleted. He was getting weaker whilst Zucharov only grew stronger. He had to finish this soon. Time was running out.

Stefan swerved aside to avoid another attack, and found space momentarily to strike at Zucharov's unprotected head. He connected only with the flat of his blade, but the blow was still enough to kill most mortal men. Zucharov was merely stunned. Before Stefan could draw breath and consolidate, his opponent had recovered. Now it was Stefan who was caught off-guard. He watched in horror as Zucharov's blade slid beneath his ribs, and a white-hot pain erupted in his gut. He fell back, clutching one hand to the wound, and collapsed against one side of the narrow bridge.

Through a red haze, Stefan watched the scene unfold. His former comrade walking towards him, slowly, almost nonchalantly, preparing to end his life. The gold band, carved with ancient runes, glittered upon his wrist. And behind Zucharov, somehow far away, Bea still trying desperately to free herself from the chains shackling her to the bridge. The surface of the bridge was slick and warm, wet with his own blood. Already the pain was starting to ebb away into a drowsy numbness that suffused his whole body. This is it, Stefan told himself. I'm dying.

He felt tired, so very, very tired. He wondered if it was always like this at the end. It wasn't right. There should be desperation, anger, a last, defiant flaring of the light. He looked up at the servant of Tzeentch as his life drained away. Zucharov was gazing down at him, a quizzical, half-smile on his tattooed face. Then he raised his sword for what would be the last time.

A sea of thoughts was running through Stefan's mind. All the friends and comrades he had known, all the battles fought and won. All had led only to this, this death, this end. From out of the torrent, the image of his brother appeared. For a moment Stefan saw him clearly, seated by their favourite corner of the Helmsman, at home in Altdorf, two pots of good ale set in front of him. Before he had set out on his journey, Stefan had made a pledge to Mikhal that he would return safe from Erengrad, that they would meet to drink and tell their stories. A week from this very day, they should have been sitting at that very table.

This isn't how it's meant to be, he told himself. It isn't supposed to end like this. And in that moment, the weariness was gone, and rage had taken its place, a rage against the dark force about to claim his life. *This was not meant to be.*

His sword was gone, lost in the struggle. He had no weapon to defend himself with but his own, battered body. Zucharov towered over him, savouring the final moment before the kill. He knew it was hopeless, but his rage would not let Stefan abandon the fight. He gripped hold of the bridge as best he could and kicked out blindly, again and again. The target did not matter now. All that mattered was to fight, and keep fighting until the gift of life was gone.

The bridge shuddered again. He heard Bea cry out. Then came a single sound, a sharp crack as a bridge strut broke in two. Zucharov spun about, suddenly realising that Bea had managed to break free. For a moment, his attention was drawn away from Stefan, and Stefan knew he had to grasp that fleeting opportunity.

He poured what was left of his strength into one final kick. His booted foot missed Zucharov but connected squarely with the side of the bridge. A tremor ran the length of the skeletal structure, and the bridge lurched violently to one side.

Zucharov spun around, surprise and confusion visible beneath the markings on his face. The sudden shift in bulk and weight caused the bridge to roll even further. Zucharov toppled forward, off-balance, towards the prostrate figure of Stefan.

One chance, the rage told Stefan. Once chance. This is it. He lifted an arm as Zucharov skidded towards him, and managed to hook his fingers around his opponent's belt.

The mutant staggered forward, trying to hold his balance on the collapsing structure. Stefan shut his eyes and rolled sideways, moving with the sway of the bridge, jamming his foot hard against the side wall. The brittle structure shattered and cracked, and suddenly, briefly, Stefan sensed only a roaring in his ears and empty space beneath his body as the bridge disintegrated.

The water was dark, and very, very cold. There was a burst of sound as Stefan struck the surface and then everything was stillness. He was alone, falling ever deeper towards the heart of Tal Dur. He knew he must be drowning, and yet the rage inside him was gone, replaced by a calm serenity. In his mind, he saw again the image of his brother seated at his table at the inn. Mikhal looked up at Stefan, and beckoned to him. No, Stefan told himself. This is not how it is when you die. This is how it is when life is given back.

His head broke the surface of the water and sweet air flooded into his lungs. He saw the moons up above, pale light shimmering on the surface of the lake. And he saw Bea, stepping from the shallows towards him, unfurling the severed links of the chain from her wrists. Stefan's sword was tucked into the belt at her waist.

Stefan lifted an arm clear of the water. To his astonishment, he discovered that he felt no weariness, no pain. His whole body felt renewed. He was giddy, drunk with newfound strength.

'It's all right!' he shouted to Bea. He stretched out, and began to swim slowly towards her. A look of alarm passed across Bea's face. She raised her hands in warning.

'Wait!' she called out. 'Stay where you are, Stefan. Don't move!'

'It's all right,' Stefan shouted back. 'I can make it.'

'No!' Bea commanded. 'Respect the power of Tal Dur.' She shed the last of the chains, and swam to meet Stefan halfway across the pool. 'Take hold of my hands,' she instructed him. 'Both of them. Tal Dur will only lend its power through one blessed with the healing gift.'

She clasped Stefan's wrists securely in her own. 'Now,' she said. 'We go. Slowly.'

Together they swam back to the shore and emerged, dripping, at the edge of the lake, amidst the rubble of the palace.

'Your wounds?' Bea asked. Stefan looked down in wonder. The gash beneath his ribs had closed. The scar lining his flesh seemed already to be fading. Other, smaller wounds had simply vanished.

'Truly,' Stefan said, 'your powers are wondrous.'

'The power comes from Tal Dur,' Bea said, quietly. 'I am nothing but the vessel.'

Stefan gazed back across the lake. 'What happened to Zucharov?'

Bea shook her head. 'Wait,' she urged. 'Watch.'

For what seemed like an age, nothing disturbed the glass-like sheen of the water. Then bubbles of air broke the surface, one or two only at first, then steadily more. Stefan felt his body tense. 'Give me the sword,' he whispered.

Alexei Zucharov rose like a ghost from the waters. Tal Dur had wrought its changes upon him, too. He seemed smaller, physically diminished. All trace of the tattoo had been washed from his body, every mark upon his skin, was gone. His eyes, when they met with Stefan's were deep, untainted blue. The eyes of a long-vanished comrade.

'Stefan–' he began, uncertainly. 'Stefan?'

Zucharov edged forward and then stopped, as if something unseen had taken hold of him. Stefan's grip on the sword eased, and then tightened again. Another change was sweeping over Zucharov. His eyes dulled and widened until only the dark kernels were visible. He looked at Stefan again but no longer knew him. His body began to shake, violently, as some invisible force began to break through from within.

One chance, the voice told Stefan again. He stepped into the waters, his sword poised high above his head. 'Goodbye, Alexei,' he said, softly.

The water around Zucharov began to stir, swirling around him like a vortex. Stefan drove forward, but never delivered the final blow. Zucharov's mouth opened in a silent scream as his body thrashed against the force pulling him down. The snaking waters wrapped around him, dragging him back towards the depths. Stefan was close enough to touch him, he could have reached out and pulled him clear. Their eyes met for one last, fleeting moment before Tal Dur sucked Zucharov down.

The earth itself seemed to shudder and cry out. Stefan felt a mighty pulse as it passed through the ground beneath his feet, spreading from the centre of Tal Dur in a shock wave through the ruins of Sigmarsgeist. The waters rose up in a great wave, then settled for the last time, like a shroud above Alexei Zucharov's head.

A PHALANX OF Red Guard bore Bruno's body down to the water's edge. He was still breathing, but he was surely nearer to death than life. Bruno was not yet within the realm of Morr, but his soul stood close by the final gates. His last moments were steadily trickling away.

'Hurry,' Bea implored the guard. 'Time is running out.' Running out for Bruno, and for Tal Dur too. Since Zucharov had been sucked down by the whirlpool, the fall of the waters had been dramatic. The lake that had been Tal Dur had halved in size in less than an hour, and the levels were still falling. All across what remained of Sigmarsgeist, the waters were draining away. Soon there would be no sign of their existence save for the ravages they had left behind.

Bea waded into the water, bearing Bruno's body into the depths. She motioned for Stefan and the soldiers to stay back.

'Wait,' she told him. 'Trust me. Trust in the healing powers of Tal Dur.'

She lay Bruno upon his back, then guided the injured man across the surface of the pool until the waters had risen up above her waist. Then, with her arms supporting Bruno's weight in the water, she bowed her head until it was resting upon his chest, and made a silent prayer.

This time the waters did not rise up. There was no turmoil, no churning whirlpool to answer Bea. Instead the stillness of the waters seemed to reach out and fill all of Sigmarsgeist. For all his desperate worry for his comrade, Stefan found himself grow calm. He looked about, across what remained of the citadel to north and south. For a moment he thought about the Norscans, whether they or any other of the Chaos creatures could have survived. But Zucharov and Anaise had gone, and with them had gone the poison that had swept through Sigmarsgeist. The heart of the citadel was gone, and with it too the rage of battle.

Bea looked up from her prayers, and beckoned Stefan towards her.

Bruno lay very still in the water, an expression of calm on his face. For a moment Stefan thought his comrade was lost, but then Bruno began to breathe again, slow and regular, like a man in the depths of restful sleep. Finally he opened his eyes and looked up at Bea. He smiled at the sight of her.

'I thought for a moment I had died,' he murmured, 'and that you were the goddess Shallya, come to receive me.'

Bea lowered her head, and kissed him gently. 'You did not die,' she whispered. 'Nor am I the goddess, though I know now how I may serve her.'

Stefan looked at Bruno and Bea in turn, and shook his head in relief and disbelief. 'Tal Dur?' he asked her.

'Tal Dur,' Bea affirmed.

'But the same waters destroyed Zucharov,' Stefan said. 'How can that be?'

'Tal Dur looked into his soul,' Bea said. 'And gave back what it found within. Evil begot evil. Tal Dur destroyed Zucharov as it destroyed Sigmarsgeist, and all evil that ran within it.'

'It could have been different,' she continued, thoughtfully. 'Theirs were once noble dreams, Konstantin and Anaise both. I'm sure of that.'

'But those dreams are buried beneath the rubble now, and Konstantin and Anaise with them,' Stefan replied. 'Evil will always find ways to taint the purest of hearts. We must be ever vigilant, lest ambition and greed poison our noble intent.'

'The gods will bear witness to that,' Bea agreed.

THEY WALKED SIDE by side through the ruins as day broke across Sigmarsgeist. The rising sun was welcome but unforgiving, exposing the full horror of the devastation that had

swept through Sigmarsgeist. Very little of the citadel had
been left untouched. The final shock that Stefan had felt
standing by Tal Dur had torn through the ruins like a hammer blow, devastating those few buildings still standing. The
dream that had been Sigmarsgeist had been left hollow, and
empty. It seemed far from certain that it would ever live
again.

The floods had continued to recede, ebbing away almost
as fast as they had first risen. Before long, nothing would
remain of the waters.

'I'm not sure that we are ready for the gifts of Tal Dur,'
Stefan mused. 'With such a power for evil as well as good,
I'm not sure we ever will be ready.'

Bea said nothing, just continued to walk at his side. Stefan
had already noticed a distance that had come between them.
They were comrades still, without doubt, but comrades now
bound upon very different paths. They walked in silence for
a while before Stefan spoke again.

'Tal Dur surely worked its wonders upon Bruno,' he said.
'I'd wager he'll recover, stronger and healthier than ever he
was before.'

'He has rested the better part of the night,' Bea replied.
'Soon he'll be ready to travel.'

She smiled, a little ruefully. 'Beyond that, we cannot say.
Tal Dur has gifted Bruno his life,' she said. 'But it will not be
the same life, the same future that he had before.'

'All our futures are unwritten,' Stefan said. 'That is the only
certainty we may know.'

He took Bea's hand. 'What about you?' he asked. 'What
hopes for the future have you?'

Bea stopped short, gazing about her at the people as they
passed by, men and women struggling with bundles filled
with clothes or food, beginning the long battle to rebuild
their lives.

'I shall stay here,' she said at last. 'This is where I belong. I
know that now. I think perhaps I always knew it.'

'What will you do?'

Bea laughed. 'Whatever I can. I don't think I'll lack for
opportunity. There is work to be done, amongst the sick, the

wounded, the starving. I can't help them all, but I will do what I can.'

'Does Bruno know?' Stefan asked. 'That you mean to stay, I mean?'

'Not yet,' Bea said, her voice very small. 'Maybe in his heart though, yes.'

'You know you could ride back with us,' Stefan said. 'To the Empire. Back to Altdorf. There'd be a life for you there.'

Bea smiled, and squeezed Stefan's hand. 'A life, maybe,' she said. 'But not your life, Stefan. Nor Bruno's, either. Your life is with the sword,' she said. 'Mine is not. Mine is to heal.' She looked around. 'I'm going back,' she said at last. 'Back to my calling, I mean.' She opened her hand to reveal the battered icon of Shallya that Bruno had worn about his neck.

'Bruno wanted me to have this,' she said. 'I don't think even he knew quite how right that was.'

Stefan looked at her, puzzled. 'I don't understand,' he said.

Bea flushed, and took a breath. 'A long time ago, before I knew I had a gift, I was a Sister,' she said. 'A Sister of Shallya, a priestess. Then I discovered that I had other powers, powers to heal that came from magic, as well as from the divine will of the goddess.'

'I still don't understand,' Stefan said. 'Surely your healing powers were a blessing, wherever they came from?'

Bea laughed again. 'Others didn't see it that way,' she said. 'What I took as a gift, others saw as witchcraft. I had to renounce my calling, and leave the Sisterhood. I thought perhaps in Mielstadt I would be left to work in peace,' she said. 'But – well, you know the rest.' She sighed, then brightened. 'But here, I won't be judged. Here I can start afresh, and use my gifts as they were always meant to be used. The goddess knows, there's work enough to be done.'

'I wouldn't argue with that,' Stefan conceded. He looked around, surveying the scenes of desolation on all sides. Most of the townsfolk who had survived would be left without homes or shelter of any sort. He feared it would not be long before disease and starvation would stalk the ruins in search of easy prey.

'Are you sure you want to stay?' Stefan asked her. 'These are dangerous times, now more than ever. The Dark Powers will turn their gaze upon the ruins of Sigmarsgeist. It may not be long before they send their armies here.'

'All the more reason for me to stay,' Bea said, resolutely. 'These people may be beaten down, but their hearts are strong. They came here to build a fortress against the evil, the dark tide of Chaos. They shouldn't be abandoned now.'

They rounded a corner, stepping across mounds of rubble and slurry. From the opposite direction, a familiar figure came into view, a well-loaded sack balanced upon his back.

'Lothar!' Stefan called out. 'Lothar Koenig!'

The bounty hunter looked up, and shuffled towards them. The contents of the sack gave a metallic ring as Koenig set it upon the ground.

'Quite a haul,' Stefan observed.

The bounty hunter glanced at Stefan, and frowned. 'I know what you're thinking,' he said. 'Dirty, plundering thief, eh?'

'There might have been a time when I'd have thought that,' Stefan conceded. 'But I'm in no hurry to rush judgement any more.'

'Well, it's all honestly come by,' Lothar said. 'From those rich enough and dead enough not to care, either.' He grunted, and peered at Stefan. 'What about you?' he asked. 'Did you find your tattooed friend?'

'Yes,' Stefan said. 'I found him.'

'And the gold band?' Lothar asked. For a brief moment a gleam came into his eye. 'Did you find that?'

'If I had, I wouldn't offer it to you,' Stefan said.

Lothar pondered a while then laughed, softly. 'You know, I'm not so sure I'd want it any more, either. There are some prizes where the price is just too high.'

'That there are,' Stefan agreed.

Lothar Koenig hefted the sack up upon his back once more. 'Well,' he said. 'I'd best be going.'

Stefan held out his hand to the bounty hunter. 'Then go safely,' he said. 'May you live and prosper.'

\* \* \*

STEFAN STOOD AT Bea's side. As he watched the bounty hunter disappear into the distance, his mind was very much on Alexei Zucharov.

'He understood about your power, didn't he?' he said to Bea at last. 'Zucharov, I mean. That's why he wanted you at the lake. He meant to channel the power of the waters through you.'

Bea nodded. 'Not something I want to think too much about,' she said.

'But–' Stefan hesitated. 'if he had succeeded…'

Bea shrugged. 'We must thank the gods that he didn't,' she said.

'Thank them with all our hearts,' Stefan affirmed. 'Truly, it's for the good that the waters have drained away,' he added. 'Let us hope they lie deep, far from all temptation.'

Bea shivered, and drew her shawl about her. 'It's growing cold,' she said.

Stefan looked at the sky. The clouds above had formed a shield of leaden grey. The first few snowflakes were starting to fall, soft upon the chill ruins of the citadel. 'Kaldezeit is upon us,' he reflected. 'The cruel season, the season of death.'

'Without death there can be no renewal,' Bea reminded him. 'We will take what fortune the seasons bring.'

'Life here will be hard, Bea. Whatever happens.'

'Life will be hard for us all,' Bea replied. 'I do not think the road you travel will be the easier.'

'No,' Stefan agreed. 'I don't suppose that it will.'

'I must go to my work,' Bea said. 'The people of Sigmarsgeist need me now as never before.'

'Yes,' Stefan agreed. 'You must go, and I must go too. If Bruno is able, we'll ride from here before dusk. We have a journey of many weeks still ahead of us.'

'Back to Altdorf?'

'To Altdorf. A homecoming long overdue.'

A silence fell between them, then Bea leant forward and kissed Stefan lightly upon the cheek. 'Go with all my blessings,' she said to him. 'And may Shallya attend you all your days.'

Stefan took her hand in his, and stood facing her for a few moments longer. Then he turned, and began the journey that would lead him home.

BEA WAITED UNTIL Stefan had gone, his words all the while ringing like a warning inside her head. She whispered a prayer for Stefan's fortune, and for Bruno's, too. She prayed that his heart, like his body, would be healed in the fullness of time. She opened her left hand again, and looked upon the locket, the image of Shallya gazing up at her.

Then she opened her right hand, and looked down at the tiny vial resting in her palm. So small, yet so precious. The last few drops, taken from the lake of Tal Dur, before the waters were lost forever. Such a tiny amount. It could do no harm, she told herself. Surely, it could only be for the good.

She lifted the vial and held it to her face. The glass felt cool against her skin. It was the right thing to do. With the healing powers of the water, who knew what might not be achieved? Sigmarsgeist could be built anew, and her people made whole and strong, free once more of all sickness and pain.

It could surely do no harm, could not be anything but for the good. Sigmarsgeist would rise again, and she, Bea, would be there to lead its people from the darkness back into the light.

She would be their inspiration. She would be their Guide.

# ABOUT THE AUTHOR

*Neil McIntosh* was born in Sussex in 1957 and
currently lives in Brighton. He has contributed
stories for the Warhammer anthologies,
*White Dwarf* and other magazines, as well as writing
for radio. Following a lengthy sabbatical, he
returned to writing fiction in 2000 with two stories
for *Inferno!* magazine. *Taint of Evil* is
his second novel.